Lovers

She and Trevor Shelby would be lovers.

Shock chilled her heated skin. It was there in his deep blue eyes watching her; the same knowledge.

A sudden need replaced all others. Panic urged her to find fault with him. But no matter how she searched the hard length of his body, the breath-stealing cut of his features, she found no visible flaw. The whispers about him were all true. He was a man to tempt the most saintly of women.

"Will you meet me here tomorrow?" Trevor brought his gaze to hers. *I want you.* But the words were silently his. Suddenly he knew, no matter how he denied it, that while Leah was frightened of him, she would come to him again. "I'll wait for you." It was both command and promise.

TARNISHED HEARTS

by

Raine Cantrell

A TOPAZ BOOK

TOPAZ
Published by the Penguin Group
Penguin Books USA Inc., 375 Hudson Street,
New York, New York 10014, U.S.A.
Penguin Books Ltd, 27 Wrights Lane,
London W8 5TZ, England
Penguin Books Australia Ltd, Ringwood,
Victoria, Australia
Penguin Books Canada Ltd, 10 Alcorn Avenue,
Toronto, Ontario, Canada M4V 3B2
Penguin Books (N.Z.) Ltd, 182–190 Wairau Road,
Auckland 10, New Zealand

Penguin Books Ltd, Registered Offices:
Harmondsworth, Middlesex, England

First published by Topaz,
an imprint of Dutton Signet,
a division of Penguin Books USA Inc.

First Printing, February, 1994
10 9 8 7 6 5 4 3 2 1

Topaz is a trademark of New American Library,
a division of Penguin Books USA Inc.

Printed in the United States of America

In loving memory of my father,
who shared his love of history
and books with me and was so proud
that I had become a writer.

Prologue

Sweet Bay Plantation
1848 Georgia

"I hate him, Tante. I'll hate him until I die."

"Hush that talk. Come help fix the dog. Leave Massa Shelby be."

Sensitive to the hate with which Tante spat out his father's name, Trevor Shelby did as she demanded and let it be. The old slave woman would never explain to him why she hated his father.

Crooning softly, Trevor gently stroked his mastiff's dull sheened coat, his face taut for every rippling shudder he felt. "Why didn't you obey me?" he whispered to the dog. "He's beaten me before. Why didn't you stay when I told you to?"

Trevor thought himself too old at fourteen to cry, but his eyes burned as he stared at the four evenly spaced punctures across the dog's massive chest. The spider webs had helped to stop the bleeding and the salve he had boiling in the kettle would help the wounds to heal. He prayed it would. Aside from love and loyalty shared, the dog was totally his, beyond his father's control. There was so much he didn't know, so much he longed to learn about medicine, that praying was all he could do.

Guilt ripped at him and his hands curled into knuckle-white fists. If he had not cried out when his father had cornered him in the stable for running off to Dr. Barlow again, Cinders never would have been speared with the pitchfork his father had grabbed to protect himself from the dog's attack.

Tante's firm hand on his shoulder roused Trevor. "Doan do no good sorrowin'. Time you work, now."

He took the bowl of turpentine from her and swung the kettle on its crane out from the fire, pouring the liquid into the boiled mix of hog's lard, white and red leads, beeswax, and black rosin. Stirring, Trevor wrinkled his nose at the smell, then set it to boil a bit more. He checked his journal, which lay open on the planked floor beside him. The salve was one of many that Tante had taught him to make, and he recorded each one he learned in his journal.

Breathing in air redolent with drying herbs, barks, and roots, Trevor cast a wary gaze over the meagerly furnished cabin, thankful that Tante had placed extra sacking over the window to hide the lamplight. He didn't want to think about what would happen if his father caught him here or learned that Tante, against his orders, had the stable slaves bring the dog to her.

"He will get better, won't he, Tante?"

"Wound's deep, youn' massa. But he be strong animal." Her dark, ancient eyes reassured him. "You make good medicine like Tante."

Tiny and wizened, she knelt at his side. Trevor raised the dog's head to his lap, prying open the jaws to allow Tante to spoon a sleeping potion into the animal's mouth. Time was lost for Trevor. He measured the dog's slowing heartbeat and watched

Tante cool a scoop of salve with the ice he had stolen from the icehouse.

When she offered him the crock, Trevor peeled back the webbing from the wound. Moment by moment, the helplessness that had plagued him disappeared, replaced by a calming peace that gave him strength as he willed, with his mind and body, for healing to begin.

His long, tapered fingers spread open the first wound. Tante's whisperings were a liquid jumble in her native tongue, soothing and steadying him as he worked the salve into the torn flesh.

The door slammed open behind them. "Devil's spawn!" roared Clinton Shelby. "You were forbidden to come here."

Trevor stilled. Devil's spawn? Yes. An apt title. Clinton made his own rules. He viewed defiance of his orders as a challenge to his authority that had to be ruthlessly stamped out. Clinton would never bend to another man's will. Trevor knew his father's demands were wrong for him. He refused to allow Clinton to mold him into someone he could not be and challenged his father at every turn.

They were alike. Trevor hated the comparison, but wouldn't deny it being the truth. He was the only legitimate son that Clinton would ever have. And Clinton despised being reminded of it.

"But I'm your spawn, Father." Trevor could ignore his father's condemning fury, but when his litter sister, Bella, whispered his name, he had to turn around. Trevor couldn't hide his shock at seeing her there with Hanson Kemps, the overseer, and Jason and Julius, two of the largest slaves. They were all crowding close behind his father.

"Yes, you're my spawn," Clinton returned with

bitterness. "The only damn one I'll have. But I'll teach you not to defy me," he declared, motioning the men behind him into the cabin. "And this time, you Gulla witch, you'll pay, too," he said, pointing at Tante.

The threat of Tante brought Trevor to his feet in a controlled rush. "Leave her be. I told her to help me. And she's mother's, not yours."

"You damned whelp! I'll break you if it's the last thing I do even if you're my son."

Crouching, Trevor watched as Hanson Kemps came toward him. His lanky frame was no match for the overseer's burly strength. He knew he couldn't win, couldn't stop whatever his father had planned, but when he saw Julius, ebony skin gleaming and muscles rippling from hours at the forge, circle toward Tante, Trevor knew he would fight with his last breath to stop his father.

The sight of the pistol in his father's hand stayed Trevor. When Clinton shoved Bella at Jason and ordered him to hold her, fear snaked up Trevor's back.

"Tried not to tell, Trev," Bella sobbed. "Don't let him hurt you again," she pleaded, struggling in Jason's grip.

Trevor had no thoughts for himself or Tante. The tears Bella shed glistened on the reddened imprint of a man's hand across her pale cheek. Hate raged through him. Before he could lunge at his father, Kemps and Julius moved, grabbing hold of him and Tante.

"Take them outside," Clinton ordered, pointing to Bella and the old slave woman. "But not my son," he added to Kemps.

Trevor stopped his struggles. The overseer's grip was too strong for Trevor to free himself. He glared at the man who sired him, stomach muscles clenching against what he sensed was coming. Two hundred years of careful breeding resulted in his father's imposing figure. His handsomeness, his mother's joy and shame, was the subject of women's whispers. No feature on the face Trevor hated was flawed, but he knew the ugliness it concealed. Rage set the clefted chin, twitched the muscle of Clinton's right cheek, and thinned his mouth, which smiled so readily to those beyond his power. Blue eyes, ringed with black—devil's eyes, the slaves called them—burned now with righteous fire.

With a sickening wrench, Trevor mirrored each telltale sign of fury. Looking at his father's face was seeing a reflection of his own.

"If obedience cannot be beaten into you, boy, I'll have my way by breaking everything and everyone you care for."

There was no other warning. Clinton fired.

For moments, it seemed Trevor's heart had stopped beating. He was unable to control his jerking body or the numbing cold that banked his defiant anger and hate. He wanted to close his eyes, wanted to turn away from the animal he loved, but mercy was not granted.

"Remember this," Clinton ordered his son. "Take him outside," he said to Kemps.

"You bastard!"

Clinton's slap rocked Trevor's head before Kemps started to drag him from the cabin. When he saw his father step over the dog and pick up his journal, Trevor cried out.

"No! Lord, no! Don't touch—" He stopped, sagging in the overseer's arms. Flames were already greedily licking at the parchment. Trevor slowly raised his head and stared at his father. He had had years to learn how to close out all feeling. Or he thought he had. He didn't know how to deal with the pain of his loss or his father's hate. Kemps pushed him outside, forcing him to face the two live oaks that sheltered Tante's cabin, set away from the neatly laid-out rows of the slave quarters.

The old woman's body was bound against one of the trees, her frail arms straining to pull free of the rope that held her. Trevor couldn't swallow. His stomach heaved. Behind her stood Julius holding a coiled whip. The flutter of Bella's white night rail drew his gaze, a ghostly beacon that seemed to draw the splintered moonlight to where she stood with Jason holding her.

Trevor raised his face toward the night sky, knowing the slaves were all awake, cowering behind their doors, none daring to stop his father. The main house was too far away. Even if he yelled for his mother, she couldn't help them.

"You are flawed, Trevor," Clinton whispered at his son's side. "You are going to destroy that flaw tonight. Never again will you display a weakness no Shelby ever had. I'll not have a son who would despoil our name."

Trevor knew the doctrine well. From the marsh at the edge of the plantation boundary, a prey's cry was suddenly stilled, but Bella's sobs rose as her understanding came. The sound filled Trevor's ears, helping him to drown out his father's insidious, controlled voice, versing him yet again in the reputation he was to maintain.

Master horseman, excellent shot, expert swordsman. Shrewd in business, but charming and reckless in upholding the Shelby ideals that governed their lives. Shelby men did not dirty their hands.

They did not dream of healing the sick or the injured. They placed their honor, pride, and wealth above all else.

But wealth could not buy freedom from pain for his mother. Not one of the doctors that his father hated so much could help her. Only Tante Celine knew the potions that brought her relief for a few days, allowing smiles and laughter from the mother he adored. Despite his father's beatings, threats, and continued punishments, Tante was teaching him her secrets. Secrets that were ashes now. Secrets that would earn her a whipping.

Trevor shook, and held on to the hope that his father would not injure Tante. He needed her skills to keep his slaves healthy, needed her to keep his mother alive and continue the illusion of his benevolence. He knew, too, that Julius was skilled at wielding that black snake.

But when Trevor focused again on those before him, Julius was holding out the whip toward him.

"Take it, Trevor," Clinton commanded.

Throat-constricting fear held Trevor silent—silent and absolutely still.

"Take it, boy, or I'll do it myself and then sell her."

"You can't! Mother needs her. She needs Tante's potions."

Clinton grabbed his son's jaw, forcing Trevor to look at him. "Yes. Now you begin to understand that I am master of all I hold."

Bella's crying reached a fevered pitch. Trevor stared at his father, and saw hell's fire burning bright in his eyes. "There's more," Trevor whispered, jerking his head free of his father's grasp. Kemps released him, but Trevor trembled where he stood from forces unleashed, uncontrolled.

"You leave for the Citadel tomorrow."

"Military school in Charleston?"

"For now. You will excel. Every defiant act will be punished, Trevor. And, since I'm removing you—"

Trevor's gaze shifted, as did his father's, to where Bella stood. But not even to protect Bella would he raise the whip to Tante.

Clinton knew his son's decision without words exchanged. "Such a futile act. Boy, you leave me no choice." He shoved Trevor forward and watched as Kemps and Julius subdued his struggles and secured him to the other tree.

"Send Bella back to the house," Trevor pleaded.

"Young as your sister is, she'll not forget this lesson."

Trevor wouldn't beg for himself, but he did again for his sister.

The whip snaked out from Julius's hand and snapped in answer. He tried to burrow his body into the tree. Above his head the whip whistled in the air, cutting free the trailing gray festoons of Spanish moss. He felt the feathery touch against his cheek as it fell, and closed his eyes, inhaling deep breaths of air that was heavily perfumed from the flowers that his mother loved. He wasn't sure who ripped his shirt apart. He thought of the cream satin smoothness of the flower and bit his lip, breaking the skin as the lash landed with a sickening force across his back.

A scream welled up in his throat. Teeth gritted, Trevor fought to swallow the rising cry, tried to catch his breath as the bite of leather slashed his skin. Flesh cringing, stomach muscles clenched, he fought with every stubborn fiber of his being not to cry out. But he couldn't shut out the sound of Bella's scream.

"Give him what he wants," Tante whispered. "Show him you hurt. Beg him, youn' massa. He stop then."

"I—" the whip snaked the air at his side, "can't whip—you." Again the air snapped with the sound of leather. Trevor was forced to brace himself, shuddering involuntarily, nauseated by the dread of another blow. Expertly wielded by Julius, the whip tore his flesh. This time Trevor couldn't stifle a moan.

"Again," Clinton ordered when he saw the slave hesitate; and to his son, "Break, damn you!"

Five more blows forced a scream from Trevor's swollen lips. Kemps was cutting him free and helping him to stand before Trevor understood that for him, the whipping had ended.

His father stood in front of him and took the whip from Julius. A red haze swam before Trevor's eyes, and pain almost conquered him, but he listened. He listened and he hated.

"You tried my patience, Trevor. Two lashes to Tante for every one you took."

"H-have—" Trevor spit blood, swallowed bile, then struggled to speak. "I beg for m-mercy."

"It's too late. Take the whip. And if I must insist again, I'll put Bella in your place. I want no doubt to linger. *You will become the son I want. You will make me proud of you.*"

Trevor's tears were of shame. He begged Tante's forgiveness. But he would never forget.

Chapter One

THE sun rose lazily this August morning of 1860. Trev watched the first rays steal what was left of the night in the sky, the faint shadows surrendering to the bright skeins of light the sun unfurled. He had the fanciful thought of an illicit lover stealing away from his lady's bower. Much like he stole time for himself.

It was yet another reminder that his freedom was near its end. Stilling the restive moves of the blooded bay he rode, he held his vantage point on top of the hill. Robert DeMoise, sole heir to Rosehall, one of Alabama's richest plantations, had lost their race and Trev waited for him.

Robert's muttered curses came from behind him. Trev smiled. As Robert damned his barrel-chested black for casting a shoe and losing their wager, he dismounted to lead the horse up the hill. The curses were now salted by the colorful language they had both learned serving two years in the western territory with the federal army. But for all his posturings, Trev knew that Robert would do nothing to harm the black, for horses were Robert's first passion.

Unlike himself. Trev had no interests which consumed him. For the past twelve years he had turned from his passion for healing and at twenty-six found he was capable of killing where he once dreamed of saving lives.

As Robert joined him on the hill, Trev knew his friend had no inkling what his invitation for a prolonged stay at his plantation meant to Trev. Here at Rosehall, where violence was unknown, Trev found a measure of serenity that allowed the frequency of his nightmares to lessen. With his army service at an end, he was free to go home. Home to Sweet Bay, where Clinton waited anxiously for the son he had molded to take the reins of heir, now that the rumbling desire of the South to secede from the Union swept their land. But as much as Trev missed his home, he dreaded returning there.

"Damn it, Trev. You're not listening to me," Robert said, slapping the trailing ends of the reins he held against one buff-clad thigh. "I demand another race, double the wager, after I have someone's hide for Mambrino's casting that shoe."

"You've vented your spleen, Robert. You would no more lay a whip on Cato's or any slave's hide than you would touch one of your prize horses. As to the wager—" Trev stopped, his voice and gaze arrested by the fluid grace of a horse and rider skirting the edges of the cleanly picked cotton fields.

"Yes? Trev, what about the wager?"

"Later." Trev wanted no distraction. The rich black-loamed earth was a foil to the dappled gray, and the sun glinted off a long length of braided hair the shade of frosted moonlight. Like a young huntress, bare-backed and bare to the knees, the young woman rode, completely unaware that they watched her.

She came closer and Trev frowned when he recognized the dappled gray as one of Robert's mares. The horse's strength and sleek lines were the result of careful breeding, but he had no clue to what breeding had produced the same in her rider. He knew every belle in the county, thanks to Robert's penchant for hunting fair game, but he did not know this one. Moment by moment he became certain he wanted to.

Robert, silent and watchful once he saw who had captured Trev's attention, waited until the rider was out of their sight before he spoke.

"You know, Trev, I've been afraid that you were still brooding over your father's summons home, but I see our local vestal has caught your eye."

Dismissing the thickening of Robert's voice, Trev shook his head and turned to look at him. "Who is she to make free with your horses?" The two men were bonded with a twelve-year-old friendship that began with their simultaneous arrival at the Citadel in Charleston, carried through training at West Point, and aided in their survival in the western territory. They often shared their money, liquor, and women.

That was the reason Trevor now carefully schooled his interest. "Perhaps I was mistaken that the mare was yours."

"No, you weren't mistaken, Trev. It is my mare. And riding her, my fine stud, is Leah. The last of Boyd's daughters. Pretty and ripe enough to have half the randy bucks in the county chasing after her."

"Boyd's daughter? I can't seem to recall—"

"The overseer, Trev. Boyd Reese kept a close watch on all his daughters, but he's married two of them off. He'd kill the man who touched his daughter without a wedding ring. Arrogant attitude for one of his station, if you ask me."

"Stop being a prig, Robert. It sits ill on you, and even you can't blame a man for protecting his daughter."

With a shrug, Robert seemed to agree and began walking his horse down the hill. And since Robert had to walk, Trev dismounted and kept pace with him. Minutes later, as Leah came back into sight riding parallel to them, he wished he were mounted. She had spotted them and waved, now close enough that he could see the strength and delicacy of her features that comprised a stunning beauty. Her body was the delectable sort to arouse any buck's attention, but for a fleeting moment he had the fanciful thought that he was watching a bird that had been set free, now returning to its cage. He couldn't help but wonder if he were transferring his own morbid thoughts of freedom to her. Not caring whose daughter she was, not questioning his desire to see her again, he still managed to restrain himself from demanding that Robert call to her and introduce them. But he couldn't help himself from wanting to know more.

"You know, Robert, I keep thinking about your remark that Reese keeps a close watch on his daughter. How is it that she rides alone?"

"Leah's made free with the horses since she was old enough to sit one. Cato trusts her, and that's enough for me."

High praise, Trev knew. Cato had run the Rose-hall stable for almost thirty years. But his curiosity was not satisfied. "I don't recall seeing her on any of the visits I've made."

"She was up at her sister's farm near Talladega this month we've been home. Seems I recall one of Mother's letters made mention that they were hoping to marry her off this summer. There are farmers aplenty in these parts who wouldn't mind marrying her. She can't look higher for a marriage prospect, no matter how lovely she is, as long as her father remains our overseer." Robert, glancing over at Trev, noticed his frowning concentration. "Why all the questions? Figure to try your hand? She's a damn fetching baggage I wouldn't mind riding."

"Virgins don't interest me, Robert. You know that." But Trev admitted to himself he was curious. He could not imagine the lovely Leah as a farmer's wife. He spoke of their new wager, wanting to distract Robert. The DeMoise wealth, and the way Albert and Frances doted on their only son and heir, had contributed to Robert's absence of morals, for all his being a master of charm if the occasion warranted it. But then, Trev knew his own morals couldn't stand too close an examination.

The nightmare wrapped Trev in its grip. Moaning, he thrashed on the bed, grabbing hold of the sweat-soaked sheet, not feeling the silken weave, but the red Georgia clay dug from the grave.

He stood at the open grave no longer a child of seventeen, but not yet a man. An echo of the laughter at his helplessness once again drove him to his knees.

Too late. The whisper taunted and haunted him by turn. He had come home too late to save them. His mother was shrouded, soon to be buried, and Bella was gone, forbidden to contact him. He had planned to take Bella this time and flee Sweet Bay. Too late.

Guilt ate at him. He should have been able to

do something, anything, to stop the insidious terror that governed their lives. "Bella," he cried out, "I promised." And laughter came, roaring in his ears.

His muscles tensed. Again he felt the heavy hand resting on his shoulder, forcing him to remain kneeling by his mother's grave. The voice he hated whispered that it was all for the best, his mother was a tormented woman who deserved the peace of death, and he, her long-suffering husband, deserved to be free of the sickness that pervaded his home.

The agony of his grief nearly overwhelmed Trev. And there was Bella, always he had to remember Bella. His plan to escape was foiled and his sister gone. *He* had known. It was never revealed to Trev how his father had found out his intent to take Bella away once he received word that his mother was dying.

Essie, Bella's young maid, hid in the corner of her cabin, frightened of Clinton, frightened of what he would do to her. But she told Trev what he wanted to know. Told how Bella was crying and afraid when Clinton took her, ignoring his wife's cries to see her baby, uncaring of the relief he revealed once he had returned and found his wife dead.

For Trev, grief and guilt mingled with a sorrowing regret that he would never again seen his mother, had never said a last word to her. There would never be freedom, never be choices of his own. Bella was hostage to his obedience. Bella, at his father's mercy, when the man never knew any.

With a jerk, Trev came awake. The trembling aftermath of the nightmare left him stunned for a few minutes until he realized where he was. Shoving aside the finely woven netting that encompassed the four-poster bed, he came to his feet in a controlled, soundless rush. A remaining tremor chilled his naked flesh while the ragged edge of his breathing filled his ears.

The balcony doors of his bedroom at Rosehall were open, for Trev could not stand to be locked in a room, and the moonlight, clean with innocence, spilled a path that beckoned to him. It was an invitation he heeded.

Thickly humid air scented with the heavy perfume of night-blooming jasmine settled over his sweat-sheened body. Trev gripped the railing, leaning over it, drawing deep breaths only to release them slowly as he forced the nightmare to withdraw.

Nine years. It had been nine long years since his mother had died and he had been summoned home. Nearly ten since he had seen Bella, for she had already been sailing toward England. If it weren't for the DeMoises making discreet inquiries among their family and friends, Trev wouldn't even know where his sister was. Not that the knowledge helped in any way. Bella was so closely watched in her private school that he was lucky if she managed to smuggle out a note once a year.

The notes, by necessity brief, never hinted of where she was in England, but the pleas, repeated in a hand that had changed over the years from a childish scrawl to a young woman's elegant script, never varied.

She wanted to come home. Trevor was the only key that could unlock her prison.

His long-fingered hands dug into the wooden rail. By his honor he had tried, but no matter how much he pleased, there was more demanded of him. More to do, more to learn, more to make the man he hated from the depth of his soul proud of him. He had borne insult, so gently hinted at by a distant aunt in response to his letter about Bella, that if he learned to temper his wild ways which were a disrupting influence on a gently bred young woman, Bella could come home. And rumors had spread. But those wild ways were what made Clinton glow with pride. And made Trev hate himself for the dual role he was forced to play.

Honor demanded that he protect his sister, love for her demanded more, but there were times when the weight settled too heavy on his soul, and he hated Bella. He longed to abandon her to her own fate. He needed peace. But he could not buy peace at the cost of Bella locked away in an asylum for the insane, as Clinton had threatened to do several times. There was the fear, too, that any day would bring the announcement of her arranged marriage. A marriage that would be to a man Clinton thought fitting, in his mold.

The costs mounted in this night's accounting. His plan to seek out medical men of learning once he began the traditional Grand Tour of Europe had been thwarted by Clinton's plan to accompany him. Trev never went to Europe, but tried making his way north, only to discover within three days that he was being followed. He gave up then, never once writing to Bella of what she cost him in pride and dreams.

"Honor can be damned," he vowed. "I will have my freedom soon."

But as he turned back to his room, he found himself envisioning the natural grace of Leah riding, once again overcome by the sense that she appeared as caged as he.

* * *

The breakfast room was a charming addition to Rosehall that reflected the pastel shades of the late-blooming garden which terraced it. Trev, dressed in rust-colored riding breeches and loose linen shirt, stood with cup in hand, finishing the last of his morning coffee, and with it, shook off the fatigue of his sleepless night.

Seated at the oval walnut table, Robert ate heartily of smoked ham, poached eggs, and sweet potato biscuits. Trev almost envied his friend's appetite for all things, for Robert never allowed anything to interfere. When he set his cup and saucer on the sideboard, Robert glanced up.

"Ready to go?"

"Military discipline seems to have made a deeper impression on me."

"I've noticed. But I wish you would reconsider, Trev. It will be damn boring without you here. The musicale at the Meagues' holds other alluring draws. And I promise," he drawled with a decided twinkle in his dark brown eyes, "to keep the younger Miss Meague away from you. Norbeck claims the young lady—"

"Norbeck's a glutton for any light-skirt."

"True. But he was telling me she becomes inspired by these evening musicales. Seems they cause a yearning to view her garden by moonlight. Preferably from the chaise in the gazebo. The lustier, the better: She likes riding on top."

Trev swallowed his distaste. Men of Robert's class would bed any that allowed, but would be the first to demand chasity in their wives. "Eat hearty, my friend, rest well, for it appears you'll need your stamina," Trev said. He started to leave and found himself stopping to ask, "Do you ever want something more from life, Robert?"

"More? Between racing, gambling, drinking, and whoring, where the devil would I find time for more?"

Trev sighed to himself, shrugging off the depression that often followed a nightmare, leading him to contemplate the stretch of empty years still before him.

"Trev, you need a woman to dispel this cynical melancholy." His cheeky grin earned him one from Trev.

"You're right, of course," Trev returned with a mocking bow, falling into his expected role. "I shall ride about the countryside seeking a willing maid to ravish."

"That's the idea."

Trev offered Robert a thoughtful look as if he were considering it. "But I'll need to find one that does not yield so quickly. The piquancy of the chase gets lost."

"Damn, Trev, have some modesty."

"I do." But his own words had conjured up the image of Leah again, and he wondered if what Robert said was true. If pursued, would she not yield?

"The trouble with you, Trev, is that you're arrogant with your assumption that any woman is yours for the asking. I'd wager against you, but I don't care to lose my money."

"But there, dear friend, lies the difference between us. I only seek out those willing to partake in brief amours."

Interest flared in Robert's eyes as he recalled Trev's decided curiosity about Leah. "I should be thankful that you didn't insist on a wager. But I do know someone who would give you a run. It would certainly remove your jaded notion that only willing women are to be pursued. Unwilling's better."

With a slight inclination of his head, Trev coolly replied, "If you like. But trust me, Robert, I would likely lose."

"A first, I'm sure."

"Your faith in my prowess is most touching." Trev's muscles rippled with tension under the fine linen shirt as he lifted both hands to run his fingers through his collar-length black hair. Clean shaven, unlike Robert, who sported a mustache, Trev conceded to the fashion of the day with a growth of sideburns which extended a few inches down his jawline. Robert would never understand his restless boredom with the endless round of calls, dinners, assemblies, and balls to welcome them home. They had quickly palled after three weeks, as had the steady diet of rich foods after the Spartan rations of the army. Conversations, on the other hand, were Spartan. He loved his homeland, but tired of its braggarts. Firmly shutting the door he had inadvertently opened, Trev knew he had to be by himself.

"I do intend to be otherwise engaged this evening and already sent my regrets to the Meagues."

"Petrie's wife?"

"Crass of you to ask, Robert."

"There's been talk."

"He's fifty if he's a day and she's barely out of the schoolroom, and lonely. A light flirtation and nothing more, I assure you."

Robert set his fork down with a clang against the rim of delicate china, scenting a new trail. "But you do admit the quarry is close to Rosehall?"

Trev slid his hands into his pockets and rocked back on his bootheels. "I said nothing about pursuing quarry. And rather than continue this verbal fencing, have done," Trev warned.

Hooking one leg over the arm of the chair, Robert smiled and ignored the warning. It was rare of Trev to become defensive over his interest in a woman. The thought was intriguing and Robert eagerly pursued it. "You were like a stallion scenting a fresh mare when you saw Leah yesterday."

"Ah, now we have it," Trev said with a nod of understanding. "You want her for yourself. Territorial, Robert? You've never been before."

There was a mocking edge to Trev's voice that angered Robert. "You don't deny it."

"You know very well I've no liking for unplowed ground."

"Unlike me? You've seen her. The face is lovely. The body, let me assure you, is exquisite, and I've never known you to refuse such attractive, easy prey."

"Prey? Listen to yourself, Robert. You're obsessed with the girl. There is no need to continue. I shall make every effort to avoid her and leave you a clear field."

"I wish I could believe you."

"If you can't, I won't waste breath to convince you."

Robert flinched. Gone was the banter and the warning. The cool disdain of Trev's voice was rarely turned on him. Trev's eyes, brightened to an intense blue which had caused more than one man to back away from him, were fixed with a piercing directness on him. Slowly unhooking his leg from the chair, Robert sat up and gripped the table. If he said one more wrong word, he risked having the cynical stranger that Trev easily became erect a barrier between them.

"I owe you an apology, Trev."

"Accepted and forgotten." He rimmed the gold edge of his cup, his voice very, very soft. "Needed or not, you've warned me off. Cease fire, my friend. Truly your concern is unwarranted. I would never bring disgrace to your home. Your overseer's daughter belongs to Rosehall; I'll respect that."

"Good Lord, Trev. I didn't mean to imply that you'd run out and rape her."

They both looked away from each other, but Trev had trouble banishing the words he heard unspoken . . . *unlike me.* Robert had raped once and Trev knew the incident had never been forgotten by either of them.

Robert broke the growing silence. "Leah is as much a part of Rosehall as the slaves. I've never denied you anything you wanted at my home. I won't begin now. I'm well aware that unlike some we could both name, you would never abuse our hospitality."

"Your faith is once more most touching."

The mocking tolerance underscoring Trev's words sent Robert's gaze searching his friend's features. "You're doing it again."

"Pardon? Doing what?" But even as he asked, Trev knew, and a small mocking smile played over his lips.

"Going off, that's what. Removing yourself. I can't explain. You're here, but not." Taking care in picking up his fork, Robert stared down at the food he no longer wanted. "I'm not imparting a bit of sense, am I?"

"Yes, I am afraid you are," Trev answered without hesitation. "I didn't think you noticed."

"Well, I have," Robert replied with resentment that Trev closed himself off too easily. Shrugging, he added, "About Leah. Tumble her if you want. It's no matter to me."

"A peace offering? Thank you." But Trev had to swallow bile at the thought of Robert's careless words said so unthinkingly. If any of their acquaintances had heard them, poor Leah would find herself flat on her back before day's end.

Believing he had indeed made peace, Robert, as was his nature, was generous. "Don't let Mother have an inkling. She's fond of the girl and offered to pay for her schooling."

"Schooling? Did my eyes deceive me?"

"No. They never do. She's seventeen or eighteen. Kept tied to mama's apron because she is the last daughter. As for the schooling, I admit it is unusual. But Reese was newly married, just as my parents were, when my father hired him. Not having daughters of her own, my mother's given a generous dower gift when the older girls married with my father's approval, for Reese has proven himself a damn good overseer."

"But Leah asked for more schooling?"

"The girl's got a notion that she wants to teach. I can't imagine more of a waste."

"A bit of a bluestocking residing at Rosehall all this time?"

"Don't poke fun at me. I've never made it a secret that I dislike books. Another of Mother's disappointments." Robert shoved his plate away. "Leah outgrew playing down at the quarters and asked Mother to teach her to read. Between Mother's effort, a little schooling, and the liberty of borrowing books from our library, Leah proved herself an apt pupil. Mother shared Tennyson with her, of all things, and filled the girl's head with trite tales of love. Leah was fascinated with our library as I never was, and Mother saw no harm in indulging her."

"And we cannot forget, you allow her the liberty of riding your prize horses."

Defensive, Robert glanced up and saw Trev's indulgent smile. His gaze met Trev's and relief came that the intensity was gone. "Aside from lecherous motives that you attribute to me, she is good with my horses. Never once abused a horse, or Cato would have her hide, even if he is slave. And it hurt no one."

"Speaking of which, I'm sure Cato is wondering where I am."

"Oh, how lovely. You are both still here," said a soft voice.

"Mother." Robert rose immediately and went to her side, careful not to crush the striped linen day gown with its wide circular crinoline that Frances DeMoise managed gracefully through the doorway. Trev watched him kiss her offered cheek, then move to pull out a chair for her while he poured out a fragrant cup of coffee and set it at her place. Smiling with genuine warmth, despite her arrival thwarting his escape, Trev returned her greeting and assured her that, as always, he had slept well.

"I despair of you, Trevor. Once again you have dispensed with Henry being here to serve. How ever are we to overcome your dislike of hovering servants?"

"I do it only for the pleasure of serving you myself," he returned, already lifting the silver covers off the dishes keeping the array of food warm on the sideboard.

"Stop flirting with him, Mother. This morning Trev's immune to any woman's charms."

"Hush yourself, Robert. It's disrespectful to talk about flirting with your mother." This was an oft-repeated scene between them, but Frances was vain and smoothed the plum ribbon- and lace-trimmed collar of her gown. She admired the flare of her pagoda sleeves, edged with the same trim, and flicked out a wrinkle in her hem. Her mirror assured her the delicate shade of cream linen she wore lent her complexion a rosy glow, and as Trev stood waiting with plate in hand for her selections, she preened under his admiring gaze.

"One biscuit, Trevor. Just a drop of honey on top, mind you." With a glance at Robert's discarded plate, she added, "And a small—mind you, very small—slice of ham. Robert, you may pour the cream." For a moment Frances ignored her son, as she was wont to do through the years when Trevor was present, and watched every move of Trevor's lithe body. Forty-three, she reminded herself, touching the small amethyst ear-bobs that peeked from sleekly coiled brown hair, was not too old to enjoy having a breathtakingly handsome young man dance attendance on her.

"Dearest Trevor, say you will be free to join me on my morning calls. You have caused a considerable stir among our belles and I do believe they become quite impatient with my continued excuses for your absence."

"But I can depend upon your generous spirit to forgive me any distress I've caused, can't I?" Trev set the plate in front of her and smiled. Frances was tall for a woman, which made shorter men uncomfortable. She was no great beauty, but everyone tended to dismiss that when she decided to charm with her vivacious and inborn coquettish manner. Unbidden and disquieting came the thought that Leah appeared tall for a woman, too.

Robert, leaning back in his chair, observed Trev's skillful handling of his mother, charming her so that her smile never once wavered, but holding firm to his regrets for not joining her. Within two years of their meeting, Robert understood that Trev had a way with women. He was too handsome, with an underlying air of recklessness always tempered by a courtly manner which appealed to women, young and old. If he didn't feel so secure in his own masculinity, Robert would have been jealous.

"You, sir," Frances intoned at Trev's conclusion, "are of hardened heart, but so sweet talkin' that I do forgive you." She blushed prettily when Trev leaned over to raise her hand to his lips. "Be off. You're dressed for riding and I can see you desire to be about your business. Do not break any more hearts, Trev, or I shall have mamas coming to call. But you, Robert," she said, turning to face her son, "you will accompany me. This time you will offer excuses for him."

"There are none. He doesn't need them. After all these years you should know that Trev never explains himself. It adds to the mystery of the man and becomes part of his most irresistible charm."

Frances sipped her coffee, her gaze following Trevor's retreat. She was pleased with the friendship that had grown steadily between her only child and Trevor. Intriguing as Trevor was—for she never believed one word of those rumors giving his behavior as the reason his sister had to remain in England—he kept Robert from the wilder excesses that could ruin a reputation. There was no jealousy in either young man for the other.

Most remarkable, she thought, setting her cup down. She knew their society prided itself on subtly goading competition among its elegant, bored, and most restless young blades.

But if the heated talk of secession did not cease, those same young men would face danger. She couldn't bear it again. Albert would return from Montgomery and tell her it was all talk, nothing more. There was no power in the world that could force the South into giving up slavery. With a sigh, she dismissed her musings. There would never be a war.

Chapter Two

"MAMA, I've been home three days from visiting Sarah, and Papa still won't tell me his decision about going to school."

"An' he won't till he's ready. I told you we'd talk about it and we have."

Leah paused in her hoeing and wiped the sweat from her brow. Not wearing a bonnet while helping her mother weed their vegetable garden wasn't so much another of her small rebellious acts as a need to feel the sun. She glanced at a new blister forming where her cotton glove was torn, resenting the fact that her hands would be as work-rough as her mother's before long. If her parents refused Mrs. DeMoise's offer to pay for her schooling, Leah knew the sameness of her mother and sisters' days was the fate that awaited her.

"If it's the money, Mama—"

"Your father has enough put by for you. But he wanted to spend it on your marriage portion. 'Sides, he won't want to be beholden to any man. That's not his way."

Leah heeded the dismissal in her mother's voice, knowing she had stated the truth. Her father had even refused to have slave help for them when Mr. DeMoise had offered. Why would he need help? he reasoned. He had three strong and dutiful daughters. It was yet another of the silent questions that plagued her and would likely never be answered. She didn't understand how her parents kept up this separation of her father's work of overseeing slaves and their family life.

Folding her hands over the top of the hoe's handle, Leah rested her chin on them, dreamily staring toward the big house. Books had opened a new world to her, one she hungered to pursue. From the quarters, she heard squeals of children's laughter as a game of sheepmeat was begun. It had been so long since she had the freedom to play the game of tag, throwing a yarn ball from one to other. Her days were ordered from waking to sleep, but even as she wished for play, Leah knew she would never be owned. If her parents had their way, however, slavery of another sort waited.

She came to with a start as her gaze focused sharply on the back lane from the quarters. Trevor Shelby was riding away and Leah felt the stab of envy for his freedom. Over the years he had visited Rosehall, she had watched him grow from lanky boy to a breathtakingly handsome man. He was Robert's best friend, but Leah sensed a difference in Trevor. She knew it was he, not Robert, that fired gossip from the slave quarters to the big houses of the country's richest plantations because so little was known about him.

"Leah! Leah! What's wrong with you? I don't know why you insist on being out here without your bonnet. There's weeds growin' while you stand there idle."

With a guilty start, Leah lifted the hoe and halfheartedly began whacking at the weeds. The kind of freedom she longed for was hers to dream about, for no one could take those from her, but she knew, as much as her parents loved her, they wanted the same for her as their other daughters. Marriage to a hardworking, sober, God-fearing man who could give her a secure home and a baby every year. Sarah wasn't even through her third full year of marriage to Nicholas and she had already carried her third child. Ruth, the eldest, had a brood of six that her husband, Martin, swore would be doubled in another six years.

It wasn't right that she had no choice. Someday she wanted a family of her own, but not now. And she wanted more from the man she would marry. The practical voice that kept her from foolish mistakes reminded her that knights brave and bold lived only in the books she had learned to read with Frances DeMoise's help.

Leah began to work with a renewed vigor, knowing if she got through the weeding, she might steal away to the library for an hour or so. The bread was rising, and her mother would let her go as long as she was home before her father. Since this was Frances DeMoise's day for calls, Leah would have the room to herself, for Robert was sure to accompany his mother.

And Trevor Shelby, with his disturbing presence, was out riding.

Nearly an hour later saw her chores finished to her mother's satisfaction and while Leah primed the outside pump so she and her mother could wash, she asked permission to go.

Thoughtfully drying her hands, Hedda Reese studied her youngest daughter, despairing of having her foolish notions ended.

"I thought you might bring the Widow Hunsicker a loaf of bread after it's baked, Leah."

"I won't be gone long. I'll take it over, Mama,

but Mrs. DeMoise sent word by Mama Rassia that she has a new edition of Tennyson and for me to come see it."

"Mama Rassia has enough to do running the big house without carrying messages. And this Tenny, I suppose it's another of those books that fill your head with—"

"Mama, his name is Tennyson, and he's a poet. I wish you would let me read you some of his words. He creates pictures in my mind." Leah saw her mother's dismay and solaced herself with the oft silently repeated verse from the poet's "The Two Voices": "A little hint to solace woe,/ A hint, a whisper breathing low,/ 'I may not speak of what I know.' "

Hedda started to reach out to her daughter, but withdrew her hand. "You get lost in your thoughts, Leah. Papa worries about that. I know you've never been like your sisters, but we love you and wish you would settle on one young man and marry. You're more than of age."

Leah, biting her lip as the harsh soap stung the weeping blister, merely nodded. She thought of the hoarded bar of scented soap in her room, a gift from Mrs. DeMoise, soap her father called sinful. But it wasn't. The perfume of Frances's roses, admired and desired by most of the county, could never be that. Nothing so beautiful could ever be sinful.

"Papa's been good, knowing how I want to keep you with me awhile longer with both your sisters gone. I do so miss having my girls about."

With a grateful smile, Leah thanked her. She knew her mother was the only one to stand in the way of her father arranging a marriage for her. Leah had managed to make her mother understand that she simply didn't care for one of the young men who had been pressing their suits these past two years. But it wasn't easy. Her parents were simple people in all their ways—in food and dress and beliefs. Her father was well paid for his work, but rarely spent money for what he called fancies. She had never seen her father without his soberly cut coat and his thinning hair combed straight back from his ruggedly carved features, which lent a stern look.

Worrying the folds of her faded apron, Hedda started for the door, only to stop and turn back. "Young Jamison stopped by to see your father yesterday, Leah." She waited for her daughter's attention, and while not pleased to see a growing wariness in her eyes, continued. "He hoped to see you after service on Sunday. We thought about inviting him to supper, if you would like."

Panic flared. The gangly built Jamison couldn't read, spat whenever he was close enough to talk, and had already buried a wife. "I wish . . . I beg you don't."

Sagely nodding, Hedda asked, "Then what Sarah believes is true? Her neighbor caught your eye? She and Nicholas speak highly of Roddy Cooper. A man of the land, sober, God-fearing, and in need of a good wife now that he has a farm of his own."

"All that is true and made most plain to me on my visit, but you know I want to teach, Mama. Going away to school—"

"We agreed to consider it, Leah. Nothing has been settled. Seeing your sisters' happiness in their marriages should have convinced you that we do know best."

"Yes, Mama." It was senseless to argue. Sarah and Ruth seemed content, as did her mother. But as Leah looked at her, she wondered why marriage meant that a woman stopped caring about herself. Her mother never dressed her fading blond hair in a more becoming style. There was a miniature, painted and sent to her father after their marriage had been arranged, that revealed a lovely young woman whom Leah resembled more than either of her sisters. Her mother's only concession to feminine vanity, if Leah could call it that, was wearing a cameo on her best crocheted collar to service. Her only other jewelry was the thin gold wedding ring she never removed.

A guilty flush stole over her cheeks for her critical thoughts. She was loved, and while her parents wanted her to step freely into the cage they believed she belonged in, they had not yet forced her into it.

"These books, Leah, give you notions above your station. A woman should be content with her lot."

"Yes, Mama. I will remember."

"There's pride to be had in making a home for a hardworking man who doesn't drink or gamble away his wages."

But does Papa ever make your blood thunder with need, Mama? The question formed before Leah could stop it, and she was ashamed to think of her parents in that way. A devil's thought planted by those books, her father would have said, but Leah couldn't believe it. What she saw for herself was the belief her mother held, giving her a serene look, just as her father wore a look of sober contentment at day's end. Was she forever to be denied wanting more?

"Wear your muslin if you insist on going up to the house, Leah. And mind you," Hedda called to her already fleeing daughter, "go in the back way.

Mrs. DeMoise may let you use her library, but she won't want the likes of you traipsing through her home."

Dismay filled her, along with worry for her daughter. Hedda slowly folded the linen towel and hung it on the doweled rack for her husband's use. She had hoped this last visit to Sarah would settle Leah down. Instead, her youngest had come home restless and secretive, but still determined not to marry.

She understood the anxious flutters that might panic her child at the thought of marrying a virtual stranger. But Boyd had been patient and kind. Nicholas and Martin were men of his ilk, not wild like Robert or his friends. Leah longed for the impossible, but Hedda hadn't the heart to tell her so.

"All I can give her is a few weeks more," Hedda whispered, and felt a strange shiver that she ignored. Leah was safe enough visiting a room filled with books.

But Leah didn't go to the library. She made her way by a twisted path that kept her from sight to the pasture where Dancer's Lady was kept. The docile mare trotted over to the fence, neighing her greeting, and Leah, needing to be rid of a stifling feeling, climbed the split-rail and mounted her. She had never learned to ride with bridle or saddle, and Cato claimed her seat was as graceful and natural as any lady's, even if she rode astride. Cato would know; he chose the mounts when the De-Moises had house parties with guests often staying for days afterward.

Riding was her secret forbidden joy and Leah refused to give it up. With a whisper to the mare, Leah urged her to take the fence. Her husky laughter was swallowed by a rush of wind as she bent low over the mare's neck, fingers tangled in the dark mane, and the horse stretched out to her full stride, giving Leah the freedom she craved.

Trev, returning across the unfenced pasture, heard the laughter and found himself watching rider and horse move as one to take the fence in a smooth flowing jump. King High, the black he rode, was a recent addition to Robert's stable and named for the high card that had won him. The stallion reared in challenge to the fleet-footed mare racing away from him, and Trev was caught unaware.

He kept his seat, but almost lost a rein, and the black took off in a ground-eating chase. He knew Leah saw him. Her laugh rang out, husky and enticing, calling to him with reckless abandon. Trev could have stopped, but he was angry that she dared risk blooded horseflesh in the heat of the day, not to mention her own neck.

Sunlight kissed the flying length of her braid and the sleek lines of her bare-to-the-knee legs. He let the black have his head following the flattened path she made ahead of them through the browned summer grasses. She was grace and beauty, but beautiful women adorned the South. It was another of its prides. Yet in Leah he fancied he saw a strength rarely displayed. Knowing about her desire to teach, understanding how futile it was, gave him a strange sense of viewing a kindred spirit being railed into an unsuitable mold.

She glanced back, then, bold as any youth, seemed to go out of her way to jump whatever lay in the path, and Trev found admiration for her skill turning to excitement with her unspoken challenge. King High began to close the distance between them. Trev could see the damp patches on her dark blue gown. His own sweat had his shirt clinging to him and the big black's body threw off additional heat.

The fluid line of her slender back had him wondering if Leah was a true daughter of the Reeses. Both her parents were wide of girth and solidly built, neither as tall as Leah. Their stature reflected the many European immigrants peopling the South, most of them farmers, or workers for the wealthy French, Spanish, and British, whose families had arrived as settlers and vied for dominance after removing the Choctaw and Creek Indians.

Trev was abruptly brought out of his thoughts as the black swerved to avoid the low-growing brush that narrowed the track. He saw that she was riding toward the bluff overlooking the Coosa River, but didn't slacken her pace. She risked herself and the mare. The surge of anger Trev felt was drowned in the primitive beat of his blood as he closed on his quarry. Cutting around a small copse of hickory trees gave him the lead. The stallion, determined to prove his dominance over the mare, needed no urging for speed.

King High fought him for control. The black moved to crowd the mare against the rise of boulders narrowing the path. Fearing injury to Leah, Trev took advantage of their closeness to wrap his arm around her waist, dragging her off the mare and up against him.

His boot was crushed between the horses. He strained against the mare's heaving side to gain room. The black tried to rear, screaming his challenge. Trev was forced to give him a vicious kick, then another, all the while keeping a tight hold on Leah. He yanked on the reins, knowing the metal bit was cutting the horse's mouth. Cursing, he pressed his knees against the sweat-flecked sides of the powerful animal, which still fought him.

The mare squealed as King High cruelly bit her neck, keeping her against the rocks, cutting off her lurching moves. Trev instantly responded with a soothing caress in his voice. He knew the break-point rage of the quivering horse whose instincts made him battle his rider for control. The black's ears were flattened, but each effort to rear was thwarted by Trev's strength.

For minutes Trev used a soft, bewitching voice that relentlessly refused to break until both horses came to a shuddering standstill.

"Don't move," he grated from between clenched teeth.

Leah instinctively obeyed the harsh order, too shocked to do anything else.

Trev had a disjointed awareness. Leah's rigid shoulder pressed against his heaving chest. His legs, taut with strain, cradled her firm buttocks and thighs. She had not fought him. Never screamed. Never uttered a sound. He didn't know when she had moved to sit crossways, her bare legs tucked tight and clear of his. The hot scent of the chase permeated his pores. The same wild heat that quivered through the stallion beneath him sent Trev into stillness. He felt the silky slide of their bodies, dragged air in as if there were none to be found, saw the bare curve of Leah's neck as she lowered her head. He inhaled the lush feminine scent of her. Fragments. Moments locked in time.

His gaze finally focused on the rough weave of her gown, then tracked the line of her shoulder where the seam was torn. He fought for control,

thankful she had obeyed him and not moved.
Thankful, too, she had not spoken.

Trembling, Leah held tight to the stallion's
mane, sensing a battle still being waged, but too
frightened to speak.

Trev knew how to deal with the sudden heat
danger sent streaming into his body. Sharpened
clarity changed his awareness, while instincts,
honed in an unforgiving western land where care-
lessness meant a man's death, told him what was
happening to Leah. Shock was sliding away. She
knew she was safe, or should, he thought, and had
to be thinking about what happened.

Her trembling turned to shudders, and the heat
of his blood turned into an aroused fierceness that
ripped into his control. He wanted her. With the
same primitive urge that had sent the stallion after
the mare, he wanted her. Now, with a surge of
hunger that demanded he take her down to the
summer grass and make love to her until day reclaimed the night.

And when she whimpered, lifting her face and
looking up at him, Trev lost his breath to see the
meld of fear and innocent desire in her large
brown eyes. Seductively lashed, they quickly
closed, and he was left staring at the faintly arched
brows that were darker than her eyes. Her brows
and lashes were a startling contrast against her
hair that stole its color from moon and sun alike.
He wanted to take her innocent mouth and teach
her a woman's passion.

Her skin was lightly burnished, sheened with
moisture, and without thinking he leaned close,
not to her flushed cheek but to press a kiss against
the torn shoulder of her gown.

"You're safe, Leah. You know that, don't you?"

But even as he asked, he heard the thick roil in his voice that he couldn't hide. Just as the intimate press of their bodies revealed the heat and heaviness of his desire.

"Loose me," she whispered, licking her too-dry lips. Leah was shaken by the piercing scrutiny of his deep blue eyes. She stared down at her white knuckled fingers still gripping the rein. She felt dazed, the stallion's scream echoing with the mare's frightened squeals while she had to fight for breath. Waiting for him to set her down, she made no move to struggle, having learned that some men enjoyed wielding their strength against anything more helpless than they. The shivering wouldn't cease, yet she wasn't cold.

Once more she bit back her pride and begged to be let go.

Fear. He knew hers as if it were his own. But seeing the slight flare of her nostrils his kiss had brought, along with the trembling lift of her breasts, had generated a surge of lustful need he couldn't temper. She was everything that Robert claimed, ripe and tantalizing enough to arouse the most jaded man's senses, and the knowledge once again changed his body to become more . . . predatory. He had frightened her and now thought to awaken her passion, but a last bit of sanity reminded him he wasn't going to touch her. He had no right to.

Trev used his boot to create enough space to release her. The stallion jerked his head as Trev forced him to move away from the mare. Leah had no choice but to touch him as she slid to the ground, quickly putting distance between them.

The sheltering boughs of the lone chestnut tree at the top of the bluff offered the only haven.

Without looking back, Leah hurried there. She had seen lust in men's eyes before this. But Trevor Shelby's gaze had been tempered with more. Pleasure. Passion. Completion. Her body responded to him while her mind rejected the knowledge. Deep inside her, a tightening sensation became an unfamiliar ache. The beat of her heart was wild, her breasts swelled until they hurt, and an unknown hollowness throbbed between her legs.

Too new, her feelings and reaction frightened her. She had never desired a man. Never thought to burn at the mere touch of his lips against her skin. But Trevor had brought that to her. She had never thought to have him chase her when she saw him riding. It was the reckless need to be free for a while that had made her laugh when she took the fence. Now she was alone with him, and he was Robert's friend. Fear chilled her spine. She had run from Robert's friends before, and a quick glance over her shoulder showed her he had dismounted and leaned against the boulder, cutting off her escape.

But he had said she was safe. Dare she believe him? Wrapping her arms around her waist, Leah moved closer to the edge of the bluff, staring down into the swirling ribbon of the river.

"I won't stop you from leaving, Leah," Trev said in an effort to reassure her and bring her back from the edge. He wished he could order his body as easily.

"You hunted me down," she returned in a breathless voice, without turning.

"No. I accepted your challenge to race."

"I never challenged you."

Trev closed his eyes, seeing again the meld of fear and innocent desire in hers. She didn't know, he had to admit that, at least to himself. "Perhaps not, and it was my mistake. But you must realize that you risked yourself and the mare with a headlong race in the heat of the day."

"I'd never harm one of Robert's horses." Curiosity had her turning around to face him. He had tied off the stallion's reins and moved closer to her, his hands in his pockets, and she sensed his threat, although he merely leaned against the rock and crossed his booted ankles.

"I've met Robert's friends before."

"And?" Trev asked in response to the unspoken accusation he heard. "I'm not like the others, Leah."

"So other ladies have said."

That damnable gossip again! But it was the arrogant lift of her chin and the wary way she watched him as his body was too slow to cool that had Trev say, "But then, you're not quite the lady, are you? Ladies, the ones I'm acquainted with, don't ride bareback and astride." It was mild compared to the scathing remarks he could easily make. His gaze lingered on the damp spots of her unadorned gown.

It was the blazing intensity returning to his eyes that made Leah forget who he was, who she was. "You're very much like Robert and the others, a strutting peacock who thinks his birth and wealth give him the right to be indulged at very turn. Men like you believe the world and all the lesser beings in it belong in your pleasure garden."

Trev came away from the rock slowly, keeping his hands clenched and in his pockets to stop him from grabbing hold and shaking her. Her insults stung, and yet reflected too much of what he believed to be true. The play was his and Trev marshaled his need to deny her accusation about him.

He was so still—still and dangerous—that Leah found she was holding her breath. But the danger was somehow beguiling. For the first time she was achingly aware of her body, of being female, incomplete and needing. Yet she was afraid of him, of what he made her feel. He didn't deny he sought only his pleasure. What she didn't understand was why, or the reason an insidious whisper was filling her mind.

Lovers.

She and Trevor Shelby would be lovers.

Shock chilled her heated skin. It was there in his deep blue eyes watching her: the same knowledge.

A sudden need replaced all others. The need to reject him. Panic urged her to find fault with him. But no matter how she searched the hard length of his body, the breath-stealing cut of his features, she found no visible flaw. The whispers about him were all true. He was a man made to tempt the most saintly of women. Even married ones like the young Mrs. Petrie.

Trev's senses were too acute not to realize the animallike wariness in her eyes. He wanted it gone. The need to prove to her that he wasn't like Robert and the others was enough to dampen his ardor.

"Will you be all right to ride back now?"

"You'll let me go?"

"It was never my intent to rape you, Leah." He ignored her cry, giving in to the urge to explain. "I was bored and restless and never meant to make you feel hunted or threatened."

"You did all that and more."

It was foolish to repeat that he already knew as much, and Trev found that he wanted to keep her awhile longer. "Perhaps we can begin anew," he suggested with lazy indulgence. And to remove the thought of being a threat, he settled himself on the ground and leaned back against the boulder. "Miss Reese, may I present myself, Mr. Trevor Randolph Shelby. Of late, I've resigned my commission in the federal army, where I served for the last two years. My conduct as an officer was without stain, and at present I am the guest of Robert DeMoise."

She fought the laughter his mocking seriousness brought, but the sudden release of tension was too much for her. Leah found herself inclining her head, the move as unconsciously graceful as any grand dame. "I am pleased to make your acquaintance, Mr. Shelby."

"And will you allow me the liberty to share the view?"

"On such short acquaintance? I believe not."

The proper answer, one a lady would give, just the right horrified tone underscoring every word, but her eyes gave the lie to it. They sparkled with a mischievous light that brought Trev to his feet.

"I'll steal it, then."

Leah didn't move. There was a more explicit promise, unspoken but there, and it ensnared her. "Are you a thief?"

"Of time."

"As I am."

Trev was stunned that the admission came from him, but more at her answer. "Leah?"

"No," she whispered, but even to herself unsure if she was admitting the truth or denying it. "I must go before I'm missed." She ran to Dancer's Lady, grasping hold of her mane and swinging herself up before he could move to help her, but when she turned the mare to start down the path, Trev blocked her way.

"Will you meet me here tomorrow?" He brought his gaze to hers. *I want you.* But the words were silently his. The awareness of tension claiming her didn't startle him, but he felt its like take hold of him. Suddenly he knew, no matter how he denied it, that while Leah was frightened of him, she would come to him again.

"I'll be waiting, Leah. Don't disappoint me."

She shook her head, confusion holding sway. Leah saw his handsomeness, felt the tug of his striking maleness, but had to refuse. He was a threat to her. Dangerous. But an image formed, faint and shadowed in her mind, and she closed her eyes, letting the shadows define themselves. Fear grew, for it seemed that he had invaded her mind. It was Trevor she saw. It was his hands she felt touching her naked body. Him inside her. . . .

With a wrenching cry, Leah opened her eyes, fighting to chase the image away. Panic spawned by the lightning-raw desire that flashed between them sent her heels digging into the mare's sides.

At the last possible moment, Trev stepped aside. "I'll wait for you."

It was both command and promise.

Chapter Three

LEAH had grown up listening each night to the soft, loving murmurs coming from her parents' bedroom across the hall. The comforting sounds had lulled her to sleep, safe and secure in her world. Their whispers had been silenced by sleep for nearly an hour now, but for her, filled with a restlessness, there was no sleep.

Tonight, for the first time, she had lied to them, not only about her lack of appetite, but about why she had changed her gown. Her mother instantly ceased her gentle probing about Roddy Cooper, expressing concern over her flushed state, and shooed her off to bed. But Leah's suspicions were confirmed that her parents were seriously considering his offer of marriage, since they had continued to talk about him after she had left.

There was little room in her mind for Roddy when all she saw was Trevor Shelby.

A strange, waiting tension held Leah supine on her bed. She was clad in a clean lawn chemise and ankle-length pantalets, her hands slightly curled at her sides. The small clock that adorned the top of the plain wooden chest kept cadence with the steady beat of her heart. But in her mind, Leah heard time running out on her bid for freedom.

From the unshuttered window a sluggishly warm

breeze carried the night sounds of field and forest. For the last few minutes the low drone of voices from the slave quarters had ceased. She listened to the gray moss brush against the side of the clapboards. The moss was draped within the branches of the live oak that shaded her room and made her think of the tattered remains of some fragile cloth.

The lush scent of yellow jasmine, wreathed in clusters among the tangled vines growing against the side of the house, made her aware of the same scent rising from her heated body. She had bathed using the finely milled soap imbued with the flower's perfume. The soap was another gift from Robert's mother that she hoarded.

Just as she hoarded the minutes spent with Trevor. He had claimed he was a thief of time and had wrung her instant admission. For that brief moment Leah was sure they had both spoken the truth, but she didn't understand why he would say it. And it was far easier to think of this and not remember those frightening moments when he had swept her off the mare or the reason she had trusted him. But she had trusted him, instantly and instinctively, not only then, but minutes later when he had stated he was not like Robert and his other friends.

No, she told herself, it wasn't a matter of distrusting him, but herself. He made her feel a yearning that was tying her insides into French knots like the stitches in needlework. He made her want . . . too much. She shivered, feeling again the light press of his lips against her shoulder through the tear in her gown. The image rose in her mind, she and Trevor entwined, bringing the inner battle she fought out in the open.

She recalled her belief, enforced by all she had

been taught, that men might desire, but a woman must remain chaste until blessed by the sanctity of marriage. No matter how it angered her, chastity and her learned wifely skills were all of value she had. No man would care about her dreams. Dreams she didn't want to give up. Roddy Cooper certainly wouldn't care that pressing his offer of marriage would steal them from her. And Trevor . . .

And someone like Trevor, who had never been denied what he wanted, could never understand what turmoil he caused her.

He had awakened need.

Leah wrapped her arms around her waist, Tennyson's epics of love lost and found by knights and ladies of Arthur's court rushing from her memory with sudden new meanings. Tales of the yearning for the forbidden, of the warnings of danger in wait for those who would not heed them.

She was wrong to think about casting aside her family's teachings. Things she had silently questioned and doubted, but knew she would never disregard. What had Trevor set free with the blazing intensity of his blue eyes and that charming smile as he tried to set her at ease? He had touched and held her and let her go, yet she felt more threatened by him than the neighboring bucks who believed the overseer's daughter was fair game, no better than white trash.

Forbidden or not, the warnings held no weight in a mind filled with the promise she had seen in his. Pleasure. Passion and completion.

With a soft, agonizing moan, Leah turned to her side, her arms squeezing her body as if to still the desire that was filling her. *Thief of time.* Those words haunted her, for she admitted now that beyond the physical yearning that deviled her, she sensed darker, more dangerous currents in Trevor that drew her even as they frightened her. What truly bewildered her was the need she had to know them, to take that momentary darkness from his eyes.

Foolish thought for a foolish woman. She was strong enough to deny him. She lay there, agonizing over a decision that held open a door to ruin. The feelings he stirred in her were terrifying in their intense pleasure, and the flush ran through her, building moment by moment, into a longing to be with him.

There was no solace to be had turning and twisting on her bed. Leah rushed to the window, holding tight to the sill. She breathed deeply, listening to the bullfrogs croaking and the whippoorwills calling. Off in the distance she heard a fox barking and the clamor raised by the hounds in their pens. These were the sounds of her world, not the unspoken whispers of a man who offered her nothing.

The full moon rose up over the far hill and made a white cape of the land below. The summer's night called to her and Leah turned away.

The clamor of the hounds drew Trev to step outside the multipaned doors of the library. A flagstone oval was enclosed by a neatly trimmed hedge nearly his height with an arched opening that led to the orchard. He sipped his brandy, regretting his decision to remain at Rosehall. There were times when he should heed his own warning not to be alone with his thoughts.

Why had he told Leah he was a thief of time? And why had he asked her to meet him? It unsettled him to know he hadn't been able to lie to her. Whatever happened to his noble assurances to Robert that he had no intention of chasing after quarry that didn't know the rules of the game?

To distract himself, Trev glanced skyward and identified Ursa Major, then located the two pointer stars of Merak and Dubhe. He tracked an invisible line from them to Polaris, the bright North Star, and noted the passing of the eleventh hour. Was Robert enjoying the favors of the younger Meague daughter? Mamas warned their darlings not to be free with their favors until after marriage and men like Robert did their utmost to seduce them from their teachings.

He couldn't stop the image of Leah's wary eyes from coming to him. No brandy, no distraction he offered himself would remove her from his mind. He watched the white flotilla of clouds skim across the moon and turned back to the darkened library. Hours of being alone after Henry had delivered a supper tray to him had Trev unconsciously attuned to every untoward sound. He glanced behind him, saw nothing, and decided the brandy he had consumed had him hearing what was not there.

Seated in one of the pair of leather wing chairs before the blackened fireplace, Trev stretched out his legs and closed his eyes, deliberately blanking his mind. Seconds later a light shuffling noise on the flagstones brought him fully alert.

Breathless from running, Leah poised outside the open doors to the library. She knew the De-Moises were away, and with them, Trevor, but Henry would never be so careless as to leave the doors open. Moonlight did not penetrate the darkened room, but Leah knew the placement of every book lining the shelves as well as the massive furniture. Still, she hesitated on the threshold.

It was her scent that identified Leah to Trev. He didn't move, curious to see what she intended. The thought crossed his mind that should he suddenly rise up from the chair, he would frighten her off. Without examining why, he knew he did not want that to happen. This wasn't the same as his heeding his own counsel to stay away from her.

Henry and Mama Rassia were in their cabin down in the quarters. He had dismissed the houseboys and maids to return to their families. There was no one here and Leah blamed her caution on the unsettling events of the day. Her eyes adjusted to the darkness, and she entered the room, avoiding the darker shadows of the furniture as she moved quickly to the far wall where her favorite book was shelved.

"Have I caught a thief?" Trev murmured in a deceptively gentle voice from behind her.

She gasped, dropping the book she had taken, and spun around to face him. He stood so close, their breaths mingled and her swaying move brought him tantalizingly near.

"Frances . . . Mrs. DeMoise allows me to borrow books whenever I like." With a spark of spirit for his accusation, she added, "I've never stolen anything."

Trev could have told her she had stolen a measure of peace from him, but didn't. "You're fortunate it's me and not Robert who's caught you prowling."

"Am I?" Leah smelled brandy on his breath. "That remains to be seen," she added, hating the tremor in her voice. It wouldn't do to show him she was afraid.

"I told you there is nothing to fear from me."

"Well, Robert's attempted to corner me in here—"

"Has he? Charming fellow. Without success, I'd wager."

"Henry came in," she admitted.

"Then you mustn't let me disturb you." Trev closed his hands so as not to touch her. Had he conjured her appearance with his constant thoughts?

Leah bit her bottom lip to keep from telling him it was too late for his advice. He did disturb her. So much that she had risked coming here so late, needing the solace of a book to chase him from her mind. The dark created an intimacy that didn't bear thinking about, and she was grateful when he moved away. Her gaze followed the lighter shade of his white shirt as he went to the side table. From the clink of decanter to glass, she wondered how much of Albert DeMoise's brandy he had already sampled.

"Why are you here, Mr. Shelby?" As if it were her right to question him! But he did not seem a man to be alone. And when he did not answer, she remembered how surly Robert became the few times she had seen him drunk. Trevor had not slurred his words. His voice had been gently amused.

Taking courage from that, she repeated her question and added, "It is rude of you not to reply, Mr. Shelby."

"After our meeting, don't you think we can dispense with formality?"

"I think not. If anything, it will serve to remind me of the—"

"Feel safer, do you?" he cut in smoothly, not waiting for a reply. "Well, I can't blame you. But since I have nothing to fear, I shall use your name, Leah. It's as lovely as you."

His voice was as soft and rich as that of a counseling angel and should have reassured her, for it was statement not flowery compliment. She felt he was watching her closely with those piercing eyes, for the warmth that flushed her had to be caused by him. *Leave now,* caution begged. Leah ignored it.

"What made me feel safe was thinking that you had gone with Robert and his mother. You still haven't told me why you're here."

Trev's eyes narrowed. "Strange, I would've sworn that you were a young woman and not a cat. No tail, no fur, and no whiskers, but you're certainly as curious as any feline."

"Which makes you a man more accustomed to making queries, not answering them."

"Sheath your claws," Trev muttered, surprised that she had the courage to bait him. "Did it occur to you that I might not know why I stayed behind? No matter, I'll set your curious mind at ease. I've little taste these days to enjoy social amenities. The thought of being called upon to play the doting swain to a simpering passel of husband-hungry belles and their overeager mamas is a role I am ill-suited for." He sipped his drink, noting that she hadn't moved, and thought again about the seductively lashed brown eyes that revealed far too much.

"In addition, Leah, I resent having to withdraw to the card room and there reassure their papas that I've most properly sown my wild oats in the requisite number of brothels. I dislike telling them what I've lost and won. That I gamble just enough to keep my fortune intact while, of course, maintaining my honor," he mocked, tossing down the last of the brandy. "Then, I must proceed to prove I can hold my liquor like a gentleman. Prove that I offer the right breeding and wealth. And last, that I have the inclination to pamper their darlings."

"I've never met a man like you."

"Like me? No, we shall not pursue that."

"It's just that I'm not sure if you explained or warned me."

"Take the explanation, Leah. It is the safe choice. I would never bother to warn you about me. But feel flattered, for I rarely explain myself, as Robert kindly pointed out only this morning."

Leah understood the mockery was aimed at himself. The swift rise of compassion made her start forward, only to stop.

"Do you find your life so intolerable?"

"Intolerable? My life is hell. Forget that. It's empty. And save your pity, Leah. You sound as if you find that hard to believe. But I rarely lie. Not about things that matter to me." Trev had to stop himself, realizing he had said more than he ever intended to, then blamed it on her perceptiveness. Leah might believe she understood, finding her own situation intolerable, but it was an unsettling thought that he wanted her to.

"It's not that I don't believe you," she began, the dark no longer threatening, but inviting her confidence in return. "It is difficult for me to see the constraints on you."

"Then you mustn't take things at face value. A lesson in the library, Leah. One you should have learned from books. Wealth is no guarantee of freedom. There are other things that can take a man's choices from him."

"And a woman's," she noted softly, drawn by his candor.

"Quite so. Like the schooling you want so you can teach. Tell me, is it marriage that awaits in its place?"

"Marriage is not what I want now," she said, watching him prowl between door and desk. "Perhaps, like you, I have no choice."

Trev disciplined himself not to respond. This conversation had already revealed more of himself than was wise. "What book were you taking?"

"One of Tennyson's."

"Robert mentioned that his mother taught you to appreciate his work. And what appeals to the lovely Leah?"

"The *Idylls of the King* are my favorite." She steeled herself, feeling vulnerable, for no one understood how the tales of love made precious her own dream of finding the same.

"The table round and Camelot," he noted softly, no hint of mockery in his voice. "Knights and vows and ladies fair. I'm sure they bring the sweetest of dreams to you."

It served to remind her how late it was, and rather than answer him, Leah started for the doorway.

"Wait, I'll escort you home."

"There's no need." But she stopped.

"I told you that you have nothing to fear from me, Leah. However, as a gentleman, I cannot let you walk alone."

"But I'm quite safe here."

"Don't be an ignorant child," Trev said bluntly. "Do you think danger walks up and introduces itself? Or gives any warning at all? You revealed far too much today, Leah, and men's lust does not present a calling card."

"Yes, I am aware of that." Leah lifted her chin, her tone defiant. "You said I could—"

"I said I wasn't Robert or any of his friends. I also said I had no intention of raping you." Trev ignored her gasp and crossed the room to her. But he didn't touch her, having that much control left. "Don't judge one man by another's actions. It's a mistake too many women make."

Cynical and tired, his voice washed over her. She sensed that whatever real or imagined danger she had felt from him had passed. A shiver chilled her spine when she thought of their earlier meeting and now. She had been terribly vulnerable. If Trevor was another man ... A small sound escaped and she found his hands on her shoulders pulling her against him. But his hands were gentle, not at all frightening, stroking her back, taking her fear.

Minutes passed until Trev felt the tremors shaking her cease and he tipped her chin to lift her face to his. "I won't hurt you, Leah. On my honor. If I was too blunt for a young woman's sensitivity, I apologize. But you are very desirable, little dreamer, and most men won't care what they steal from you." Trev brushed his thumb across her bottom lip, then pressed it against his own. "For as long as I am here at Rosehall, Leah, you'll be safe with me."

Leah brought her hands up to his chest, seeking his warmth and the strength beneath. His voice was dark and soothing, cutting away fear and setting free her own yearning to be held by him.

"Lovely Leah," he breathed over her mouth, framing her face and touching his lips to each temple before he closed each of her fluttering eyelids with light kisses. "Lovely eyes, lovely name, just simply lovely."

She thought she imagined the touch of his lips to hers. He released her so quickly, stepping away, that she found herself bringing her fingertips to her mouth to hold the bare touch there.

He picked up the forgotten book and handed it to her. "I'll escort you home now or it will be too late."

Unsettled by the sensations he raised, Leah nodded and couldn't object when he took her hand in his. There was a strange gentleness within him, although the desire was there, too. He simply compelled her to know more about him with every passing moment they were together. She allowed the intimacy of his fingers laced with hers, needing to touch him.

Trev stopped beneath the sheltering trees that bordered the short path to her home. "Will you be able to get inside without anyone hearing you?"

"I've done it before."

He thought to warn her about Robert's interest, but his own was still in question and he was the man's friend. He raised her hand to his lips. "I bid you good night and the sweetest of dreams."

Leah acted without thought and drew his hand to her mouth. "And you, the same." This time she knew there was a subtle tension in his body; she felt it tightening hers and wanted him to kiss her.

"If you want to ride, send word to me through Cato. No one will know. Robert plans to stay over in Montgomery with his parents." Trev didn't press for an answer, but left her. It was enough that his head had cleared from the brandy and he sensed that Leah, young as she was, had a power all her own to have wrung the admissions she had from him. He would have better served her and himself had he issued warnings about the danger she presented to him now. He couldn't afford to care about anyone.

Damn his honor! He should have taken her mouth and showed her what she risked. But the thought of bruising her lips, or using passion to frighten her no matter his good intent, was tantamount to his desertion of Bella.

There was no one to hold him accountable to his promise to protect Bella from their father. Nothing but his conscience and sworn word given to his mother. Nothing but his damnable honor.

Leah would come to him again. The certainty did not come from his arrogant assurance, as Robert termed it, that no woman would dare say no to him. It was simply the power of the need he felt that left no room for doubts.

And lovely Leah, though she had tried to hide it, felt it, too. That alone would bring her to him.

And what lessons could he teach a bird about to be caged?

Chapter Four

FOR the next three days, Leah recklessly stole minutes from every chore to find time to spend with Trev. Robert and his parents had extended their stay in Montgomery to attend a slave auction, so no matter what time she managed to slip away, Trev was waiting for her.

He brought laughter with a droll wit, recounting stories of his days as a cadet in the Citadel and later the army. Trev listened to her, never once belittling her hopes and her dreams. If she despaired of hearing about his dreams, she was forced to dismiss it because of his rare gift of friendship. If the blaze of desire for her had been blanked from his eyes, Leah comforted herself that her building longings were foolish imaginings, and basked in the warmth of his smile when he saw her coming to him.

Hedda, believing the fever-bright desperation in her daughter's eyes came from knowing her father's eventual refusal to continued schooling, allowed Leah her time alone. Marriage would settle her, and not one slave's whisper came from the quarters that Leah was never alone. Leah was the dreamy one, different from her sisters, and she was the last child, which made Hedda intercede when her husband thought to question Leah.

Trev, in truth, became a thief, recklessly ignoring yet another summons home from his father. He stole the innocent haven Leah gave him, storing each laugh, each shy smile against the day he would leave her. He battled the intense desire he felt for Leah when he was with her, and lost it each night in the dreams that had replaced his nightmare. Her trust brought more of his own, although he knew she wanted more than he could give her or anyone. There was no artifice in Leah; her joy in being with him chased the enemies of his soul.

So it was that on this fourth day, he waited for her beneath the lone chestnut tree on the top of the bluff. He stared down at the dark, churning water of the river, letting the serenity of the land and moment seep into him. From the deep shadows cast by trees on the river's bank, Trev watched a doe and half-grown fawn come to the water. The doe protectively kept watch as the fawn drank, and Trev's acute senses heard Leah's breathless arrival.

"I'm glad you came," Trev said without turning, holding out his hand. "There's a doe and fawn at the river." He clasped her hand and drew her to his side, enjoying her silence as he did everything about her, until the doe and fawn retreated into the forest below them.

"They were so pretty and graceful," Leah murmured, glancing up at him.

"Like you. But come away from the edge. I don't want to lose you."

Leah was about to object, but couldn't. Trev's eyes were as luminous as the sky above them and even in her dreams he never appeared so overwhelming male. His linen shirt was open at the throat, seeming to define the power of the muscled body that fascinated her. His dark riding breeches revealed rather than concealed the muscular length of his legs, and suddenly Leah wanted to touch him. She closed her eyes, but still saw him, sunlight bathing him, its warmth burning in his eyes, caressing her, warming her blood.

"Leah?"

"I . . . You are right. I was too close to the edge."

Trev glanced down at the battered leather case on the quilt he had spread beneath the tree, and wondered how wise had his suggestion been that she bring her wildflower sketches for him to see. It would mean sitting close to her. When she looked at him as she had a few moments ago, Trev doubted his control to keep from touching her. With a rough shake of his head, he reminded himself of his promise. Had done so too many times to count. But his fingers clenched tight wanting to free the captured shades of sunlight and moonlight of her hair, braided and coiled at back of her head.

Seeing him staring at the battered case, Leah hesitantly asked, "Are you sure you want to see my drawings? They aren't very good, but—"

"But I shall enjoy them despite your claim," he cut in smoothly, smiling and forcing the tension to ease. With a glance down the track, Trev frowned, seeing his black alone. "Where's Dancer's Lady?"

"I didn't take her. I walked here. I couldn't manage the case and what's beneath it."

Trev dropped to one knee, as her teasing voice demanded he find what was hidden. "Pralines? Mama Rassia chased me off when I tried to take a pan."

"Ah, but she knows they're my favorite," Leah said. "She always make extra for me." His crestfallen expression brought her husky laugh, which suddenly stopped when a wholly male smile creased his lips. Leah caught her breath, feeling the increased beat of her heart. "I've really brought them as a reward for your patience."

Trev instantly thought of sweeter rewards he'd like to claim, but merely set the pan aside and said, "I need none. Will you come sit and show these to me?" He set aside the pan and case, making room for her beside him. With a new sensitivity that was solely for her, he saw that her large expressive brown eyes held an awareness of the desire he tried to hide. For a moment he thought she would bolt and run. "Leah, remember my promise to you?"

Her lips parted, the trembling of the bottom one so telling that she held his gaze a moment more before turning away. Why was today different from the others? He had done nothing to make her afraid, but then, with innate honesty, Leah admitted that Trev wasn't who she was afraid of at all. She was afraid of herself.

"Would you rather leave, Leah?"

"No." The word tore from her quickly. She was too inexperienced to deal with him. She couldn't tell him how he made her feel, couldn't ask that he kiss her and end the ceaseless need to know from his lips what passion tasted like.

"You can't know how that reassures me, Leah. I don't ever want to frighten you."

"It's not you, but myself that I'm frightened of," she whispered with candor.

Trev had to discipline himself not to answer. He knew what frightened her, and knew, too, that he dared not open a door best left closed. Denial was his only choice while he had the strength for it.

"There's no need to be. I am not a connoisseur of artwork, merely a friend who wishes to share your interest. Will you set your mind at ease?"

Leah nodded, knowing she had no choice, but she knew it was not her mind she wanted eased. His expression was impassive, too controlled. She longed to see in his eyes the indecision that plagued her. Foolish thought. She had no experience to bring that about.

Trev leaned back on one elbow, his long legs stretched out, and waited, dismissing a hundred smooth, coaxing ways to draw her near. Leah had to come to him on her own, had to believe he would do nothing more than look at her sketches and share a stolen pan of sweets.

Drawn by her need to be near him, Leah sat on the quilt with her legs curled up beneath her gown and took up her case. She untied the ribbon, lifting out the sheaf of parchments covered with her penned drawings.

"You'll promise not to laugh, Trev?"

"Solemn oath." He covered the top sheet with his hand, his gaze holding hers. "Before we begin," he intoned with mock seriousness, "there's a pan of sweets of which to decide the dispensation, Leah."

"We'll share equally."

Shaking his head, Trev offered her a wolfish grin. "Not so. You're greedy about sweets. The other day you had three dried apple tarts to my one."

"I'm not greedy. You eat too slow."

Her prim voice and decidedly pursed lips brought his laughter, but when Leah joined him, another chain containing the need to taste that captivating, husky laugh from her lips tightened with near unbearable intensity.

Trev was the first to stop, demanding, "You forfeit a square for every flower's color I name correctly."

"You cannot," she quickly returned, disappointed in his choice of forfeit.

"You doubt that I might know them?"

"Not at all, Mr. Shelby. But Mama Rassia never cut the pan." Leah couldn't resist giving him a smug look.

"Easily remedied, Mistress Smug." With a casual move, Trev sat up and reached into his boot, withdrawing a flat bone-handled knife from its sheath.

Leah's gasp arrested his move to take the pan. Her gaze rose from the wickedly glinting blade to his face. "You . . . I've never known a man to carry a knife in his boot."

"A habit I picked up from an old scout. For survival, Leah, nothing more." With precision, he cut the pralines into neat squares, too aware that she watched his every move. He wiped the blade on the edge of the quilt and replaced it into the sheath sewn to every pair of handmade boots he possessed.

"Ready to begin?"

Nodding, Leah couldn't stop the warmth unfurling inside her when the sleek elegance of his body reclined once more. Desperate to distract herself, she began showing him her inked drawings of the herbs in her garden, declaring him a cheat when he named them all green. There was delight to be had in explaining the varying shades and seeing his exaggerated wonderous expression grow until he couldn't stop laughing and begged her to cease.

Setting these aside, Leah turned the others over

so he could not see them. "I demand a forfeit for each of them. Ten in all, Mr. Shelby."

"If you hadn't brought such a small pan, I would gladly give them to you, greedy miss. But you can't claim a forfeit until we are done. Proceed."

Trev waited, and with an eloquent shrug of her shoulders Leah set the drawings to rights. He admired the delicate hand that had captured the fragile stems and flowers, not the sketch itself. She turned them over slowly, and he knew she didn't believe his constant denial that he didn't know their colors. Color existed in the shimmering light of her hair, in the dark brows and lashes that veiled the slanted looks she cast his way. Shadings came from the flush stealing into her cheeks lightly burnished by the sun, and the deeper rose that painted lips he wanted to kiss.

Desire prowled inside him, deep and sharp-set, so he sat up, bracing his arm against his raised knee, and leaned closer to her, determined to end his own torment as well as their time together.

"Now, this," she said, "is a moccasin flower and blooms from May to—"

"It's yellow, shaped more like a lady's slipper, and is spotted with—"

"All right. I concede your knowledge. But you won't know this one." The drawing she revealed showed a heart-shaped bloom with lancelike leaves.

"No hint?"

"One." Leah turned. "It blooms for a single day."

Her words whispered over Trev's mouth, the sweet breath of mint taken inside him, chasing good intent beyond his caring. "And if you were given one day to bloom, little dreamer, what would you have?"

"Love," she murmured, holding the intense blue of his gaze with hers. "A love so blinding, so powerful it would cast time in stone so the day would last forever."

"Do you know what you ask?" He never meant the words to be harsh, but need grew and expanded until he felt his blood heat.

She withdrew, and stared down at her sketch. "I merely answered you. And this time you do forfeit, for you haven't given me its color."

"I can't give it to you, Leah." He knew she understood. Her bent head revealed the tension in her bared neck, and her fingers crushed the edge of the parchment.

She wanted to leave, but could not force herself to move. Quickly then, trying not to let him see how his denial hurt, she pointed to the next one. "Windflowers can be found at the edge of the woods."

"Pink or white. Very delicate. A flower to handle with the utmost care."

"And this is trillium, which loves a rich, moist soil and leaves red berries after it blooms."

"It's white, Leah. The color of purity."

Her heart lurched and raced, the dark velvet murmur of his voice both enticement and warning. She felt the tremor that began inside, spreading warmth as she chose to hear only the lure that desire cast and not the warning. "I can't tell you this one's name, for it is its color."

"Some call them bluets and others name this one innocence."

"And this," she said quickly, knowing the trembling was visible, "the beard-tongue with two lips—"

"A light shade of red, like your lips. The only

two lips I'd rather explore with my tongue than continue this charming discourse on wildflowers." Despite the taunting quality of his voice, Trev gently turned her to face him. "Let me make the warning plain. You're heedlessly baiting a danger you know nothing about, Leah. I'm trying to stop it any way—"

"And if I don't want—"

"You should. And I'm the wrong man for you."

Silenced by the ruthlessness of his claim, Leah sensed the darkness was back, the darkness that drew her to him and made her long to soften it. But Leah found that she had pride to aid her.

She withdrew slightly and gathered up her drawings to set them inside the case, and carefully re-tied the ribbon. Before Trev could stop her, she came to her feet and walked away from him.

"Leah?"

"You would know best. I haven't an inkling what came over me, Trev. I never meant to spoil our time together." She had not wanted to admit that to him, but it was true, and he could make of it what he would.

Trev let her have the balm of her pride. He had wanted to hold her, kissing her senseless and seducing her before she could utter a sound. He still could. He found himself brutally dismissing the idea. Leah was the one who risked more than she knew; he only risked another night tossing from need.

Yet he couldn't let her remarks go unanswered. "You were meant to be a wife, Leah, not some man's lover."

Leah wrapped her arms around her waist, closing her eyes. Lovers. The image she had never banished from her mind came to the fore. But he didn't want her. "Once again, I bow to your wisdom. I forget all my wifely skills recommend me for that position and no more."

The mere thought of marriage had Trev stepping carefully around the trap she unwittingly opened. Never would he marry while Bella was under his father's control. Or while the man lived. Marriage meant taking a wife home to Sweet Bay, where Clinton would have himself another hostage. Leah had to be disabused of any notions she harbored about him and marriage. But the easy choice of cruel words he thought to speak never came forth.

"The only wisdom I have is to protect you, Leah."

"Can you teach me to protect myself, Trev?" she pleaded without looking at him. "Have you wisdom to share to remove the dreams that plague my sleep? Can you tell me what way I can stop wanting a man who doesn't want me?"

She faced him with those last words, and he saw the longing in her eyes. Still he fought a battle not to go to her and show her the lie she believed. Yet when he spoke, he knew he had lost. "By your own declaration, I am wise. But wisdom dictates that I walk away from you, Leah. Now. Wisdom doesn't enter when a man's blood heats at the sight of a woman. Telling you I want you isn't wise at all, but it's the truth."

He came to his feet, hands clenched at his sides, closing his eyes briefly, trying to recapture shredded promises. There was no gentleness in the gaze that raked the soft cling of her plain nut-brown gown. When Leah came to meet him, she didn't wear the layers of under garments most women wore that he was skilled in dispensing with. She stood in full sunlight, aiding his searching look over the delicate set of her features, from the graceful length of her neck down to the agitated rise and fall of her breasts. He spared her innocence nothing in his gaze, lingering on the thin cloth draping taut nipples. Her arms, wrapped around her slender waist, didn't hide the soft suppleness which eliminated the possibility of her wearing a corset. Her stance only gathered the cloth to reveal the gentle swell of her hips. At most, his cynical eyes observed, she wore a single petticoat beneath her gown.

"Stop it, Trev. You've never looked at me like this. You make me . . . make me feel undressed."

"Do I?" he queried. "A most deliberate intent." His eyes came to rest on her mouth, then targeted her eyes. "I simply wanted to remove any doubt you hold that I didn't want you." He barely controlled the need to have her body beneath his, her lucious mouth silenced by his own, and risks, along with his conscience, could be damned.

Leah moved to pass him, but he easily blocked her way. "The truth, Leah. I want you. It's a truth that hasn't changed. Won't change," he added softly, exercising every discipline he knew not to take her mouth. But he couldn't resist reaching out with one finger to trace the delicate arch of her brow, noting again how its shading, like her seductive lashes, was startling against her fair skin and hair.

She stilled, the faint catch of her breath holding him, before the warmth of her breath rushed out to touch his wrist. The top of her head reached the bridge of his nose and Trev had only to close the small distance separating them to kiss her. He didn't coax, as was his wont; he didn't touch her to subtly cajole her into compliance with his desire. He stood, waiting, taking the slowly heating scent of her skin inside himself, letting it simmer with the need coursing through his blood.

He sensed her hesitation, felt her shiver, and offered no solace. Her lashes feathered downward, hiding her eyes, but her head tilted back a bare fraction, and still he waited.

Waited until the tension grew heavy and tight to know the taste of her mouth with his. He wanted Leah to feel it, wanted her to want him with the same blinding hunger that had held sway over him from the moment he had seen her. Denials meant nothing now. She was too close, far too desirable.

The insidious pull he so effortlessly exerted sent reason fleeing from Leah. Time and place seemed to disappear until there was only Trev filling her world, Trev and the passion he promised. She found herself raising her lips to his.

"Be sure, Leah," he whispered, stealing the scent of mint, her mouth so sweetly spiced with its taste, her lips shy, far too shy to share when he rubbed his against them, coaxing her mouth to open.

Trev didn't press her. A woman's mouth told the secrets of her passion. The discovery of Leah's brought the devotion of total concentration. The shyness was lack of skill. He offered his own. And she was generous letting him learn the shape and texture of her lips. The warmth of them quickly heated under the teasing play of his kisses. Her mouth was mobile, following his every lead, reluctant to release his when he lifted his head for a moment.

Her lips glistened, irresistibly delicious, and he tasted them as one would nibble a sweetmeat, wanting to dissolve the spiced covering to get to the potent liquid center. And there was incredible softness, like the gossamer wings of thistle down, in the tentative play of her returned kiss.

But Trev found his infinite store of patience escaped him. He wanted hunger. The same hunger that had prowled his hours, robbing him of peace and sleep. He wanted, needed, with an unmeasured depth, the shy flowering of her mouth to burst with passion's bloom.

"Trev?" She parted her lips, naively seductive, waiting only his taking of her unspoken offer, never wanting the gentle kisses to end. She whispered his name again, lost in the sensations that came from his lips brushing against hers, the tender caressing pressure as his mouth moved from side to side, drawing her instinctive need to be closer to him.

He was compelled to deepen the kiss, knowing how rough his mouth was, knowing, too, he could no longer help himself.

Leah pulled back, eyes wide as he cupped her cheeks to keep her from turning away. She stared up at his face, the angle of sunlight accenting the intriguing shadows under his cheekbones. His eyes were dark blue and deep, and she could smell the deeper, more secretive scent of his skin. She swayed toward him, without will of her own, ensnared and so tempted.

His skin was warm beneath her hands. She caressed his cheeks, his neatly trimmed sideburns drawing her fingertips to explore the masculine lines of his jaw.

Temptation. He was so still, yet she felt encouraged to fill her need to touch him. Curiosity teased her, so that without thought she raised her lips to the slight cleft in his square chin and lightly kissed it. Leah heard his ragged breathing above her own, heard, too, the low groan that seemed to be drawn from deep inside him when she tasted his mouth with the same tender play he had offered her. And when minutes passed, she lifted her head, licking at the faint spice of mint that was hers, melding with something hot and needing from him.

She wanted him. Had never wanted any man this way. It shocked her, as heat raced through her like wildfire. She went willingly into his arms and held him against her. The unknown ache that had begun days ago spread with painful intensity as she felt the thud of his heart against the swelling of her breast.

"Leah, lovely little dreamer," he murmured, nuzzling the tender skin of her flushed cheek, "I've never wanted anyone as much as I want you. Don't turn away. I need you."

The words, so softly uttered, penetrated deeply and found a private unforseen hope in her heart. Her hands slid from his face to his shoulders. But Leah never spoke, for they both turned at the shouts below them.

Trev glimpsed the fear that paled her face as he shoved her toward the concealment of boulders and ran to block the way up the path.

Chapter Five

HIS curses made no allowance for Leah hearing them when he spotted Robert and identified the rider with him as Arthur Norbeck.

Trev glanced behind him, making sure that Leah was hidden, for he couldn't bear that she should be discovered here with him. The hesitation cost him the time needed to stop Robert from dismounting and running up the path. And there was Norbeck, whose predatory eyes went well with his reputation, though his ruddy skin was marred with old pox scars.

"What's this? No greeting for my return to alleviate your boredom with country life?"

"Surprise, Robert, I haven't been bored." Trev noted his friend's fever-bright eyes and slight slur. He coolly stepped onto the path and blocked Robert from coming farther. "Isn't it a bit early for you to begin drinking?"

"Actually, we haven't stopped. Have we, Norbeck?" Robert barely heard Norbeck's reply, for he had spotted the quilt beneath the tree. "Ah, I see that you haven't lacked for a companion to while away the hours, Trev." Leaning closer, his gaze most indulgent, he whispered, "Petrie's young wife still needs some consoling?"

Throwing one arm over Robert's shoulders, Trev

turned him around and forced him to walk down the path to where Norbeck waited with their horses. "Now, Robert, you know I would never divulge a lady's name, even to you."

With an awkward shift, Robert managed to straighten himself and disengage Trev's arm. "Know you for a gentleman, Trev. Of course you can't. And you can trust me not to say one word. Norbeck will have to make do with my company until you return."

Trev helped him mount and stood there watching until they were out of sight.

When Norbeck could bear the silence no more, he reined up and looked at Robert. "Well, was it true? Is Petrie's wife available?"

"Trev wasn't with Petrie's wife. He wasn't with anyone's *wife*."

"But that little yella-skinned gal said—"

"She was wrong. Norbeck. Trev isn't with anyone. C'mon, I'll race you back."

"You're on, but Robert, that little gal—"

"Fancy her, do you? Well, if Sulla Mae's willing, she's yours if you win, Norbeck. Trev'll tell you I'm most generous with my friends about everything that belongs to Rosehall."

That Robert had grated the words and belied their spirit was dismissed as he took the lead and Norbeck struggled to overcome him.

Trev had stood in the path for so long that Leah thought he had forgotten her. She came out from behind the boulder, rubbing her arms to rid herself of the chill that beset her. When Trev finally turned and walked back, she acted without thought and ran to his arms.

He rocked her trembling body against him, seething with the possessive force that held him in its grip. He knew he would have violated every code of honor governing friend and guest if Robert had attempted one move toward discovering Leah.

After moments, she lifted her head from his shoulder, her hands cradling his face. But Trev made no move to kiss her. She appeared too fragile. The loose tendrils of her hair had escaped her coiled braid and clung to the oval shape of her face. Her eyes were still dark with unspoken yearnings and the unexpected pleasure he had silently promised her. He longed to whisper reassurances, but the storm breaking inside him left him without resource to the glib murmurings that often came so readily to him.

Believing the sudden appearance of Robert and Norbeck had served to remind Trev of the difference in their class, Leah felt an immediate cooling of her ardor. Inadequacy made her try to push him away, but he held her tight.

"Trev, listen, please. Robert's coming—"

"Means nothing. I won't let him near you."

Leah silenced him by pressing her palm against his mouth. "You don't understand. It's the way you live. You and Robert. Your lives are idle, filled with pretentiousness and selfish—"

"Have I been selfish with you, Leah?" he demanded, pulling his head back.

The blaze in his eyes left her no quarter to lie. "No," she finally whispered, unable to hold his gaze.

"Before Robert came, I said that I need you. I—" he stopped trying to explain the fight he waged within not to frighten her. But he showed her his need, tempered now, rubbing his open mouth against hers, the touches brief and tantalizing. Robert's coming served to remind him that he wanted to make her his. As the need to be one with her thundered through his blood, Trev used his tongue to mate with hers, the only way he allowed himself to take possession of all that was virgin about her.

The thrusting forays of his tongue built an unbearable tension between them, until Leah felt the tightening of her body, clamoring for release. His mouth lured her from the path to salvation and the kneading motion of his hands, gently shaping her body to the strength of his, guided her toward a gateway to the unknown.

There were no hidden intentions. She knew there could not be. The power of his lean body pressing her against him made her soften, dying a little inside.

"Please," she moaned, dragging her mouth free of his. "Please, Trev, I cannot do this."

"There's nothing for you to do." Husky, impatient, his voice was lush with passion. His lips warmed the sensitive skin below her ear while his hands skillfully stole the sudden tension from her body with the gentle abrading dance he made of brushing her against him. "Just kiss me, Leah. Just as you have been. That's all. All," he added, racked with a shudder.

Her fingers wound through his hair, her mouth once more pliant and yielding beneath his, and she clung to him, feeling the intangible bonds of his need surrounding her.

This was her vision come to life. Passion and pleasure. A seducing of her will, not the force generated by lust.

Lovers. She was lost in the consuming sensations he called from her, all emotions drawn taut and sharp as a razor's edge. She shook from the fervency kindling inside her.

And Trev savored the softness, the gradual giving over of fear to surrender. He recaptured a measure of control, willing to lavish patience when the reward would be so sweet.

He cradled her hips between his hands, leaving her no shelter from the fiercely aroused state of his body. Leah came to him as dawn came to the night, bathing him in the soft, heated glow of her colors, chasing the darkness that haunted him, ending his isolation.

Trev knew he should stop. Now, while he was yet able, but she answered the press of his body with an intense trembling of her own as fire swept her. With small sounds of pleasure and a deeper parting of her mouth, she invited him to share the warmth. Leah slid her hands over the hard muscles of his arms, clinging to him, her touch less than gentle, for she needed him to keep her balance or fall. He had spoken of need, but not of a raw wildness that made her hunger.

And he couldn't let her go. Her passion was untutored, and he wanted the same exquisite sensual pleasure that held him in its grip to capture her.

As he wrapped his arm around her slender waist, the slow sliding thrust of his tongue had Leah arching her head back, lost in a swirl of sensations that went beyond her dreams of him. He stroked her quivering side until the fullness of her breast nestled in his cupped hand, stilling her momentary lunge for freedom when his thumb with tender delicacy discovered one taut nipple. Helplessly she said his name, pleading indulgence to have the fevered ache end.

Her cries flamed his desire as he learned the

shape of her, gently caressing her sensitive flesh. Leah's fingers were threaded into his hair, her kiss becoming demanding, and she was unaware that her hips moved against him with instinctive need.

Trev knew her invitation came from the same hunger that ripped through him. A hunger that left no room for anything but having Leah. His hand smoothed her throat, his lips trailed open-mouthed kisses, stopping to savor the race of her pulse and to take desire's mist from her skin. Her moan of pleasure fed him as wood fed fire. He felt the slow clenching of her fingers in his hair when he bent lower and slowly drew her into the heat of his mouth.

Leah couldn't hold back the cry he wrung from her. She was defenseless against the fever that rose inside her, feeling his teeth and tongue move over her, first gently, then suckling her with a tender wildness. Shuddering as the fever built, she fought to reclaim sanity. But her body had craved this, wanted the sear of his mouth. Wanted, and never knew the depth of the passion he could call from her.

More than passion ruled Trev. He knew he felt something more for her, emotions more tender and tangled that made him long to ravish and protect her. He wanted to sweep her up into his arms, then carry her over to the quilt and make love to her. He longed to teach her about small deaths and rebirths, to ignite inside her the fire that burned him to core. And he knew just how close to the edge he was of doing exactly that.

He had no right. Leah was vulnerable, trusting him more than she knew. Reluctantly, he reclaimed her mouth, making a slower, intimate search of her spiced sweetness. His arms tightened around her, drawing her up against him, and he had to force himself to end the kiss. Her eyes, once innocent, were dark, near black, glazed with passion, her breaths uneven and shallow as his. He touched her cheek, rouged with the desire that told him she was as aroused as he.

Drawing her head to his shoulder, he rocked her gently, stilling his hunger, his murmurs meant to soothe her the only way he allowed himself to. When he tried to end the embrace, she nestled closer, her hands gripping his arms.

Leah shook like a leaf under the storm, trying to understand his dark velvet murmurs of promises and honor, knowing only that he had consumed her, teaching her the potency of man's passion. And awakening her own. She had dreamed of this. Dreamed of the flashing raw lightning that teased her as it teased the skies, promising surcease from the heat if it rained. Every kiss, each touch of his offered ease from the fever that had not abated. Bewildered, she finally made sense of his words, speaking denial no matter how softly, and cried out.

"It's too late, Trev. I never heeded my own warnings."

"Heed mine," he demanded, cupping her face and raising it to his, still warring to control the strong emotions that roughened his voice.

A flooding chill of shame washed over her. She could barely order herself to speak. "Let me go, Trev."

Her eyes revealed the hurt he caused and the lingering desire. Knowing he wasn't ready to let her go, he slid his hands to encircle her neck, caressing the line of her jaw with his thumbs. "You don't want that, any more than I."

His rawly sensuous smile left a sudden path of heat snaking through her. Leah lost her breath, the implicit sexuality of it making her swallow hard, finding the same promise reflected in his eyes. "I don't understand," she pleaded in a strained voice. "These feelings—"

"—are too new, and frightening, and all my responsibility, lovely Leah. I never meant . . . It matters not what I intended; I take blame for letting this go too far."

"Frightening. Yes." Leah only latched on to that one word, denying all else that he said. But she needed more. "I don't know how to make these feelings stop, Trev." She couldn't go on, for the blaze in his eyes had been quelled to a cool blue wash, and she tried to pull away. He wouldn't release her. Leah closed her eyes. Didn't he ache with the same hunger? Like a small forgotten thread, memory pulled out gossip about him. Temptation for any woman. Defeated, Leah bowed her head. Her innocence could never please him.

Trev had to leave her to wage her silent battle. He did not utter a sound. He had shamed her, he knew it as if the shame were his own. There were words enough to murmur, easing and soothing it away. There were touches and kisses that would give them both what they wanted. His body lured him with the knowledge of skillful caresses that would bring passion to flame once more. But he used none. He was stilled on the edge of a primitive precipice, where his blood demanded he ignore every promise he had made her, and with it, his honor. He had no need to finesse her virginal trepidation, for Leah had come to him driven by the same hunger that drove him.

Hunger and its ease was all that he could offer

her. He could not, would not explain the shame of his own life. The tenuous hold he had on himself tightened with the reminder.

Feeling his tension and sensing it had little to do with the desire that made her fight with herself, Leah looked up at him, her hands resting on his shoulders.

"Trev, I have no one else to ask. How can I make this ache inside me leave? Do you see how wrong you are to claim the choice is yours alone?"

Her choice. He countered his instant thought. "You don't know what you're saying, Leah."

Once again, his experience and her innocence rose in her thoughts. Could he lie with his kisses? With his body, which left no doubt he wanted her? There was too much about him she didn't know. But Leah understood that for her the warnings he gave had come too late.

"Shall I beg you?" she whispered, in agony that he would release her and she be unable to stop him.

Beg? Even as his gaze searched her taut features, he knew she could not have used a more potent word with him. He had learned how little begging gained. "You cannot," he uttered in a defeated voice, and abruptly let her go.

She watched him walk to the edge of the bluff and stand with his back to her, raking his hands through the rough silk of his black hair. With shaking fingertips she touched her lips, feeling the throb of heat, measuring their hunger for his. She still tasted him. Was there nothing she could say to him? Ruthlessly, Leah stopped questioning herself. She had to get away from him. No matter how her body craved the lean strength of his.

Gathering her courage, she lifted her hem and started to run.

Trev grabbed hold of her before she reached the bottom of the path. "I'll take you back."

"No. I made my own way here and don't need—"

"I know what you don't need, Leah. Me. But I will take you back." His grip tightened on her arm, and he was aware of causing her pain by the wince she didn't try to hide. "There is no choice in this." Each word was evenly spaced from between his gritted teeth. "No discussion at all." She opened her mouth, but he shook her. "I won't have you go back alone."

"Why? Why should you care? You're willing enough to let me go. You *know* what awaits me, Trev." Panting, clawing at his hand to free herself, Leah yelled, "You don't worry about sending me to another man's bed with the desire you brought to me."

"Then I shall expect his thanks!" He saw the recoil in her eyes as she caught his meaning, but he was beyond caring. Her words had slashed him. He was not willing to let her go at all. He dragged her closer, using his strength to overcome her struggles. "Do you," he said harshly, holding her gaze with his, "know anything about needs? Shall I tell you of mine? Shall I not spare your innocence? Need, Leah, is dictating that I carry you back to that quilt and find out how well I can teach you to ride me."

Her palm slapped against his cheek. She felt singed by the blazing anger in his eyes, at the harshness of his voice, which was still vibrating with the passion that still clawed at her.

"You're crude and insulting. You're—"

"All that and more."

He still denied her freedom. Leah narrowed her eyes. "You deserved that slap. You deserve to be horsewhipped for what you've done."

"And I'd risk it and more to have you." The words were out before he could stop them.

She stilled. How could anger last when there was candor?

Trev had to recover what he lost and spared her nothing. "Truly, little innocent, we do differ on what I deserve. My patience should have been rewarded," he assured her acerbically, "by a most pleasant tryst, free of virginal recriminations."

"Bastard!"

"Yes. And remember that, Leah." She paled and he felt through the cloth of her gown how chilled she became. But it was her eyes, tears glittering, deep down, like the drowning reflection in a well, that made him add in a deadly soft tone, "Do you think I want to lose what little peace I've managed to steal for myself? Do you believe any man wishes to have every waking and sleeping hour beset with a craving for any woman? Do you?"

Leah, drawn close by his grip, couldn't look away. The darkness that lured and frightened her was back. Why was peace for himself something he needed to steal? Compassion overcame all else.

"Can you believe, Trev, that any woman wishes the same torment?"

"Go home, Leah. You're right. You came alone and should be safe enough."

She had only thought she felt shame before, but it was as nothing to the burning flood his rejection brought.

Trev watched her run and made no move to stop her. He couldn't. It was the only way to protect her.

He walked back to the quilt and stared at the forgotten pan of pralines and Leah's case. Both reminded him that the sweet innocence which had marked their times together were at an end.

Trev realized how foolish he had been to think he could be friends with Leah. He wanted her so badly, he ached with need.

But Leah was a threat to him. She wanted more than a man's passion; she wanted love.

And Trev had none to give any woman. He was the wrong man for Leah. It was that simple. Simple and inescapable. He had promised her she would be safe with him and believed it to be true when he said it. Now he knew his words for the lie they were. Leah wouldn't be safe with him. And he knew she wouldn't stay away from him.

There was only one way to protect her. Trev took her case with him when he rode back to Rosehall. And all the while he ignored the nagging voice that asked why he cared about protecting Leah at all.

Chapter Six

"HENRY claimed you two were in here brooding, but I didn't want to believe him," Trev said from the doorway to the drawing room.

Robert, sprawling in a wing chair, nursed a drink and morbidly swung his leg, sparing a single glance at Trev. Norbeck rubbed his bloodshot eyes and forced himself to sit up.

"Have you returned with the intent of joining us?"

"More than join you, Norbeck. I propose a round of debauchery to please even your jaded tastes." Freshly bathed and attired in formal day wear, Trev had armed himself since his return. He had captured Robert's attention as well.

"Have you truly become bored with the country scenes, Trev? Not an hour ago I wagered Norbeck we'd never drag you away."

Robert's direct gaze revealed to Trev that he wasn't drunk. "See for yourself," Trev stated, offering a showy bow, "you've lost your bet. Is not my neckcloth tied in its most elaborate knot and are not my trousers creased to Henry's perfection? Come, Robert, admit that under Mama Rassia's supervision, my collar is starched and linen as snow white as you could wish. The only thing your country scenes have provided," he mocked with a gleam of cynical amusement, "is to hone muscles and provide a smooth fit for my waistcoat."

Still befuddled by drink, Norbeck tried to focus his gaze and ended up shaking his head. "Does he mean us to return to the city, Robert?"

"Aye. And the devil is on Trev," he said, setting his drink down and standing. "You'd do well to come, Norbeck. Excitement is always lured by Trev's recklessness. The women are willing, the liquor the best, and gambling fevered." He looked at Trev. "That's what you want, right?"

"It's what I need."

Coming forward, Robert lightly slapped Trev's shoulder. "Then we're off." Softer then, so that Norbeck couldn't hear, he asked, "Was it another summons home that set you off?"

"What else could it be? I've no more wish to take up the reins of heir than you. Let's make merry this night, my gallants, for tomorrow . . . ah, hell may demand its accounting tomorrow."

Leah learned at supper that Trev had left with Robert and Norbeck for Montgomery. She fought not to react, but dismay filled her. Feeling her father's watchful gaze, she hurried to bring the platters to the table.

"So, there we were, Mr. DeMoise and myself, waitin' to go over the accounts, when Henry comes to tell him that Robert and his friends are gone. Fair furious he was with his son. Even I thought Robert would be settlin' now that he's out of the army. He shows no interest at all in takin' up the reins and learnin' the workin's of Rosehall."

"He's still a young man, husband," Hedda softly reminded him.

"That's no reason for his carousin' 'round the countryside with Shelby and the others. They won't teach him what he needs to know to keep his land."

"Then let us be thankful that Robert is not your child. You are not responsible for his actions."

Leah set the last platter on the table in their dining room and began to serve in her mother's place, since this had been Hedda's day to visit the parish poor. She caught the silent look they exchanged and fear spread through her. Had they somehow discovered she had been sneaking off to meet Trev?

With unsteady hands, she served her father first, filling his plate with two thick slices of baked ham, the largest roasted potato, and a heaping spoonful of fresh-picked peas. She handed the heavy crockery plate to her mother to add a slice of corn bread and wished she had thought of some excuse not to join them.

"Leah?" her mother prompted. "Will you not finish?"

Coming to with a start, Leah quickly made up a serving for her mother. She averted her gaze from her as she handed over the plate, knowing both her parents were watching her now. She had to stop this. They would certainly question her if they knew her nervous state.

Taking the smallest slice of ham for herself, Leah almost spilled the spoon of peas into her dish. She took her place on the high-backed wooden chair next to her father, keeping her eyes on the well-mended linen tablecloth. There was little she could do about her chilled hands as they joined with her parents to say grace. Guilt sent a flush over her when her father made special effort to give thanks for her being a good, dutiful daughter. Invoking the Lord's blessing on her made Leah's stomach churn.

"Mama tells me you don't want young Jamison to call after service on Sunday, daughter."

"Yes, Papa."

"Has another young man caught your eye?"

Leah stared at the plate. "I hope you'll let me go to school before I think about marriage."

"Leah, I told you—"

"No, Hedda, I'll be tellin' her. Your talk did little good if she's harborin' these foolish notions."

"But, Papa, the money—"

" 'Tis of no matter. I've enough to provide what you'll be needin'. We'll hear no more talk of schoolin'. Ain't fittin' for our kind. Supper's coolin'."

Leah gripped the edge of the table, hearing the final dismissal, seeing in her mind's eyes the shattering of her dream. She couldn't speak, couldn't argue; she would only be reminded that she looked above her station. She needed to run, needed the comfort of Trev's understanding— Lowering her head, she bit back a moan. There was nothing more to be had from Trevor Shelby. And if she didn't stop, she would have her father knowing that she had not only met in secret with a man, but had allowed him liberties that belonged to a husband.

There would be no dismissal of that, but a whipping as punishment for her sins. Her mother averted her gaze when Leah sent a pleading glance in her direction. She was alone and could only sit there, longing to flee their stifling presence.

Fleeing was a thought that Trev echoed later that night, but it was considered bad form for a gentleman to leave a card game when he was the only one winning. Trev had led Robert to believe this was what he wanted and needed in order to exorcise the devil riding him. He was wrong. All he wanted was Leah.

Once in the city, there had been no choice as to where they would spend their evening. The hotel had procured a carriage, since they had ridden their horses and deposited them after a short ride in front of a mansion outside Montgomery. Lavale's boasted classic Greek Revival lines in its building, was exclusive and expensive, and drew only the wealthiest and most profligate with its lavish appointments that satisfied every whim and fantasy. Its gaming rooms witnessed the winning and losing of fortunes, and the private parlors offered a man his choice of exquisitely beautiful courtesans of either sex, skilled in the erotic arts.

As simply elegant and discreet as the small hand-painted sign beside the front doors, arrangements for a companion required merely a nod, or a soft murmur to the properly begowned young women whose sole purpose was to ensure their patrons' pleasure. Lavale's did not employ men to serve in the bar or gaming rooms. Women, he claimed, provided pleasure for the gentlemen that frequented his establishment. They beguiled and refused any crass measures to discuss cost. Should a man balk when he was presented with his bill upon his leaving, he never crossed the threshold again.

Waiting for another fresh pack of cards to be brought to the table, Trev again wondered what had possessed him to suggest coming here. He had forced himself to match Robert's amusement upon their entering the wide, marbled hall, and Norbeck was quick to desert them for a pair of petite red-heads, gowned identically in black silk. Trev had declined to wager on Norbeck choosing to be participant or voyeur, having no desire to avail himself of the peepholes in every room.

Refusing to allow his somber mood to show and thereby bringing Robert's questions, he made his way to the bar and found two of their friends more than willing to gamble.

His thoughts were distracted at the lightest brush against his arm, and Trev glanced up to see that his cognac had been replenished with a new glass. He ignored the veiled invitation in a pair of liquid brown eyes which far too quickly reminded him of Leah's, and set several gold pieces on the tray the young woman held.

"*Merci, monsieur.* You are most generous to Angeline."

"He can afford to be," Clifford St. Thomas stated before Trev could answer. "He's the only one winning."

"Then, *monsieur,* you must allow me to console your losses when you are finished."

Eyes hooded, Trev watched the byplay as Clifford, son of the DeMoises' cotton broker, and Jon Paul Childers, whose family claimed one of Alabama's largest shipping lines, vied for Angeline's attention.

Robert, having the new deck, called a stop and began to deal another hand. Trev bet on the blind, to the annoyance of the others, and even Robert's skill was no match for Trev's uncanny luck.

Trev sipped his drink, intent on banishing Leah from his thoughts, but someone passed behind him leaving the faint scent of roses. It was enough to trigger the taste of Leah's skin, warming under the ply of his lips, the same scent rising from Leah, clouding his senses until he realized that Clifford was actually shaking his arm.

"Are you in, Trev?" he asked, seeing that he had caught Trev's attention.

"I'll play these, Clifford."

"Again, Trev?" Robert asked, eyeing him from where he slouched in his padded chair.

"The devil's own luck seems to be mine tonight." He was thankful there were only nods of agreement, but Trev still felt apart from the others. Robert's family raised cotton, the St. Thomases sold it, and Childers lines shipped it to fill the increasing demand in England and France. He truly did not want to spend the rest of his days with only the concerns of the planter class that ruled the South to interest him. But that was the fate that awaited him.

"Norbeck's been gone nearly two hours," Robert mentioned. "Care to make a wager, Jon Paul? He has two, and might last the night if he doesn't drink."

Deep in thought, Trev ignored them. Bringing Bella back from England was a start toward freedom. He still had to confront his father. Confront him or kill him.

"Cards, Trev?" Clifford asked.

His tone indicated it was not for the first time. Trev picked up the hand he had been dealt, forcing himself to concentrate. Folding wouldn't serve. He had won too much. "I'll play these," he answered, hoping that one of them could beat a pair of kings. He anted his share into the pot, not caring who took cards or how many. The room was suddenly stifling, or perhaps he needed to escape his thoughts.

He tuned out the flow of conversation, hearing Leah's voice, her plea, her candor, the pleasure sounds he had called from her.

"Damn it, Trev, you haven't drunk that much. Stay with us. It's only sporting to allow us a chance to win back what we've lost to you." Jon Paul's eyes were fever-bright, staring at Trev's winnings.

Robert, quick to read the sudden challenge in Trev's gaze, motioned for the box of cigars to be presented, with John Paul offered the first choice. "Clifford mentioned that building was still going on at Fort Sumter when he was there in April. His father attended the Democratic party's convention. I told him, Trev," he said, selecting a thin cigar for himself, "that you and I have extremely fond memories of Charleston."

"A city as lovely as her women."

Robert, so attuned to Trev's moods and voice, sensed his friend was not remembering any woman from Charleston when he spoke. But he let it go, having accomplished a distraction.

"Her people know how to cherish our way of life," Clifford stated, rolling his cigar between his fingers. Satisfied with his choice, he waved the young woman away. "It is our hope that all of the South will hold to our strong beliefs so that no northerner's demand for change will be listened to."

"There's not one of us," Jon Paul said, glancing at each man in turn, "who will stand for wearing Lincoln's yoke if he's elected."

"Never happen." Robert laughed and raised his glass. "A toast, gentlemen. Lincoln's a fool thinking to ask us to give up slavery along with our states' rights. It's like asking a lady to surrender her virtue."

"No man," Clifford declared, "who calls himself one ever asks."

"If he doesn't," Trev stated just as their glasses touched, "then he takes. We still call that rape, gentlemen, and perhaps that is what Lincoln will do to those who oppose him."

Oaths aimed at Lincoln erupted, until Clifford once again spoke. "You voice concerns we've all heard, but I swear to you it will never happen. I have the assurances of our brokers in England and France that should we require aid to put down this upstart farmer that dares to dictate to gentlemen, they will stand by us." He waited until the toast was finished and set his glass down. "They need our cotton, Trev. They won't allow the North to interfere with their industry."

"Trev doesn't agree. Do you?" Robert asked, placing his cards facedown as their talk replaced their game.

"Why ever not?" demanded Jon Paul. "Your family raises cotton and rice. Georgians are known for bucking the federal government time and again. My daddy claims they'll be the first to raise arms if any dictates come from Washington, unless they're the ones they want. It was Georgia who made the dangerous proposal of a southern convention when South Carolina attempted nullification of the new tariff bill."

"You're reaching, Jon Paul," Trev warned softly. "That happened almost thirty years ago. But I will admit that what you say about Georgians is true. They don't back down to the wearing of anyone's yoke."

Dead soft, Clifford asked, "Does this mean if we go to war, sir, you will not fight beside us?"

"That's liquor talking, Clifford," Robert chided,

never intending that Trev should come under attack. "I never said that Trev wouldn't fight; he would serve his state with the same honor he gave as a federal soldier. You should apologize—"

"No. There's no need." Trev glanced at Clifford. "I believe you meant no insult."

Clifford took the out. Trev was a good shot, perhaps better than himself, but Clifford's father swore to cut off his allowance if there was one more duel. "Damn right, I didn't, Trev," Clifford said. "But what the devil did Robert mean?"

"Simply that I don't believe either England or France will embroil themselves in a war, should it come to that."

"Let the federals try." Jon Paul swept up the cards he had been dealt. "We have the better fighting men. We're not farmers but gentlemen with the advantages of our class. They'd never win."

"Stop sounding like a pompous ass," Robert said, then smiled at each man in turn. "I'll place a wager now, that there isn't a southerner worthy of his name that can't outshoot any northerner."

Trev let them make their bet, knowing how wrong Robert was and how quickly he forgot the men they had served with. Wealth and privilege were not theirs exclusively. But he refused to dwell on this. He would fight if it came to war, not to keep slavery, not when he had worn a similar yoke these past twelve years, but he would fight for the states to have the right to decide the issue for themselves.

The talk served as yet another reminder of how apart he was from the others at the table. He now played recklessly, losing one hand after the other, folding and betting heavily, to have them believe his luck had finally changed. The thought of war and what it would do not only to the land, but to their women, brought Leah to mind. If she married the farmer her parents wanted her to, she would be in northern Alabama. Her husband's loyalties would likely be with the Union, for they were a breed apart from their southern brethren. A damn fool thought. But he didn't want Leah marrying any farmer. *You can't marry her,* he told himself. *You can't marry anyone until you break the shackles Clinton holds.*

Disgusted with his thoughts, Trev began losing his money. When Angeline came to serve another round of drinks, he took advantage of her not so subtle invitation to leave.

Once out of the card room, Trev placed five twenty-dollar gold pieces in her hand.

"*Monsieur,* for you, I do not need extra."

"*Au contraire, Angeline,* it is not for me. Robert is very fond of you. If you would entertain him for a few evenings while I tend to a personal matter, I will make arrangements with Lavale myself to have the same amount credited to your account for each night."

The matter was quickly concluded, Trev thankful there were no questions. He declined the offer of a carriage, deciding to walk back to the hotel. The night was clear and sultry, and Leah filled his thoughts. He needed time to be alone and think carefully about the risk of seeing her again.

But he wanted to be near her. Needed to, more than he realized, and it was the strength of that need which he fought.

Distance between them meant nothing, and he the fool to commit himself to spending several days in the city. The lovely Angeline was only one of the pleasures to be found as a cure for Leah. He could have stayed the night.

Surely a skilled woman, whose only desire was to please, would have removed the feel of Leah's untutored mouth and hands. And Leah's laugh? Her taste? Her total responsiveness? Were they, too, to be found in another woman?

Nothing short of having Leah was going to stop this war that he waged.

He had been a coward about enough that mattered. He would not hide behind lies now. What he felt for Leah was not going to be easy to overcome. It was something he could barely control.

What's more, he no longer wanted to try.

Chapter Seven

FOR the third night Leah escaped from the confines of her room after her parents were asleep and ran in a headlong flight that whispered of momentary freedom to the bluff.

Sleep was impossible. Trev haunted her. And with him, the shattering of her dream.

It had been an impossible hope from the first, but she had grasped it tight, praying that her parents' love for her would urge them to seek her happiness rather than follow their belief of what was best for her.

The walls slowly being built day by day were closing in on her, and she knew there was no real escape. Just as there was no escaping Trev's place in her heart and mind.

Trev had understood. He had listened and silently shared her dream. Then gave her another. The passion between them was unexplained, barely controlled. Branded in her memory was her complete willingness to abandon herself to him. But from the moment Trev had kissed her, Leah knew she would make him her world.

Unconsciously, she rubbed her arms, feeling chilled. He had proven she would never be content with the civilized marriages her sisters had made. She could not imagine placid Sarah and Nicholas, or staid Ruth and Martin being senseless from the heat and fury of their passion.

But she knew the beginnings of a less than civilized desire. Trev had taught her that much. And left her. He had ripped aside her safe world. It was madness she felt along with a deep hollow ache when his mouth had moved on hers.

She swayed where she stood, shaken by the memories of being held and caressed by a man who had ruthlessly turned her away. He never told her how to stop this longing to feel him against her, flesh to flesh.

Appalled by her thoughts, Leah paced, fighting to stop the need twisting through her. Trev was in her thoughts constantly, bringing daydreams of dark, steamy nights, simmering with the same wanton promises that whispered seductively from his eyes.

Moonlight peeked from beneath its bank of clouds and showed her how close to the bluff's edge she walked. She stared for long minutes at the darkness below, then carefully stepped back, wishing she could take time with her.

The wild beating of her pulse raced beneath the fingertips she placed at her throat. There was no longer solace to be had here, no way to end the torment, for Trev had stolen her heart. He was the man she wanted to love without knowing she had dreamed of him.

Love? she asked herself, and knew it was true. She longed to spend every waking and sleeping moment with him near. She ached with the memory of his kisses. She needed his understanding and laughter as deeply as she needed his desire.

She was in love with Trev and he didn't want her. She had nothing. Wiping at the tears suddenly blinding her, Leah turned, desperate to escape her thoughts and this place.

Trev stood waiting.

Leah closed her eyes, afraid she had summoned him with her imaginings. She knew she had no defense against him.

But his whisper of her name was real. She took a blind step forward before she opened her eyes.

"Trev?" It was a helpless plea. He stood before her, bathed in the bright full moonlight, dressed as she had last seen him, the ties of his linen shirt undone, his breeches molding the length of his legs tucked into calf-high boots.

She was shaken and had to swallow several times before she could speak. "Why are you here?"

"I came looking for you."

Resentment curled through his words, and Leah buried the rush of joy she felt. "I don't understand. Why were you—"

"The reasons don't matter. I found you." He stepped closer to her, but her defensive stance made him stop before he was close enough to touch her.

"The reason matters to me, Trev," she whispered. His nearness caused an insidious flow of warmth inside her and she looked away from him, fighting the sensual pull he effortlessly exerted. "It's very late. Why were you looking for me?"

Trev raked his hand through his hair, his patience shredded. "I can't stop wanting you, Leah. It's that simple."

"No. It's not simple at all," she murmured, surrounded by his husky declaration that left her vulnerable. But she couldn't be hurt by his rejection again. "I wasn't waiting for you. That's not why I'm here."

"Something drove you from your bed, love. Don't lie to me. I abhor liars," he warned, watching her with an intensity that narrowed his eyes. He knew he had hurt her, but Leah didn't understand at what cost to himself.

"My bed? You went looking for me in my room? You risked—"

"I said," he noted with ill-concealed harshness, "that I want you."

"Now, not before. You left me, Trev. You said—"

"I was trying to protect you the only way I could."

"You lied to me." She could hardly breathe, so great was her agitation. She had to look at him. The moonlight was not kind to him; his features were hard-set against the black thickness of his mussed hair. His eyes seemed leached of their intense color, but no less piercing. Leah saw the uncompromising set of his tense jaw, and her chin rose with agitation.

"What is it you want from me, Leah? I'm not lying when I say I want you!"

Harshness and yearning. And Leah heard the unspoken words clearly. *I'll have you, too.* She knew the love she felt for him, the intense need she had to ease the darkness that seemed to haunt him and make him hold himself apart from her, would not let her deny him. Yet she was afraid that he would take all she gave and leave her with nothing.

He paced, a restless tension filling him as he fought the urge to go to her and convince her with passion as words could not.

"Answer me," he finally demanded, unable to stand the silence. "Do you believe me?"

"Yes, I believe that you want me. But you don't

need me, Trev. You make me doubt myself. I can't trust my feelings."

His gaze rose slowly up her arms, over the curve of her shoulders, to her face. His breath caught to see pain reflected in her eyes. "Have I taken that from you?"

The anguish in his voice brought her own. She rubbed her arms, feeling as if he had touched her, unable to look away from the mesmerizing power of his gaze. "You don't understand. I—"

"It's you who don't understand, Leah. You must know why I had to leave you?" he asked with a deadly softness.

"Your honor drove you to hurt me to protect me. That is what I understand. In a twisted way it even makes sense," she added very softly, feeling the ache intensify inside her.

"Yes, to protect you. And to stop stealing your innocence."

"You've taken nothing from me that I did not give freely." Leah started toward him and stopped herself.

"I wish I could say the same," he countered. "You've taken my peace, my sleep, and even the solace of drink. You fill every waking hour and haunt the night until I was driven to seek you out and put an end to—"

"Stop! You claim to want me, but it angers you." She watched him move to block her way. "No more, Trev," she implored, sliding her arms around her waist, praying to stop the turmoil churning with every passing moment. "I never asked you for anything."

"You ask," he stated, ruthlessly coming toward her. "Your eyes plead silently for trust, and peer into a man's soul until you strip his secrets from him. And I can't stay away from you, Leah."

She released a shuddering breath. "You don't want to give me your trust or tell me your secrets. You don't want to share with me, Trev." She backed away from him, afraid that if he touched her, she would be truly lost.

"I've never had pleasure that equals being with you." He stopped stalking her. "I can't give you more. I can't give anyone more."

"I know you believe that," she returned in a saddened voice. Would it be enough? If she loved him, would he ever learn to love her?

Her gaze found him turned slightly away from her, staring off into the night. She responded to the utter loneliness he portrayed. If she gave him her trust, went to him and told him she loved him, would he believe her? Before Leah did more than ask the question of herself, Trev turned to her.

"The desire I feel for you is as new to me as it is to you, Leah. But I won't seduce you with lies or make promises I can't keep."

"Can you make your body lie to me, Trev?"

His soft knowing laughter made her look away. "Lovely little innocent. No, my body didn't lie about the desire for yours. No man could keep the changes passion brings to him hidden. We haven't the advantages of a woman, who can keep the changes desire brings to her body concealed."

Leah knew he had only to touch her to know that her desire for him wasn't hidden at all. She thought of her lost dream of freedom that teaching could have brought her, and knew that marriage to a man of her parents' choice awaited her. But she wanted Trev. His last words brought more than faint, unknowing images. Her body was already reacting to the passion and pleasure she could have in his arms. *And completion. That* he had denied her.

Trev withdrew the unfurled bud of a rose from the open neck of his shirt. He saw the way Leah warily watched him and raised the bud to his lips, his kiss as delicate as the pale ivory color of the rose itself.

"Take it, Leah. It's the scent you wear that haunts me. I've taken care to remove the thorns, so you can have the pleasure of holding it without injury."

Their fingertips almost touched, for she couldn't stop herself from reaching out. She had only to take a step more and lift the rose from his hand. Still, she hesitated and knew she had brought his anger. The days and hours without him, the needs that he aroused and left unfulfilled, all battered against the lone warning that told her to run now or she never would.

Leah took the bud and brought the rose to her lips, its fragrance heady.

"You've stolen this from Frances's garden." The softness in her voice reflected the easing of tension in her body and she glanced at Trev's eyes, sighing to see their deep color returned and a wicked grin creasing his lips.

"Do you see what you've made me become? A thief, Leah. But then, that makes us a pair, for I've already told you what you've stolen from me."

No lies. Not to herself and not to him. Time and distance had not eased the hunger between them. He claimed she had not been out of his thoughts and she knew he had never really left hers. Confronted by his candor, having him near, made fear and warnings fade. *Pleasure. Passion.*

Completion. All that he had promised awaited her. With the loss of her dream, this was the only freedom of choice she was to have. A lifetime of never knowing a world filled with Trev stretched before her.

Trev read the sorrow in her eyes and turned away. He would not beg. He would not take. He had come here hoping his memories of their time together would allow him to be close to her. He never expected to find Leah, had at first thought he had lost his mind and breathed life into the vision that haunted him. She would never know how she eased the loneliness that plagued him. He could never tell her that she alone allowed him to be gentle and tender in a world which scorned a man for revealing such weaknesses.

The need that clamored in his blood would never know its ease. Need that whispered in her voice, calling his name. Need that surrounded him like the sultry night air.

Leah called to him again, knowing she wanted the passion, not a safe stability. The velvet softness of the rose she held offered her the hope of tenderness and when he turned, slowly closing the distance between them, she prayed that Trev would feel more than desire for her. She tensed when his hands circled her neck, forcing her face up to see him.

She was too close and he wanted too much. Trev forgot all the rules of civilized seduction and tightened his fingers to hold her. There was luminous fire in her eyes holding his gaze, almost challenging him, and he pulled her against him, taking her mouth.

She parted her lips and he demanded, then coaxed, needing more than she had given him before. Her gown was pooled between them. He urged her closer, stroking his hand down her back, shaping the taut muscles of her buttocks, sliding his leg between hers. Her trembling body was a cry of surrender, softening and curving to mold itself to the hard planes of his.

Leah thought she knew the hot taste of his fierce desire. She was wrong. This went beyond fever to a sweeping storm so shattering it consumed her. She couldn't hold him close enough, hungry to have the dark, spiced scent of him filling her. This is what she had longed for, the madness that kindled fire. Time stopped in this moment, a moment that went on and on, just as she told him she wished.

She wanted to understand how Trev took her from herself and replaced her with a creature so greedy for more of him. She found no answers. Only need. She wanted him with an inescapable truth that made her cry out.

Her fingers locked in the thickness of his black hair, welcoming the thrust of his tongue, teaching her to retreat and duel, then conquer when she claimed his dark taste for her own.

Trev tightened his arms around her. His hands sought her, skimming under her gown and petticoat to find the soft, heated skin he had dreamed of possessing. His name was a fevered litany from her lips, pleas or demands, he knew not, for something wild burst inside him.

His mood was to claim, and every kiss, every touch fed that possessive fury. He felt her begin to shake, the first edges of unleashed passion taking hold of her. As he would. Her total responsiveness fed him as wood fed fire, but he held a last measure of sanity that forced him to jerk his head up.

Staring down at her face, flushed and shimmering in the moon's light, his breaths mingled with the erratic rhythm of hers.

"Be sure, Leah. Very sure. There's no going back for either of us. You may not have wanted me in your life, but I'll be the only man there."

The words snapped a leash on passion and Leah pulled free of his arms, the crushed rose falling unheeded to the ground. She couldn't order her senses, couldn't tell him what he had demanded was impossible. She backed away toward the shadows beneath the chestnut tree, hating him for stopping, hating him for making her verbalize her choice.

The midnight moon glided his darkness and all Leah could do was call his name. Eyes wide, she watched him tug his shirt free of his breeches, carelessly bunching up the linen as he yanked the shirt over his head and tossed it aside.

Her slipper caught on a small rock hidden in the thick grass and Leah stumbled. Her hem twisted beneath her foot and she fell back, her left hand and hip taking the brunt of the fall. Leah curled her fingers around sweet-scented grass, knowing Trev would not seduce her, but only come to her if she asked. She couldn't meet his intense gaze. Her eyes skimmed across his bare shoulders, down the demarcation of a thin dark arrowing of hair on his chest. There was no line to distinguish his waist from his slim hips that tapered into powerful thighs.

Her first sight of him came to mind. But she hadn't kissed him then. Only dreamed about it.

She had not known how heady passion tasted from a man's mouth. Trev's mouth.

"Leah." Her name was the only word Trev whispered, abandoning all the lavish, seductive phrases he knew. But his body berated him with racking demand that he go to her. And when he knelt close within the curve her body made, he waited until she looked up at him. "Say you want me."

His voice was low and beguiling. She knew he sensed her desire and her fear, but wondered if he understood how stripped he made her feel that he should know them at all.

With his thumb, Trev gently shaped the tender swell of her mouth. "Shall I offer you words that would seduce the answer I want from you? I can," he noted with softness, but not arrogance, sure of his knowledge. "I will," he added when she didn't respond, "if that is what you want from me."

She searched his features, knowing he was not lying. Trev could and would salve her way if she asked him to. Leah had to touch him, caressing his cheek, feeling the heat of passion beneath her fingertips, a flush the shadows hid from her sight. A tremor passed between them and Leah lost whatever thought of sin she had. To deny Trev was to deny herself.

"I want you, Trev, and all that is honest from you," she murmured, brushing one finger over his lips.

He caught her hand with his, pressing a kiss to the center of her palm before raking his teeth over the fleshy pad below her thumb. His smile was wholly male as her thick lashes feathered the high curve of her cheeks and the softest of moans escaped her lips.

"Look at me, Leah," he commanded, drawing

her hand down to his chest. He shuddered as her hand touched him, splaying wide with tiny kneading motions, then stilled. He was unable to hide what she did to him, unable to still the wild beating of his heart that she measured with a light touch until their breathing kept cadence with it.

He drew her to her knees, pulling her against him. "Kiss me, Leah," he whispered, his eyes hungrily targeting her mouth even as he lowered his head. "Give me that kitten-soft tongue that's far too shy."

"Trev—"

"Now, Leah."

She gave him her mouth, and shyly stole the heated darkness of his taste, kissing him as he had kissed her, passion and hunger trembling inside her with each deeper invitation his mouth made. Her hands sought the hot coiled male strength of his arms and shoulders, before sliding into his hair to hold his head. Even as she deepened the kiss, she felt him caress her sides until his hands cupped her breasts. Her skin burned through the thin layers of cloth when his fingers teased her nipples until they were taut peaks awaiting his kiss.

And she knew that he wanted her with an honesty that went beyond words, beyond her dreams. She felt the shudders that racked his body as they did hers. Heard her soft moan of need find answer in his. She ached and was inflamed by the strength of his hands kneading her hips against the hungry desire of his.

Trev drank her broken sounds, lightly raking his teeth down the arched curve of her neck as her head fell back. He wanted to claim and taste and possess every bit of her passion, of her sweetly heated skin, and then claim the softer, sweeter heat hidden inside her until she burned as he burned and he gave her what she once asked for, time stopping still.

He wanted her hands on his aching flesh, and drew one down, his dark murmurs coaxing her, but her fingers gripped the edge of his breeches and he leaned back.

"Leah, don't be afraid," he whispered, framing her face, his voice gently hushed and thick with need. "Does it shock you to know how much I want your touch?" With one finger he circled the swell of her breast, closing the circle, knowing she watched him. "You ache here, don't you, Leah?" But he wouldn't touch the taut peak her gown clung to.

Leah shook from the sensation that spread through her. She turned her face. "Trev, what I saw in your eyes that first time shocked me, but no more than my own thoughts." Nuzzling his hand, her voice a bare thread of sound, she whispered, "The dreams of you, the hunger to know completion in your arms leaves little room for fear."

He leaned close, the tip of his tongue lightly shaping the delicate whorls of her ear. "I know about the dreams, Leah, and the hunger. . . ." He captured her earlobe with the edge of his teeth. *But mostly the fear.* The words were his, dark and silent as he uncurled her fingers from his breeches and rubbed her hand over the heat of his damp skin, showing her how much he needed her touch. Trev watched her eyes until her gaze locked with his. He tasted her lips with a kiss of controlled passion and hid nothing of his need when he drew her hand to rest on his aroused flesh.

"No fear?" he asked, knowing how little control

he had left, but fighting to retain it if Leah showed the slightest hesitation.

"I should be afraid. It's what I've been taught." But even as she spoke, her fingers shaped him, heat and strength that made her feel powerful when a groan escaped his lips. "No matter how much my parents tried to shield me from what goes on down at the quarters, Trev, there is little hidden. The slave women talk and—"

"And you enjoy knowing you can make me ache for you."

"Yes," she murmured, holding his gaze, giving him back the honesty he silently demanded.

"I told you no man could lie about his desire for a woman. One woman. One man. You, Leah. For me." Trev held her face within his hands, bringing his lips to hers. Her mouth was warm, wine-rich, and hot, and he feasted on the luscious taste of her as he bore her down to lie on the quilt. "I hurt with wanting, Leah. Do you ache, little dreamer? Does the hunger prowl awake or asleep until you feel mad with need?"

The relentless softness of his voice bathed her in yet another heat. Held against him, she knew reason fled with the flame and power he offered her. Sensation was the ruler. The only one. His mouth allowed her no hesitations, no shyness.

A last fear filtered to the surface. She would lose her heart to him. But his skin was hot and damp to her hands sculpting his muscular arms, trying to draw him closer as he dragged up the skirt of her gown and petticoat.

He no longer gave her gentleness, nor tender wooing. Leah could not demand it. She didn't want gentleness. Her lips clung to his in a wild, urgent kiss, her body arching up to mold itself to his, unable to bear the knotted tension that burned inside her.

Trev covered her with his strong, hard body. There was no finesse when he reached between them to tear open the constricting buttons on his breeches. Buttons tore cloth and fell from the strength of his hand, but he didn't care, for Leah welcomed him and cradled him between the warmth of her thighs. The thin lawn drawers were her last protection, but he let them be, rocking against her with the same thrusting rhythm of his tongue stealing every virgin secret of her mouth.

From her hair, from her skin rose the subtle scent that was hers alone, heated and sultry as the night, clouding his senses with a desperation to possess her that he had never known. She had brought him an end to his isolation, for her total giving demanded its return from him.

He lavished kisses and still she gave him more. Her pleasure cries, the hard raking feel of her fingers against his naked back drove him to the edge. She was slender, her body supple and strong, all feminine heat whispering silent pleas that crumbled his purchase on the edge moment by moment, move by surrendering move.

Hunger. Leah knew it now. He tore his mouth from hers and she felt his teeth lightly score her neck. She shivered to feel his hand cup her breast, his lips closing over the taut nipple. The ache was instantly soothed, until he suckled and her blood kindled with a new fire, sending a wild, primitive beat through her body. He shifted and she strained to follow, knowing the promise of his passion, knowing what it meant to want with every caress of his hands, every taste of his lips.

"You feel it now, don't you, Leah? Like a fever that can never be cooled?"

"Yes." The word was dragged from her lips. There was no shame in touching him, no sin in taking from him and wanting still more. She heard the tearing whisper as the last cloth barrier was ripped away and felt the steamy night air touch her bared skin before his hand closed over her.

She was suddenly vulnerable, but her body had stolen all control from her mind. Trev was whispering, praising her, darker and darker words that drew her into a world where only needs mattered. His teeth raked over cloth to her other breast, and her fingers dug into the skin of his shoulders, her body rocking to the stroking of his hand. Biting back her cries, she arched up, opening to him, feeling his arm slide beneath her neck as his mouth found hers once more.

Leah reveled in his body, the lean hardness that met her every touch. Her mouth was as greedy and demanding as his. She could feel the heat of his blood beneath his skin, her own becoming fired to an unbearable degree.

Passion. She understood it now. Every breath needed to be drawn and filled with his scent. Every cry he called from her had to be echoed by his. She surrendered to the shimmering web he spun, twisting and turning, following his lead. A strange new tension gripped her. She could feel it build, feel it tightening with a savageness that allowed her no time, no breath. Tremors shook her. She couldn't find air. Only Trev. His mouth. His hands. Opening her, taking her even as the first crashing shock of completion and joining captured her.

Heat. Her softness surrounded him. With every nerve straining, calling upon every bit of his will-power, Trev went still above her. He saw the glisten of tears seep from beneath her closed eyes and cursed the rampant desire that drove him to forget her innocence.

"I'm a bastard for hurting you." No matter how hushed, the declaration was brutally harsh. He fought against moving as he fought the draw of silky heat that held him, but died a little with every tremor that enclosed his flesh with the fire of hers. "Open your eyes, little dreamer."

And when he saw her eyes luminous with the sheen of tears and a drop of blood welling from where she had bitten her lip, Trev started to withdraw.

"No." Her hands held his hips. His features were harshly drawn, shadowed above her, like his tormented voice. She would not lie to him.

"You didn't hurt me, Trev," she whispered. "I dreamed of this, of having you inside me. I want all the silent promises. Pleasure. Passion and, now, completion."

"Yes," he breathed over her lips, knowing it was what he wanted as badly. He was too aroused to do more than bury her denial of pain. Leah called him with a subtle tightening of her taut thighs and he lost himself in his need for her.

Pleasure intensified. Passion flamed anew and completion was hers as he pulled her legs around his hips and joined with her in an intimacy that she had never known.

She shuddered, again and again, reaching for his strength, clinging to him. This was the madness. The image she had first seen. Trev inside her, claiming her even as she knew she held him. Dying a little. Finding Trev was there.

Leah clutched his arms, slippery with sweat, understanding that she wasn't dying but being born. She sank her teeth into his shoulder, crying out with a pagan demand that drove her, as he did, past all reason. Darkness filled her vision as he answered her plea, and she gave herself over to him, to the final shattering that came without warning, taking her as it took him.

Chapter Eight

TREV held Leah close as they rode out the trembling aftermath of their lovemaking. He had to drag air into his lungs; there didn't seem to be enough to allow him to breathe freely. Reality came with the sounds of the night around them, trickling into his consciousness. He had never lost control of himself with a woman before Leah. Trev knew himself, or thought he did. He understood the hunger that had built in him to have her. He didn't know he would pay with a part of his soul.

He lifted his weight from her, feeling a piece of himself was being torn as he moved to lay beside her. With his arm beneath her neck, he cradled her against his shoulder, facing the dim understanding that more than desire had flared between them. The scrape of one boot against the leather of the other served to remind him that he had never taken them off. Another first for him. And Leah . . . He forced himself to look at her.

Free of her heavy braid, tangled waves of her pale hair curled damply against her cheek and shoulder. Her eyes were closed, her body warm and pliant against his. But the moon, as if to aid his need, seemed to brighten, and he saw the ravages he had left. Her slender legs were bare, her gown and petticoat bunched between them; her lips, parted with the shuddering breaths she still released, were swollen from the greed of his kisses. He lifted his hand to smooth her hair back, wished she would open her eyes and look up at him, afraid that she would do just that. But he had to know.

"Leah," he whispered, using one finger to stroke her still flushed cheek, "are you sorry?"

She didn't want to be called away from where she lay, filled with peaceful lassitude. She was shy, too, of what she would see in his eyes. The warnings, every one she had been given and knew so well for herself, came flashing back. She fought her mind not to recall them, but the opening was given with Trev's withdrawal. She had wanted to hold him, to keep him a part of her, but she knew men didn't want that. At least, she reminded herself, Ruth and Sarah said as much.

But could she trust her sisters' knowledge when neither one could have known the passion she shared with Trev? Her hand uncurled from where she had pressed it against her breast, and, very tentatively, touched Trev's still warm skin, measuring out his heartbeat. Within seconds, the quickening beneath her palm satisfied her need to know that she was not alone in feeling the shattering aftermath that had rocked her world.

Her sigh brought Trev to lift his hand from her waist, cupping her chin to tip her head back so he could view her face. Leah's mouth wore the hint of a smile. He distrusted what he saw. Leah had been innocent, he would swear to that, even if he had not felt the tearing of her maidenhead. And he, Trev cursed himself, he had been less than the finessing lover of his unwanted reputation.

"Open your eyes, little dreamer," he urged softly

as he slid his arm from beneath her neck, setting her head down gently. Elbow bent, his hand braced his head so he looked down at her. He had asked her if she was sorry. The smile hinted she was not, but Trev couldn't trust his own instinct now, even if Leah was resting contentedly at his side.

"Am I dreaming, Trev?" she asked with a note of wonder. Leah struggled to open her eyes, her lids feeling as heavy as her body. But she, too, wanted to see him. Her courage had been used to take what she yearned for and was not as yet replenished. His thumb played at the corners of her mouth, shaping her smile until it fully bloomed.

"That's better," he noted with masculine satisfaction. She burrowed her face against his chest before he could stop her. Trev tangled his hand in the silvered sheen of her hair, gently tugging so he could see her, but Leah resisted him.

"What's wrong? Are you ashamed?" Her muffled sound made no sense to him. "Did I hurt you? he whispered, feeling her fingers tighten against his chest. "If I did, I'm sorry, Leah. I was very . . . aroused."

Leah lifted her head and slowly turned onto her back. "I know," she answered, cupping his whisker-rough cheek.

He saw the smile curving her lips and watched a sensual shiver take her. He waited until she opened her eyes and then a wholly male smile of satisfaction creased his lips. "I wasn't gentle with you."

"I didn't want you to be." The blaze of desire meeting her gaze kindled hunger anew. Leah closed her eyes, her hand sliding down to test the heat and strength of him. He was smooth and hard, flushed with heat, and Leah shivered as she caressed him. "Trev? I . . . please. . . ."

"Please you, yes, I want that, too." His mouth closed over hers, the heavy beat of desire flooding him, her gentle caresses arousing him to an unbearable degree.

He shouldn't want her again. But the inviting shift of her body, the quick little catches of her breath, her whispered plea for him to show her how to pleasure him, all combined to send him over the edge again. He loved her slowly, tenderly, hearing her cry out, before he began all over again, giving her with his body what he couldn't give to her with words.

Her whispered cry of loving him echoed in the night as he drove into her one last time. A cry that melded with those of wild demand and pleasure found.

Leah knew, even as he held her tight to ride out the tiny convulsions, that he heard her. She could feel his withdrawal, emotional and physical, as he sheltered her in his arms. But this time she wasn't going to be silent.

"You heard me?"

"Yes."

She flinched at the flat hardness in his voice. "You misunderstood me, Trev. I won't take back the words of loving you but I'm not asking you to say them."

He was silent for so long that she raised herself up to look at him. Leah found the effort of holding his intense gaze almost unbearable. "Have you ever desired something so badly, Trev, that you spent every moment dreaming of it?"

"Yes. I wanted you like that."

Wanted. Her breath shuddered from her. "Tell me, was it more than you dreamed?" She knew as soon as the words were spoken that he wasn't going to answer her. But something drove Leah to say more. "I wanted you like that, too, and for me it was more, much more. You made me feel alive, Trev. Free." She sighed and slowly lay down beside him, fighting the anger for thinking she could reach beyond his shadowed walls.

Trev closed his eyes, unable to look at her. *You made me feel alive. Free.* Her words replayed themselves, no matter how much he wanted to shut them out. She had driven him to shred what little claim to civility he had. His honor had him swear to protect her from himself. She shredded that, too. Just being near her drove him to passion's edge again.

"Was my honesty too brutal, Trev? Does my saying I love you make you feel guilty? Or is it enough that your lust is satisfied?"

"No, Leah. My *lust* is not satisfied." He loomed over her, holding her hands to either side of her head. "And your honesty is not brutal. Just words I've never heard from a woman before. I asked what you wanted from me. I told you what I could give you. That's all there is. Pleasure shared, Leah. No love. No marriage. No commitment," he grated from between clenched teeth as the thought of Leah his, truly his, rose in his mind.

She made him want to spill the secrets of his soul to her. And he never could tell Leah about the twisted shackles that bound him.

He understood the grave danger she was to him. But his body wasn't listening to his mind. He wanted her, and anger rose that he should still feel this sensual prowling hunger for her.

Leah tried to pull her hands free, but he wouldn't let her go. She had spoken her truth and lost him. "I need to go home," she whispered, swamped beneath a flood of shame.

"Leah," he murmured, his voice thick with guilt. "I—" Trev stopped, wishing he could change what was done, knowing he couldn't. Self-contempt lashed at him. He could be brutally honest with himself. He knew he would do it all over again. He had wanted Leah and would kill to be inside her now, but she would demand the payment of his soul if he allowed her to get any closer.

He had not felt this vulnerable since that long-ago night when Clinton had torn his life and dream apart. He had sworn then, a vow he had repeated at his mother's grave, that he would never let anyone else find a weakness to use against him.

Trev released her and sat up with his back toward her. She had come to him. Leah, with dreams in her eyes and truth on her lips, bringing him a tiny corner of the world where passion burned clean and bright, untainted by the darkness that haunted him. He couldn't stop the shudder that slithered down his spine when he felt her stroke his back. She whispered his name, coaxing him to share with her what was wrong.

Despite his harsh words, Leah was on her knees, touching him, begging him to talk to her. She longed to ease the corded tension in his neck. "Trev, you made yourself a part of me. I won't ever let you take that back. Can't you trust me a little?"

She wanted what he didn't know how to give: trust and love. Leah, sweetly heated fire, showing him how dark and empty his life had become.

"Candle in my night," he murmured, gently drawing her forward as he turned, kissing her with the same gentle restraint that he held her with, hearing again her soft cries, remembering how she tasted, sweetly spiced, soft, heated, and hunger beyond physical need growled both demand and warning.

Love her and end loneliness. Love her and be shackled with another hostage.

Cherished. His kiss had given her that and no more. Leah let him go, understanding at last that Trev gave all he could, all he would for now. She had come here tonight with shattered dreams, buried one and had the other mended with the giving of her heart. No matter how gentle, he was still rejecting her. Pride was the only aid she had to force her to move. She sat up, fumbling to pull her clothing into order.

Leah stared down at the remains of her pantalets, then crushed them into a tight ball, seeing them as a reminder of all she had risked. She wanted to confront Trev, wanted him to talk to her, to help her understand the confusion that was surrounding her. She clamped her lips tight, gritting her teeth, no longer able to trust herself not to plead with him.

Very deliberately, Trev forced her hand open and took the torn cloth from her. He came to his feet in a controlled rush, walking to the edge of the bluff, where he tossed them. Raking his hair back, he stood watching the fluttering drift of white cloth until the darkness below swallowed it.

His breeches clung to his damp skin. One button hung by a thread and he used it to secure them closed, feeling again the sense of his life hanging by a matching tenuous hold.

"Leah, I'll buy you new ones."

"No, I don't want that from you. I want—" her

voice caught on a sob, instantly stifled by her clenched hand pressing against her mouth. She would not cry.

Trev tensed, unable to turn around. No, she didn't want cloth easily replaced, and he couldn't replace the veil of innocence he had torn. And he didn't want to let her close, didn't want her to make a place in his life. Her words of coming here to bury a dream rose from his memory. Was that why she had given herself to him?

"You never told me why you came here tonight, Leah."

"There's to be no school for me." She stared at his naked back, unable to marshal any defense.

"I could make that happen for you. I could give you money to go away."

"Money?" she repeated. Anger began to churn. "Payment?" she whispered, realization dawning that she had been so wrong about him. He was like Robert. Spoiled, rich, and the bastard he named himself. "You'd cheapen— No, I won't let you do that to me! I don't want what you can buy." She scrambled to her feet, every ache and twinge a reminder that she couldn't walk home.

Biting back denials, Trev let her believe her claims. Anger would serve him as nothing else could. And he needed distance between them almost as much as he needed her.

"Take me home," she said suddenly.

He turned slowly at the demand. She stood, hands rigid at her sides, hair wild, her stance defiant, watching him. He had sullied what they had shared, just as she said, and its taint was bitter in his mouth. He merely nodded.

Leah's fear rose as he came toward her, her protest dying when he swung her up into his arms.

His eyes were cold, his lips tightly compressed, and she could see a muscle twitch in his cheek. She hated having to touch him now. "You've forgotten your shirt."

He ignored her reminder to retrieve his shirt and carried her down the path to where he'd left his horse.

The silence began and lasted through the ride home as Leah struggled not to touch him. The efforts left her exhausted. He rode around the quarters. To avoid waking the dogs he kept away from their pens, riding up a back path that ended at her mother's fenced garden.

Leah roused herself then. "Stop here or we'll be seen from the house."

Trev was in no mood to argue. His mind supplied all the right and good reasons he had withdrawn from her, but his body had hosted the pressing heat of hers despite her rigid insistence to ride astride. He wasn't so insensitive that he didn't know she was hurting, but it was with unaccustomed force that he drew rein and slid from King High's back.

"Leah, much as you may hate this, I have to put my hands on you to lift you down." She closed her eyes, and Trev had to accept that as the only answer she'd give him. But he did so gently, caging her between him and the horse.

"Let me go."

"I only wanted to give—"

"What, Trev? More offerings?" she hissed. "You had no right to toss my pantalets away. I could have repaired the damage. They were mine, Trevor Shelby. Not yours to do—".

"You can never repair the damage done this night." He gripped her shoulders, forgetting that he had sworn not to touch her again. She lifted tear-filled eyes to his and anger washed away. "Leah, I've made a mess of this. It's nothing to do with you." The lie burned his conscience, but he ruthlessly thrust it aside, wanting to spare her recriminations. "There are things about me you don't know, things I can't tell you."

"You won't trust me." Vibrating with anger, Leah managed to wrench free of his grip and turn to run, only to stop and face him. "Damn you, Trev. I made the choice of coming to you, believing I would find more than passion in your arms. It was the only choice I'm being allowed. But I was wrong. So wrong." Desperate to get away from him, Leah bit back a cry of pain and ran.

"You weren't wrong," he found himself whispering, long after she had gone. It didn't matter whether or not she had heard him. It was enough that he knew he spoke the truth.

It was a scraping noise that brought Leah from a fitful, exhausted sleep. She lifted heavy-lidded eyes and turned to see the curtain fluttering at the window. The sun was already splashing muted shades that promised a cooler day, and with a sigh, Leah closed her eyes, turning her head to nestle deeper against her pillow.

Her softly inhaled breath brought the scent of roses and she smiled, one hand reaching up from beneath the sheet to draw her pillow closer.

But it wasn't the rough linen weave her hand encountered. She tensed on her soft feather tick, almost afraid to open her eyes even as her fingers touched velvet. Still caught between the throes of sleep and waking, she slid her head back a bit and looked at what she touched.

On her pillow rested a dew-drenched rose. Her gaze barely focused on the blood-red flower before she was cupping it in her hand, drawing it close to her lips. A rose—

The noise she heard . . . the rose . . . She struggled to twist free of the tangled sheet, dropping the flower and coming off her bed so quickly she almost fell. Her gaze darted from the window to her bed and back again to the curtain, now stilled. The soft thud below her window made her turn, understanding dawning that while she slept unaware, Trev had come here.

This was the Trev she loved, not the withdrawn stranger he had become last night. *Loved? He doesn't want your love.*

But why, then, had he come to her room and left a rose?

Leah didn't have an answer. She stared at the flower a moment longer. Every passing second had her backing away as exhaustion fled, and with it the pain of rejection. She thought only of the time when his passion had brought her completion, believing as she so needed to that he did feel more for her.

The trill of bird song drifted through the window along with the low-chanted spiritual led by Old Silas. Leah shook her head, recalling where she was, wanting to believe that today was as any other that she had awakened to the work song Old Silas began and the other slaves joined when they headed out to the fields. Rosehall and her own place within its boundaries was not marked by the violence she knew existed on other county plantations. Her father used no whip, families were not sold off and separated, there was no talk of rebellion, there were no runaways.

But Trev had come and she no longer had order in her life.

From below, her mother called out to her. Leah would be expected downstairs, dressed and ready to begin the day, as if nothing had happened. Her parents would have put the denial of what she had longed for from their minds. And Trev? Why had he risked coming into her room to leave a rose?

The flower drew her back to the bed to pick it up. She stared at the bloom, one finger edging the petal's silky velvet. Apology? Message? Good-bye? Why had he come?

It was a similar question that Trev asked himself as he leaned his arms on the split-rail fence surrounding the horse track that Robert had ordered built four years ago.

Beside him, Cato held the stopwatch in one bony coffee-shaded hand, the other held high over his head, ready to signal the boy on Mambrino's back. The three-year-old bay loved to race, as evidenced by his restive moves, but Cato, with a patience Trev admired, merely waited for the horse to still.

Trev glanced at the small tear in the loose sleeve of his shirt and knew Cato had drawn his own conclusions about his sudden arrival at the track, disheveled, his breeches grass-stained from where he had slipped and fallen, along with his boots muddy enough to be a gentleman's disgrace. For all their familary when discussing horses, the slave would not give away the fact that Trev had come from the lower pasture which led to the overseer's house.

It was worry for Leah's emotional state that led to his foolishness of stealing another of Frances's roses. The same excuse that made him implusively leave Robert and Norbeck in the city. No sleep and a body that still hungered for Leah had sent him searching the garden for a perfect bloom to give her. She needed to know that he was not callously disregarding the precious gift she had given him.

Excuses. Nothing more. He had to see her. That was what sent him to her house, climbing up that massive oak and into her room. There had been barely enough light to see, and he had never given a moment's thought to being caught.

Deeply drawn into his thoughts, Trev missed the signal which set Mambrino around the track in his ground-eating stride.

"Give 'em 'is head, boy!" Cato shouted as the thundering horse and rider swept passed them.

Trev tried to focus his gaze on the watch Cato held over the rail, but all he could see was Leah, asleep. The bed's netting had never been untied, and the weak gray light only offered him sight of her shadowed form. He didn't need light. She was branded in his mind, from the husky laughter, gentle as a spring breeze that enticed like a soft caress, to the mischief sparkling in her eyes when she teased him. He could see himself lean close to brush the tangled hair from her face, one tenacious curl clinging to his fingers as he withdrew his touch. He had blown a kiss and left the rose, satisfied that she slept, but wishing for her forgiveness.

The anger that she had managed to breach the walls he had so carefully erected these last twelve years had seeped away in those moments. But Trev knew he had to make ample amends. He would take full responsibility, no matter her declaration that the choice was hers. A rational decision he could live with, when all he wanted was Leah again. As they had from the moment she uttered them, her words of belief that she would find more than passion with him returned with a vengence.

What the devil did she want from him? Trust? He could not, would not give that. It wasn't money. She was sure to throw any offer of monetary compensation in his face after the way he had bungled the offer last night.

Guilt made him dredge up marriage.

The most honorable restitution. The most forbidden to him. Trev gripped the rail, his gaze unfocused. Marriage equaled insanity.

He had no doubts that Leah had been a virgin, although when he had finally thought about it, he realized she was unaware that riding astride had likely torn her maidenhead. And it had been too late to care. The moment he was sheathed inside her, he would have bargained with the devil before denying himself surcease. And that is just what having her once was: a temporary respite.

Marriage was, like his once-held dream of being a doctor, impossible for him now. Not only with Leah, but with any woman. But he didn't want another woman.

Closing his eyes, blocking out the world, he envisioned her face. Her skin, lightly burnished from the sun's kisses, making a striking contrast to the pale blondness of her hair. Those wide, far too expressive brown eyes framed with thick, seductive lashes as dark as her brows. And her mouth, parted, generous, taking as much as giving. She was storm and moonlight and he was surely killing himself to stand here and think about her.

An obsession. That was all she was. All he could allow her to be. He surely wasn't in love with her.

But then, his mind countered, what did he know of love? Bella was the only person he had loved enough to sacrifice his life for once his mother had died. And even that love had been corroded by the hate he felt after paying with a loss of dreams.

And a loss of freedom. An involuntary shudder ripped through him. No bride of his for Sweet Bay while Clinton lived. He could never expose a woman to that man's cruelty. The mere thought of Leah hostage to his father's demands upon him sent a roil of sickness churning inside.

It was the height of folly to believe he would ever have a life of his own while Clinton lived. He had wished the man dead these long years past, but something stayed his own hand from committing the deed, no matter how his father had goaded.

And what if the same savage insanity that had made his father the man he was dwelled within him? Trev refused to follow the oft-opened path the past beckoned him toward. He had tried to understand, once the wrenching despair of being torn from his home had eased, even tried to forgive the man his taunting punishments which brought pain to everyone around him. But Clinton was the devil on his back.

Time would give him his freedom. In four more years, when he reached his thirtieth birthday, the money and land entailed by his mother's estate would be his. Clinton couldn't stop it from happening. Four more years of staying away, of using his skill at cards and taking the generosity Robert offered him.

But he couldn't forget about Bella. His conscience never really allowed him to do more than set her aside. And now it placed Leah beside his sister.

"Marse Shelby, you be feelin' poorly? You're groanin'."

Trev jerked away from the hand that held him, staring, then realizing what his action meant to Cato. "Too many unpleasant thoughts caught up with me, Cato. It was nothing you did." *Groaning? Just how close to the edge was he?*

Pursing his lips in a thoughtful way, Cato nodded. It was as close to an apology a white man could make. And Marse Shelby was more decent than most, asking after folks when he came to visit.

"Gets me to wonderin' if it's somethin' catchin. Take Miss Leah, now. She's always down 'ere, seein' as how she purely loves 'em horses of Marse Robert's. Ain't seein' her 'round 'ere must be near a week. Wish I thought to ask after her. 'Course her papa doan much like that." He busied himself folding the square of muslin he used for a starting signal, since slaves couldn't handle guns, but knew he had Trev's full attention.

"Never did get to tell her 'bout Marse Robert sayin' as how we's goin' to Kentucky. He figures Mambrino's 'bout ready to race with de best of 'em blu'grass horses."

"Robert dreams of beating one of Elisha Warfield's thoroughbreds," Trev answered, wishing his own dreams were as simple to plan and carry out. "Robert also would like to be invited to the Lexington Jockey Club, Cato. It's the oldest one in the country."

"That's what he says. Older than me." Cato glanced up and smiled, but with uncanny sense turned the conversation back to where he wanted it. "Miss Leah's right fond of Mambrino. She helped me pick out who his mama was gonna be an' Marse Robert says yes when his daddy wrote him. Miss Leah's folks doan know 'bout that. There's lots they doan know 'bout her doin's. But she's a fine lady. Takin' her books down by the quarters, teachin' folks to make 'em letters an' such."

"That's against the law, Cato. Someone should warn Miss Leah about that. Not that it makes any sense."

"It's white man's law, Marse Shelby. Doan need to make no sense. Miss Leah ain't a one to be carin' 'bout breakin' rules."

Cato waited expectantly, hoping the sugar bit he offered about Leah would be taken up. Marse Shelby was about as restless a stallion as he'd ever seen and Miss Leah a sassy filly. He sighed at the silent man beside him.

"Like I was sayin', Miss Leah's a fine lady. Shame she's cooped up with her mama today. That little gal sure do like bein' out in de sun not locked up in de house."

"Why, Cato?" Trev no longer tried to hide his interest. He knew he had been carefully baited, even as he understood the underlying warnings Cato issued. Nothing escaped the notice of plantation slaves and any man who believed it did was a fool. He turned to Cato, repeating his question.

"Why is Leah locked in the house today?"

Chapter Nine

"DOAN be takin' on with me, Marse Shelby. I'll tell you. It's Thursday, suh. An' bein' that, de minister man comes to call. He's got powerful thoughts for salvation. Miss Leah, now, she says he come for her mama's brandy cake. She give me a piece once, an' I'm partial to agree."

"Cato," Trev warned, then strove for patience. Trying to shake the rest out of the man would do no good.

"Seein' as how Missus Hedda raised up her gals like ladies, Miss Leah's got to sit by an' listen good to his preachin' even if she was feelin' poorly. Figure it has to be that what's keepin' her away. Gots to say, that man can fire de brimstone iffen he sniffs sin near a body."

"Miss Leah," Trev intoned very carefully, feeling heat climb into his cheeks so that he looked away from Cato's too-knowing gaze, "is not a sinner."

"Ain't for de likes of me to argue with white folks. You say she ain't a sinner, she ain't. Me, now, I'm asinnin' aplenty. I got this fine day, good fast horses, an' Marse Robert's gonna bet all my saved-up Christmas dollars when Mambrino races. It's a sure bet, sure as that preacher man takin' on helpless Miss Leah iffen he has a min' to."

"You've spun your tale and kept me here, Cato. But it's nothing to me what Miss Leah does with her soul." Trev abruptly started to walk away, then turned back. He had made a promise to Leah that while he was here he would protect her. Too bad he didn't remember it when it counted.

"Cato, I'll add a five-dollar gold piece to your stash. And remember, betting is only a sin if you lose."

"Iffen you say so." Cato slipped his arm around his youngest son as the boy climbed under the rail fence, but he watched Trev's long-legged stride take him toward the big house.

"He see me ride?" the boy asked.

"Marse Shelby's got his own devil ridin' him, boy, an' paid you no min'."

"Where's he runnin' to?"

"Ain't our place to be questionin' what white folks do, boy. I tole you that. But I'm bettin' that Marse Shelby's gonna take his devil an' go wrastle with de servant of de Lord to save him a soul."

"Who's he gonna save, daddyman?"

"Ain't knowin', boy, ain't knowin'."

Leah, hands folded primly in her lap as she sat in the parlor, couldn't decide if the minister's call was blessing or punishment. It was a blessing that his arrival, which she had forgotten, prevented her from seeking out Trev; she had been once more willing to cast aside pride and forgive him his rejection. She had come to the understanding that Trev had given her what he could of himself. Each time she had tried to breach walls, he had attacked her, and it was only later, upon reflection, that she realized what the problem was.

The punishment was hers, for every day of freedom lost could never be regained, now that her parents declared school was out of the question. Freedom had somehow become entangled with Trev, so in denying him, she denied herself. And it was agony to school her features into a mask that revealed none of her thoughts. Her mother had already remarked several times about the shadows beneath her eyes, deliberately ignoring her plea to be excused from this visit.

She glanced at her mother. Hedda perched on the edge of the mahogany side chair, her back as straight as the chair's own, a freshly starched white linen collar and cuffs relieving the severity of her deep blue gown. Both Leah and the minister watched Hedda carefully slice slivers of her special brandy-soaked walnut cake. Cecil Kavan's greed was apparent in the way he eagerly reached for the good china plate that held two slices. Leah had never told her mother that she believed the minister had a fondness for her cake and the spirits that flavored it more than he had any desire to save their souls.

Declining her mother's offer of cake, Leah felt her stomach flutter when Mr. Kavan began a discourse on the wages of sin.

"My dear, you are truly blessed by the Lord, having raised yourself three virtuous daughters. I'm despairing of saving those two Brewster girls considering their family's slovenly ways. Sin is what those folks teach their young'uns. It pains me deeply to be hearing folks call them thieves, believing them no better than white trash in addition to all their sinning."

While her mother murmured praise for his charity, Leah saw that he gobbled up his cake, having provided his customary bit of gossip. As for the

Brewster girls, they had spread their favors through the countryside for more years than Leah knew what *favors* was referring to. And their brothers were no better. But guilt for what she had done made it difficult to meet her mother's gaze or the close-set eyes the minister directed toward her. Had they said something she was supposed to answer?

"Mama?"

"We were concerned, dear, you've gotten quite pale."

"I was reflecting on the minister's words."

"But you have nothing to do with those Brewster girls, Leah. Surely you didn't think our minister—"

"Hark to your mama's words, girl. You keep company with sinners, they'll be leading you down their path to ruin. Near time you were wedding. Young Jamison seems to have marked you out for special attention. Fine boy, Missus. You be sure to tell her papa I've said as much."

Leah deliberately chose the straight chair nearest the window, and hoped they would both forget she was there. Cecil had claimed the settee to accommodate his portly frame, with her mother's chair close beside it. The drone of their voices praising young Jamison's worth was easily dismissed. Leah thought of Trev's offer to pay for her schooling.

Did she want to teach so badly that she would accept money from him? It would mean leaving her family. Her parents would never forgive her. Did she want to be another Miss Gilbet, depending on the generosity of her students' families to ease her lonely lot? Miss Gilbet had been the first to praise her, but had warned her, too, of the difficulty women faced. Unless she could secure a position in a girl's school, she would be forced to take whatever was available, for most people wanted their children taught by male tutors.

That point was driven home when, after three months, Miss Gilbet had been replaced. Leah never knew where she went, leaving the desire to share the world she had opened to a hungry child. While her sisters and parents had never fully understood that world, they had never denied it to her until now. And what would happen to her if she took money from Trev?

She would be cast off, a wanton sinner, having her dream and losing her family. The need for love and approval made her send a guilty glance at her mother, who was engrossed in cutting the minister yet another slice of cake.

Leah turned back to the window, her guilt hitting a new level when she saw the man walking up the path to the house. Trev was mad! Darting a look between her mother and the window, she gripped the edges of her chair.

The knock at the front door was so soft that at first Leah hoped her mother didn't hear it. But that hope was dashed when it was repeated and her mother looked up.

"Leah? See who's come to call."

"Yes, Mama." Dread marked every halting step that brought Leah out of the parlor and into the hall. She could see Trev through the curtained glass of the tall side window which framed the door.

She had never seen him wear a gentleman's formal day clothes and was not immune to the impact of his handsomeness. Her gaze rested on the snowy white neckcloth that nestled a gold stickpin before skimming the double-breasted frock coat that fell to the knees of his gray doeskin trousers. The coat was open, revealing a small patterned dark gray waistcoat the same shade as his gloved hand, which was raising a walking stick to knock again.

Leah jerked the door open.

"Miss Leah, I've come to call," he announced, sweeping his hat from his head.

"What are you doing here? How dare you come?"

Her low-voiced tirade was given with an anxious look cast over her shoulder. Trev, grinning, leaned against the open door so she couldn't close it in his face, and wished again he could dress Leah in something other than the drab russet gown she wore. The plainly cut collar and cuffs reminded him of the Quakers he had seen, and he despised the tight coil of her beautiful hair.

"Who is there, Leah?"

They both sent glances toward the doorway of the parlor, Leah's guilty, Trev's amused.

"Aren't you going to invite me in, Leah?"

"Tell me why you've come."

"Did you find your rose this morning?"

Leah couldn't stop her instinctive move to touch her breastbone, where the rose was pinned to her chemise. "You risked getting shot if my father had seen you."

"Would you care?" Her eyes revealed shadows, and his grin faltered upon seeing them. He had to touch her, but when he raised his free hand to her cheek, he was forced to shield what her flinching away did to him. "Don't fear, Leah. I've come to rescue you."

"Leah?"

"A moment, Mama," she called out. "As for

you," she said to Trev, "I don't need rescuing. I need you to be gone."

"We need to talk—"

"Leah," Hedda asked, coming to stand in the parlor doorway, "who are you talking to?"

Before Leah could move to stop him, Trev stepped over the threshold. "Mrs. Reese, allow me to beg your pardon for calling without a proper introduction. I am Trevor Shelby, Robert's friend, and houseguest of the DeMoises."

"I'm well aware of who you are, Mr. Shelby." Hedda came forward, barely noticing that her daughter stepped aside while Trevor made a formal bow.

Leah, watching them both with disbelief, realized she'd never viewed Trevor's effect on other women, only listened to gossip about it. He was every inch the perfect gentleman. Her mother, to her surprise, offered him her hand, a sign of her acceptance, and, to Leah's mortification, invited him to join them as she took his card.

"I would be most happy to, but beg your indulgence while I explain the reason for my calling. Mrs. DeMoise has received a crate of books, and I, thinking to make myself useful while she paid her monthly call at the orphanage, offered to unpack them and place them in the library. It pains me to admit that I am not at all familar with her methods of shelving her books."

Trev couldn't resist his smile, for he had caught the mischievous sparkle in Leah's eyes as she watched her mother become his captive audience.

Clearing his throat and swallowing a laugh, he continued. "When Henry and Mama Rassia discovered my dilemma, they quickly suggested I beg the assistance of Miss Reese."

Leah's brow rose and she bit her bottom lip to keep from smiling. He was being a charming rogue and she had no doubt that her mother believed his every word, especially when he mentioned Mama Rassia, who ruled the big house with an iron hand. And Henry, her husband, was at times more formal than his masters.

"But surely, sir, upon her return, Mrs. DeMoise can direct you?"

Leah held her breath for a moment, suddenly wanting to escape from the minister's visit and his talk of sin and marriage.

"Madam, I beg your understanding. I've given my word as a gentleman to see this small chore completed upon her return." He met Hedda's clear and candid gaze. After thinking a second, Trev added, "You are concerned of course, with having your daughter properly chaperoned. If one of the housemaids won't serve, I'll ask Henry to stay in the library with us."

Sensing Trev had dispelled her mother's silent worry and had her wavering toward giving her permission, Leah knew that she wanted to go with Trev no matter what scheme his fertile mind had conjured.

"But the minister . . ." Hedda protested in a weak voice to Leah, "he wanted to talk to you about young Jamison." She caught Leah's imploring gaze and remembered how she felt about the young man. "I suppose it will do no harm for you to accompany him, Leah. But mind you, watch the time." To Trev she explained, "My daughter tends to forget herself whenever new books arrive. And Mrs. DeMoise is so generous to allow her the use of their library."

It was both an evil imp and need for revenge

that whispered to Leah she should not allow Trev to escape without making the acquaintance of Cecil Kavan. She suffered guilt, and prayed the minister wouldn't find out what she had done. Cecil would condemn her for the sin of giving herself to Trev without the benefit of marriage. Yet, even as she turned to her mother, Leah wondered why she had never thought of what she felt and shared with Trev as sin.

"Mama, it would be rude to leave without Mr. Shelby being given the opportunity to meet our minister. You've always said his stirring words of wisdom are of a guiding benefit to all who hear them. We cannot, in good conscience, deny Mr. Shelby a brief word or two which might set him on the path to salvation."

Trev could have throttled her. Leah's mother smiled at him, her eyes brightening at the thought. With a curt nod to Leah, he handed over his hat and walking stick, removed his gloves, and said, "I shall endeavor to find a special way to show you my appreciation for this opportunity, Miss Reese."

Leah, letting him precede her into the parlor, took his warning to heart. His look had been furious and she wished to call back her impulsive words.

Once the introductions were over, Trev adroitly handled the minister's probing and, while declining a cup of tea, did enjoy the cake. There was no pretense to his lavish praise, for Cato's claim that Hedda's cake was the best he'd ever tasted was true. He took note that Leah did not have a piece of cake as she rigidly perched on the edge of her seat, ready, he was sure, to pounce on him if he said one word that dared to indicate how well acquainted they were.

The talk had been social to this point, but when Kavan asked about the reason for Trev's call, Hedda was the one who answered.

"Well," Cecil said, "we must excuse them immediately. Anything to assist Mrs. DeMoise. A fine lady. A God-fearing woman and one most generous in her support of our building fund for our new church. While I don't hold with book learning for our young women, Mr. Shelby, I shall make exception to Leah accompanying you, as I'm sure her mama has done." He took Leah's gasp as surprise that he approved, not as the outrage she had intended. "Be sure to extend my best regards to Mrs. DeMoise, Leah."

The moment the door closed behind them, Trev took Leah's arm. To all intents he appeared the gentlemen, but he was making sure she didn't run off. "Thwarted your scheme of putting me on the coals, didn't I?"

"You needn't sound so smug. You know you did. We've already agreed that I don't have your skill to lie. But raked over coals is only a small measure of what you deserve."

"I know."

Leah stumbled and looked up at him. "You mean that, don't you?"

"I take full responsibility for what happened. And my rescue mission today was for selfish reasons. I wanted to talk to you, too. Leah, you must agree—" Ignoring the nearness of her mouth was no longer possible; nor could he resist the sudden longing in her eyes that had to mirror his own. He leaned close, touching his lips to hers for a breath and no more.

"Good morning," he whispered, "I wanted to

wake you like that," he added, wishing they were far from watching eyes.

"Trev, last night—"

"Ended badly," he cut in, leading her down the path.

Leah was unsure of why he had come for her and didn't answer. The brief touch of his lips to hers served to remind her that it wasn't enough, would never be enough. It was as if the harsh words, the hurt they caused, never happened, for the love she felt for Trev had the power to wipe them from her mind.

"Are there really books to be put away, Trev?"

"On my honor. But then, you have no reason to believe I have any."

Her fingers tightened on the cloth of his sleeve. "Don't say that, Trev. I told you the choice was mine. Without hope of school, I have marriage to look forward to, and it's a cage I never wanted." She glanced up at him. "You know about cages, don't you, Trev?" she asked softly, feeling his tension. She hid her disappointment when he didn't reply.

"About the books, Leah," he said after a few minutes. "There are a few that Robert and I picked up for her. I did make a mess—"

"A deliberate one, I'm sure."

"Yes. And Henry thought I should ask you for help. I suspect Mama Rassia put him up to that after I asked her to prepare a luncheon for us."

Leah kept pace with his long-legged stride, every step adding to her determination not to allow him to evade her questions. "Then I assume you went to a great deal of trouble to have your way. But there was no need, Trev. I would have come to you."

"The lady requires candor?"

"The woman does, indeed," she returned.

"Admitted. But it was because I knew you would find a way for us to see each other, and that's what we need to talk about."

"And you came like a thief into my room with the intent of talking to me?"

"Should I have stayed and ravished you?" he teased, striving to turn the seriousness of her mood into a lighter one.

"I'm sure you have the skill to have accomplished that without a soul being the wiser that you were there."

"The hell with this!" He yanked her off the path against a massive oak and leaned close. "I didn't sleep for thinking how I'd left you. The rose was atonement. A foolish—"

"Not foolish, Trev," she cut in, cupping his cheek. "It was another of the tender expressions you've given me. But please, stop before you are caught. The reds are Frances's favorites. We'll both pay if she finds out what you've done with them."

Pressing a kiss to her temple, Trev closed his eyes. "What have I done to be graced with your forgiveness?"

The anguish in his voice tore at her. She wanted to tell him again of her love, but knew he wasn't ready to hear it or believe it. Trev's cynical turn of mind might even have him believing that her declaration was a either a trap or her way to soothe her conscience if she accepted the money for school.

"Leah? Was I wrong?"

"No, Trev. But I, too, made harsh accusations—"

"Deserved. Every one of them." He took her arm

once more, pointing with his walking stick. "We'll take the path up through the gardens and you'll see for yourself that Frances will not miss one rose. She's nearly stripped the bushes, replenishing every vase and bowl with pinks and reds, and even took a basket to the orphanage with her. There, at least I'm on safe ground. It's your feelings I'm unsure about, Leah."

The bantering tone was gone and Leah stopped short, uncaring of who could see them. "My feelings are plain enough. It is yours that remain hidden."

"I'll explain what I can," he finally answered, after they had followed the winding stone path through the scented garden. At the door to the side hall, Trev stopped and opened it. "You know where the library is; I'll join you in a moment. I want to tell Henry we're here."

"I'm sure he knows, Trev. Henry, like Mama Rassia and every other slave at Rosehall, knows everything that goes on."

He tipped her chin up. "Does it bother you that they know we are lovers?"

"Are we, Trev?" she countered, her gaze direct. "*Lovers* implies an intimacy of more than one night." But her courage to take this further fled, and Leah slipped through the open door.

"I'll promise you that and more."

She didn't answer. She couldn't. He didn't understand they stole time for a little while from where they both must go. Trev said he would never marry her or anyone, but his place as heir to Sweet Bay demanded like marry like. She could bring him nothing but herself, and his needs for a wife demanded more than what Frances or her mother had taught her.

Once again, she knew that, even if such a marriage were possible, she would lose her family. Her father would never allow a marriage between them. With a sad smile, Leah knew that people who did not live with the rigid codes that governed the conduct of classes in the South could ever understand. In their own way, her parents were as bound by social dictates as Trev had to be.

Leah went to the library to wait for him.

Regret for what could have been colored her gaze as she entered the room and glanced around the floor-to-ceiling shelves that covered two of the walls. Trev hadn't lied about needing to bring order to the room. The desk before the multipaned windows held a stack of volumes; others were in crates piled one upon the other. An open crate sat on the floor. The oval table in front of the fireplace, flanked by high-backed leather chairs that invited one to enjoy the warmth of the fire and a good book on rainy days, held the wrappings she assumed the new books had come in.

Leah stepped into the room, noticing yet another stack of books, which had to come from the empty shelf above them. What had Trev been doing? She went to the desk, curious, and began picking up one book, only to set it down and take another. She had never seen these medical journals. Opening one, Leah found Trev's name written on the flyleaf. One after the other, she discovered they all belonged to him.

Careless as she replaced *Culpeper's Complete Herbal and English Physician* on the desk, Leah knocked a small book to the floor. Bending down to pick it up, she saw the folded paper sticking out from its pages. It was more than curiosity that made her open and read what turned out to be a letter. Anything that would refute Trev's claim that she didn't know him, didn't want to know him, was fair territory.

The letter was dated ten years earlier, addressing the board of the University of New York and requesting information about the university's fees and study requirements for the school of medicine with the goal of obtaining a degree.

Her hand shook as she stared at the signature.

Trevor Randolph, Rosehall Plantation, Augusta County, Alabama.

What was the lie? Trev lived in Georgia. Sweet Bay was his home. He had told her that. And Shelby? Why wasn't the letter signed Shelby?

Quickly, then, she reread it. There were no inkblots to mar the strong, masculine writing. The letter was perfectly legible. She stared at the date, rapidly figuring that Trev, if the signature was his, had been about sixteen when this letter was written.

Leah wasn't sure what alerted her that she was no longer alone.

Chapter Ten

S HE turned to find Trev standing in front of the closed door, and while she watched, he reached behind him to lock it. With his thumbs now hooked into the pockets of his waistcoat, he appeared at ease, but the rigid set of his cleft chin told her otherwise.

"Truly, Leah, you've been a distraction. I quite forgot I left those books here. Have you found me out?" he asked very, very softly.

She ignored the softness and heard not only the underlying accusation for her intrusion, but his obvious resentment. "The book fell and this letter . . . this letter—"

"Ah, a forgotten letter. Was it some impassioned youthful plea for the notice of some young woman?"

Leah saw the way his unruly black hair tumbled forward over his forehead. She was warned by the cool blue wash of his eyes where a colder fire burned. "Stop it, Trev. You're furious. The letter is not a love note, but to the board of the University of—"

"Oh, that. Toss it out, Leah. The letter means nothing."

She did not believe him. "Was this merely a draft?" She held it close to her, afraid that he would come and snatch it away before she had her answers.

"No, Leah, it's not a draft. It's nothing."

"You wrote it for a reason. Why didn't you send it?"

"Have you," he asked with exaggerated sarcastic emphasis, "aspirations of breaking all social, moral, and gender barriers to become a lawyer, Leah? If you do, I am acquainted with several young men who would eagerly take you on and teach you all the skills of inquisition."

"I've already broken moral and social barriers," she snapped back. Leah was sure he expected her to wilt beneath the blaze of his eyes, but she had made herself a promise and refused to back down. "I asked you a civil question. I would expect the same in reply."

"Another lesson in the library, Leah. Let me explain the rules that govern lovers. Questions are considered in bad taste. Especially when one indicates a desire not to discuss matters pertaining to the past."

"I can't accept that. I want you to answer me. I need to know."

"It was a boy's prank."

It was the bleak look in his eyes that made her glance at the books and shake her head. "I don't believe that."

"Believe what the hell you like. I did not bring you here to hold a discourse over some damn forgotten letter!"

His powerful figure loomed arrogantly, seeming to fill the room with his presence. Carefully folding the letter, Leah replaced it in the book. "As you wish, Trev." She turned and gazed out the window. "If the letter means so little, why lie about it?"

She waited for his reply, counting off seconds that stretched into minutes. Tense, silent minutes that finally forced her to turn around.

The floral-patterned carpet had quieted his steps; he now stood before the fireplace. She watched him repeatedly rake his fingers through his hair, sensing with an attunement which no longer had the power to surprise her that the darkness in him was back.

Leah could no more stop herself from going to him than she could stop her need to bring him ease. She resisted the urge to touch him, understanding that Trev waged his own battles.

"Is it so much that I ask you? Tell me why you never sent the letter."

"Why the devil does it matter?"

"I shared every dream, every hope, all my thoughts with you. And you listened to me, Trev. You left me without a defense against you. You claim I didn't know you, but you were wrong. Are wrong," she repeated, seeing his lips compress. "I know a man who is gentle, not the cynical stranger you become whenever I get too close. And then you dared to claim I didn't want to know you. We both understand that for the lie it is. You said we're lovers, but love means to share the good and bad without judging."

"It's that important to you?"

"Yes, it is."

"My mother died and I had to return home for her funeral. That's why the letter was never mailed." It was close enough to the truth.

"And the books? They are yours. Surely afterward you could—"

"The DeMoises were kind enough to store them for me while Robert and I served in the army.

There were other matters that claimed my attention after I buried my mother."

The note of finality was one she heeded, even if Trev left her with more questions. The amount of books and their cost indicated a strong desire to pursue his thought of becoming a doctor. Leah gnawed her bottom lip. Was the denial of it what turned him bitter?

"Will your mother come looking for you?" he asked abruptly. She shook her head and before he gave himself time to think, he drew her close and kissed her.

Leah knew the power of his kiss. She was helpless against the desperate raw need his mouth fed to hers.

She came to him, as Trev knew she would, without coquetry, without pretensions, all feminine softness that gave and gave with a generous spirit he could not, would not deny himself.

In her arms, with her kisses, he could forget the lost dream, the aimless wandering, even the revenge he longed to have. She narrowed his world to sharing her joy. Sharing all she gave, all she allowed him to be.

Even as his need rose to bury himself deep inside her, her soft moan came, revealing her own highly aroused state. But Trev wanted to give her more than an uncontrollable passion. He eased his kiss to mere brushings of lips to lips, slowly withdrawing, unable to let her go. With his hand gently clasped around her neck, he tilted her face up, watching her reconcile herself to opening her eyes.

He toyed with stealing every pin that held the silky luster of her hair tightly in place. Her seductive lashes framed her dark eyes. Trev leaned close to kiss each brow. Trailing a string of light kisses on her cheek, he knew she was as shaken as he.

"Forgive me?" he murmured, planting a kiss on the tip of her nose, glancing around at the discreet knock at the door. "Just as well I stopped kissing you or Henry would find no one answering."

Leah sought one of the wing chairs, hoping it would shield her as Trev went to the door. What if it weren't Henry? What if she were caught here with Trev? It didn't matter. She would dare anything to be with him. She sat up when she heard the door close. Trev came to her side.

"I know a lovely spot for a picnic," he said, taking her hand in his. "Down by the duck pond beneath the willows."

She hated to steal his wicked grin, but one of them had to show sense. "Trev, I can't traipse about the plantation with you. Not in the open where anyone can see us."

"You never worried about it before."

"Don't withdraw, Trev. I wasn't your lover before. If my father found out—"

"You're right. Not that it matters to me, Leah. I'd take on the devil himself to be with you." Her stricken look brought his smile and a lighter tone. "Well, since I can't take you outside, we'll have our picnic here."

"Here? In the library? But—"

"No buts allowed. New lessons, Leah. For both of us. And there is no better place than right here."

Within minutes, Trev had snapped open and spread a snow-white damask tablecloth and unpacked the basket Henry had just delivered. Leah listened to him whistle, watched him remove his waistcoat and neckcloth, then come to her.

"My lady," he said, making a bow and taking her

hands, "my very lovely lady, your cold collation awaits. As I do," he added softly.

Only too happy to have him tease and see the dark shadows lifted from his eyes, Leah's mischievous spirit entered into his play.

"And pray tell, my fine gallant, what lessons would you teach?"

"To myself, how to make amends." Leah rose at his urging, but made no move to come closer. "You need to be courted—"

"Trev, that can't be. My father would never allow you."

"Yes, I know. You've mentioned his opinion about Robert and me." His smile coaxed hers, for he refused to dwell on anything serious. "Let's see . . . I could teach you how to seduce me." He brought both of her hands to his lips and kissed them, holding her gaze with his.

"Do women *seduce* men, Trev?"

"All the time. Just the way you look at me, pleading for a kiss, is a seduction I can't resist. But then, I have the excuse of my desire for you, which has not been sated," he whispered, turning both hands over, exposing the palms to his lips. He watched her eyes darken as her pulse increased. "Not for me," he added, "and not for you."

"Trev, tell me what you want from me."

"For as long as I can have you, I want you in my life."

"Yes. I want that, too." She nestled against him then, resting her head on his shoulder.

"Lovely Leah, you may be as much of a fool as I to think we can make such a promise."

She smiled against his shirt. "Oh, Trev, don't you see? First you call us both thieves. Now we're fools. It appears to me," she murmured, feeling his arms enclose her, "that we share much more than desire."

"You won't regret this, Leah. I promise you won't."

Leah chased the shiver of apprehension that crept up her spine. No price was too high to pay for loving Trev.

Passion and love twisted together, forming an unbreakable chain entwined around Leah's heart. She waited for the coming of night, when dreams lived in a softer, silent world, benediction to all that she and Trev shared.

The bluff became their private haven. The tall chestnut tree with moonlight gilding its sheltering branches was their only witness as she learned to seduce him, overcoming shyness, drawing from Trev the power and understanding of indulging her own sensuality.

Trev was all seduction and laughter, teasing and claiming her mouth was as fickle as spring sunlight for deserting him. The wind was the only sound as she came to him, loving him, renewing her own needs.

To get through the days, she hugged an inner serenity knowing that he waited; she cherished his telling her that the tranquil murmur of her voice steeped him in peace.

His eyes lost their dark shadows. Leah gloried in love.

And like a quenchless flame, desire spread, as rich and heady as the apricots steeped in brandy they had one night, greedily stolen, greedily eaten.

Greed that made them stretch the hours of the night a bit longer, only to end with tormented whispers. . . .

"I don't know how to leave you, Trev."

"I never needed anyone the way I need you."

Kisses stopped the words neither one could speak. The words of love, of forevers.

And this night, as a gray light filtered into the sky, Trev held her tighter, his kisses conveying an urgency he couldn't put into words.

He didn't tell Leah about the note from Bella he had received before supper. Bella had suddenly returned from England, was home and waiting for him at Sweet Bay. She had begged him to come, writing that her need for him was desperate.

The DeMoises understood his decision to leave immediately. Robert knew he would travel light, and gave him King High, a horse bred for speed and stamina.

But in making a decision to leave immediately after he saw Leah, Trev hadn't figured that he would be unable to let her go. He held her longer than he should have, blocking out the argument he had had with Robert when he asked his friend to give Leah the money he set aside for her to have after he had gone. Robert thought him mad when Trev told him what he had planned.

He kissed Leah now, stilling hunger, and storing her sweet, generous giving. Nothing was going to stop him this time from getting Bella free of Clinton and away from Sweet Bay. Then he would come back and claim Leah as his. But he couldn't tell Leah that he loved her. Those were the words of a free man, words of a man who could ask his love to marry him. He could only murmur she was what he often called her: his candle in the darkness.

The moment he tore his mouth from hers and cradled her close, he wanted to kiss her again. The ever-lightening sky was his warning that he had to leave.

"Leah, I want you to wait for me. You've taken me on blind trust and I'm asking you to do so again. I've got to be away for a while," he said, his fingertips on her lips silencing her. "I still can't make promises to you. I just don't know what's going to happen. But wait for me."

"I love you," she whispered against his hand, suddenly frightened. He pressed her close to him and let her go.

"Trev?" she murmured, seeing him already leading his horse away before she turned to cross the back garden. A chill of foreboding slithered down her spine. Leah turned, hearing the faint sounds of King High's ground-eating stride that took her love away. Then she, too, saw how light it was becoming and hurried to let herself in the back door.

Something was wrong. Why didn't she question him? Why couldn't Trev trust her enough to tell her where he was going?

Her silent questions ceased abruptly.

The door was jerked open from inside. Before Leah could move, her arm was grabbed in a punishing grip and she was yanked over the hall's threshold. She threw up her free arm to shield her eyes from the sudden flare of light.

"Harlot! Who were you with?" Boyd Reese bellowed, dragging his daughter closer and slamming the door closed.

"Papa, please, I—"

"One word," he demanded, crushing her arm when she tried to pull free. "Give me the bastard's name."

Leah blinked back tears of pain, shocked into

silence by the sight of a wild-eyed man who now
bore little resemblance to her father. Veins stood
out in his forehead. Corded tendons bulged in his
neck. He had both hands on her arms now, shaking her. Leah saw her mother, standing near the
back stairs, holding the lamp, but she was blur in
Leah's tear-filled vision. The roar of her father's
voice drowned out whatever pleas her mother
made.

"Tell me! Who dragged you down to sin? Who
made you a scarlet woman?"

Feeling her neck would snap with the next forceful jerk, Leah couldn't have answered even if she
wanted to. She had no thought but to protect herself. Her arms were numb from his crushing hold.
No matter how she struggled, her strength dimin-
ished against her father's. The demands went on,
but she made no sense of the words now. He was
forcing her to her knees, his grip in her loosened
hair shaking her head.

"Tell Papa, Leah. Tell him what he wants to
know."

"Harborin' a viper . . . in my house . . . listenin'
to you, woman. Give her time an' she'll come
'round. Got 'round to bringin' shame on me, is all."

"Boyd! You're hurting her."

"Always wantin' to go off by yourself . . ."

Their voices dipped and swayed in and out of
her hearing, and the hall faded in and out of her
vision. Leah tried to raise her arms, but was
stopped by needlelike pain as her initial shock receded. She saw her mother's robed figure near the
stairs. She had to get away, escape to her room,
but the stairs were as black and out of her reach
as the doorways leading back to the separate
kitchen and the closer one of the parlor. She dug

for purchase on the smooth-planked floor, ignoring the burning tear of her hair, desperate to crawl free. But her father jerked her back.

"Answer him, Leah," her mother begged. "Please. I've never seen him in such a rage. Answer him."

"Answer me, harlot!"

Leah couldn't see him anymore. But she could feel. Her head rocked back with the sudden open-handed blow her father landed. She tasted blood. Fire spread from her jaw and cheek. Someone was screaming. The second blow sent her sprawling on the floor.

Into the shocked silence, before blackness roared up to claim her, Leah saw her father's boots. *Why was Papa dressed?*

It was late afternoon of the next day before Leah made sense of where she was. She had been drifting in and out of a blackened void, sensing her mother's presence, feeling her touch, but unwilling to give up the safety offered by the darkness that enfolded her.

She felt the cool cloth against her swollen jaw, and swallowed the coppery taste in her mouth to hold back a cry. Her body ached. Tears slipped from beneath closed lids when she felt her mother's gentle hand brush the hair back from her face.

"Mama?"

The croaked whisper brought her water to drink, but Leah barely managed a sip. She opened her eyes, the night rushing back with clarity when her mother averted her gaze and stepped away from the bed.

"I'll tell Papa you're awake."

"No. Wait. Talk to me."

"Why, Leah? What did we do, that you thought to bring such shame to us? Not once in all the time I've been married to your father have I seen him raise his hand. He's ashamed." Hedda came closer to the bed and leaned over her daughter. "You've got to tell him who it was, Leah. It's only right this man be made to do the honorable thing and marry you."

Leah wanted to curl away from her. She wanted the darkness to take the sound of her mother's voice, steal the painful look of her eyes. But the pain Leah felt in her body, her heart and her mind, refused to let her escape. Her father had never hit her before; she had never seen such rage in him. Her mother had never before had such sorrow in her eyes and voice.

Hedda couldn't look at her daughter's bruised face, but though she turned back to rinse another cloth in the washbowl, she didn't ignore Leah's silent plea.

"It was after midnight, or close to it," Hedda said, "when Papa caught the Brewsters trying to make off with the sows he was fattening. Old Silas saw them hanging around at the edge of the wood by the pens the last few days. He was keeping watch, and when he heard them coming up through the wood, he ran to get Papa. I came to tell you not to worry, but you weren't here, Leah. And when papa came home, he knew it, too. I couldn't stop him from what— I just couldn't stop him. He was waiting down there in the dark, just waiting for you."

Hedda hunched over, shoulders shaking as she sobbed, and Leah turned her head, tears spilling down her cheeks. By now the whole plantation would know what had happened to her. There was no way to protect herself, but she could protect Trev.

A deeper, aching pain spread inside her. She squeezed her eyes shut, fighting to think clearly, and hurting, hurting so bad. . . .

"You listen to me, Leah, and listen good. Papa's gonna ask, and ask again, keeping you locked in your room till you tell him who you were sneaking out to meet."

"Mama, please—"

"There's nothing I can do. He's blaming me for not letting him marry you off last year. We raised you right. Didn't we? We taught you to not to sin."

"No sin, Mama. Stop—"

"Why? You've got to hear what you've done to us," Hedda declared, sniffing into her hankie and coming back to the bedside. "I can hardly stand looking at you. You can't be denying to me that you were with a man, Leah. I *saw* what you looked like. Gown half buttoned, not a petticoat in sight. Mouth all bee stung and your neck and cheeks reddened by some man's whiskers. Hair wild as a slattern's."

"You make it sound dirty—"

"It was dirty. Is. And sinful, too. Do you know how you've hurt me? Here I was believing you'd settled to the thought of marrying, an' you're off meeting some man."

Leah covered her ears. She didn't want to hear more. *It wasn't dirty and sinful,* she longed to cry out. *I didn't mean to hurt anyone. I just wanted Trev and his love for a little while.*

"Don't be hiding, Leah. I know you can hear. You were always the different one. Dreamy-eyed and going off by yourself with those books and drawings. Never should have let all those fancy notions take hold." Hedda straightened, then tucked her damp hankie into her cuff. "I've taken my blame for this and asked your father's forgiveness for my neglect to keep you chaste. But you'll do the same, Leah."

Ignoring her own pain, Leah twisted on the bed, reaching up to capture her mother's hand. "Mama, please believe me, I didn't think I was sinning. No one can blame you."

"Child, oh, my dearest child," Hedda cried, sinking to her knees and hugging her daughter close. "What have you done? I loved you best, child. I've never told that to a soul, but it's true. I knew there'd be no more after you. But you've got to tell, Leah. Let Papa set this all to rights. That man has to marry you," she pleaded, stroking Leah's tangled hair.

"He can marry you, can't he, Leah? I mean, he's free?" Feeling Leah burrow her head against her, Hedda rocked harder. "Tell me he ain't got a wife. I can't even think who it is. I know you wouldn't be sneaking off with young Jamison. There ain't a man— Leah!" She pulled back, uncaring of the cry she wrung from her daughter, eyes widening, knowing even as she tried to deny it. "It wasn't him. You wouldn't sin with one of Robert's noaccount friends. You didn't . . ." The truth was in Leah's eyes, shimmering with tears, and Hedda closed her own, rocking back and forth and moaning.

"I love him, Mama. I love him."

Hedda held her daughter tight, overwhelmed by the need to protect her. But Leah wasn't a little girl anymore. She was a woman. There was nothing Hedda could do. Boyd could rant and threaten all he wanted, but he couldn't force a man like

Trevor Shelby to marry their girl. And everyone in the county would know she had sinned.

"Pray, Leah," she whispered. "I'll tell Papa you're sick. But tomorrow, by this time, you'll have to tell him his name. You hear me?"

"I hear," she answered, her voice muffled against her mother's chest. "I just can't do that to him, Mama."

In desperation, Hedda dug her fingers into Leah's back. "You've got to. You slept with him, didn't you? What if you're carrying his child? You pray like I told you. Pray your papa don't go gunning for him."

Pain was nothing, measured against the fear. Leah prayed. But not for guidance. To protect him, she prayed that Trev was really gone.

Chapter Eleven

IN a mood of bittersweet melancholy, Leah divided her hours between the agony of waiting and solitary reflection. The new moon marked the last days of the month as she sat on the floor near her window, recapturing moments from memory, letting the time flow by, too cowardly to think of what the day would bring. She was a fugitive from the consequences her decision had brought and thought only of her time with Trev.

The treasure of his murmuring voice, the exquisitely tender touch of his hands, the kisses that silently, but so eloquently expressed his feelings.

"Dear Lord, he's gone," she whispered, no longer able to summon tears.

Leah knew she would never have revealed his name until her mother mentioned the possibility of a child. Was she so blinded by love—was he, for that matter?—that the thought never came to mind? Not once in their stolen hours had they talked about it.

She had told him she wished for a love so powerful it would make time stand still. Time . . . She could remember every moment of the first day, but couldn't recall when she'd had her last menses.

Blind panic took hold of her. What was she thinking of? She gripped the sill so hard, splinters pierced her fingertips. Panic grew. Leah was frantic to pull the splinters out. She didn't want to think; she needed this small pain.

She wasn't respectable.

She could be with child.

And Trev . . would he want her? Would he be willing to marry her to give their child a name?

"Is that what I want? Trev forced to marry me?" The night held no answers, and morning brought her father's summons to the parlor.

Leah dressed with care, choosing the same russet gown she had worn the day Trev had come to rescue her from the minister's visit. She didn't want to think of its significance. Her mood was strange, as if all thoughts were suspended, and she had no time to decipher it as she brushed and coiled her hair.

The small mirror hanging over the washstand revealed the purpling bruise on her jaw and the crescent marring her cheek. If she were the harlot her father had called her, she would have rice powder to cover it. No matter who named her harlot, Leah would never accept it. She loved Trev and no one was going to sully it.

There was no reason for her sudden turn at the door. Her gaze skimmed over her few possessions, memorizing their place, a dim understanding coming that she would not be the same when she returned here. If she did . . . Leah abruptly turned her back on the echos of laughter and tears, the faint images of a girl dreaming, a woman holding a rose. The past did not matter. Yet she closed the door very softly behind her so as not to disturb the elusive moments of pleasure and pain that had brought her to this moment.

She kept her gaze directed at the closed parlor

doors, unable to look at the spot where shock, fear, and rage had exploded. She had to wipe her damp palms before she knocked at the door, and spent the few minutes waiting in dread before her father opened one door and stood aside to allow her to enter.

Leah stumbled, barely catching her balance when she saw Robert waiting in the room. He stood with his elbow resting on the mantle, one gleaming boot braced on the edge of the woodbox. From his expertly tied white neckcloth which accentuated his somber countenance, to the perfectly tailored bottle-green frock coat, Robert appeared what she had always called him: wealthy, spoiled, and arrogant. He barely greeted her with a curt inclination of his head, and chilled her with the frosted anger in his eyes. Fear began to course through her. *Why was he here?*

"Sit down, Leah."

She started at her father's command, the first words he had spoken to her since he had hit her. It gave her no pleasure to find that he couldn't look at her, but Robert stared at the bruises. Leah took the straight-backed chair near the window. She needed Trev. But he was gone.

"Well, say whatever it is you've come for," Boyd demanded.

"I told you I wanted to speak to Leah alone, Reese."

Robert had not moved, but his tone conveyed his displeasure and Leah was thankful he ignored her father's belligerence.

"An' I told you that you'll say what it is in front of me. This is *my house*."

Leah flinched. *His house. Not his daughter.*

"Your house, Reese? Need I remind you that this

house was built with timber milled from Rosehall's forest? It sits on Rosehall land. The clothes you wear, the food you eat, all are paid for from Rosehall's profits."

Staring out the window, unable to bear her father's humiliation, Leah noticed the opaque grayness of the overcast sky, which was as dark and threatening as Robert's silky voice. A thin layer of smoke hung in the air over the quarters' outdoor baking ovens and she wished she were down there.

"Your father is a gentleman, but you're not cut of the same cloth, for all your fancy ways."

"Men of your ilk should never pass judgment on their betters, Reese. My father has nothing to do with this matter."

"We'll see. I'll be goin' up—"

"He's not there. He's gone back to Tuscaloosa, where matters of grave concern occupy his attention to ensure there will be no military crusade upon the South if Lincoln is elected. *I want you to leave the room.* Don't force me to exert my authority in my father's absence."

"Stop it, Robert! You've no right to speak to my father—"

"I'll not have the likes of you defendin' me, girl," her father snapped.

"Shut up, Reese. Neither your daughter nor anyone else, for that matter, could defend you if I choose to take insult from your manner. Don't ape your betters. You haven't the proper stature for it. And I shan't ask you again to leave us. I'm ordering it."

Leah couldn't stand watching them and closed her eyes. She wondered if being Trev's lover had allowed her to absorb his skill of being in place, listening, but sealing off all feelings. Surely the lashing dismissal of her father's voice should have hurt. Was the gray void that now surrounded her the place where Trev disappeared to whenever someone came too close? If so, she welcomed it as the door closed and she was left alone with Robert.

"You know why I've come, don't you, Leah?"

Her fingers demanded her attention as she clasped the fingers of one hand with the other. "No. But you'll tell me."

"Boyd shouldn't have hit you. It's a sin to mar such a lovely face."

His voice was still silky, just as dark as before, but the threat came from another direction. Leah didn't move, didn't answer him. She couldn't breathe properly. The air was suddenly thick. Reminding herself that this was Robert, Trev's friend, offered no consolation. All she could remember were Trev's warnings about him.

"He's gone, you know."

"Gone? Who is?" she asked very softly.

"Don't play coy, Leah. I know about you and Trev, have from that day I saw your leather case up on the bluff. I must say I was disappointed that you would choose Trev over me. I can do so much more for you."

Silk and dirt. Leah felt her body tighten, needing to curl up and hide somewhere. She hadn't felt this sullied under her father's rage or her mother's agonizing accusations. But Robert made her feel dirty. Robert gloated that Trev was gone. She was alone.

Robert had wanted her complete attention, just as he had wanted her. But when she lifted her face and he saw her eyes, he had to harden his resolve to save Trev from his own foolish plan. He couldn't look at her a moment more. Her eyes were those of the dead. One of Mama Rassia's walking dead, he found himself thinking and remembering. "Just like that," she'd say, snapping her thick black fingers in front of his nose, bending over him. "Suck de breath right outta de body. Take all de color. All de life. Den leave de body."

And that is how Leah appeared now, all color leached from her face, even the bruises appearing to fade. He had intended to draw this out and have his satisfaction, but now he wanted it over quickly.

"Trev left money for you. He said you'd know what to do with it. But it's a paltry sum for what you've given him, Leah. I can afford to double it." She rocked in the chair as if he had hit her. Robert tamped out the flare of pity he felt. He understood, far better than Trev, how being a woman's first lover clouded a man's thinking. And that's all it was between Trev and this overseer's daughter. All it could be.

"Would you—" Leah swallowed, then tried to moisten her lips, "please go."

"I haven't finished. Damn! But between you and your father I've received little respect for my place. The money is up at the house. So are your drawings. He left them and he won't be back. Should you find yourself needing consolation, Leah, you'll find that I'm far more generous with my lovers than Trev."

"Get out, Robert."

"You're upset. Of course. Whatever schemes you hatched are foiled. And as a warning to you, don't offer your favors to any more of my friends. Sulla Mae, who has no illusions about her place, is better suited to service their needs."

"Dear God! Get out . . . get out," she grated

from between clenched teeth, rocking faster, her
arms wrapped around her waist. She tasted copper
from the blood welling where she had bitten her
swollen lip. Robert preys on fear, she warned herself. Don't show him any and he'll leave. Oh, Lord,
he's touching me. *Trev? Trev, I need you.*

Robert curved his hand over her shoulder, his
warm flesh chilled by the cold seeping through the
cloth of her gown from her skin. "A last thing to
tell you, Leah. Trev's good, but I'm better. When
you're thinking clearly, you'll realize he did you a
favor. You are far too lovely to grow old warming
some farmer's bed."

Leah raised her head slowly, for it required an
effort. She felt dry and brittle, ready to shatter,
but forced herself to gather whatever moisture was
left in her mouth. She held Robert's cruel gaze for
a second more, then spat on his gleaming boot.

He knew she was braced for him to hit her. And
he would have. But his voice was very soft when
he spoke. "You'll pay for that, Leah."

"No. I've already paid."

He left her rocking, and barreled into Boyd as
he opened the door. "Get out of my way, Reese."

Boyd caught Robert's arm. "Not so fast. You'll
give me this man's direction. He'll do the right
thing by her."

"Take your hand off me, Reese. And you will do
nothing about this. I will not have my friend bad-
gered over this trifling. If you feel some compensation must be made for the loss of her viginity, I'll
pay it, and that's the end of the matter. If you dare
bring this up to my father, I'll have you thrown off
Rosehall."

"Thrown off?" Boyd repeated, shaking his head,

only to stop and stare up at Robert's arrogant features.

"You've thought yourself above your station, man. Rosehall is mine. Do you think my father will gainsay my decision to dispose of you if I tell him you're thwarting my efforts to take more responsibility? And make no mistake. I'll do it."

Robert shoved Boyd back, gathering his hat, gloves, and walking stick from the hall stand. "There's to be no talk of Trev doing the right thing. He's already done that by leaving here. Heed my advice. Marry her off quickly so the talk will die down. I don't want her on Rosehall land." With a last glance inside the parlor, Robert added, "Castoff goods don't sell well, but there's money to sweeten the gall for some fool to swallow taking her now."

He closed the door on silence, absolute in its devastation.

There was no pride left in the man who walked back through the connecting hall to the kitchen and faced his anxious wife.

"Boyd?"

"You heard the last? I'm to be thrown off if I try to get Shelby to do the honorable thing and marry her. Thrown off, he says, like my sweat these years means nothing'. He'll do it, too."

"And Leah? Where is she?"

"Where he left her. Where you'll be leavin' her. She's needin' to reflect on her sin. Shamed an' disgraced us in one blow."

"Listen to me," Hedda said, coming around her worktable to put her arms around him. "She's still our daughter, and she needs us, husband. I hate seeing you so beaten, but Boyd, please, set aside your pride. She's hurting. Leah told me she loved him. No," she said, putting her fingertips to his mouth, "let me finish. She's done wrong, but we'll stand by her. I've not asked much of you through these years of our marriage, but I'm asking for this, Boyd. Help our child."

"Should I be takin' that devil's advice," he asked, patting her back and moving aside, "an' find a fool to marry her now?"

"If you want to keep your position here, you have no other choice."

"I've worked this land like it was my own."

"And did a fine job of it. Nicholas and Martin respect your advice when it comes to their land. And that neighbor—

"Cooper. Roddy Cooper. He was wantin' permission to court her."

Hedda stopped him from leaving. "Let me talk to Leah. She won't give you any trouble. She'll do what's right." His curt nod sent her running to her daughter.

Hedda didn't bother to knock at the parlor doors. She opened them, then stopped on the threshold, blinking at the darkness.

"Leah, it's quite dark in here. Why didn't you light the lamp?"

"No, light, Mama. Please."

Compassion for her daughter made Hedda stand behind Leah and gently touch her shoulders. "You're chilled to the bone. Come away from the window. It's going to storm and you've never liked lightning."

You're wrong, Mama. The storm's over. And I learned to like lightning. Trev was like that. Bright and fierce. Filling my world, filling me.

"Come along, Leah. We'll have some tea. That'll

warm you. And then we'll talk about what needs to be done."

"Where's Papa?"

"Don't be afraid. He's gonna give us time to talk."

"He's not going after Trev, is he?"

Hedda drew Leah up off the chair and cupped her cheeks. The shadowed light didn't allow her to see her daughter clearly, but she felt her trembling, heard the panic.

"You heard what Robert told him. He'll lose his position here if he does."

Leah leaned forward, resting her weight against her mother. "I'm glad he's not going. Trev—" *Tell her!* "Robert said he used me. He doesn't want me. I don't believe him, Mama. I don't want to believe him. I can't believe him!" she cried out, tearing free of her mother's arms and running blindly up the stairs to her room.

Boyd came rushing in just as the door slammed above them. "Was that her answer? Runnin' off to hide?"

"I told you, Boyd, she's hurting. Leah will come around."

"She'd better, or I'll take a belt to her." Stepping closer to the stairs, he yelled, "You hear? I'll take my belt to you an' show you what hurtin' is!"

Leah heard him. She lay dry-eyed on her bed, staring up at the ceiling, knowing no one, not even her father, could make her hurt as much as the pain ripping inside her.

"He's gone, you know."

But only for a little while.

"I know about you and Trev. Have from that day on the bluff."

What else did he know about us? Did you tell him more? Where are you, Trev?

"Wait for me, Leah." She whispered his last words to her. Wait . . . wait . . .

"What am I waiting for, Trev? Did you send Robert here to me?"

"He left money for you."

"I don't want his money."

"I'm far more generous . . . don't offer favors . . . service their needs . . . Trev's good . . . did you a favor . . . you'll pay for that . . . pay . . . you'll pay . . ."

Her fingers tore into her hair, the heels of her hands pressing her temples, twisting and turning, while she tried to stop hearing Robert's voice. Tried to stop the words.

She came off the bed in wild flight, fed by the urgency of despair. She had to know for herself. She couldn't trust Robert. She ran down the stairs, the first fat drops of rain hitting her as she flung open the door and met the gusting wind. Henry would tell her. Mama Rassia would know. And Cato. Cato knew she loved Trev. Cato would tell her the truth.

Driven by the need that filled her, Leah fought the slash of rain that tried to blind her, the wind that bent and twisted branches to stop her, even the silent scream building inside, telling her he was gone.

She dragged air just as she dragged the sodden skirt of her gown, refusing to stop, circling the quarters, heading for the stables. She couldn't breathe and had to. The lane was muddy, her legs trembling as she forced them to run, falling and unable to stop herself. She sprawled there, the rain beating down on her, rousing herself to spit the mud from her mouth while thunder pealed in the sky like a devil's laughter.

Her fingers clawed at the mud, finding purchase despite the violent shivering of her body. She pushed herself to her knees. Where had her strength gone? Had Trev taken that as he had taken her trust and her love? Had he betrayed her?

"No!" she screamed, defiance overcoming weakness and helping her to stand. But she couldn't run anymore. She was barely able to walk to the stable doors. As the storm raged, so did Leah, crying and calling, banging on the doors for Cato.

She fell into his arms when he opened the door, and let him drag her inside. The sudden warmth and familar smells offered no comfort.

"Tell me," she begged, clawing his shirt.

"He's gone, Miss Leah. Marse Shelby left almost two days ago."

"Trev's coming back."

"You're cold, Miss Leah. Let me get you on up to de house."

"C-Cato. He's coming back."

"Never said that. Marse Robert say he gone home. Had Henry pack all his—"

"H-hush." She looked up at him with fever-bright eyes. "H-heaven's cryin', Cato. Mama Rassia s-said when I die, heaven's gonna c-cry."

Chapter Twelve

THREE days of an unabating storm front forced Trev to detour north across the state line of Georgia and seek passage on the Muscogee railroad. King High took exception to being confined in the car. The big black settled down quickly once he had grain and the company of other horses.

Trev was exhausted from his hard riding, battling wind and rain, but the private compartments were all taken. Rather than share close quarters in compartments with strangers, who inevitably would get around to asking questions, he chose a seat in the passenger car. The smell of damp, close-packed bodies rose to meld with older, staler stenches embedded not only in the tightly woven straw seats, but in the very walls and floor of the car itself.

Slouched in his seat, hat pulled low, Trev closed his eyes as the train pulled out of Columbus. He ignored the rising and receding babble of voices, children's cries, and the curses from two slovenly drunks that came and went along with the ebb and flow of passengers in the next hours. The small towns along the rail passed in a blur of names.

The hiss of steam, the warning blasts of the whistle, and the slowly building momentum of metal wheels clacking against the rails formed a background for his silent litany. Home. Bella. Freedom. He hadn't sent a message ahead that he was arriving. He refused to give Clinton any warning at all.

His ears became accustomed to the grinding screech and the conductor's shout announcing another station, his body accommodating the lurch and slam as the train stopped and started, following the slightly northern curve of the rails. At dawn they stopped in Fort Valley, where he watched as a few cars went onto sidings awaiting the Southwestern Railroad's train. He was hungry, but no one stirred on the platform.

He dozed on the way to Macon, where the car took on a rowdy family, excited by their first trip south on the Macon and Western. Trev had the fleeting thought that if there was war, Georgia's rails could move troops and supplies as well as the vast rail network of South Carolina. He found a black woman selling ham-filled biscuits and bought two. He managed to get a cup of coffee only with difficulty, for the morning was chilled and the line long.

At Gordon, where the train nearly emptied for the spur line into the state capital of Milledgeville, a woman caught his eye as she strolled along the platform. Her hair, what little of it he could see beneath a beribboned and feathered bonnet, was nearly the same shade as Leah's. The thought of her waiting for him, loving him, made his lonely vigil bearable as he changed to the Central railroad and began the last part of his journey.

Once past Bostwick, the rail followed the winding of the Ogeechee River, which emptied into the inlets near Fort McAllister. Leah would love the islands. She had never seen the ocean, with its glistening sand beaches, but she would, he vowed. She would see all that and more once he was free.

He disembarked in the small town of Eden, dubbed Eden number two, for a little ways south was a larger township with the same name. King High was well rested, full of spirit for running, and Trev, thankful for the cool, dry day, was more than anxious to ride him across the Ogeechee southeast to Sweet Bay. He rode without stopping out of Bryan County into Liberty, passed ponds and creeks and sluggish streams. He rode through forests of long leaf pines cut in half by the dark cypress swamps, gray moss hanging still, and from the sea came the faintest breeze carrying to him the beloved scent of magnolia, pine, and jasmine.

At the fork he slowed, ignoring the black's prancing, as he rode closer to the Midway Congregational Church. The white frame building stood in a grove of pines and moss-draped oaks, its clapboard sides lined with shuttered, small-paned windows. He remembered climbing the square tower that rose from the roof, surrounded by an open belfry, and, to the dares of his friends, trying to make it up the tall hexagonal spire. Service had not yet begun and that had been one of his mother's good days. Clinton had been away, and she never chided Trev, but praised his daring as she led him inside.

He was tempted to go in to see if the pews were as stiff as he recalled, their hinged doors standing on the wide-planked floor, all separated by aisles. Up above them was the circular gallery used by the slaves, but he had been directed to keep his eyes on the clergyman in the high pulpit.

There was history here, beyond his own memories, for the church was the cradle of Revolutionary spirit in Georgia. Two of its supporters, Lyman Hall and Button Gwinnett had signed the Declaration of Independence, and two others, Daniel Stewart and James Screven, became brigadier generals in the Revolutionary army. In his mind he heard his mother's lovely drawl, telling him how the parish was honored with the name Liberty for its marked patriotism.

He turned away so as not to see the small pavilions built to allow the families rest and refreshments during the intermission between morning and afternoon services. Old feelings of hate rose with the memories of Clinton holding court, the women flirting in their discreet ways, the men seeking out his advice. Eight miles to go before he saw the boundary marking Sweet Bay's land.

Yet he found himself holding King High to a walk, wondering how his father had fooled a planting community that boasted deep religious convictions, gentle social refinement, and wealth. Their piety was the very cornerstone of their lives. He knew these people; they were industrious, observant of their place and obligations, known to be humane in the treatment of their servants. The men gave their sons the traditions of patriotism, high standards of honor and integrity. Was his home the only one that hid beneath its prosperous facade a rot so deep, so insidious, that death seemed the only escape?

Two horsemen cut across a field at a gallop, attracting Trev's attention. He wasn't close enough to recognize them, so he couldn't call out. Too many years had passed, separating him from the boys he knew who went to the state university in Athens or to the northern universities of Yale, Harvard, and Princeton. But the horsemen served to remind him that he was lingering when he should be hurrying. The quicker he got Bella away, the faster he could return to Leah and ask her to be his wife.

It was late afternoon when he dismounted and walked up the long avenue that led to the main house. Sweet Bay comprised nearly one thousand acres. Twenty acres were pockets of lawn shaded by the live oaks and sweet bay trees, cedars and pines, gardens of sweet and sour oranges, figs, pomegranates, olives, and grape arbors that surrounded the house. These were the scents of home, the ones that he carried with him in his forced exile.

He didn't know the pickaninnies, whose sole jobs were to keep the lawns and gardens weed-free. But then, slaves were sold and bought like the coming and going of seasons here. So unlike Rosehall. But he needed a clear mind for what waited and couldn't allow thoughts of Rosehall's tranquillity or Leah's love to distract him.

Trev found it near impossible to keep comparisons from coming to mind. There was no singing from the quarters, the rice house, and ginhouse. Figures scurried from mill house to barn, the chickens in the poultry sheds making more noise. He stood halfway up the long drive, closing his eyes and marking the placement of brick kitchen and dairy, smokehouse and washing sheds. He wouldn't be able to see the carriage house or wagon shed from here, or the huge stable. But he didn't want to remember the stable at all.

With every step he took, the past came alive, and he, weaker than he thought, couldn't stop it.

He opened his eyes, walked the distance until

the house rose before him. Rationally, Trev knew it was the play of the late afternoon's shadows that made the house appear alive, whispering, warning, but waiting for him. He used Leah's love, a love that deemed him worthy, to combat the regretful haunting of lost hopes and dreams.

The wide, encircling veranda was empty of life—but then, Clinton had never been one to sit rocking in the chairs unless there was company. The whitewashed house rose to two stories, eighteen rooms in all. He wondered where Clinton was at this hour.

From around the corner came a sullen-faced boy of no more than eight, better dressed than the pickaninnies he had seen—but then, his job was to take care of visitors' horses and Clinton was always careful to make the proper impression.

"I takes yore horse, suh."

"What's your name, boy?"

"Pickins, massa," he answered digging the toes of one bare foot into the dirt. "It's on accounta Tantalou sayin' as how I's pickin' up dis an' dat."

Trev didn't hand over the reins. He felt like a stranger, for he had no idea who the boy was talking about. But any source that would help him deal with what waited inside the house had to be used.

"Who's Tantalou?"

"She took Mammy's place in de big house."

Another one he didn't know. "Do Julius and Jason still work in the stables?"

"Doan know nobody called dem names. We gots JimmyJack an' Bishop an' Elijah, he's de smithy."

"And Tante Celine? Is she still here?"

The boy shook his head, toes digging harder, churning up the dirt. He wriggled his skinny body from side to side, and as suddenly as he started, he stopped. "Massa, why you askin' me 'bout folks ain't 'ere?"

"I lived here once," Trev replied, reaching into his waistcoat pocket and palming a half-dollar, before he realized it would cause trouble for the boy. He fingered a half-dime and handed over the silver five-cent piece. Trev smiled when the boy turned it over and over before bobbing his head and thanking him.

"You be de massa's boy what got hisself whupped jus' like you was a nigger boy?"

"Just' like you're gettin' whupped iffen you doan stop botherin' de gentlemun an' take his horse," came a voice from behind.

Trev turned, not recognizing the massive black man coming down the steps, moving quickly for all his bulk. When he saw that it was the man's intent to cuff the boy, Trev stepped between them. "There's no need to hit him. He said nothing wrong."

"Massa Shelby doan want—"

"*Massa Shelby* isn't here. What he doesn't know won't hurt anyone. But I won't stand for any cuffing while I'm here."

"But yore Massa Shelby, too, suh."

Trev hated the term, but it would do no good to say so. The man's broad unsmiling face showed the ravages of a fighter and Trev wondered what his father had been thinking of to make this man— it was obvious from his neat sackcloth suit—the majordomo.

"I'm afraid you have me at a disadvantage. I haven't been home for a long time. Pickins withstood my asking about former slaves."

"Beg yore pardon, suh. Massa Shelby, now, he

call me Monk, on account of my stayin' away from de black wenches. Had me a wife when Massa Newberry owned me. Had me the name of Shagato when I was fightin' for 'im. Them Newberrys, they fell on hard times an' sol' us off. Massa Shelby say he doan need no more wenches, no more pickaninnies. Ain't seen 'em near two years. Ain't knowin' where they got off to." He turned to the boy. "You take real care with that fine horse of Massa Shelby or I'll tan yore hide good."

Trev took his saddlebags, admiring the quiet dignity of Monk, even as he pitied him. But Trev pitied anyone who was subjected to Clinton's whims.

Before he followed Monk up the wide steps, Trev took a last look around. "Monk, do you know what happened to Tante Celine?"

"The ol' witch woman?"

"Is that what they got around to calling her? She wasn't a witch, but a skilled healer on the island she came from."

"It ain't my place to be sayin'." He held one of the double doors open. "Mistress Bella, she'll be right glad to see you. Been askin' every day."

"My sister will never be mistress of Sweet Bay, just as I will never be its master. Remember that, Monk." Trev stepped inside to the entry and gave Monk his bags and hat.

"Yore room's been kept ready since Mistr—Miss Bella's come home. I'll get Silvy—she's one of de chambermaids, so's you know—an' tell her to get water hot for yore bath. You'll be wantin' one after all that ridin'."

Trev had no problem smiling, or thanking Monk for letting him know yet another name. It made him feel less a stranger. He glanced up the two sets of stairs that rose from the entry hall and formed a balcony. The double doors on either side led to the drawing rooms, the left opening into the large dining room and the right into the library. Behind them, yet again separated, was his father's office, small parlor, and smoking room, while the other side held the sewing room and what had been his mother's office. But he made no move toward any of them.

He knew he should bathe and change before seeing either his sister or father. He sent a rueful gaze over his dust-laden boots and clothes, felt his beard itch from not having shaved in five days.

"Monk, is my father's man Gilbert around? There's not even a clean shirt in those bags, and I'm not sure what was left here would fit me."

"Massa Shelby got hisself a new man named Caesar. Gilbert, he was gettin' on in years. Couldn't move fast. This Caesar's right uppity, even if he was raised a house nigger. But he do a fine job brushin' out yore clothes."

Trev nodded, and Monk left him. He couldn't bring himself to ask if his father was home, and, if he was here, where. He was dirty and tired, yet his steps dragged as he started up one side of the staircase, fighting memories battering him from every side.

"Oh, my Lord! Trev? Trev, is that you?"

He was halfway up the stairs, caught in the curve, when a feminine bundle of silks and lace came flying toward him in a blur. "Bella?" Black hair. Blue eyes, A head shorter than him. Skin as white as magnolias. Small-boned as she was, her slender arms hugged him so tight he couldn't break free and look at her. She was crying and laughing, then murmuring his name over and over.

"Oh, Trev, hold me, hold me. It's been so long. I can't believe you're really here. I kept waiting and hoping. Trev, you're home. We're finally together again."

The soft childish drawl was gone, and now he held her tight, closing his eyes, trying to adjust to the fact that the slender young woman in his arms was Bella. The image he had carried with him had little resemblance to who she was now: pale, skinny, eyes too big for her face. But he rocked her as he braced himself against the wall, overcome by the tears she shed that soaked his shirt.

When she lifted her head, Trev let her pull back and cup his bearded cheeks with her hands, while he stared down into the face of a stranger.

It took him minutes before that sense of strangeness began to leave him. The cascade of pinned-back curls were as black as his own hair, and the widow's peak he used to tease her about came from their mother. Her tear-filled eyes were a lighter blue than his, but as thickly lashed. He held her with one arm and touched her deeply arched brows, his fingertips making her real to him. Her nose still had a little bump from when she had fallen out of a tree trying to keep up with him. She wasn't lovely, not like his Leah, but when her wide, mobile mouth curved into a smile, dimples formed and the small imperfections were forgotten.

"Too many years, Trev. You're not the boy I remember." Bella wiped at the tears that wouldn't stop, once more hugging him close. He was different, Trev, and not the brother she once knew. His eyes were hard, without the warmth she had dreamed of. But she had missed him and told him so. "Be patient with me, I've missed you. I just need to hold you and know you're really here."

He murmured soothing sounds, all he could manage. She had grown up away from him, and he found himself fighting the rage that was surfacing. He wasn't there to see her pin up her hair for the first time, or see her hems let down. He wasn't the one who teased her, if anyone had, about the shy looks exchanged after church service with some boy. His guardianship had not extended to the joyful events of her life. That had been stolen from him. From her. He had never offered brotherly advice on dancing and gowns and friends, but he knew of others who had shared such things with their sisters.

The bond they had was more than blood. And Trev knew he had to have time alone, away from her, without hurting Bella or himself. Time to arm himself.

He slowly disengaged her arms, forcing a smile that never reached his eyes. "Thank goodness the stairs are wide or we'd both have tumbled down, Bella."

She took his hand, hiding how hurt she was. Beyond her name, he'd said nothing. Not a word of missing her, not a word that he found her grown up. He even seemed reluctant to follow her up the stairs to his room. "Monk will have hot water for a bath, and when you are ready, come to my room, Trev. We need to talk before you see Father."

He let her turn away and take a step before the pouty bottom lip revealed in profile sent him spinning back to the past and a little girl who made that same gesture not to cry.

"Bella," he called softly. "Who held you when the nightmares came?"

"No one," she answered, turning around. "There was never anyone who cared but you, Trev." She stared at the carpet runner, unable to believe the warmth in his blue eyes meant she had her adored brother back and not the cold-eyed stranger who had thinly masked his hate.

"I still care, Bella. I always have, always will, but seeing you is like meeting someone I thought I knew, but really don't know at all."

"And for me it's the same. He stole twelve years from us, Trev. Twelve long and, for me, lonely years. I prayed you would come and rescue me when you grew up. I—"

"Yes, Bella. Long and lonely." He took a step toward her, just as she did toward him, both freezing at the bellow from below.

"Why wasn't I told he's here? Damn you, Monk, I'll have your black hide for this! Get him down here. Move, damn you!"

"Go to your room, Bella."

"No. You're not going to face him alone. I remember what he did to you. I won't let that happen—"

"I'm not a boy anymore. And you're not locked up in a school across the ocean where I can't get to you. Now go to your room and wait for me."

Old emotions, like old scars, ravaged her brother's features and Bella saw the hard-eyed stranger was back. This was not the reunion she had dreamed about, or hoped for. Where were the quiet walks? The chance to talk and share the missing years of their lives? He came abreast of her, his look ordering her obedience, but Bella grabbed his arm.

"Trev, listen to me. I'm not a child. I said I had to talk to you. Now there's no time. I'm in love,

Trev, and I want Father's permission to marry, but he's refused to even meet Howard."

"In love?" he repeated, motioning to Monk at the top of the stairs to stay where he was. "A schoolgirl's infatuation."

"Massa Shelby, he's—"

"Tell him to wait, Monk. I'll be down directly."

Bella marshaled her arguments, knowing this was not the way she had intended to tell him. His tone was dismissive, just as her father's had been. Her grip tightened on his arm, stopping him from leaving her.

"I'll be eighteen in two months, Trev. I'm not a child but a woman. Howard is good man. Nothing like father. But if you fight with him, he'll keep refusing, to spite you and punish me." Her eyes implored him for understanding. "Trev, haven't you ever fallen in love? Hasn't there been someone special in your life where just being with them enriches every moment? Are you listening to me?" she pleaded, both hands squeezing his arm, desperate to reach him.

Hate reared its ugly head, and Trev felt it tear at him. Once more she pleaded for herself. One more sacrifice for him to lay at his father's alter. He wanted to lash out and barely stopped himself. Bella's pleas, soft, urgent, rang in his ears. She was almost eighteen. *Old as Leah. You can't discount Leah's love. Age never mattered. Leah asked for nothing. Bella asked for everything.*

He peeled her fingers off his arm one by one and walked away.

"Trev!" she cried, running after him. "What are you going to do?" He was already halfway down the stairs when she repeated her demand. Gripping the thick wooden railing, Bella leaned over, not caring if her father heard her. "Tell me if you'll speak on my behalf. Please, Trev, nothing has ever mattered so much to me."

At the bottom step he turned and looked up at her. His countenance was like raw lightning and Bella staggered back with a cry. His face was as inanimate as a mask. Only his eyes showed life, darkening until blue warmth all but disappeared. She didn't know this man. He was dangerous. Frightening her so she forgot it was Trev staring up at her, his lithe body ready to spring the distance between them and kill her.

"Trev, wait," she whispered, lifting one hand to implore him. "You don't know about him. Trev, please."

He held her gaze a moment more, then spun on his heel and walked through the drawing room doors Monk held open for him.

Chapter Thirteen

"**I**'VE answered your summons." Trev closed and locked the doors behind him. He leaned against the solid wood, giving his eyes time to adjust to the near-dark room. The only source of light came from thin slivers of the fading day between the drawn blue velvet drapery gracing the floor-to-ceiling windows of the two outside walls.

"Kept me waiting, boy."

"Your pardon," Trev intoned with ill-concealed fury. "I attended a long-awaited and desired reunion with my sister. But I'm here now. Shall we begin the celebration?"

"Silence your foul tongue! Think I'd order a fatted hog slain for the return of the prodigal son?"

"Touching thought. Your welcome overwhelms me." He could hear that Clinton was at the far end of the room. The rank musty odor of decay permeated the air and the darkness enclosed him like a tomb. He had had enough of darkness. Hate filled his mouth like spit, but he swallowed it. If he let it free, it would ignite like fire, consuming all in its path and be just as deadly.

"Why haven't you ordered the lamps lit? Or does the dark help you ruminate upon your sins?"

"So the bantam cock tries to crow?" Clinton's laughter filled the room.

Trev waited out the sound, clenching the protruding door handles behind his back until the well-remembered carved relief was imprinted on his palms. And when there was silence, he said, "I beg your pardon. An error in judgment on my part that I did not polish my manners in the barnyard before presenting myself to you."

"Insolent bastard. I can still take a whip to you."

"I'm not a boy, Clinton."

"But Bella's home. Did you forget that in your puny effort to prove you're a man?"

"It's your puny effort to use Bella that needs to be forgotten." Trev knew the taunt had pierced his father's shield. He heard the rattle of decanter to glass and smiled, hoping Clinton needed liquor's false courage. His breathing slowed, then held, and in those few moments he heard the slurp of Clinton drinking. Suddenly he wanted to see him, needed to. He stepped into the room, avoiding the large square pedestal table in the center, and began yanking apart the velvet drapes on window after window.

Trev clung to the last drape, his breathing harsh as if he had been running, hate welling up, slipping from his leash. He was so close to Clinton that he couldn't avoid inhaling his smell. He gagged, angry that Clinton heard, but the man smelled like the foulest tavern swill, bringing bile rising, just as the past rose, forcing Trev to fight for the courage to turn around.

And Clinton knew. "I've poured you a drink for Dutch courage, boy. But you'll have to turn around to get it," he taunted. "Can't do it, can you, *boy*? Guess I finally beat all that cockiness out and still couldn't make you a man."

Don't listen. Don't turn around now while you

could choke that goading voice into absolute silence. Don't let him foul you, as he fouls everything he touches. Think of Leah, dreams in her eyes and love in her heart. You can't go to her with his blood on your hands.

"Get the hell out if you can't face me."

Trev released his grip on the drape and slowly lowered his hands to his sides. With every slurred word that came from Clinton, Trev felt fear dissipate and control return.

"You saw Bella. Fancy piece of goods—"

"She's your daughter for Christ's sake!"

"At least marrying her off will bring me something! Unlike you. Worthless bastard that you are."

"If I am deemed worthless in your eyes, Father—" Trev began, turning. He stared, for there was nothing else he could do.

He had wished Clinton dead too many times to count. Now he stared at a dying man. Or what was left of the man he had been. A broken old man, to whom time had brought the ravages of his excesses. Ignoring the venom pouring from Clinton, Trev noted the open sores on his forehead, the sparse head of hair, more gray than black, the lesions that disorted the shape of his vile mouth. Trev didn't know how long he stood there before he realized that the glazed eyes he thought were staring at him were marred by small cankers near the corners. The way Clinton blinked, turning his head slowly from side to side, brought the understanding to Trev that Clinton was losing his sight. Justice had come.

"Shocked you silent, bastard?" Clinton's frail body heaved forward in the corner chair, his arm knocking against the side table, drawing Trev's gaze to the coiled whip, the decanter, glasses, and bottle clearly marked LAUDANUM.

The fetid odor of decay in the room increased with the foulness of Clinton's breath. Trev saw his mouth working, his protruding tongue covered with grayish cankers. Trev didn't need his small store of medical knowledge; he had seen enough in dockside taverns and saloons to know the last stages of syphilis. Like its evil host, the disease ate its way to the core.

"Go on, say it. I can feel you gloating. You know what I've got. You think it's killing me, and you're already digging the grave. But you'll wait and rot before that happens. It's been eating at me for years. But I'm winning. Beating it! Hear me? I'm the master and no one rules but me!"

Clinton rose from his chair, his gait the staggering of a drunk. He had to hold on to his elbow, pushing his arm up, clenching the fingers into a fist. "Damn weakling! Get out! Where's all your fine talk of doctors now? Quacks, the lot of them. That's what you wanted to be. Another of those damn bloodsucking leeches. Taking a man's gold and lying to him. Telling him he can't bed his wife or she'd bear him a poxed idiot.

"Curses on their heads! What the hell did they know about a man's need to forget the puling excuse of a woman he wed? I damn the lot of them. Ravening crows know nothing about a man needing the fire of his loins cooled. Trying to make me believe one of those pious bitches flipped her skirts and spread her legs for one too many men. Fools and thieves. Saved you from that, boy. A man knows how to cure the pox. Whiskey'll do it. Whiskey an' virgin's blood draws the poison. There's a cure you won't find on their lying lips."

Trev saw him fall back in his chair and wished, for one insane moment, that he could summon pity. Perhaps for a stranger there would be compassion. But not for Clinton Shelby. Trev felt rage that simmered, then cooled. Revenge cried out and was silenced. For years he had lived with the loaded and unseen gun this man had held to his head, feeling the jerk of the leash he had kept around his throat, desiring to rend the flesh and spill his blood. Once he had been schooled in the torments of the Greek tragedies, he had understood the enormity of the crime he had longed to commit. Patricide. Death of the father for freedom of the son.

"Say something, you mealy-mouthed weakling. Or are you swaying on your feet, ready to faint like that weak-kneed sister of yours?"

Exhaustion had stolen the thunder of Clinton's voice, the insidious voice of Trev's nightmares. Trev couldn't summon any feeling. "It appears that justice has been served," he stated in a dispassionate voice. "It's obvious that your extravagant pursuit of pleasures of the flesh led to your gluttonous indulgences in all the deemed vices. The laudanum and whiskey won't be enough. Perhaps there is a God and He's extracted a price for your sins that I never could attain."

"Pompous ass! Stop that drivel. Where's your caring for your father? Why the devil do you think I summoned you home? You're here to carry out my orders. Your sister is to be wed. You'll run Sweet Bay as I command until I'm well. You'll give me honor, you bastard. The honor that's mine by right. You can't forget it's the seed from these loins that made you."

Trev had stood there too long and borne too

much. "If there is a God, may he forbid my ever remembering that." He deliberately spaced each word, watching the flinching moves of Clinton's pitiful body react as if Trev had truly delivered whiplashes.

"Where the hell are you going? I can hear you, boy." He fumbled for the whip on the table, knocking over the drink he had poured for Trev. "I whipped you once, boy. I'll do it again. Don't you dare walk out on me. I'm your father. I'm still the master here!" he cried, lurching forward.

Trev heard the snap and coil of the whip hitting the floor behind him. He kept walking to the door, feeling the eyes of his mother's portrait following his every step. But at the door he turned and saw Clinton holding his glass.

"You are done, Clinton Shelby. Finished and no longer master of anything but this room. You've come to a more fitting end than I could have begged as payment from the devil. Hell is waiting, old man. I hope its fires are cool so that you'll burn for a long, long time."

He unlocked the door, but before he opened it, glass smashed above his head. Shards fell in a shower over his head and shoulders, the thick, weighted bottom of the whiskey glass hitting and slicing his cheek. Trev ignored it, just as he ignored the weakened shouts that followed him out into the entry hall until he closed the doors. He stared at the solid wood, sealing off his feelings, burying the past, and turned the key in the lock. The silence that followed along with the air he dragged into his lungs made him feel as if he had truly left a tomb.

"Massa—"

"Don't," Trev began, turning around to Monk,

"use that servile tone or that term addressing me."
He pocketed the key and saw Monk's gaze following his move. "These doors are to remain locked
until I am out of this house in the morning. Is
that understood?"

"Yessuh."

"The other doors that lead to the library through
this room are to be locked, too."

"Ain't a need, suh. Massa Shelby, he keep 'em
locked all de time. You best let me tend that cut."

Trev absently wiped the back of his hand across
his cheek and looked down at the smear of blood.
Once before he had spilled his blood upon leaving
Sweet Bay; it seemed somehow fitting that he do
so again. He shook his head, keeping the past
locked away, and roused himself to move, for there
was much to do before he could leave.

"Suh, yore bath's waitin' an' Tantalou fixed some
vittles."

"The bath can wait, Monk. Forget the food and
go down to the cellar and get me a fresh bottle of
bourbon. Bring it to my mother's office. And,
Monk," he added as the big man moved off, "tell
my sister to start packing."

"You's leavin'?"

"Tonight, if I can get done what I need to do."
Trev lit the lamp on the side table and opened the
drawing room doors. This had been his mother's
domain—her ladies' parlor, she liked to call it,
since the dining room opened to it. The cream-
and-rose-striped wallpaper revealed missing paint-
ings with the clean, sharp outlines of their frames.
He held the lamp aloft, finding the tables stripped
of the delicate porcelain figurines that had been
his mother's passion. Only the portrait of himself
and Bella remained above the mantel. Not that it

mattered; he knew he would take nothing from this house but Bella with him.

Memories crowded close and he beat them off, hurrying through the open doors of the dining room, sensing its disuse. A short hall led off this room, doors opening to the sewing room, his mother's office, and, farther back, to the enclosed dogtrot that ended in the huge brick kitchen.

Trev went into the office and set the lamp down on top of the inlaid writing table. He imagined he still smelled the lingering trace of his mother's scent as he rolled back the dust-laden top of her desk. His fingers trailed along the thin brass railing that edged its top, idly tracing the faded flowers lacquered on the wood, before he caught himself and withdrew her inkwell set. It was dried out, and he wondered what he had been thinking of, to believe he could use it. He heard Monk in the hall and without turning said, "I'll need ink and paper from my father's office. A fresh pot of coffee, too, Monk."

"I brung the vittles, case you wants 'em. There's clean water an' a cloth to tend that cut, an' the spirits. An' Miss Bella's waitin' to see you."

Not now! Trev raked his hands through his hair. He wasn't ready to give her explanations. "Tell her she'll have to wait." But he had no sooner broken the seal on the bottle and poured himself a much-needed drink when Bella burst into the room.

"Why am I to pack? What— Oh, Trev, your face! What did he do to you?"

"Nothing to concern you."

His callous dismissal stopped her forward move. "Trev? Please, tell me. Don't make me feel like a useless ornament."

"Useless? You? Never that, Bella. You've had a

major role to play." He tossed back his drink and refilled the glass, leaning against the writing table and facing her. "I want you to pack. Now, Bella."

"My God!" she cried. "You sound just like him."

Like him? Like Clinton? Trev stared into his glass. Never would that happen. But it brought him up short to realize that Bella was their father's victim, too. The meld of hate and love he had for his sister wasn't easy to dismiss. But he made an effort to speak calmly.

"I want you to pack because we're leaving here."

"Leaving Sweet Bay? But you've just come." Bella saw the second drink disappear as quickly as his first. She wished she could reach him, but didn't know how. Trev was a stranger to her. A stranger who was in the room, but somehow distanced. His coldness hurt, but she had survived these lonely years by not allowing anyone to see how vulnerable she was.

"If you refuse to tell me what happened with him, will you at least tell me what he said about Howard?"

"Howard? Who the devil is he?"

"The man I love, Trev. I told you father withheld his permission for him to call. Refused to even meet him. He sent his man of business to the ship when we arrived. But Howard is waiting for me in Savannah."

"It never stops with you, Bella. More complications."

"Have another drink. Soon you'll have father's arrogant tone down to perfection. And there is no complication. Howard wants to marry me. With or without father's permission. He can provide a good home, since his family owns mills and a bank."

Once again Trev heard her accuse him of sounding like their father. He didn't like it one bit. But the bitter waste of the last years churned inside him and wouldn't release him.

"Are you deliberately being obtuse or just selfish, Bella? Pardon my asking, but I've had my fill of sacrifice. Beyond missing me, as you claimed, do you give a damn what the past twelve years have been like for me?"

She withdrew from his acid tone as if he had slapped her, but refused to cower. "I cared deeply. But you're a man, not a helpless woman. Society is cruel to women who attempt to escape their fate. I cannot marry a man I do not love. I will not end like mother: old, broken, and so sick that my husband hates the sight of me and the children I bore him. I, too, have scars, Trev. Not that you care. You're so wrapped up in pity for yourself, you've forgotten the threats I had to live with."

Her impassioned plea, and her accusations of self-pity and Trev's similarity to Clinton, broke through the bitterness and hate. His fingers tightened around the glass. Had he lost himself in pity?

Trev looked at Bella and found her direct gaze disconcerting. He had accused her of being selfish. While he had remembered that she, too was Clinton's victim, he had forgotten how young she was. She had lived with the threat of being locked away in an asylum for the rest of her life or being forced to marry a man exactly like their father. He had given up so much for Bella and now had her thinking he didn't love her, didn't care. He was not and never would be the man his father wanted him to be.

"Bella, I didn't forget, but I lost sight of the hell he put you through. But we can end it tonight and be free of him. This time I will allow nothing to stop me." He held out his hand to her, beckoning her to his side. "Freedom, Bella. An end to my emasculation and the beginning of your emancipation."

She came to him hesitantly, asking his intent.

"I'll write out passes and letters of manumission for every slave. And you said this Howard is waiting for you in Savannah?"

"Yes. I said I'd send him word. But Trev, you'll have every planter in the county enraged if you free the slaves."

"Since I won't be here, they can find some other way to vent their outrage."

Monk knocked on the door. Bella took the tray from him and poured coffee for her brother while Trev set the paper and inkwell on the writing table. Trev's accusation that she didn't care about him hurt. Perhaps the years had stolen more than time. The love they shared appeared to be gone from Trev. But she refused to allow his accusation to remain unanswered.

Bella looked up at him. "Trev, you accused me of not caring about you, but it's not true. If freeing the slaves will give you satisfaction, I'll help you write the letters. I'll even get the key to father's strongbox, since I know where he's hidden it." She had to fight to remain calm under his impassive look. "I only ask one thing of you, and if you grant it, I will never ask for another."

Once more Trev had to confront image and reality. "Bella, in my mind you've always been the little girl needing protection, no matter the cost. I swore to mother, swore on my honor, that I always would protect you. It is difficult to reconcile your acceptance of my plan with that little girl." He offered her the glass, and this time she took it. "A chance to begin anew. But just a sip for you; I can't have you tipsy while you're writing. Drink to us, sister mine, to our freedom and dreams."

Bella touched her lips to the glass, hating the smell of spirits. She remembered the rages drinking brought in this house. "And to you, Trev. I wish you find love as I have."

"Perhaps I will," he replied, unwilling to share Leah with her, with anyone. "Is Howard worthy? I assume the one last request you would make of me is that I give my permission for you to marry?"

"It's more than you're being of age and able to do it, Trev. I want Howard to know that every word I spoke about you is true. You see," she said, coming up on tiptoe to kiss his cut cheek, "I love you despite your holding yourself away from me. Howard grew quite jealous of you, for I made you my knight and when I knew I loved him, only then did he claim a place in my heart alongside you."

In the soft lamp light, he saw the love in her eyes and within him there snapped the last bond of reserve. He cradled her against him, rocking and soothing the rush of words, agreeing they would talk of their years apart, but not now.

"I know how much he's stolen from us, Trev. I don't know all it's cost you. But you were all I had, my only hope. He frightened me with his threats of forcing me to marry, then of locking me away if I refused. There were days when I prayed to get a note smuggled out to you. I was desperate, Trev, so desperate to see you. If it weren't for Frances's cousin being on the school's governing board, I don't know what I would have done."

"Hush, little love, hush. It's all over, Bella. No one will hurt or threaten you again. And if Howard is worthy to be your husband, I'll do all in my power to see you wed."

"Father will pay for his crime against us, won't he, Trev? I want him to suffer as he had made us suffer. I never knew," she whispered, unable to stop the tears, "if you were all right. I lived with being watched all the time, having my belongings searched. Howard's youngest sister became my best friend, but when he asked to let me accompany them on outings when he was in England on family business, they told him I had to be watched. They told him," she sniffed, rubbing frantically at her wet cheeks, "you would corrupt me and mustn't be allowed near. He would never tell me more."

Trev gently cupped her cheeks, pulling back so he could look at her. "Bella, they're right. I am corrupting you. I have asked you to write—"

"No! I offered to help—"

"Does it matter? But I will take full responsibility for this. No more of this rot that lives on Sweet Bay will touch you."

"As it has you? And I won't allow you to claim full responsibility. We are together in all things once more."

"Together, Bella." He held her while she cried, for herself and for him, while he withdrew every memory of Leah. He wanted to tell Bella about her, about her love, her goodness, which gave him back a belief in tomorrows. But he kept his love secret, needing to hold it safe so that nothing and no one could snatch it away.

Leah was his strength and he wanted to go to her cleansed of hate. And to remove the stain of the times he had thought Bella a hated burden, he confessed to her. It was in the moments following that Trev fully understood that age did not make a woman, or bring her wisdom, but love could and did.

"My dearest brother, do you believe I did not cry out and rail against my lot? I had the same shameful feelings of hate and despair being held hostage to your obedience. You are a man of honor, Trev, and I ask your forgiveness, for I am twice blessed to love two such men and you are alone still."

"There is nothing to forgive. I do love you, Bella, even if you've soaked my shirt."

For a moment she was startled; then a smile lit her eyes, slowly curving her lips. She hugged him, then accepted his offered hankerchief. "You'll like Howard, Trev. He's a man of honor, too. He refused my suggestion that we elope before we ever left England, refused to change passage on the ship so we could go to his home. He even," she teased, needing to see his smile again, "refused to make me his mistress."

"Mistress? And what do you, with your sheltering, know about mistresses? Never mind. I'll have a talk with Howard."

"Yes. Yes, about all good things. That is all there is for us, Trev, only the good things that love can give."

He promised himself that if Howard did love her, he would arrange their marriage. But not in Savannah, where they were known. He would have to take them to Charleston, where he still had friends. It would not be the wedding Bella had envisioned, if it was to come about, but this was the only way he could provide one.

And as she sat beside him through the long hours of the night, writing even as he did, after taking Monk into their confidence to supply the slaves' names, Trev felt the pain of his years of slavery ease. He did not need to watch the hands of clock moving the hours toward his own freedom. Every breath he took counted the time for him.

When dawn came, they were done, and his hand ached. He thought about writing a note to Leah to tell her of his delay, but Monk interrupted with the news that his father was tearing up the room, demanding that the doors be unlocked.

"Bella, have your things been packed?"

"I left Silvy to do it."

"Monk, have a wagon brought 'round and saddle my horse." And to Bella, "He'll think about smashing the windows, for he's not yet crazed. But we'll be gone, Bella. Go see to the loading of your belongings. I'll meet you outside."

The moment she was gone, he gathered up the letters and passes they had written, placing them on the tray for Monk to hand out. He then opened the strongbox, surprised to find his mother's jewelry case, nearly two thousand in bank notes and a hefty sack of gold coins. It was unusual for there to be this much cash, but then, Clinton may have given in to a need to have his wealth at hand. Trev took the bank notes and the jewel case, leaving the coins for Monk to disperse among the slaves. It was small compensation for whatever they had to suffer, and more would cause unwanted attention.

He gave the room a last look, realizing he felt no regret in leaving. Sweet Bay was no longer his home, hadn't been for a long time. And Leah was waiting. The exhaustion fled at the thought of her and he walked outside to the dawning of a new day.

Bella was up on the wagon seat, competently holding the reins. At Trev's look, she smiled. "Howard taught me to handle his team when—"

The explosion of glass and curses from the side of the house made them both freeze. Trev recovered first, tossing the jewel case to his sister, shouting for her to go. He started back toward the house, but Monk came running out the front doors.

"You go on an' leave. I'll see to Massa Shelby. An' take the Lord's blessin' with you. He likes winnin' his fights same as me."

For a brief second, their gazes met with perfect understanding. It appeared to Trev that not only had Monk lost his servile tone, but his slurred, liquid speech. Big as he was, Monk stood taller, now proud as he inclined his head to Trev's nod. Trev set his heels to the big black and rode to catch up with Bella.

They were nearly to the church when something urged Trev to look back. He was glad he never asked Bella to slow down, for above the trees, against the clear blue sky, there rose the black curl of smoke.

And Trev rode on, finally free, believing for the first time there was a God, and that Monk knew Him well. He had won this fight with the devil.

Listless from the fever that had ravaged her body for days, Leah cried out silently in despair. There was no God. He had stolen her love, then battled her will to die, leaving her hopeless. But alive. . . .

With trembling hands, she searched beneath her pillow for the carefully pressed rose that she had begged her mother to leave there. She wanted to believe Trev's last words. She did want to wait for him.

As the days passed without word from Trev, Leah's strength returned to her body, but her mind was battered by turns, first by her mother, then her father, and even Frances, all denying her hope that Trev was coming back. There was no place on Rosehall she could go without his memory haunting her, but she tried, unaware of the conspiracy going on about her.

It was Frances who began it after hearing from Robert that Leah developed a *tendre* for Trev which he did not return. Frances had no doubt that she had been told the truth. She knew Trev's attraction for women, and knew Leah for a dreamer.

Leah had taken to wandering the rose garden most mornings and it was here that Frances found her.

"You're looking better, Leah," she said, cupping a full bloom within her hands. "You've had us all worried about you. People, I've learned, are very much like my roses. You can give them sun, water, and a good soil to thrive in. But you know what it is that makes my roses so admired? They respond to love, Leah. Just as we do. And for women, dear girl, it is not enough to love, we must be loved in return.

"We need passion in our lives. Do not ever believe a woman has but one passion. We do not. We learn to fill our days with many. That is what makes us strong," she stated, looking directly at Leah. "Marriage, a home, and children fill up the empty hours. You may not believe it now, Leah, but there is joy to be had when you have nurtured something and helped it to grow. Like my lovely roses."

Like my love for Trev. . . . But Frances had reached her as no else. Love could not survive without nurturing and hope.

"He's not coming back, Leah. Accept it."

She couldn't. Not until the continued emotional battering brought her to a state of fear that she carried Trev's child. The knowledge forced her to go see Roddy Cooper. If she had to marry, she would use her pride and do so on her terms.

Chapter Fourteen

AFTER almost four weeks of delay in Charleston, Trev was about to see Bella married. All he needed was the return of his friend Charles Berrien's brother, the Reverend Joseph.

Once Trev had realized that he wasn't going to arrange the marriage as quickly as he wanted, he had sent a note to Leah in care of Robert. He had rewritten the note many times before he simply told her that he loved her and would be coming back to ask her to marry him. All she had to do was wait for him. Since Robert knew this is what he had planned, Trev was sure he would see that Leah received his message.

Trev hated lying to Charles, who was a lawyer, for they had been good friends at the Citadel, but the lie he told served his needs. Trev told Charles of the small wedding they had planned to hold at Sweet Bay, and how the plans were threatened due to their father's illness, the suddeness of his death, and the fire that left them homeless. Charles offered his home and his help.

As for Howard Paxton, Bella's fiancé, Trev quickly decided he was all that Bella said he was, and more. Howard had drawn Trev aside at their first meeting, declaring that he would marry Bella with or without Trev's consent, with or without a dowry. It was with unaccustomed candor for men of their time that he proceeded to tell Trev how much he loved Bella. There followed a talk about his family history, the family's holdings, and his own prospects.

Trev grew to understand Howard's unabashed emotions toward Bella and his youngest sister, Mary Eliza, Bella's friend and schoolmate, who had accompanied them home from England. The two Paxtons extended to all the loving warmth and caring they had grown up with.

Howard proved himself an ally as news of Clinton's death spread. Without details, Trev filled in a few gaps of what Howard had already surmised. Howard also used the death and the loss of Sweet Bay as a reason to his parents for not delaying the wedding until their arrival, lying, as Trev had, about plans to go back and rebuild Sweet Bay.

Charles Berrien and his wife, Laura Elizabeth, not only offered their home, but did all they could to make an intimate celebration for Bella's wedding. Charles spoke to his brother, Joseph, a minister who had been away escorting his wife and infant daughter to visit her parents upcountry. Charles explained about Clinton's sudden demise and assured Joseph that Trev was her guardian and gave his permission for the marriage.

Marriage was very much on Trev's mind as he escorted Bella to church in the carriage, with Mary Eliza standing as her bridesmaid. Howard followed with Charles in a separate carriage, as custom dictated. But Leah was who Trev thought about as he gazed at Bella.

The white satin gown brought out the blue of Bella's eyes and the blush on her cheeks. Her ebony curls were drawn back from her face. He longed to see Leah dressed as his bride. The long white-blond veil of Valenciennes lace enfolded Bella in a gentle beauty as she raised the sprays of early-bloomed orange flowers to her nose. Trev would see Leah carry roses, for he could never look at one without thinking of her.

Bella turned her head at something Mary Eliza whispered and Trev saw the sun catch and reflect from the pearl and diamond ear-bobs she wore. He had given Bella all of their mother's jewelry, but for one ring that had belonged to his grandmother.

Meeting Bella's sparkling gaze, Trev smiled, sharing her happiness. Being able to grant her desire to marry Howard had given him another sense of freedom from the past, easing the darkness he had lived with for so long. He fingered the ring in his waistcoat pocket, feeling the shape of the small gold hearts that fit into each other. The story attached to the ring, which his grandmother had told him before she died, was that if a woman accepted a man, she returned the ring closed, and if she refused his suit, she would return it open. He was sure the simplicity of design would please Leah, just as he was sure that she would return it to him closed so that he could slip it on her finger and pledge his love.

At the church Mary Eliza fussed with the train of Bella's gown. "Thank goodness the day is perfectly clear. If it rains when the bride and groom leave the church, they'll have an unhappy marriage. Or a great brood of children," she added with a mischievous smile. "Don't forget to cry a little when Howard first kisses you as wife. If you don't, all your life will be filled with tears."

So it was with laughter they entered the church

where Trev, wearing a pearl-gray frock coat and trousers, as did Howard—for even the bereaved were forbidden to wear black mourning to a wedding—led his sister to the altar. He held Bella close before he relinquished her.

"My dearest Bella, I wish you happiness and love for today and all the tomorrows." He kissed her cheek and heard her whispered wish for him as Howard took his place at her side and Joseph began.

"Truly, those of us here are the dearly beloved . . ."

Trev felt an ache spread inside him. He longed for Leah. When Joseph solemnly intoned the wedding vows, he repeated them silently, speaking them to Leah in his mind, counting the days until he would hold her in his arms again.

"Will you, Isabella Lenore Shelby, take . . ."

"And will you, Leah Ann Reese, take Roderick Cooper to be your lawful wedded husband . . ."

Leah barely heard the vows the minister spoke. What was she doing, marrying a man she didn't love? *You must marry.* Was the reminder her own, or the words she had heard over and over from her parents and from her sisters when they came to help pack the family home and move them to Talladega? She didn't know. The last week was a blur once she had given in and done what they all wanted.

She couldn't claim her dream of her wedding day was tarnished. For she had never had a dream of what it would be like. Her family as well as Roddy's was here in the small country church. If there were few smiles, she blamed it on the solemn occasion, or the rain that began as they entered the church. The one thing she was sure of was that

Roddy came to the marriage knowing the truth of her feelings for another man. He only knew there was the possibility of her carrying her lover's child and not that she did. He accepted it. Just as he had accepted the generous dowry her father offered. There were no dreams left. While her heart cried out in despair for what she had shared with Trev, she knew she could not have managed alone. Frances would only have given her the money set aside for school if her father had approved. It was a wedding gift instead. But even if she had gotten some money, it would have run out, and she would have been left alone in a strange place. How would she have managed with a child alone? There had been no choice but marriage.

Yet she couldn't help wishing it was Trev at her side, taking her hand in his. Not Roddy. Her hand was lost in his large, square-shaped one. Leah stared down at the blunt fingers with the light sprinkling of hairs on the backs. He would have the right to put those hands on her tonight. And every other night. Roddy squeezed her hand in warning, and she came to with a start to find the minister staring at her.

"Say I do," he prompted.

Leah looked up at Roddy. His ruddy skin seemed to darken. His jaw thrust forward, adding to the rugged, somber cut of his features. He was barely taller than her, his thick hair the color of burned straw and flax. The line of his mouth firmed and he turned to glare at her. A wide band of paler skin cut across his forehead, attesting to his working with a hat in the sun. Beneath thin, straight brows, his blue-gray eyes were cool and proud.

He wasn't a handsome man, not like Trev, who stole her breath, but Roddy was sturdy in build and nature. His shoulders were broad, his neck thick where it emerged from between them. The neckcloth he wore was carelessly tied, its yellowed color revealing its disuse. *Remember he is your only choice.*

"Leah?" Roddy asked, squeezing her hand again.

The child. You must think of the child. "I do take thee, Roderick Cooper, for my lawful wedded husband and promise . . ."

Bella and Howard were married. Trev kept remembering the moment when they had turned to each other and kissed for the first time as man and wife. A painful envy came to darken his happiness for Bella, a regret that he wasn't sharing that moment with Leah.

The wedding breakfast was over. It was time for Bella to withdraw. The wedding cake, which occupied the center of the table surrounded by flowers, had been cut. He had made his toast to the bridal couple and each guest had offered compliments and kind wishes.

He had promised Bella he would stay until the ship sailed on the morning tide. Then he would be free to return to Leah. When Charles asked him to join him in his library for a drink and talk after the guests had left, Trev accepted. He needed a diversion to pass the time.

Once Charles served their drinks, he began questioning Trev about the political climate in Alabama. Ever since Trev had met him, Charles displayed a passion for politics.

"I'm sorry to disappoint you, Charles, but my recent sojourn at Rosehall left little time to find out."

"But you must be concerned. Both here and in

Savannah, Trev, the local elections have tried to ignore national politics. For Charles Jones, the new mayor of Savannah, the ploy worked. He didn't even solicit the nomination made while he was absent from the city. But he is moderate in his thinking, as are a few others just elected. Moderation won the elections for them."

Charles leaned forward in his chair, cupping his glass between his spread knees. "Trev, there are those of us in Charleston who are deeply concerned that the election of Lincoln appears a fixed fact. In view of recent correspondence I've had from friends and fellow lawyers in Pennsylvania, Ohio, and even Indiana, there's little doubt of it. The Republicans claim New York by a clear majority of over forty thousand. We fear that if Lincoln is elected, the action of a single state such as South Carolina or Alabama may precipitate us all into war."

"The only thing to do, Charles, is to trust to Providence to influence the minds of those fanatics toward compromise and hope it will avert war."

Setting his glass aside, Charles rose and began to pace. "I wish your solution could happen. There are incidents of scoundrels attempting to induce Negroes to leave the southern states. I am anxious to have the result of a case coming up. Free black men are being charged with inducing slaves to run North. We can't have these men forgetting their place. Gambling, smoking, and drinking in the streets will not be tolerated."

"Have you ever considered how we call a man free, then attempt to curb that freedom?" Trev asked with gentle mockery.

Astonished, Charles stopped his pacing and

stared at him. "Are you mad? These are Negroes, not whites."

"That is the thinking which will bring the South to her knees. This attitude is precisely what the North hates."

"Listen to yourself, Trev. You're one of us. Do you mean to tell me that you wouldn't stand with us if one or more of the states decides to withdraw from the Union after Lincoln's elected?"

"No. That is not what I said. I will fight for the states to have the right to choose. I can't imagine anyone advocating the right of free states to wage a military crusade on the South." Trev tossed back his drink now that Charles had stopped bristling.

"There is one other thing to consider," Trev said. "What benefit will there be if the North makes an attempt to subjugate the South? Surely men of business would do everything to prevent this from happening."

"You're right. And we must think of them as being in violation of the Constitution. The right of self-government on the part of the people is the very cornerstone of our nation. Those states that wish," Charles intoned, resuming his pacing, "have a right to withdraw from any suggestion put forth that denies it. We have a right to life, liberty, and equality."

Yes, as long as your skin is white. But Trev never said it aloud, for it was an old argument among him and too many of his friends. Later, in his room, once a letter of instruction to his father's man of business was in Charles's hands, Trev stood and watched the brilliant stars. Bella would receive all monies from the disposal of the estate that were not entailed to him. And tomorrow he could begin his journey back to Leah.

*   *   *

Dry-eyed, Leah watched those same stars. She had left Roddy upstairs snoring and had come down to the small parlor to be alone. In *Roddy's* home. She must remember that.

He was not pleased with her. He'd had little patience with her. Leaning her head against the cool glass of the window, Leah let the tears come. She must remember to never open her mouth when he kissed her. Never touch him below his shoulders. He had told her to lie still and turn her face, like a good woman, until he was done.

She had obeyed him. And bitten right through her lip to still her scream when she was made to feel violated by his every touch and his crude grunts. Now that it was too late, she understood the mistake she had made. She should have taken the money Trev once offered and run as far as it would have taken her.

Her hand curved over her lower belly. She couldn't run. Her father cursed her for being a whore, but she knew the whoring came from marrying Roddy. Despite having said her vows to him, she stood in his home and thought of Trev. He would never know how much she loved him. Leah had to summon her pride, the same pride which had sent her to speak frankly with Roddy before she had agreed to marry him.

Trevor Shelby would never know if there was a child. Roddy had agreed to claim a baby as his, and few of their neighbors would dare count the months on their fingers openly, since she had been in Roddy's company when she had visited her sister. It was another reason why she had chosen him. Being away from Rosehall and Trev's haunting memory was the other. But she didn't believe there was a place for her to run to, or hide in, that would take Trev from her thoughts.

She had to remember the vows she had made this day. She could not tarnish them with a love that had abandoned and then betrayed her. Trev had asked her to wait, but without one word from him, she had to believe he wasn't coming back.

With a last look at the night sky, Leah turned and gathered the hem of her nightgown to make the climb up the stairs and into her husband's bed. Never again would she allow a ghostly lover to come between them. She would be a good, dutiful wife. She would, she vowed, if God granted that she bore Trev's child.

"Gone? How can she be gone?"

"It's just as I said, Trev." Robert tossed aside the newspaper he had been reading and rose from the sofa where he had been lazing the boring afternoon away. He repeated for the second time since Trev had burst into the room, demanding to know where Leah was, "I told you. They packed up and left. Good riddance, too. Reese was getting uppity as a nigger. I found his presence on Rosehall near intolerable."

"But why?" Trev asked in an agonized whisper, still unable to believe it.

"They wanted to live near their daughters. Leah decided to marry that farmer near one of her sisters. Copper or Coper—"

"Cooper. His name is Roddy Cooper."

"Yes, well, that's it. Come tell me the news you've gathered on your travels. Since Lincoln was elected by popular vote and South Carolina seceded the same day, rumors are flying."

Not once in this had Robert looked at Trev. He

still could not bring himself to do it as he poured out a drink for himself. Tossing it back, he spoke quickly. "Clifford said the government officials have resigned and that they hoisted the Palmetto flag. Father believes we shall soon see a southern confederacy. That," he stated, pointing to the newspaper he had discarded, "is a copy of the *Mercury*. I know you won't believe this, Trev, but I was reading the Honorable Charles C. Jones's speech given at Fort Pulaski. Savannah's mayor preaches caution. Most of Alabama's men believe that should it come to civil war because of us forming a confederacy, it will be preferable to submission to Black Republicanism. There isn't a planter in the South who's not aware that the North intends to crush us."

The chilled black silence forced Robert to look at Trev, who gripped the edges of the sideboard, shoulders hunched over as if he had taken a blow. Guilt sent a flush to color Robert's face, deepening when Trev turned around. Trev's bearded face and dust-laden clothes added to the dangerous gleam of his eyes.

"Gone? Married?" he repeated with icy contempt. "Didn't you give her my note?"

"I tried, but she refused. Took the money, though. Well, she didn't, but her father came asking for it and Leah was the only one I told that you had left it for her."

"I'll need a fresh horse, Robert. I've run King High to the ground getting back here."

"Where the hell do you think you're going?"

"I'm going to find Leah. I want her to tell me that she doesn't love me, never did." He shook his head to clear it. "I can't believe she married, knowing I'd return. I needed to know she was waiting.

Leah was the only thing that made this time away bearable for me. I want to hear why she did it from her own lips."

"Damn it, Trev, don't be a fool. She's not worth—" The door slammed and silenced him. He stood there, staring at the door, understanding at last that Trev had meant every word. He loved Leah. He had intended to ask her to marry him. And Robert had not believed him. He had dismissed the talk as the heat of passion and nothing more.

"My God, he really wanted to marry her."

"Marry? Who's that, Robert," Frances asked, sweeping into the room. "I thought I heard voices, but no one is here."

"Trev was. Here and gone. And he's the one who wanted to marry."

"Trev? Are you tellin' me he wanted to marry Leah? But you claimed . . . Oh, Robert, what have you done? He's your friend, closer than a brother all these years." She ceased the moment she saw her son's eyes. "Where is he?"

"Getting a fresh horse. He's going to see her."

"Well, you've got to stop him, Robert. Leah is married now. She mustn't have Trev upsettin' her with vows of love. It wouldn't do a bit of good. Make her miserable, an' nothin' more."

"I can't stop him. You're a fool to think I'll try. I'd have to tell him what I've done. And I can't. I won't. If Leah loves him, she'll save me that. She won't explain, won't say a word about my part in this. And stop looking at me as if you're ashamed, Mother. It's nothing to what I'm feeling."

He came to stand before her, his hands gripping her shoulders. "Swear to me that you will never tell Trev what I've done. Swear it!"

"Take your hands off me, Robert. I'm still your mother. The remorse I see in your eyes is the only thing that stops me from cursing you. From the time he came to us as a boy, we have known what his life was like. Robert," she said, seeing despair meld with the remorse, lifting her hand to his cheek, "if you can live with this foul lie on your conscience, I will never say a word to Trev."

She started to walk away, then turned. "But if you are his friend, go with him. He'll need you after he has seen her."

This thirtieth day of November was blustery and cold as Leah returned from ministering what help she could to her sister Ruth, who had taken with the broken-bone fever. The onset was quick, the pain in the joints unbearable, but its duration was short in most cases. Martin's mother had come to relieve her, but Leah was in no hurry to make her way home.

She had been married for two weeks, and each day the realization of her mistake grew. The man did not like her books, so she hid them. He did not want her wasting time picking wildflowers to brighten up the kitchen. He did not ... Leah stopped herself from repeating the list of Roddy's want nots, must nots, should nots, wishing he would add one, just one, to his unrelenting list. She longed for him to tell her not to come to his bed each night.

Carefully stepping over the deep wagon ruts in the lane, she hugged her winter cloak close, chilled as she was whenever she thought of the agonizing long hours of the nights. She had tried to talk to Roddy about wanting to please him, trying hard to wipe the memories of Trev from her mind. But

Roddy's answer was to tell her it was shameful talk, he'd have none of it in his home. And she was left alone without any warmth, without the least show of tenderness.

It was condemnation in a prison of her own making. Lost in her thoughts, Leah did not hear the drumming hoofbeats behind her until the rider swerved to avoid her. She jumped back, tripping on the cloak's hem, and fell into the bushes with a cry.

Stunned by her fall, she looked up, but the sun blinded her. The rider had not dismounted, but Leah felt the tenseness that suddenly gripped her. She knew before she shaded her eyes, knew with the way her heartbeat quickened and every sense came alive, that Trev had come. His lithe body swung down from the horse, moving toward her, the body she knew as well as her own.

Stop! she thought to cry out, unable to move. In a flash she saw her chance to grow whole again disappear when he reached out his hand toward her. She cringed, scratching her cheek on the twigs that entangled her hair.

He stood leaning over her, blocking out the weak sunlight, taking the very air she tried to breathe. Dark and forbidding, he was a Trev she had never seen. It wasn't the thick stubble on his face, but the bleak despair in his eyes that frightened her. She was afraid to move, afraid that she would shatter, so great was her shock at seeing him. Leah clasped the tie of her cloak, holding the cloth together as if it would somehow protect her.

"I had to know if it was true," he said in a voice marked with bitterness and exhaustion. His gaze locked on her hand, staring at the sun glinting off the gold of another man's wedding ring.

"It's true, Trev. I'm married."

"Why? Why didn't you wait for me? Not even a damn month—"

"Seven weeks. Seven weeks and four days."

A fire spread in his belly. She was married. Married and counting the days. "Are you so joyous in wedded bliss that you count each day? Don't bother to answer. I don't want to know. Just give me your hand so you can get up, and stop cowering as if I'd beat you."

Leah didn't want him to touch her. He had no right to be angry with her. She had tried to wait for him. But the child .. Oh, Lord, she couldn't tell him about the child. He might try to claim it for his own once it was born.

Trev needed to touch her. He grabbed her and dragged her up before she could twist aside to avoid him.

"Why didn't you wait for me? I need to know, Leah. I told you to trust me. I asked you to wait. There were things . . . none that matter now, but they kept me from coming to you. Just tell me why," he demanded, his eyes ablaze.

He pulled her close, unable to stop himself from giving in to the need of having her in his arms again. Her struggles were easily subdued by his strength, but he couldn't understand why she refused to answer him.

"You told me you loved me," he said, cradling her face between his hands. "Don't close your eyes, Leah. Look at me. Listen to what I'm saying to you."

Her expressive brown eyes were dull and filled with fear. But Trev was so set on having his say that he ignored the fear. "I trusted your love, Leah. I believed you when I believed in nothing else. I can't . . . I won't accept your love was a lie. Do you hear me? I won't believe it was a lie!"

Leah knew what she had to do to protect her child and herself. She couldn't let Trev think she still loved him, but the words seemed to choke her each time she tried to speak.

Her silence defeated him as no words could. Trev pulled back and released her. He stared at his clenched hands and slowly lowered them to his sides.

The burning inside him receded, replaced by an coldness that seeped into his bones. "I'm begging you for an answer, Leah." He drew a shuddering breath and released it, fighting for calm.

He turned away just as she started to reach out to him and Leah let her hand fall back. "Roddy asked me to marry him. You never did, Trev." The words were soft, but as chillingly cold as the numbness that seeped inside her. He said he loved her. *Now he said he loved her.* But when she tried to walk away, he blocked her.

"No. I'm not finished. You were mine. I told you I was coming back."

Wrapping her arms around her to stop the shivers, Leah stared at the ground. He wasn't going to let her go. She had to pray for the strength to withstand him when all she wanted to do was be held in his arms.

"You never said when you would come back."

"Was your bed lonely? Is that why you ran off and married him? Or didn't you believe me?"

Leah closed her eyes. She hated him so much at this moment that she was afraid to answer him. All the torment, the emotional battering she had from everyone pushing her into marriage would come free in rage and betrayal against him. She had to remember how close to home she was. Roddy must never know that Trev had come here. Roddy must never know about Trev at all. Her hand slid beneath the cloak so the move was concealed from Trev. She took courage from the tiny life she held.

"You don't have any right to question me, Trev."

He turned toward her. "I have no right," he repeated with disbelief. "I have every right. I'm the man you betrayed with your damn lie of love."

"No!" Leah shoved at him, knowing she didn't have the courage or the strength to take any more.

But Trev caught her up against him with one arm and held her chin so she had to look up at him. Her eyes were wild, like a trapped animal's. Her skin had paled to white and he could feel every shiver that rippled through her body. But his fury cooled, for he had never seen Leah like this; she had never been frightened of him.

"Do you understand what you've done to me, Leah? I never trusted anyone but Robert until I met you. Do you know what it does to a man to have that trust betrayed? You took my money and betrayed my love—"

"No," she whispered, shaking her head until she was free of his hold. "I never touched your money. I told Robert I didn't want it," she cried, the memory of that day and how sullied Robert made her feel coming back. But there was no fight left in her, none in her words, for the weeks of fighting with everyone had taken their toll.

"Robert told me your father came at your request for the money."

"Robert said that? But it's not true. I never sent my father to him." Stricken that he would not believe her, Leah stopped defending herself. Why had Robert lied to Trev? She stopped herself from asking. Trev had said he trusted no one but Robert until he had met her. No matter what she said, she would never have his trust again. It was too late for them. She was married. She had to remember her vow to God. She would be a good wife to Roddy if He let her have Trev's child.

"You took my money and married another man. Do you know what that makes you? Do you?" he demanded, struggling against the knowledge he had lost her. He couldn't stand touching her and knowing she was not his. Never again would Leah be his.

He turned his back to her. Leah knew she could walk away from him. But there had always been a need within her to ease the darkness that haunted him. His voice was as bleak and despairing as the look in his eyes. The money didn't matter. If Robert had given it to her father, or if her father had demanded it as payment for her shame, it would change nothing. The damage was done. She would still feel betrayed that Trev had left her for so long. She would always carry the memory of Robert making her feel sullied by what she shared with Trev.

Leah couldn't hate Trev. He had not lied to her. He had kept her in his life for as long as he could. If he had once said he loved her, she would have waited forever, no matter what anyone said or did.

She started to walk away, only to have him stop her once again.

"Why did you refuse to take my note from Robert?"

"Your note?"

"Yes, my note," he repeated with harsh impatience. He couldn't look at her. Trev knew he would reveal the pain her betrayal caused him. He had never begged her, but he would. He had to know, had to fully understand why she didn't wait for him.

"I sent it to you once I knew I would be delayed in Charleston. Robert said you refused to take it. Had you already made up your mind to marry Roddy?"

Horror spread inside her. His accusation stung. He thought she had plotted to marry Roddy while claiming to love Trev. Robert had lied to him. Robert had never tried to give her Trev's note. Robert, the only friend that Trev trusted. Words of denial sprang to her lips, but Leah couldn't speak them. Betrayed. They had both been betrayed by Robert.

Leah swayed where she stood. How could she hurt Trev by telling him about his best friend's betrayal? It was agony to be tormented by this decision. She wanted to tell him the truth. She longed to defend herself. Years of sharing had gone into the trust and friendship that Trev had with Robert. Could she destroy it? Would Trev even believe her over anything Robert said? Trev had no one but Robert. She couldn't take that from him. She loved Trev, but he was lost to her. Hurting him would only hurt herself more and she couldn't do it.

It pained her to look at him. "I must get home. My h-husband is waiting for me."

For long moments Trev searched for some sign of the love she had given him. Leah's eyes, always so revealing of her feelings, were now blank. He stifled the rush of pity he felt upon hearing her weary sigh. She stood waiting for him to let her go to another man. No, he clarified. Not just another man. Her husband.

The hopes and dreams he planned to share with her now that he was free came crashing down on him. And the pain inside him grew. Trev had never used the desire between them to hurt her. But he was fighting the despairing blackness that threatened him.

He caught her and pulled her to him. "I haven't had a chance to kiss the bride, Leah."

"Don't do this," she pleaded, forming the words against his lips closing on hers. God help her, she couldn't fight him. This was her love and he had been cruelly taken from her by lies. And she had never denied him.

Tears came for the bitterness she drank from his kiss. She could only cry out silently in pain for the truth she withheld from him. His lips were cold, as if there were no warmth left inside him. And she could do nothing to ease the heartache she tasted in his kiss.

It was too much to stand there and not give in to the need to give and receive love from his lips to hers. Leah summoned the strength to do it. Trev would end up hating her, but she loved him too much to hurt him again.

When he lifted his head and stared down at her, Trev held her cheek so she couldn't look away from him. "I want you to know that I loved you. I wanted you for my wife. I would have beggared my soul to have you share my life," he ended with deadly softness.

Leah didn't feel her tears until he wiped them away. "Have I made you sad, Leah? Are you crying for what we could have had? No man will ever love you as much I did. No man could ever treasure the gift of that love as I would have."

"No m-more. I c-can't—" She bit her bottom lip

to stop herself. Lost. He was lost to her. And she was imprisoned in a marriage without love. Her chest became tight with the need to draw a breath that was free of him. "What else do you want from me, Trev?"

"To never forget what we shared."

Fear formed a hard knot inside her. If she had his child, she would never be able to forget him.

"Did you ever love me?" he asked with anguished torment, raking his hand through his hair.

"Yes."

"But you couldn't wait—"

"They said you were gone. Gone and never coming back," she answered in a deadened voice. Soon, let it be over soon, she silently begged, hurting as she never had, aching with the despair of how they had both been sentenced to be apart.

"And you," he whispered so softly she had to strain to hear, "believed everyone but me?"

"Yes!" she cried out. "I believed everyone."

His sigh echoed her own. Why was he continuing to question her? She was married and lost to him. Yet he couldn't accept it. He couldn't accept losing yet another heart-held dream, and live with the intense pain that spread without end. His hand trembled, caressing her cheek, but he had no pride left to try to hide it.

Leah looked into his eyes. They were as dark and empty as a night without stars. She had had to be strong before, and now she demanded more of herself. But he made a choked sound and held her tight, and she had to steal a last moment for good-bye.

Her cheek was pressed against the soft wool of his cloak, listening, as she had so many times in the past, to his heartbeat.

And Trev whispered his final retribution.

"Can *he* make you tremble with his touch, Leah? Do you look into *his* eyes and know you are the only woman he loves? Can *he* bring a cry from you, begging him to come inside you to make you feel whole?" His lips brushed her temple, her cheek, and lingered at the corner of her mouth. "When you lie in his arms filled with completion, does he hold you as if you are the sunrise, warming everything you touch? Does he?" he repeated, breathing the words over her trembling mouth before he barely touched them with his.

"I loved you like that, Leah. You taught me to dream again. To hope and to love. And you stole everything back, leaving me nothing."

He spun on his heel and walked back to his horse. Leah swayed where she stood. Robert stole from us. It wasn't me! she longed to cry out. When he set his heels to the horse and galloped past without looking at her, she clutched the edges of her cloak. She mouthed his name, wanting to call him back . . . wanting what she could never have.

Dreams, hopes, and love. Shattered. She didn't know how long she stood there before the cold bite of the wind forced her to move. Every reluctant step took her closer to a loveless prison.

When she stumbled, her hands protectively folded over the slight swell of her belly. "Candle in my endless night," she murmured. She had lost Trev but had his child within her. He was stripped of everything.

And Roddy, standing as a silent witness in the woods across the lane, watched his wife's every step with his cold, proud eyes.

Chapter Fifteen

"TREV? Trev, you've got to climb out of that bottle long enough to hear this." Robert glanced around the hotel room, then roughly shook his friend's shoulder to rouse him. At least he was sitting up today, Robert thought, stepping back when Trev focused bleary eyes on him.

"I've had a letter from my father. He's with the governor in Mobile. Governor Moore is asking all the banks to retain all gold and silver in their possession as of December fourth as a matter of state. Father goes on to say that there is scarcely a doubt that Alabama will secede from the Union before the fourth of March in the new year. Do you know what this means, Trev? We are going to war."

From the mind-numbing, liquor-induced haze, Trev managed a smile and reached for the bottle on the table. He drank deeply, then offered it to Robert. "Calls for a celebration. A war? Men die in war, Robert. Do you think they'd have me?"

"I think you've had enough." But Robert made no move to take the bottle away from him. It had taken him two weeks of following Trev from one tavern to another, as Trev sought the lowest company, before he had managed to bring Trev home to Rosehall. Trev hadn't had a sober day since. But Trev retained enough sense not to inflict himself on his parent's hospitality and had moved to a hotel in Montgomery. Robert had been splitting his time between plantation and hotel ever since. But no matter how he tried, he couldn't rouse Trev to care about anything.

Guilt forced Robert to hide his disgust with Trev's slovenly appearance, as well as the condition of his room. He didn't bother to argue anymore, but went and rang the bellpull. His anger had not worked; Trev laughed it off. His biting mockery that Trev was wallowing in pity, earned him the sharper edge of Trev's tongue. When he pleaded with Trev to stop, Robert saw Trev withdraw.

But Robert had had enough. "I'm ordering your room cleaned and hot water for a bath for you, as well as valet service. We are dining out this evening, Trev. I won't take no for answer."

Trev's reply was another drink. His walls of defense had crumbled, and he wasn't able to shore them in place for any length of time. With a weary sigh, he leaned his head against the high back of the sofa, wishing Robert would leave him alone.

Poor Robert. He tried so hard to get him to care. A man couldn't have a better friend. Robert just didn't understand that he had lost everything: Sweet Bay, his dream, and Leah. Bella was cared for and loved. He had nothing. And he knew the import of the letter Robert read. The South would go to war unless cooler heads prevailed and some compromise was reached quickly.

Men died in war. Guns offered a sudden, clean death, not his cowardly choice of crawling into bottle after bottle. *Like my father before me, I have found the solace of drink when life has become unbearable.*

But he didn't ever want to be like his father.

Leah had held out the hope he could save himself. Leah. The forbidden one. He had to bury her. Bury her as deep as he had buried the past.

Trev heard the door open and close, listened to the murmur of Robert's voice giving orders, and he smiled. A man could go to hell and back with someone like Robert at his side. He should get up and thank the man.

"Robert, my friend, have I thanked you?"

"Thanked me for what?" he asked, opening the drapes.

"For whatever it is a man thanks his friend for when he's as stubborn as you. My company has not—"

"Trev, it doesn't matter. Nor do I want thanks. We're friends, just as you said." Robert came over to him, and this time he took the bottle. "There's a new girl at Lavale's I want you to see. He's holding an auction for her first night."

"First nights are not my pleasure."

Helping him to stand, Robert grinned. "Wait till you see her, Trev. Exquisite from the top of her blond hair—"

"No blondes!" He shoved Robert aside and staggered over to the window. Lights were ablaze in every building. Another day lost. Leah was lost. Leah and her damn silky hair. He couldn't stomach the sight of pale blond hair. The memories were still too sharp and cut too deep.

"There's Angeline or those Chinese twins. Just come with me tonight, Trev. Get out of this hole you've buried yourself in. No woman is worth what you're doing to yourself."

"Do you think I care? It's not just her." Trev turned slowly and faced him but locked his fingers around the carved molding of the sill. "I blame myself for what happened. If I had told her why and where I was going that night, she would have waited until I came back. There were a hundred times when I could have said that I loved her. But I never did. I sent you to her, never realizing that Leah wouldn't trust you."

Robert turned away and stared at the bottle. *Tell him.* But he choked on the confession he should make.

"I didn't mean to hurt you, Robert. But since I'm making these admissions, I want you to know that I added to Leah's distrust of you."

"I don't think I want to hear anymore, Trev. Your bathwater should be here and once you're cleaned up, meet me downstairs in the bar. Norbeck and Clifford will be joining us. We haven't been together for a good game in a while."

Trev slumped back against the window when Robert left. Now he had succeeded in alienating the only friend he had. He shouldn't have told Robert how Leah felt about him; nor should he have confessed how he encouraged her to feel that way. Robert did not deserve to have any blame placed on him for the mess Trev had made of his life.

If going with Robert tonight would make up for his surly behavior these last few weeks, he had to do it. And with this understanding, Trev realized he had reached yet another turning point.

He would give Robert tonight as he had asked, but no more. There was a time when he had courted danger and survived; perhaps there was mercy somewhere and he wouldn't this time.

But when the hotel valet arrived and Trev was undressing, he found himself withdrawing his grandmother's ring from the pocket of his waistcoat. No matter what condition he was in, the ring stayed with him. He opened and closed the hearts, slowly clenching his fingers over the ring in his palm. A reminder and no more. There wasn't anything worth caring about. And never, ever another woman.

The hot water made him sweat, and he closed his eyes as the man bustled about, setting the room to rights. He had one last memory to drag forth and then he would be done. Trev had avoided thinking about the way Leah looked on that blustery day. There were deep bruised shadows beneath her eyes as if she had not slept. He had cast aside how thin she had felt to him when he had held her. And he had to recall the desperation, then the frantic look in her eyes. Had to listen again to her husky voice speaking of denial, of her marriage, of her vows.

He had loved her and she had betrayed him. He had trusted her and she denied him.

Too many shattered dreams had taken their toll. He couldn't afford any more. He simply couldn't care.

And later at Lavale's, he found himself ready to begin his new life.

The cards were hot, the liquor smooth, and the women like silk.

When he returned to the card room in the wee hours of the morning and joined yet another poker game, Trev found he was envied his luck.

"The devil's own," one player said, throwing in his hand.

Trev didn't smile, didn't even attempt to rake in the pot he had just won. But he answered the man. "You're right, you know. It's the devil's own luck I have. You see, I was born in hell."

Robert heard the last as Trev shoved back his chair and walked away. He stared at the winnings left behind and quickly motioned to one of the young women to gather them up and give them to Lavale, who would keep them for Trev. Then he followed his friend.

Love was not in Roddy Cooper's eyes as he watched the twisted turnings of his wife in their marriage bed as her body fought to reject the child she carried. He didn't know if he should pray that she kept this child or that she should lose it, for Leah had refused to tell anyone whose child she carried. It was a somber mood that lay over his home with the comings and goings of his family and Leah's, and the well-meant neighboring wives with their advice.

He suffered their pitying stares and whispered words to have hope, to pray that Leah would not lose their child, while he longed to expose her for the whore she was. But he had taken the dowry money he had needed to enlarge his farm to raise himself to the position that he felt was his stolen birthright. It was all that kept him silent while the prideful bitch he had married dared to tell him she had taken a lover who then abandoned her. He had lulled her into believing he would accept a child if there was one, raising it with his name, as his child. In return he would have Leah's loyalty forever.

Bitter gall rose when he recalled that not even two weeks after their wedding she had betrayed those vows. And without knowing whose child she carried, he dare not get rid of her.

Roddy cursed his grandfather to the blackest pit of hell. If he had not lost their rich lands when

Georgia sold land to them, land that later became part of Alabama and Mississippi, he would be a wealthy planter today. But the man had had no backbone, giving up before the Yazoo land fraud case was settled in the family's favor by the federal court, losing the wealth the family had. His father had barely managed to buy this small farm and hold on to it, but Roddy knew he could do better.

Leah thought him a stupid man, but he was already seeing the turn of the tide with the talk of war. His hate of every landed Georgian, every slight and slur the Alabama planters had laid at his door, would be paid back. And he'd keep Leah, not because he wanted her, but to deny another of those hated Georgians, Trevor Shelby, from having her.

If she lived, if she gave him a son and if there was justice, that would allow him to have his revenge on her.

We, the people of the State of South Carolina, in convention assembled, do declare and ordain, and it is hereby declared and ordained, That the ordinance adopted by us in convention on the twenty-third of May, in the year of our Lord one thousand seven hundred and eighty-eight, whereby the Constitution of the United States of America was ratified, and also all acts and parts of the acts of the General Assembly of this State ratifying amendments of said Constitution, are hereby repealed; and that union now subsisting between South Carolina and other States, under the name of the "United States of America," is hereby dissolved.

Done at Charleston the twentieth day of De-

cember, in the year of our Lord one thousand eight hundred and sixty.

South Carolina's declaration was repeated in the weeks that followed until Trev could recite it, if he wanted to. He allowed himself to be swept up in the celebrations of the coming holidays and the fervor which accompanied every ball and dinner he attended as talk of secession escalated.

And Robert was always with him, watching as Trev's withdrawal became complete. Trev was cyncial and remote. He attracted women's attention, but they meant nothing to him. No one would partner him at the fencing schools, for his blade was wielded with a skill that cut through a man's defensive moves within minutes.

It was Frances who thought of a solution that would break the destructive cycle. She was proud that Robert shouldered his responsibilities for overseeing the plantation with old Silas's aid, but guilt for her unwitting role between Leah and Trev prompted her to go to her husband.

"Robert and Trev have military training, schooling, and are loyal, Albert. The governer asked you to recommend men to him."

"And who, pray tell me, wife, will run Rosehall?"

Snuggled against him in their velvet-draped bed, Frances said, "Silas taught Robert and can do the same for me."

"My dear, think about what you're proposing. Running our plantation is an unending round of work."

"But if we should go to war, Albert, Robert will be called and you'll be in the capital. Who else can see to Rosehall? Widow Charmers has had the management of her estates for four years an' made a fine job of it, too. Even you said so."

"It's Trev that has you worried as well. Don't bother to deny it, dear. I've seen what's happened. All right, I'll do it."

Frances lifted her face for his kiss, praying she was right.

Once Albert presented his proposition to Governor Moore, who agreed they were good choices to act as messengers for correspondence which could not be sent by regular routes, Robert and Trev were summoned.

Robert saw this as an opportunity to redeem himself in his mother's eyes as well as his own. And it could be Trev's salvation.

Trev was bored with Montgomery's offers of entertainment. His recklessness, far from bringing him a challenge that would release him from hell, earned him a reputation which had men speak softly or not at all to him. Few resisted gambling with him, for all his devil's luck. And when his voice took on that hard edge bordering on insult, thoughts of the two men he had already killed in duels made others back away.

Robert's hope that Trev would take interest in what they had to do was quickly dashed. While he was with Governor Rector of Arkansas, learning Rector was disposed to Alabama's view to secede, Trev honed his knife-fighting skills in taverns. Robert had to force himself to concentrate on what the governor was saying.

"You must express my deep concern for the counties bordering the Indian nations. The Creeks, Cherokees, Choctaws, and Chickasaws have them worried. They are reluctant to vote for secession and leave those tribes under the influence of the government in Washington. The Indians receive large stipends and annuities and unless I can be assured that the South will do as well as the North for them, I cannot hope to induce them to change their alliances and dependence."

Robert took his leave, promising to return in the morning for a formal letter, and went to find Trev. An apple-cheeked barmaid was using Trev's ripped-off sleeve to bandage the cut on his arm when Robert finally located him.

"Got careless, Robert, but it's just a scratch, so don't frown. I'll live."

"And you're none too pleased about it," Robert snapped, gathering up Trev's coat and neckcloth.

"Such truth deserves a drink. Draw a pitcher of your best ale, lovey," Trev said to the barmaid. He saw the resignation in Robert's eyes and grinned. "Just one; then I'll leave with you." With his good hand he reached into his waistcoat pocket for a coin. For a moment Trev stared down at the ring he carried, and without a word or change of expression, he tucked it back into the pocket and tossed the gold coins on the table.

Robert watched, then resigned himself to drinking the ale. Trev never mentioned Leah, but he carried that ring with him. And Robert wondered if the love Trev had for her would ever diminish or die before Trev's own death wish was granted.

They only spent two days in Montgomery before they were sent to Louisiana. Rights, honor, future peace, and safety were words on every southerner's lips, but privately to Robert, Trev mocked them as words without substance. Arriving too late to deliver the governor's message to the Louisiana legislature, Robert insisted that Trev help him speak to the men still present in the capital.

But one representative's son, Anton Chevette, recognized the bored, reckless look in Trev's eyes and quickly suggested he accompany him. Robert was due to have a private meeting with the governor and couldn't go. He thought of warning the Creole about Trev, but knew if Trev found out, he would just disappear. So while Robert listened to the governor's conclusion that there was no hope of justice for the South except in separation because of Lincoln's election, he thought of Trev's hopelessness. And despaired of helping his friend, just as the governor related his own despair that Lincoln's opinions and ideas of constitutional duty were wholly incompatible with the South's.

It took Robert two days to find Trev this time, going from cockfights to gambling dens, then every bordello in the city. Directed to Rampart Street, where Anton had a home for his quadroon mistress, Robert discovered Trev loading a pair of dueling pistols that Anton provided.

"What have you done this time, Trev?" Robert asked, after being served coffee. He watched the lovely, near-white Danielle withdraw at a signal from Anton and close the doors.

"He had no choice, Robert," Anton answered. "A Creole's blood runs hot and one took exception to Trev following his wife into a shop."

"Trev?" When he didn't answer, Robert sighed and shook his head. "She was blond and slender and you thought—"

"Nothing, Robert, I thought nothing. It was a mistake that will be satisfied this morning behind some cemetery."

"When does this stop, Trev? When are you going to start caring?"

"It stops, my friend," Trev said, looking up with a cool gaze, "when I find the knife blade or pistol shot with my name on it."

But it wasn't to be that morning. Trev fired first, his aim deliberately off, and when his opponent raised his pistol, every man there cried out as Trev, ignoring the gentlemen's rules governing duels, stepped forward to present a better target. The man was so shaken that he missed him, but honor had been satisfied.

As they began their hard ride back to Alabama so Robert could make his report, he reminded Trev of a conversation they had had. "You asked me if I ever wanted more from life. I—"

"You answered that your racing, gambling, drinking, and whoring left you no time for more."

"But I never wanted to die, Trev. You've got to see what you're doing to yourself." But all Robert received was a cynical look as Trev set his heels to his horse.

Trev could never admit to him or to anyone that he was still shaken by the sight of that woman among the crowds of holiday shoppers. It wasn't drink that had clouded his mind and made him follow her, it was her resemblance to Leah. Would she never stop haunting him?

The night after their return to Montgomery, Trev wished he could refuse the governor's invitation to dinner, but Robert and his parents insisted he go with them. Robert told his father what he had reported to the governor, while Trev half listened, wondering when Robert had become so serious.

"New Orleans is their great commercial depot

and their great concern, which is why they are taking a course of reflection. The governor did say that if Alabama announces its intention to secede as a foregone conclusion, the other states would promptly respond. There's no doubt that having Louisiana will add dignity and importance to the movement. She is a state that is essential to secure the respect and recognition of foreign nations and the support of the hesitating states."

Frances and Albert basked in Moore's approval of the job their son was doing, and, unaware of Trev's misdeeds, included him. When the ladies withdrew after dinner, Frances told several women that she had given serious thought to hiring a secretary to handle all the invitations arriving for Robert and Trev. The two men, it was agreed, made a handsome pair, often surrounded by the loveliest belles wherever they went. But Frances thought of Trev's distancing himself from all that went on around him. At least he had not refused to come tonight, as he had several times earlier.

She had debated about telling him of the hastily scrawled note she had received from Leah, begging for a meeting between the two women. Leah had accompanied her husband to the city. At first Frances wasn't going to go, thinking it best that Leah be cut off completely from the past. But she feared the young woman might still harbor a *tendre* for Trev and had to know. When she first saw Leah, she had to still her conscience, for there was little to remind her of the lovely girl she once knew. Leah was pale, her brown eyes lifeless. Frances heard about her coming child and wondered where was the joy it should have brought Leah.

Frances kept their meeting brief, answering Leah's questions about those she had cared about at Rosehall. But her control softened when she saw the longing in Leah's eyes after she had told her what Robert was doing.

"It's Trev you want to know about, isn't it? Well, he's fine. Working for the governor, just like my Robert. You're a married woman expecting your first child, Leah, and must forget Trev," Frances sternly reminded her.

But even now, amid the warmth and charming company of the dinner guests, Frances felt chilled when she recalled the bleak despair in Leah's voice, asking, "Will you tell me how to forget him?"

She had to dismiss the incident from her mind as the ladies rejoined the gentlemen. When Albert told her the governor had proposed a toast to Robert and Trev for the exemplary service they rendered Alabama in these troubled times, Frances was proud. Perhaps her son's desire to serve his state had come from lies and misunderstandings with Trev, but Robert had matured. Learning they were going to Kentucky immediately after the new year, she hoped that Trev would find the peace he was looking for so desperately.

Beriah Magoffin, the governor of Kentucky, issued a proclamation the day after their arrival, convening the legislature in extra session for the seventeenth of January. He asked for two days to consider the lengthy missive Robert delivered. Once again, Moore had expressed his hope that while each state would determine its own reaction to the grave issues facing the South, the decision makers would take into account the identity of common interests, sympathy, and institutions in the slave-holding states. It was his wish that these things would lead to the frank consideration of common grievances and the measures necessary to correct them.

For once, Trev accompanied Robert on his rounds of Frankfort, Kentucky's capital, gauging the temper of the Kentuckians, not only in the private clubs where their status gave them entry, but in the taverns as well.

Southerners repeated their grievances, convinced that the Northern states had violated their sister state's rights. Trev chose a corner table, nursed a drink, and listened to the passion, wishing he could find it within himself, as Robert recently had.

It was simply beyond him to make the effort. He served as a bystander while Robert held court at the bar, reminding men that slavery existed in twelve of the thirteen states at the time the Constitution had been adopted. Four billion dollars was the estimated worth of slaves in the southern states now, which formed an important element of their political power.

"We all know," Robert stated, after buying a round of drinks, "that the North has waged war to destroy our power for nearly a quarter of a century. We have conceded to the northern states every right secured to them by the Constitution. We have protected the lives and property of their citizens when they come before southern jurisdiction."

"That's right," several men quickly agreed. One added, "And when southerners try to reclaim their fugitive slaves—their own property, gentlemen— they are set upon by mobs and are lucky to escape with their lives."

"It's fanaticism!" yet another man put forth, pushing his way through the crowd. "I know my slaves were stolen. Two prime bucks. And when I made a requisition through the governor to have the thief brought to justice, that northern bastard dared insult us and claim there was no felon, nor had a crime been committed."

"War is our only means of redress!" someone yelled, as glasses were raised.

Robert motioned to Trev as he slipped away and, once outside, asked Trev what he thought.

"Oh, I agree, Robert. War is the answer they're all looking for. I might even find my own answer there."

Robert understood the mockery, but since Trev agreed to stay with him, he didn't remark about it. And as the night progressed and the incidents of the past summer were raked up by men all over the city, Robert realized that Trev was growing very quiet. He would give anything to have Trev's insights, but it was a useless wish and he carefully made his own mental notes of what angered these Kentuckians the most.

Liquor loosened tongues and Robert had the money to buy. He learned of the abolitionists who burned whole towns in Texas and poisoned slave owners to the cry of "Alarm to their sleep, fire to their dwellings, and poison to their food!"

The sufferings of Kansas came up, having gone on for years, leaving death and desolation. The armed incursion into Virginia for the purpose of exciting a servile insurrection among the slaves and arming them for the destruction of their owners brought a near riot in one club. It was with horror that one man recounted the sympathy manifested in the North for John Brown, leader of a raid into Virginia, who died on the gallows a condemned felon. In the North he was celebrated as a martyr to liberty.

"And who needs a squadron of our navy maintained off Africa to enforce the laws against the slave trade?" one overzealous man demanded of Trev. He grabbed Trev's arm and spilled his drink. "I'll buy you another, sir. Hell, if you can answer me, I'll buy you a bottle."

"That will not be necessary," Robert replied, holding on to Trev's arm. He was afraid of what Trev would do and added, "We are leaving." Trev's gaze held a rare show of temper. Robert had to remind him that he was to gather information, not attack those who spoke freely.

Trev shrugged off his hold.

"I tell you all," the man continued, "we're payin' for it. Payin' for the navy to be kept afloat on the seas and not one damn coin is spent by Congress to protect us and our property. Those northerners preach 'bout equality. Tell me, any one of you, where is the equality for us?"

"Don't forget," another man added, his voice hushed to draw complete attention, "the final insult we are to bear. The black day of November sixth shall live as an outrage to every true southerner when Lincoln and Hamlin were voted into office!"

Trev and Robert slipped away to the shouts of never submitting and the belief that the South would prevail with glory. Robert had his information and Trev a case of aged bourbon to take back home. But while Robert presented Governor Magoffin's idea of a united southern presentation to Congress, stressing the hope that just demands would be conceded and the Union preserved, Trev went to Rosehall to pack his belongings.

Frances tried to talk him out of it and informed Robert the moment he returned. "Talk to Trev," she pleaded with her son. "I'm afraid of what he'll do, Robert."

"You think I haven't tried!" Exhausted from the hours of talk, Robert rubbed his eyes. "If I can't stop him, Mother, I'll have to go with him. You and I know I owe Trev that much."

"I worry that if he goes to war, Robert, he'll be killed and you won't deal well with losing him. We were wrong to interfere, no matter what you believed. Help him. Something has to make him care about living again."

But Trev, who rarely showed anger these days, made it clear he did not want Robert to come with him.

"I do not need a nursemaid, which is the role you've chosen to play, Robert. I'm sick of it!"

"Well, you can't leave without seeing Moore. He's got to release you. Damn it, Trev, at least tell me where you're going."

"Lawton is forming a brigade. I'm joining him in Savannah."

"There's no need to pack your things. You can leave them at Rosehall. You did before. You always called this your home."

Trev finished placing his shaving gear into his case. "I can't stand the sight of the place. There is too much here for me. And I need to be alone, Robert."

"That's too much to ask of our friendship," he protested.

"That's the hell of it, Robert. I'm not *asking* for anything from you. I don't *want* anything from you."

And guilt-ridden Robert let him go.

Trev resented the time he wasted going to see the governor. He pointed out that there were other men better suited to carry Moore's message to Governor Joseph Brown, but Moore wouldn't even consider it. Trev didn't bother to argue; he listened to Moore and counted the minutes.

"Trevor, his excellency should hear my words from a native son of his great state. Although, I admit, I've come to think of you as an adopted son of Alabama, I do understand your wish to return to the state of your nativity. Invoke our brother, the governor of our glorious mother state of Old Georgia, to give us his counsel and advice. Events now transpiring must unite us all, as loyal sons of the South, in the defense of the South.

"Remind him that we should make ready for the conflict which is nigh well upon us. Delay is dangerous; hesitation, weakness; opposition, treason. And while we honor the gallant act of our sister state of South Carolina, we want word from Georgia on where she stands. It is only accident and fortuitious circumstances that have placed South Carolina in the front of the battle. Our state will be there, too."

Sure that Moore was finally finished, Trev rose from his chair. "Sir, I did not make myself clear. I will not be returning. I've been assured a position on Colonel Lawton's staff."

"Ah, the lure of action for the young. Words are the swords of old men and you're anxious, like most young bloods, to see fighting with real weapons. I pray daily that it will not come to pass. Find me someone reliable to bring the governor's reply and know that I wish you well."

There was no sense of freedom once Trev began his journey back to Georgia. Leah and the memory of their last night together haunted him without mercy.

Once she had taken the nightmares away from him and replaced them with dreams of her. Now the nightmares had returned, but she led the cast of players, calling out to him while he searched in vain to find her. Robert never asked about the nights Trev had awakened, drenched in sweat and hearing his own tormented groans. Trev knew there had been a deeper bond, aside from the love he shared with Leah, that refused to allow him to find peace.

He found no solace in liquor. Other women had satisfied a physical need, but none could touch the hunger of his soul. He had given Leah a part of himself that he had once buried, and now Trev found it far too easy to return any gentleness, any show of tenderness or compassion, back to its grave.

Chapter Sixteen

TREV met with Governor Brown and delivered his message. Since Colonel Lawton was away from the city, Trev was left to his own amusements. He told Robert he wanted to be alone, yet volunteered for temporary duty on the governor's staff to fill the hours. By the end of January, the resolutions made by a caucus of senators from seven of the southern states in Washington revealed the opinion of these states to secede. In addition, a provision was made for them to organize a confederacy and to meet in Montgomery no later than the middle of February.

Nights when he gambled, he stopped listening to talk of the latest dispatches that were sent from one state to another. As disillusioned as Trev was, he could not provoke those men whose rage grew when they learned the Republicans refused to consider the Border-State Compromise and pledged to sustain the president. Mississippi passed a resolution to raise a committee to draft the ordinance of secession, with plans to secede immediately. Florida followed. Volunteers were requested to man forts. And with the dispatches came word that the ordinances were passed to strike out the words "Constitution of the United States" and to call the state militia into active service.

Trev was at Fort Pulaski when Robert showed up, Georgia's troops just having seized the fort. Robert was dismayed when Trev shrugged off his explanation that he was joining Trev in Lawton's brigade because Robert was sure they would see action long before any Alabama troops. He volunteered, along with Trev, to inspect armories for possible purchase, the only job Trev could find that would keep him on the move.

The two friends were the first to learn—being with Governor Brown at the time—that Edwin Morgan, the governor of New York, condemned the seizures by Georgia and her sister states. All post offices, customs houses, monies, and fortifications within the states that had once belonged to the federal government were seized by the state governments.

"Treasonable acts. Insurgents, he names us, gentlemen," the governor stated. "He will devote fortune, lives and sacred honor to uphold the union and the Constitution. And what of our honor?"

Honor. No one spoke of anything else. Trev sickened to hear the word, thinking of the cost honor had demanded of him. But men all over the South, motivated by patriotism, resigned their appointments in the navy and army of the United States and tendered their service to their home states. On February 8, the Constitution for the Provisional Government of the Confederate States of America was announced. Jefferson Davis was unanimously elected president. Frances wrote to Robert, who shared the excitement and celebrations going on in Montgomery with Trev.

Robert didn't tell Trev that Leah was expecting a child in late summer. He didn't mention her at all.

Lincoln was inaugurated. The Confederate acts were passed to provide for a war department, munitions, and the purchase of armories. Trev anxiously awaited his orders.

Far from the active service Trev had envisioned, he and Robert were assigned as aides to the newly appointed Brigadier General Lawton. Due to their military schooling, the general insisted they remain in Savannah, as he was charged with the defense of the city, harbor, and coast.

Robert hid Trev's drinking, wishing his friend would stop. Their pay of ninety dollars a month as lieutenants was supplemented by thirty-five dollars more as aide-de-camps, but Trev won and lost ten times their pay in a night. Robert watched Trev pace like a caged animal if he was idle for a few minutes, and knew he volunteered for whatever extra duty kept him too exhausted to think. Trev drilled troops, but found no pleasure in hearing their admiration for his skills.

Lawton refused to allow Trev to go north, commanding him to check the garrisons at Fort Pulaski and Fort Jackson. Robert prayed Trev would never find out that he had taken it upon himself to speak to the general. Robert was left to visit the ladies of Savannah engaged in preparing cartridges for muskets and cannons, while others employed their sewing skills making flannel shirts and rolling bandages.

Trev began to hate Savannah. The sight of lovers strolling arm in arm and the frenzy of sudden marriages sent him into a deeper depression. Four months he had waited, and when April came along with new shirts from Frances, he knew the wait was over. The great principles of political and civil liberty upon which the Union had been founded and stood for eighty years was at an end.

He was going to war.

Spring came slowly to the hill country of Alabama, but Leah welcomed every sign of life. She had to hide the old papers she gathered from every source, waiting until Roddy was asleep before she read every line. Alabama was proud of her sons who were already serving the South and she knew that Robert was in Savannah and Trev had to be with him.

It was late May before she read about the blockade of the Georgia harbor by the *Harriet-Lane* and learned that Trev had been there when the ship fired on a Spanish brig, then chased it off. The reporter lamented the fact that the ship remained out of Fort Pulaski's gun range, but bottled the harbor much the way the *Niagara* blockaded Charleston.

Disappointed that nothing more was mentioned, she folded the paper and placed it beneath her mending in the sewing basket. Rubbing her back, which seemed to ache more as the days passed, she thought it strange that Roddy had very little to say about the war. He was happy enough when the state announced that the war department would purchase all corn offered for sale, but whenever Martin or Nicholas mentioned the fighting at Manassas, the first victory for the South, Roddy was silent.

But then, she reminded herself, Roddy didn't have much to say to anyone these days, while she awaited the birth of her child. If it weren't for her sisters coming by, she would get no news at all, for this late in her pregnancy she was forbidden by a rigid code of what was proper, to be seen by anyone but family.

Taking up her candle, Leah went into the kitchen for a drink of water. The pump handle still squeaked when she primed it. Roddy kept saying he would fix it, but never did. Small repairs were being left undone all over the farm, yet he was gone for most of the day. Leah had learned not to question him. He had a temper that flared as suddenly as the spring rains.

Now she heard the creak of the stair and knew he was coming down to see where she was. Leah tossed out the rest of the water and snatched up her candle. She reached the parlor just as he appeared on the last step.

"This is the third night in a row you've left our bed. They say a woman walks at night when her time is near."

"I told you the child isn't due for months yet." Leah stared at the bare feet and hair-dusted calves his nightshirt didn't cover. She wished it were concern that had made him get up to look for her. But there was no concern for her in his voice, or his eyes. There was disgust for her ungainly appearance. And with a silent sigh, she waited for him to start back upstairs, then followed him.

Lying beside him in the dark, she thought of Frances telling her that all things needed love and nurturing to survive. She was given none by the man she married. And as the hours passed, she wondered if Trev had found love that would help him survive the war.

The men he served with called Trev the "devil's own," for no one took more risks in a battle, none was as reckless to court danger, yet he remained whole.

After the Seven Days Battle, in which nineteen thousand raw Confederate soldiers were killed, Trev began to believe that even death didn't want him. The moans of the wounded were drowned in his drink, but even liquor couldn't wash the taste of bile from his mouth. If he had been old enough to fight his father on the day his fate had been sealed and become a doctor, maybe he could now be of use. Robert was there at his side in battle, and later when he passed out from drink, always covering for him. But Trev volunteered for every mission that promised death for a careless man. Trev came to believe that he really did have the devil riding on his shoulder, for he couldn't find a shot with his name on it.

The days were a blend of danger and carnage, but he never reached the callous stage that some men did. His nightmares about Leah melded with the screams of the wounded men in the field tents, begging for doctors.

Robert saw to it that Trev ate. When the generosity of southerners allowed, they had mouth-watering pot likker, made from ham, cabbage, potatoes, and corn-meal dumplings. When times were lean and supplies were left rotting due to lack of transportation, they made do with black-eyed peas and cornbread. Robert's mother's letters begged him to take care of himself. She knew why he had to be with Trev, but she feared that he was the one who would be killed.

Trev always led the reconnaissance missions. Only once did he lose a man to sniper fire.

"It should have been me that died."

And all Robert could answer was, "Keep trying,

Trev, you've got months yet of fighting, with the way the war is going."

The days ran together. Skirmishes took one toll on the men, boredom another. When the diseases swept through the camps, the death toll mounted from dysentery, typhoid, chicken pox, and raging infections. Trev found it impossible to stay away from the field tents. But not one man dared to tease him, not within his hearing when he fought to instill the need for basic cleanliness in the medical tent. More than a few found that Trev's temper was like the hair trigger on his Henry repeating rifle.

But that didn't stop the men from speculating among themselves about why Trev had fought with the doctor and insisted on burning all the blankets and uniforms of every man who had the pox.

"Maybe he figures the smoke'll finish off the Yankees when that fancy repeater of his runs out of cartridges," one young and very new recruit said.

"Yore jus' jealous 'cause you can't buy yore own gun on thirteen dollars a month. That Henry's worth eight soldiers shooting from cover."

"Ain't that right," another hardened soldier agreed. "Yore so wet behind the ears you can't be knowin' that damn Yankee gun Shelley got tradin' with a picket can be loaded on Sunday an' fired all week.

"An' whatever you do, boy, don't tweak that devil's tail. Better men than you tried and failed."

"Tried and failed" was the refrain Leah repeated to herself. As on every other Sunday afternoon, her sisters and Roddy's two cousins, along with their husbands and children, had come to call. The children had eaten, played, and now most of them napped. The women sat in the shade of the wooden porch while the men were down at the barn sampling Roddy's home brew. Her smile masked her thoughts as they chattered about her coming child, Roddy's proud strut, and how anxious she must be to have the heat of summer over. They managed to admire each other's needlework, too.

Leah discovered that if she nodded every once in a while and kept smiling, they would talk for hours and she wouldn't need to say a word.

Being married had not bridged the gap between her and her sisters. Roddy had never offered to rub her back as Ruth claimed her Martin did for every child she carried when her time drew near. And she couldn't imagine Roddy walking the floor with a baby to let her sleep as Nicholas had on occasion done for Sarah. Even Kate, Roddy's cousin, who was expecting her fourth child, had some kindness bestowed by her husband. As did the shy Agnes.

She could not share with them the silences that filled her home, nor tell of the brooding way Roddy watched her. She shared with no one the forbidden thoughts she had of Trev, and again, because of Roddy, had little news of the war, so she didn't know where he was.

There was the shameful secret she never told: Her husband found her ugly as her time drew near and slept in the spare room. He didn't like sitting down to supper with her, and when he did, he refused to talk. She understood his need to know whose child she carried, and this, no matter what it cost her, she refused to do. He had made her a promise that he would accept the child if it was Trev's, not that she had given him the man's name, but something had happened to make Roddy change soon after the last time she saw Trev.

Frances had been sparse with information the one time they met. And Leah knew Frances was right to tell her to forget Trev. But she was still trying to find out how. There were nights when she couldn't sleep, when the nagging backache that had so plagued her today kept her walking the floors. The way she soothed herself was with memories of Trev, then she worried about where he was and if he was hurt.

And she would remember the last touch of his lips, not the words or the pain in his eyes the last time she saw him. Suddenly Leah sat up straight. She felt as if someone had taken a knife and sliced across her back. Swallowing her cry, she grabbed hold of the chair edge on either side. She had the same warning pain when she was near to losing the baby. The child couldn't be coming now, she thought. But another pain cut across her middle and sweat broke out.

"Leah, honey?" Ruth started, reaching over to touch her sister's hand. "Leah? Agnes, get Roddy. He's got to carry Leah upstairs."

"Ruth, is it the baby?" Leah demanded.

"Now, don't get scared, Leah. I know it's too soon, but you'll be fine. I promise you Sarah and I will stay."

Leah held both her sisters' hands. She looked from Ruth to Sarah and bit back another cry of pain. "Don't . . . l-let Roddy be . . . alone—"

"Doan you know anythin', Leah?" Kate cut in before Leah could finish. "Roddy'll stay with the men down to the barn, gettin' drunk while you're doin' the birthin'."

Leah glared at her, then pulled on Sarah's hand

so that she leaned closer. "The baby. Don't let Roddy be alone with my baby."

Sarah shared a look with Ruth. "We'll see to everything, sister. Don't fret now. Save your strength and worryin'."

But Leah grew frantic with worry. The baby was full term, a week late by her reckoning. They all believed the child was early. Roddy would know this was her lover's child. Not his. And Roddy already hated her.

Pain gathered in another forceful wave and left her panting. Gently, Leah cradled her swollen belly. Trev's child. Impatient to be born. She closed out the voices around her and thought only of having Trev's child to hold and love. Hers alone. As Trev never could be.

"Leah," Agnes said, taking hold of her hand, "let Roddy carry you upstairs."

Pain gripped Leah just as Roddy lifted her into his arms. She met her husband's fierce gaze. And she cried out, afraid.

At the same moment, Trev sighted his rifle, fired, and missed. A strange prickle of danger slithered down his spine. He closed his eyes and in his mind he heard Leah scream his name.

"Damn, Trev, that's the second one you missed." Robert didn't bother to hide his annoyance. "Rabbit's about all we're having for supper, and not much of that if you can't shoot straight."

Trev ignored him. He couldn't explain what had happened. It wasn't the first time his aim was off. Waking or sleeping, he could hear Leah call out to him. Like a mist stealing up to conceal the enemy's presence, so Leah stole into his thoughts. She was a danger to him. He wondered when he would stop thinking about her.

With no other game in sight, Trev and Robert returned to camp, where they found orders waiting for them to move out.

The days began to blur together. There were a few skirmishes, there was a great deal of waiting, and then they were sent to Maryland.

They were badly outnumbered at Sharpsburg. Trev agreed with most of the men and officers that only the Union General McClellan's piecemeal attacks against them allowed General Lee to present a strong force at every turn. The Confederate soldiers were ordered to take the land and hold it, relinquish it when they were overcome, then reclaim it once more, the land blood soaked and covered with bodies.

In September, a wounded General Lawton was sent home to Savannah. Trev had been fighting nearly eighteen months and was ordered to count the dead of his brigade. Nearly half of the eleven hundred men were lost, along with five of their six regimental commanders.

Trev was sick after he made his report. But he never regretted his lack of medical knowledge more than when he walked by the field tents of the wounded and heard their cries. He did what he could to help, but he was ordered to ride out with another Georgia brigade under the command of General Braxton Bragg. Robert and half the remaining men filled the depleted ranks and the Confederacy passed a conscription act as the cost of war kept mounting in the number of dead and wounded.

Trev and Robert were in Perryville, Kentucky, when they missed being crushed by a larger Union

force. Rains turned roads into impassable mo-
rasses, and when Trev and Robert could ride, they
traveled sometimes fifteen miles in a day, only to
find the enemy had slipped away—that is, if the
enemy had even been there in the first place, for
there were incidents in which Union sightings
were the imaginings of volatile cavalrymen. In November, their division commander, McLaw, told
his four brigades that Lieutenant General James
Longstreet had appealed for their meat rations, but
there was delay in getting them.

As the new year of 1863 approached, they were
once more on the move. Trev brought information
to General Bragg that Union forces under General
Burnside were at Knoxville with twenty-three thousand men. The Confederates left Sweet Water to
take up positions near Jackson's Ford on the Little
Tennessee River.

There was a misty rain and Trev could barely
see. Robert was at his side, and three raw, very
nervous recruits followed them as they scouted
ahead of the main force. Trev wished the young
soldiers were country men, who knew how to move
quietly, not these city-bred boys who were tramp-
ing noisily through the woods.

They had been out almost two hours and had
seen no sign of the enemy. Trev knew it didn't
mean the enemy wasn't out there, but only that
they were well hidden. He had just turned to Robert when a shot was fired, sending him spinning,
and a burning spread in his thigh where he was
hit. Robert shoved him to the ground, crouching
over him, taking four shots in his arm before he
could raise his rifle.

"Fire, damn you!" he ordered the recruits before
he gave in to the ripping pain and passed out.

Trev pushed Robert aside, raised his repeater, and fired. He didn't hear the cry that told him he had hit one Yankee. His mind wasn't on what he needed to do. He couldn't let Robert die. When his rifle was empty, He took up Robert's, covering the recruits while they reloaded their single-shot rifles.

In minutes they were surrounded by their own force, but Trev wouldn't let them separate him and Robert. He managed to keep a seat on someone's offered horse, then took Robert up in front of him. Trev's hand was covered with Robert's blood. The way Robert's arm hung uselessly warned Trev his friend would have to lose it. He had regretted his lack of skill, cursed his father for stealing his dream of being a doctor, but now a deep well of black bitterness rose, for he knew what awaited Robert.

Trev's pants leg was soaked with blood from his own wound when he rode into camp. He couldn't get down fast enough to stop them from taking Robert. When he tried to follow, one of the aides stopped him.

"You don't want to go in there, sir. We ran out of chloroform two days ago. And that leg of yours needs to be looked at."

"Then do it while I hold him," Trev answered, pushing his way inside the tent. "And send someone for the whiskey in my tent. We'll all use it."

Trev stood by Robert's head, holding his face between his hands, talking of their times together. Talking over Robert's screams, over the sound of the saw, swallowing bile, and never once looking away from Robert's glazed eyes. And when it was done, he stayed with Robert, wondering how he was going to repay his friend for saving his life and losing his own arm. How could Robert do it, when he knew Trev's self-destructive wish?

There was fighting, but Trev heard none of it. He cared for Robert through his fever, ignoring his own wound. The shot had passed through the fleshy part of his thigh. Trev would have a scar, but would heal whole.

It was long after midnight and the moans of the wounded were a never-ending sound when Robert woke. He screamed, seeing the stump that remained of his arm. Trev held him when the tears came, rocking him as he would a child, but begging Robert to tell him why he had risked his life for him.

"You know I was looking for that shot with my name on it. By all that's holy, Robert, why did you get in the way?'

Clear-eyed for the first time, Robert looked up at Trev and with his one hand gripped Trev's arm. "You're my friend. More. The brother I never had. But you'll repay me, Trev. You won't let me live like this. One shot. That's all I ask. Don't let them send me home a cripple."

Trev didn't waste time feeding Robert the platitudes that a thousand men had been given when they lost a limb or an eye. But he could and did refuse Robert's repeated pleas that Trev should shoot him and let him die.

Frantic, Robert tried to sit up, only to find his balance was gone. He was desperate enough now to get Trev to do what he wanted. "You've got to do it. You're the only one who will. It's my fault that Leah married Roddy. I lied to her. Lied to you. I never told her you were coming back to marry her. I never gave her your note. Do you hear what I'm telling you, Trev? You lost her because of me."

"There have been times, Robert, when you've spun some tales—"

"The truth. The goddamn bloody truth! You still don't believe me. I'm the one who told Boyd about the money, and he took it to give to Roddy. And if that's not enough to make you pull the trigger, I offered to make her my whore." He fell back against the thin mattress, panting, wild-eyed, as Trev slowly rose and stood staring down at him. "I went to her the day after you left. I knew Boyd had beat her, and so did I with every word. She looked like the walking dead. You remember Mama Rassia teasing us about their eyes. Leah's eyes were like that. That's what I did when I said you left money for her but that I would double it if she'd be my whore."

Trev shook his head, half knowing Robert was telling him the truth, but still needing to deny it. All this time, Robert, always with him. Robert, his friend. Robert had stolen the only thing that offered him hope. Leah lost because of Robert. Leah called a whore. By Robert. Fury built inside him.

"You'll do it now, won't you?" Robert begged.

"No."

"I lied to my mother. Told her you didn't want Leah. She talked to her, convinced her to marry. Now?"

"No."

"We all worked against you. Boyd wanted to go to you. I threatened to throw him off Rosehall if he dared. That's why they left. Now, Trev?"

"No. No," he grated from between clenched teeth.

"I didn't believe you could love a fancy piece—"

"Shut up!" Trev felt the wound opening, not of the flesh, but of his heart and his soul. Leah! Yet he couldn't walk away.

"I wanted her. Would have had her, too. I knew you were with her that day at the bluff. Was she good, Trev? Did she pleasure you? Tell me, Trev. We've always shared. Did she spread her legs—"

"Don't, for Christ's sake, don't—"

"It wasn't rape, was it?" Robert goaded, kicking aside the thin blanket and struggling until he sat up. He tried to grab hold of Trev's arm, but Trev backed away. "Do you want more? Go get your pistol, Trev. Or better yet, use your hands. Take your revenge. Killing me would service us both."

"I can't kill you. I couldn't kill my father when I thought he destroyed me. I won't kill you, Robert." But he gazed down at his clenched hands, shaking with the need to choke off his truth.

"Bastard!" Robert yelled. "Where the hell are you going?"

Trev dragged his wounded leg and shoved through the small crowd that had collected in the tent. He was torn and broken, like the scattered remains found in the carnage of the battlefields. But rage was exploding and he knew if he didn't get away, he would do what Robert begged. He would kill him. Yet he turned at the entrance and looked at Robert.

"I won't kill you, but I'll kill any man who grants your wish. I'm taking you home, Robert. I want you to live. Live and remember that you destroyed me. Live with what you condemned Leah to. Just live, Robert," he whispered in a soft, so soft, but deadly voice. "And when life becomes hell, maybe the devil will pity you. Maybe God, if there is one, will forgive you. But I never will."

He left him, left men staring after him as whispers flew through the camp. Not one man tried to stop him when he crossed their picket line and found a hole in the woods to crawl into.

It had been fifteen years since he had felt the hot, burning sting of tears. He had been a boy then; he was a broken man now. But Trev didn't shed one tear for himself. They were for Leah, the woman he accused of betrayal and believed a whore. His love, who had believed Robert's lies, just as he had.

Trev had warned Frances about her son's injury and attitude about it. He didn't do it to spare her feelings, but for himself. Trev was not going to deal well with her tears, for on the long ride home Robert never stopped telling him what they had done to Leah.

Trev wouldn't go into the house. He waited silently while Henry and the houseboys carried a fevered Robert inside. Frances went to tend to her son, shivering at the cold-eyed stranger Trev had become and who now called her Mrs. DeMoise. She knew without being told that Trev had found out what she and Robert had done. It was buried in his weary eyes, eyes that had seen too much and survived. She sent one of the boys to tell him to wait for her, for she couldn't let him go without talking to him.

Cato was still down at the barn, but had little to do these days, since the blooded horses were all gone. But when Trev asked him about Leah, Cato told him that Boyd caught her that night and beat her. He spared Trev nothing of the way they all had gathered around her like a pack of wolves, tearing at her until she gave in.

And Trev listened to how his love had been alone, sick and frightened, with no one to turn to. His punishment, his guilt that he had left her.

Frances found him helping Cato feed and water his horses. It hurt to know he hadn't even taken them from their traces, making clear his intent to leave immediately. She found she needed more courage to talk to Trev than to face what had happened to her son. But the years of war had brought her the understanding of how strong a woman could be.

"We did what we thought best for you, Trev. Robert was able to tell me he confessed to you the part we played. But I swear to you," she declared, gazing into the piercing blue of his eyes, "that I did what was best for Leah. I believed my son, who loves you like a brother." Frances stepped forward and cringed inwardly when Trev stepped back before she could touch him.

"Forgive me, Trev. Forgive my son. We've all suffered—"

"Mrs. DeMoise, I have no forgiveness for anyone but Leah. And I see that Cato is done, so I'll take my leave."

"What will you do? Trev, don't—"

"Do?" he repeated, climbing up onto the wagon's seat and taking up the reins. "What can I do? All of you destroyed my life."

It was his deadened voice that made Frances cry out, "Then go to Leah. Tell her. She loves you, Trev. She's never stopped, and I will carry the memory of her tears and what we've done to both of you to my grave."

"Then I wish for you what I wish for your son. May you live a long life. Both of you."

Chapter Seventeen

LEAH escaped to the rolling hill-country woodlands whenever she could. Today she desperately needed the solitude the woods offered. How could she come to terms with what she had just learned?

Roddy was a traitor! There were Yankees in their barn. He had been hiding them, and others, all along. She couldn't doubt what she heard for herself. She couldn't.

She had believed him when, to account for the wound in his leg, he said that he had fallen and his gun had gone off accidentally. He was left with a limp and unable to answer the conscription call. But now she knew it for the lie it was. All the while she had cared for him, hoping they could still have a chance to make something good of their marriage, he had been laughing at her. Now that final, slim hope was crushed. Roddy, a traitor, who had made her one, too.

Unwittingly, she had supplied him with information to give the enemy. Her eyes were bleak as she looked back at the chimney of their house, hating herself for leaving her son with him. There had been no excuse she could think of to take the baby from Roddy when the child enjoyed being with him. She had to get away from Roddy.

What could she do? How was she going to live with knowing that she may have sent men to their deaths?

Damn him! Roddy made a mockery of every vow he had made before God.

Leah rubbed her arms through her cloak. Her skin felt as if it were crawling with unseen things. She was sick that her own husband had used her. He had placed them all in danger by giving aid to the enemy.

It was all she could do to stop from heaving. Like most of the women in Coosa and Talladega counties, she had offered what help she could to ease their soldiers' lot. Now that the fighting was right over the northern border in Tennessee, the wounded men were being sent into Alabama. Once her chores were done, Leah spent time at the church, reading to the soldiers. She knew where they had been wounded and where they would be sent once they were healed. How many times had she filled the silence at supper and told Roddy what she knew?

And what if Trev had been with those men? What if she had somehow caused him to be hurt? Leah hoped that whatever help she gave to the soldiers, the same would be offered to Trev if he needed it. Frances was the only one who knew how she felt.

She and Frances had come to an understanding. As the president of the Society of Mothers, Frances had visited every farm, plantation, and town in the county to solicit aid and cooperation, gathering supplies or offers of care for the wounded. When she came to the farm a second time, telling Leah she needed quinine, Leah bargained with her. She told Frances how to make the desperately needed quinine from the berries of the dogwood trees, and a soothing cordial from blackberry roots for dysentery. In return she wanted news of Trev.

Frances never gave her much. But it was enough to know that Trev was alive and whole, even if he was in the thick of the fighting in Maryland. As supplies dried up due to blockades and lack of transport, Frances came more often. They compared whatever information there was to be had about wild plants and barks that could be used not only to make medicines, but as substitutes for foods, tea, and coffee.

Now it was clear why Roddy never once objected to Frances's visits. Often he would stop work to come up to the house when Frances arrived. Leah had been proud of his helping to load Frances's wagon with the supplies gathered by themselves and their neighbors. How many times had he packed the barks of wild cherry, poplar, and wahoo trees from their woods, knowing they would be boiled down into an extract for chills and ague? All the while, Frances would talk, and Roddy would listen. What had happened to the captain or colonel who had been sent back to his brigade? Roddy, nodding, his smile false, telling her he wished he could be out there defending their homeland, while he gathered troop movement information to pass along to the Yankees.

Leah leaned against a sweet-gum tree, rubbing the ache in her back. Who could she trust to tell? And how could she betray the man whose child she carried? He had waited months after William's birth before he rejoined her in their marriage bed. Months in which she was terrified he would harm the child. She knew he watched the baby's soft downy hair grow into a light brown and the unfocused eyes that gradually became a deeper blue. He had never voiced the question she'd find burning in his eyes: Whose son was he? Leah always looked away. William's birth had been difficult. The child was small, so small they had feared he wouldn't live. But she had loved him so fiercely that she had willed him to live. Despite the gloom of those first months of his life, William had survived and grown into a sturdy little boy who would celebrate his second birthday on July second.

She thanked the Lord every time she looked at her son and saw only a resemblance to herself in his changing features. But all these thoughts brought her back to the fear of those Union soldiers being discovered on their land. How could Roddy not only betray the bond of the Confederacy, but put them all in danger?

And if he knew what she had found out, what would Roddy do to her? She was alone in deciding this, as she had always been alone. Except for the time spent with Trev. But Trev was lost to her and she mustn't think about him. For the need and longing to be with him, to know again the joy of their times together, would overwhelm her with grief. And the passion that was hers had been replaced by the nurturings of motherhood.

With an almost frantic haste, she began picking the round globes of the sweet gum. These had become a substitute for those who could not get tallow for candles. It was Frances who had passed this along from women on the south Alabama farms. By placing melted lard in shallow bowls, then letting the sweet-gum globes become saturated, they could be lit and floated in the oil, giving off a fairylike light. She always had a few baskets to give Frances, and it would be better for her if Roddy knew why she had been away from the house.

Fast as she picked, Leah couldn't shake off the despair that Roddy's betrayal brought her. He could have passed along information that may have gotten Trev killed. Trev and so many others. Someone had to stop Roddy. But who? Did her father know? Were Martin and Nicholas involved? Neighbors? Friends? Her basket was barely filled, but she stopped gathering more. Maybe those Union soldiers would be gone by the time she got back. Maybe she had mistaken what she overheard. And maybe the two stolen sows they had been fattening would be back in their pens.

Leah pressed a hand to the aching small of her back, then lifted her basket. So many incidents became suddenly clear. How many times had she held William and stood by the window as a detail of Confederate soldiers rode up the lane and Roddy went outside to meet them? No matter what they wanted, their arrival would precipitate Roddy's anger. Not that he allowed it to show.

She hated his cowardly lying when those very soldiers risked their lives to protect the land he claimed as his. Roddy took their gold when they had it, cheated on the weights for the grain and corn he sold to them for horse fodder, and denied he had more stored away. He thought she didn't know about the burned-out remains of an old cabin and the stone cellar in the woods. Roddy hid sacks of grain there; she had never suspected what he was doing with them until today.

Her father would be no help, even if she could summon the courage to go to him. He treated her with a cold contempt and forced her mother to stay away, too.

Could she betray Roddy? She knew what her fate and William's would be. If they weren't burned out, they would be ostracized. She didn't care for herself, but there were her children to think about. One born and one to come.

How much more was she to bear? Her steps dragged over the path. Somehow she had to find a way to deal with this and still protect her children.

But when Leah returned to the house, Roddy was gone and William with him. Standing on the porch, pulling her cloak around her, she gazed at the closed double doors of the barn. It was too early for milking, a chore Roddy had taken over a few weeks ago. She had thought it was due to her awkwardness and inability to sit on the three-legged stool since she had passed her sixth month. But now she knew it was to keep her away from the barn and from finding out what he had been up to.

Another small hope that their marriage might work had been crushed. She couldn't bring herself to go into the barn. The baby would be safe enough. He'd just learned how to say "mama," and not much more. He adored Roddy, though Roddy spent as little time as he could with the boy.

She knew Roddy would be different with this child she carried. This one he had no doubt about. And she would never tell him what he longed to know. But these deep thoughts added to her agitation and she didn't hear the creak of a wagon's wheels coming up the lane.

Leah heard nothing of the wheels, but she did hear the whisper of her name. A whisper from dreams, a whisper born of her longings, a soft murmur repeated over and over with an added entreaty for her to turn around.

When she did, her first impulse was to run. Her body wouldn't respond to the frantic message her mind sent. Torn between pleasure and fear, she breathed deeply, her heart beating heavily, for the sun was at his back and all she saw was a black silhouette. From nightmare and dreams came the vision she wanted, the vision she had not seen for two and a half years. She simply stared at him.

Shock held her, just as the blue of his eyes did. That piercing blue that turned almost black with passion. And she felt the thin layers of protection she had carefully built being ripped away, leaving her vulnerable once more.

With a cry, Leah closed her eyes, denying what she saw, denying that she loved him still.

"Leah?" he whispered, his voice naked with longing despite its gentleness.

Hope and fear melded; love tore fear away. "Trev? Oh, Trev, is it really you?"

Time stopped in those moments, stopped as it had so often for her, and she beheld the only man she would ever love. Leah didn't remember moving toward him, his name a cry on her lips. She didn't remember him climbing off the wagon seat to enfold her into his arms. It was as if he had never been gone, never believed she had betrayed their love, and when he lifted his gloved hand to caress her cheek, she sighed his name yet again, lifting her face for his kiss.

The cherishing feel of his lips on hers was balm to her soul. She took his strength, his warmth, swallowing the emotions that threatened to erupt and steal her dream. Trev holding her, kissing her . . .

It was a sweeter, wilder passion that held sway over her senses, like the first time their lips had touched. His gentle coaxing deepened the kiss, and for Leah a shower of sensual memories spread inside her. Just as they did when she dreamed of him.

She needed to touch him. Her fingers slid up the soft wool of his coat, then clung to his shoulders, wanting him to be real. Trev, taking her back in time, until there was only the two of them. Leah knocked off his hat, threading her fingers into the thick black silk of his hair, holding him closer. Her move to press nearer was stopped by the rounded swell of her belly, and with a wrenching cry she pulled free of him.

Trev didn't want to let her go. After two years of unholy, unjust, brutal war, he had tasted life. Once he had thought that war would bring him a clean, sudden death. He even thought all feelings, everything good in his life, had died when he lost Leah. But watching her turn away from him now brought an understanding of what death really meant.

He had come to beg her forgiveness. He craved that from her. But when he called her name and she came to him, he could no more remember that she was another man's wife than he could stop breathing.

A blind fury rose, which he stifled, when she folded her arms protectively over the rounded swell beneath her cloak and turned to him. She should have been carrying his child. She should have been his wife. His!

"Why have you come here, Trev?" Leah finally asked. She hurried around to the side of the house where they would be out of Roddy's sight if he looked out from the barn. She found the courage to look at him. His face was gaunt, his body thinner. But now there was the unmistakable stamp of cynicism etched on his features as if repeated disillusionment had tarnished his view of the world. Leah wondered if her face revealed the same to him. Compassion for what he must have seen in the war almost sent her back into his arms. But if Trev felt the desire his kiss had conveyed, it was not apparent in the cool fire of his eyes. And she was left with her fragile walls shattered.

She asked him again why he had come.

"To see you. To beg your forgiveness. I know the truth now, Leah."

"Whose truth is that? Yours? Robert's? Or mine?" She heard the mocking bite of her words, but he seemed determined to ignore it, for his gaze softened. She watched him pick up his hat and saw that he was a captain now.

"Leah, I—"

"Just answer me."

"You've every right to hate me. I swear to you I never knew until a few weeks ago what Robert had done to you. They were lies." He couldn't meet her direct gaze, and toyed with his hat brim. "I wish I could see the compassion that was there a moment ago in your eyes. I've a wound that never healed, Leah. I never stopped loving you."

"Don't," she pleaded, closing her eyes briefly. "You can't—mustn't—say such things to me. It's all in the past, Trev." She wanted to walk away from him, but once again her body refused to obey the dictates of her mind.

"We need to talk. You can't deny me that. I didn't know, I tell you."

"But it doesn't matter, Trev. We can't let it matter."

"Is your husband home?"

Instinctively, Leah looked toward the porch.

"You risk kissing me with him inside?"

"No. Yes. Yes, I risked it, but Roddy's not inside. He's down— I'm not sure where he is. Please, you've got to leave."

"Leah, don't be afraid. I won't do anything to cause—"

"You don't need to do anything. Your presence here brings enough trouble."

Trev tossed his hat on the wagon seat, then raked his fingers through his hair. "Does he know?"

"I never named you." She had to lock her hands together not to touch him again. "What purpose does it serve to bring the past back? And why are you here in Alabama? I heard—" Leah bit her lip. She hadn't meant for him to know she was keeping track of his moves.

"I've brought Robert home. He's lost his arm and begged me to kill him. I wanted to, Leah. When he told me what he did to you that day, I wanted to kill him. I understand now how frightened and alone you must have felt." He was unable to remain this far away from her and closed the distance between them.

He thought of the ring he had meant to give her—the ring he still carried with him—but Leah turned as if to run. He flattened his hand against the wood, cutting off her escape. The only thing he would kill for would be to see the love in her eyes again. All the love that was his when he was afraid to claim it, afraid to admit how much he needed her love, needed her. And he knew he was a liar, because he couldn't keep from touching her. He cradled her face, lifting it so he could look into her eyes.

"I would do anything, give anything, including

my life, to take away what you went through. But it's for myself that I've come. I need you to forgive me, Leah. My sorrow rests with all the harsh, cruel things I said to you. I loved you, and never stopped. Can't. You claimed my heart."

She saw the truth of every word in his eyes, but her fingers bit into his gloved wrists, pulling his hands from her face. Pain filled her and she knew by the way his expression changed that she was not hiding it.

"If I—I forgive you, will you go, Trev? Will you let me keep what little peace I've found?" Trembling, both from fear that he would discover Roddy's secret and from fear that Roddy would discover them together, she lowered her head. "Go," she whispered. "Please, I beg you."

Nothing prepared her for his hands pushing aside her cloak, both gently splaying wide across her rounded shape. The wall at her back stopped her from moving.

"Trev?" And when he looked up, she couldn't swallow the soft, shattering cry that escaped her lips. He gazed at her with such love, such intense longing that far surpassed any dream.

"Leah, if you want, I'll take you and your child, even this unborn one. I'll claim them as my own. But if you are loved, I swear I'll walk away from you. Can you tell me that?" he pleaded. "I never would admit, even to myself, how many times I dreamed of seeing you like this, carrying my child."

Speak the lie. Tell him you love, Roddy. He'll leave and you'll protect him from the Union soldiers hiding in the barn. And you'll protect your children and yourself. Trev will never know that you are married to a traitor. Tears spilled down her cheeks, Trev's name a soft litany. "If only you knew . . .

Trev . . . if only. Hold me. Once more, then go. Please, you must go."

But his arms were her haven. His lips were the cup which caught her bitter tears, then whispered the words she had yearned to hear.

"I love you, Leah. Love you," he murmured, scattering kisses across her cheeks. "Then, now. Always." Suddenly he was silently praying that she would not tell him her love belonged to another man. He brushed his lips against hers, needing to speak words he had kept bottled up until it was too late. Now he had no right to say them. But death had stalked his days, the death he had courted so daringly, and he had learned not to count on any tomorrows.

Softly then, rocking her gently, he said, "I want you to know that I dreamed of you. I'd hear you crying out my name, calling for me, and I despaired of finding you, Leah. There were nights— no, I won't tell you of the nights. I can't speak to you of death, when you were and always will be light and life to me."

Leah held his face within her hands. Her love for him had never died. She had lost him once and it had nearly killed her, but now . . . now she knew she needed the strength his love would give her. Leah kissed him, all the buried yearnings, all of her love welling up from inside her, given to Trev along with her heart. And his kiss made her feel cherished, desired, and loved in return.

"Love, listen to me," Trev murmured. "I never told you why I left or couldn't say that I loved you and wanted to marry you. But I say it now." And he bared his soul, telling her how his father had killed his dream and held Bella hostage to get what he wanted. The words were rushed, for he was aware of the risk to her of his presence, but he had to make her understand what he had kept from her. Trev spared himself nothing in the telling, and when done, he was drained.

He brushed the glisten of tears from her eyes and held his fingertips over her mouth. "I've come to give you what you've wanted, Leah. Your dream to teach. You can't tell me that you love him. You can't want to stay with him. Come away—"

Trev broke off and stepped back away from her. There were hoofbeats coming up the lane.

"Not now," Leah whispered, horrified, rushing back onto the front porch. "Dear God, not now."

Chapter Eighteen

TREV stared at her, not understanding. But he quickly followed, standing protectively in front of Leah, shading his eyes with one hand, while the other opened the leather flap of his holster.

"The uniforms are gray, Leah," he said almost immediately. "There's nothing for you to be afraid of. It's only a small patrol, likely looking for stragglers. I'll deal with them if you want me to."

"You should have left when I told you to go, Trev." She was stricken by the thought of those Yankees in the barn, but was too frightened to even turn and gaze down that way. Dear Lord, she prayed, please don't let Roddy come up to the house until these Confederate soldiers are gone. "Get rid of them, Trev, please."

He shot her a puzzled look, but stepped off the porch as the patrol drew to a halt.

The major returned Trev's salute, while Trev summed up his men. Three were raw recruits and two had the hardened look of men who had seen war, as did the major. But what drew Trev's gaze and held it were the two men riding double, dressed in Union blue, a rope secured around their waists and then wrapped around the horse's belly.

"Major James Thomas Gee, sir," he offered,

holding out his gauntleted hand on Trev, "late of the Tucaloosa School of Instruction, on assignment to track down Yankee scum crossing our borders."

"And good hunting, too, I see," Trev returned. Then he introduced himself. "But I am well acquainted with Mrs. Cooper and attest to her loyalty. You won't find bluebellies here."

Leah, listening to them, knew she had to get rid of them and Trev quickly. If Roddy came out of the barn and saw them here, there was no telling what he and those Yankee soldiers hiding in the barn would do. She wasn't sure, but she thought there were more than six of them. Leah knew, too, she had to do all she could to protect Roddy, and in turn protect her son and her unborn child. Incidents of whole families being dragged from their homes, the men beaten and the buildings burned because they were suspected of being northern sympathizers, rose in her mind.

Before she thought of something, the major turned to her. "Ma'am, we've had a hard cold ride these last two days and would be most grateful if you could spare us somethin' warm."

"I've soup on the fire and could make you coffee," she answered, unable to deny them food, but she didn't see the look Trev shot her way, hearing the underlying resentment in her voice.

"Coffee?" one of the men asked.

"It's not real," she hastened to explain. "Coffee's nearly sixty dollars a pound now, but we've used roasted okra seeds and the taste is mighty close." Leah forced a smile while murmurs of appreciation went through the men. As they were dismounting, she heard William calling her.

"Mama, Mama."

Leah rushed off the porch and stopped just beyond the rail to scoop up her little boy, noting with a desperate gaze that the barn doors were open.

When she turned, holding the boy protectively in her arms, Trev felt gut-shot. The chubby undefined features were Leah's, but his eyes . . . "The boy's eyes are blue," he managed, searching for the truth in her expressive brown eyes.

But Leah wasn't looking at him now. She placed a kiss on her son's hair. "Yes. William has his father's eyes."

Conscious of the other men, Trev couldn't ask another question, but it burned his tongue to hold them back. His gaze followed Leah as she came up the porch and stood before the door. The longing he had felt to touch her, round with child, was nothing to compare with the hunger that now rose and nearly consumed him. She held a boy who could be his son.

Not knowing what else to do, Leah, terrified now, invited them inside. She stepped over the threshold, only to stop and spin around with a choked-off cry when the major ordered his men to take the horses and prisoners down to the barn. Her gaze met Trev's, saw his hunger directed at her son, and she ached for him. But William's safety had to come first. She could only try to protect them both.

"Not the barn, Major," she said quickly. "Our cow just died. There might be lingering disease. And I'm sure your prisoners could do with food and coffee as well."

Wild yells and two shots threw the men in the yard into a melee of orders and rearing horses. More than a dozen Union soldiers came around from both sides of the house to encircle the Confederates. Trev shoved Leah inside, shouting for her to slam the door, yanking his Colt revolver from his holster, kneeling and firing. The major drew his saber and attacked the two men who tried to grab both him and his horse.

Leah cradled William tight, running to the window and tearing aside the lace curtain to watch. Prayers tumbled with no sense from her lips and her son began to cry. She couldn't see Roddy, but Trev was fighting with a burly man who slammed his fist into Trev's jaw and sent him sprawling. The horses were in the midst of the confusion, their dangerous hooves rising and falling as two Union soldiers gathered their reins. Trev had reached into his boot and pulled his knife as one attacker closed on him, and Leah felt everything blur and shift to a day when Trev had used that wickedly sharp blade to cut squares of pralines. William wailed and she hushed him.

"They can't win or get away," Roddy said, coming up behind her.

His hot breath touched the back of her neck, and she shivered, suddenly chilled. But Leah couldn't turn away. Pressing William's head against her shoulder she heard the shot that sent one of the gray-clad young men staggering back, his hand grabbing his shoulder where blood seeped.

"Stop it, Roddy! They'll kill them all."

"You think I don't know who he is? I hope to God they kill him." He pushed Leah forward until her forehead touched the glass, and crowded her from behind. "He can't last much longer. Him and that major are the only two left standing. And look at that cowardly Reb, running off."

Leah did see the wounded young man grab hold

of one of the milling horses and, despite his wound, manage to haul himself up onto the saddle. He flattened himself, setting heels to the horse as shots were fired, but he held on and was soon lost to sight.

The major ran his saber through the man he had been fighting, only to turn and find himself confronted with three Union men holding their guns on him. He set down his sword and slowly raised his hands. Trev fought alone, and now the Union soldiers turned their attention to him. Leah saw the war in his eyes, she who knew every mood those blue eyes conveyed. *Don't die*, she silently begged him. *Give up, Trev. I love you. Live for me.*

And as he stood there, chest heaving, his fine new uniform ripped and filthy, she was sure he had heard her every plea, for his gaze came to rest on the window where she stood, and in the next moment he handed over his knife.

His defeat and despair were Leah's. Weakened by the moment, she didn't realize that Roddy was herding her through the door and outside to view the results of the attack. Two Union soldiers lay dead, as did one of the Confederates. The major had a gash in his thigh, but it was to Trev that she was forced to look.

The skin of his right cheek was scraped raw and his eye was already swelling, along with his jaw. With the back of his hand he wiped the blood from his cut lip and raised his gaze to hers. Why? he seemed to ask, but Leah had no chance to say anything. She was shamed by the praise of the Union captain to her husband, thankful that William's cries had subsided.

"It's not me, but my wife you should be thankin'.

She's the one that held them here until you were in position."

Leah cringed when the officer turned to her. She didn't hear one word that he spoke, for the condemning stares of the men in gray made her feel as if she had taken physical blows.

"Don't you dare lay your own traitorous acts on me, Roddy. I did not stall them. I didn't betray them. You're the one who brought this shame here. You and your—"

"Silence!" His large square hand slammed across her face, sending Leah and the child she clutched reeling back against the post of the porch roof. She held William tight, his terrified crying renewed, and remembered another man making her feel as helpless with a blow. Leah banished the memory and the burning sting of her cheek to soothe her son and didn't see the Union officer move toward her, quickly checked by Roddy, who stood in front of her and the child.

She could feel the pull of Trev's gaze demanding that she look at him, and tried to resist, but their bonding was too strong. Raw fury lit his eyes and she gave him a quick shake of her head when he fought the constraints of the two soldiers holding his arms. But even the plea from Leah's eyes couldn't silence him.

"You're a cowardly bastard, Cooper. If it takes a lifetime to hunt you down, I'll do it and kill you for hitting her."

Roddy spat in the dirt at Trev's feet. "Reb scum. Make all the empty threats you want. Where you're goin' you ain't gonna survive." Hitching up his pants, Roddy ignored the stares of every single man. "Well, Captain Bixby, I said I'd help you and did. You owe me ten dollars apiece for the enlisted men and twenty for the two officers. They should have plenty of information you can use. And I'll have my payment in gold."

"Judas money," Leah whispered as Roddy held out his big blunt-fingered hand and the officer took coins from his pouch, counting them out, but dropping them into Roddy's open palm as if he couldn't bear to touch him.

Leah wanted to run and hide. Not even the days when she wanted to die, believing that Trev had betrayed her, brought such black despair. Roddy had sold these men to the enemy. He had sold Trev. She fought and found courage, needing to stay and learn Trev's fate.

"Since my wife was willing enough to feed this Reb scum, you and your men are welcome to the food," Roddy offered, his hand clenched tight around the coins.

Captain Bixby looked at each of his men in turn and found that silently they agreed with him. But it was the soldier near Trev's wagon who saved him from trying to find the words that wouldn't insult Cooper's wife.

"Cap', there's provisions here for all of us. An' that Reb that got away is sure to be comin' back. Seems as how we got what we came for."

"Yes, we have. Secure the prisoners, and bury the dead before we leave." Turning to Roddy, he said, "You won't mind if we find a suitable spot in those woods to bury them, will you?"

"Not if you bury 'em deep so no animal can dig 'em up."

Bixby started to turn away, caught the gazes exchanged between the Confederate captain and Cooper's wife, who still bore a livid imprint on her cheek, and issued a warning for her sake.

"Think about that Reb coming back here with reinforcements, Cooper. If I was you, I wouldn't be around to explain what happened here."

"Wait, please," Leah cried out. "Where will you take him—them?"

"It's not for me to decide, ma'am. I want to apologize for what you have been subjected to. It was never our intent—"

"None of that matters, Captain," she interrupted, longing to have a private word with Trev, but they were already securing his wrists and leading him over to his wagon.

Trev held that last look at Leah, barely able to stop himself from telling her that he loved her, he would come for her, no matter how long it took or where she was. The only thing that held him quiet was the gloating look on Roddy's face and the knowledge that he was powerless to stop Roddy from delivering any retaliation he wanted on Leah.

A gust of wind blew up, whipping Leah's cloak and the hem of her gown. Trev stared at her, not seeing the movement of the troops around him, not caring about the rope biting into his wrists. She pressed her lips to her son's head, returning Trev's gaze, just as the boy turned and nestled against her shoulder. Trev couldn't hear what Roddy whispered, but his hand on Leah's arm made it clear he wanted her to go inside. Leah resisted. Roddy leaned closer and whispered something that made her face pale, while her eyes grew wide with fear.

Trev had suffered agonies which had plunged him into a helpless bleak despair, but nothing had torn his insides as Leah's last frightened look at him, before Roddy shoved her and William into the house. Roddy's gloating look sent Trev lurching to his feet, fighting to find his footing on the loaded wagon bed. He struggled to free his hands, every civilized restraint snapping under the lightning-raw need to protect Leah.

A bluecoat swung his rifle butt against the backs of Trev's knees, knocking him forward. Only the major's twisting turn prevented Trev from falling. But when Trev tried to jump off the wagon bed, the bluecoat cursed him and jammed his rifle butt into Trev's belly, shoving him back.

A sharp reprimand from the Union captain made the bluecoat stand aside. To Trev, who still struggled to deny his pain and get up again, Bixby said, "You don't strike me as a foolish man, but this is the height of stupidity. Don't force me to have you restrained further. Understand you're making it worse."

Trev looked at him, caught the warning in his voice, and followed his gaze to where Roddy stood. The man was glaring at them with cold, wary eyes. When the captain once again turned to Trev, he saw pity within his eyes, a frown deepening the lines of his face.

"Shelby, is it? I thought that's what I heard when the major here arrived. Well, you've seen action, by the look of you. The war brings about acts which no gentleman can bear, but the constraints of my office do not allow me to interfere. Will you give me your word of honor, Captain, that you will attempt no further disruption while we are here?"

Leaning closer, seeing the drops of sweat beading Trev's face, he added, "If you won't give your word, I'll have you trussed up like a bird ready for the spit."

"Do it, Shelby," the major urged, for he had

been close and knew the force of the blows Trev had taken.

"I haven't any choice," Trev muttered, pain encompassing him. But he looked up as Roddy rushed inside and slammed the door closed. The wood offered no barrier to his shouting.

"Get your things together quickly! Move, woman. We're leaving before those Rebs come back."

"Roddy, please. Wait. Go without us. You can leave us here. William and I will go to my parents."

"Your father doesn't want you! Damn you, obey me and hurry!"

"I beg you, Roddy, don't do this. I'm carrying your child. Stop it! You can't take William," Leah screamed over the wails of the child. "Coward! Liar! Give me back my son."

"Captain," Trev yelled, hearing a crash and cry from the house. "Stop him before he hurts her. Move. I'll swear on my word of honor that I won't try to escape. But show some pity and stop him."

"You've mine as well and my men's," Major Gee added.

Bixby accepted their promise not to escape with a curt nod and hurried up the steps to pound on the door, knowing the cost of his prisoner's sworn word. It was the sacred duty of every officer to attempt escape from the enemy. When Roddy finally opened the door, he met the man's fury with his own.

"Cooper, you'll cease your abuse of your wife or I'll take back that pass I gave you to see you safe through our lines. We're pulling out, but I can send word along to keep a watch on you. Damn it, Cooper, find more fitting targets than a woman or forget calling yourself a man."

"Get off my land! You got what you came for, so go." From his side, Roddy raised his rifle on them.

Trev was the only one who realized it was his Henry rifle that Cooper held.

Bixby, confronting a repeater and not a single-shot muzzle loader, motioned to his men already mounted to form their line. He ordered a private up on the wagon and told them to move out. There was nothing more he could do.

Trev twisted and turned to keep the house in view, Leah's cries ringing in his ears. When he couldn't stand more, he closed his eyes, but the sounds of her voice wouldn't leave him.

Nine months later, Trev knew the soul-sickness of war held no measure against the sufferings he witnessed that went unrelieved in the Rock Island prison in Illinois.

Smallpox, pneumonia, and fevers took a toll of death that brought the attention of the acting surgeon general of the Union army. The barracks were overcrowded, there was no drainage, there were no decent rations, and the orders to the guards did not preclude brutal treatment of the prisoners. They were not allowed to converse with the prisoners, nor allow them to collect in squads, especially at night, and they could fire upon any prisoner rushing the fence. The cornbread, supplied from outside the prison, made so many ill that their ration was cut. The post quartermaster was a drunk and rarely did the prisoners receive the letters and packages addressed to them.

Trev and the other officers did what they could to keep morale high, but their task was nearly impossible. The bed straw rotted and filled with vermin before it was changed; blankets were rags before new ones were issued. Nearly one hundred survivors of smallpox had their clothing taken and burned, but were given nothing to replace it until another inspection brought a demand that was answered.

Men poured in from St. Louis, sicker, and badly clothed. Measles broke out and Trev despaired that he could do no more to help. Orders came that the prisoners were to hang their blankets out to air every day, but did not take into account the days it rained and they were left without blankets. The war dragged on and life became a wretched struggle for survival. Trev joined in plans for an escape, helping to dig the tunnel under their barracks to directly outside the parapet. Only ten of the original eighteen had the strength left to try, and they were in such a weakened condition that the last two were caught. Trev went back, but heard behind him the firing and yells which revealed that only three men made good their escape.

The remaining men in the barracks, as well as those who were caught, were beaten and put on rations of one small loaf of bread, when three loaves were needed to make a pound, and a piece of meat two inches square and so fouled that only the most desperate would eat it. Men began taking the Union oath to escape this hell.

Trev received two letters from his sister, written a year apart, telling him of her happiness that she finally had given birth to a daughter. The second letter asked why he had not acknowledged her packages to him, which he had not received, and vowed renewed efforts to get permission to visit him.

Trev received another letter. He recognized

Frances's handwriting and couldn't bring himself to open it. But something held him back from tossing the letter away.

He carried it around with him, fingering the paper until the edges frayed, forcing himself to finally open it.

She began with her prayers for him to remain hopeful and strong. Albert was getting involved with the prisoner exchanges, but there were numerous delays. There were a few lines concerning Robert's continued bitterness over the loss of his arm and his beloved horses.

Trev read as far as Frances's expressed hope for his eventual forgiveness before he threw the letter down. It was then that he saw the postscript on the other side.

Leah's name had him snatch up the letter and hold it with hands that shook.

> *I have managed to learn that Roddy has taken Leah and their son to the Northwest Territory. It is believed that he has been hired to work for the Overland Stage line. I wish I had more to tell you.*
> *Frances.*

As the conditions in the prison worsened, bringing Trev a deep depression for the wounds he could not heal, the illness he could not prevent, not only for lack of skill but for lack of the basic supplies, he focused on Leah. Light to his darkest hours, thoughts of her willed him to live and find her no matter how long it took.

For it wasn't only the news of where she was that kept him sane and fueled his struggle to survive, it was the realization of Leah's admission when he had first seen her son.

"*Yes. He has his father's eyes.*"

Not my husband's eyes. Not Roddy's. But his father's eyes.

He remembered the cold, haughty look of Roddy's blue-gray eyes and thought of his own color.

Was William his child? Had Leah borne him a son? His need to know burned daily. When the call came that Confederate soldiers were to be offered a chance to take the oath to the Union and serve an enlistment in the Western territory, Trev knew he could no longer stand with the five thousand strong who refused to consider it. He could not die here in this rotting hole without knowing if he had a son. Without holding his love close once more.

Soldiers were needed to fight the rising threat of Indians, as troops were called back to replenish the depleted ranks of the Union army. Men were reduced to eating rats if they could catch them. A wearied soul such as Trev's examined the oath he had sworn to the Confederacy and thought of all those other vows and promises he had been forced to break through the years. The honorable choice was to stay in prison. Or he could, with a small measure of privacy, take the oath to the Union. He would have to answer four questions composed by President Lincoln. Once done, he would be separated into what was called the "calfpen," where other former Confederate soldiers awaited their new orders and uniforms of blue.

It was a desperate and emaciated Captain Trevor Randolph Shelby of the Confederate States Army who left the cattle yard called the bull pen. He and others just as disreputable in appearance sent a last sweeping gaze over the silent group swarming with vermin that watched them line up for an the oath-taking that would free them. He had been savaged by the war and prison, had lost faith in himself and his dream, but would vow to the devil himself if he could have the chance to find Leah again.

She alone meant life to him.

Chapter Nineteen

LEAH, seated beneath a spring-leafed cotton-wood while ten-month-old James slept at her side, smiled to see the serious concentration on William's face. He was wading at the edge of the stream, calling to the fish that were just stirring from the cold winter. William imagined himself a skilled Indian hunter and she didn't have the heart to stop his pretend play, for he had little enough to enjoy.

Gathering up the remains of their picnic lunch, Leah thought about the old miner, Giddon Ellis, who had stayed at their Overland Stage home station while he recovered from painful mountain fever.

The miner had filled William's head with tales of Indian hunters. For a reason known only to William, he had latched on to the description of Indians luring fish to remain still, then catching them with their bare hands.

It was harmless, but Roddy grew angry when William refused to stop. It was one of the few things William would be stubborn about when Roddy confronted him. But then, Roddy did all he could to belittle any imaginings William had, just as he forbade her to take her books with them.

She had accepted Roddy's growing embitterment

with her and their marriage, but he couldn't steal her joy in her sons. She could have found a measure of peace and even happiness after their flight from their home.

The home station Roddy was finally hired to run for the Overland stage and mail line was in a broad, saddle-shaped valley, filled with cottonwoods, willows, and wild apple trees. After the incredible journey through the Rocky Mountains and the wide plain of sand and sagebrush at the end of the Wind River Range, this place was an oasis.

Here along the creek, the wild roses were beginning to bud, soon to perfume the air with their scent. But Leah no longer thought of gathering their petals to make soap; she neither had the time or cared enough to do it. Roddy would only begin his tirade that she was a Jezebel, not fit to be a wife of a decent man. And she had no defense against it.

No matter how she tried not to let memories of Trev interfere with the need to make a stable home for her sons, she was guilty of keeping those memories alive. The news recently passed on by the soldiers from Fort Bridger as they rode their patrols to escort the stages from the station ten miles southwest to the fort was that troops of Confederate prisoners were going to be sent here to the Utah Territory to replace the Union forces needed to fight the continuing war to the east. Whitewashed Rebs, was how Captain Emerson George described them.

She didn't know which prison Trev had been sent to. When they waited in St. Louis for Roddy to be approved as a stationmaster, she had attempted to have a letter to Frances posted, but Roddy found out and destroyed it. Since his threats against her didn't always work, he had taken to threatening William. Leah didn't try to write again.

There was no question in her mind that Trev was alive, despite the horrid conditions of prisons on both sides. It wasn't just her heart that knew; she had a link which reinforced her belief.

With a quick look around, Leah withdrew a gold ring from the small deerskin pouch where she kept her storeroom key. From the moment she had discovered the ring of twisted gold hearts in the yard where Trev had fought, she knew it belonged to him. The gold was near pink in color, but always warm no matter how cold the weather. She held the ring tight, praying that Trev would have the strength to overcome whatever horrors he was forced to endure. Her prayers never included seeing him again, but she wished that he live and find not only love, but find a way to become a doctor. For her, it was too late to dream of more than escape.

Little James stirred restlessly in his sleep as if her thoughts had reached him. Leah leaned over to brush his flaxen hair from where it curled over his forehead. She had labored for two days to give birth to him on the nightmare journey west. If it weren't for the women in the wagon train with them, she wondered if she would have survived. Not only had they tended to her, but they had taken care of William while Roddy brooded and drank. Far from the joy she had expected from Roddy when James, a son unquestionably his, was born, Roddy ignored the baby as much as he ignored her. William was now his target, except at night.

Roddy's drinking alarmed her, even when it kept

him from claiming his husbandly rights. Roddy had taken to trading meat for "Valley Tan," Jack Robertson's locally made cheap whiskey. She had gathered courage to ask the mountain man to stop, but he had as little respect for women as Roddy. She lived in dread of the nights when Roddy would try to attempt to bed her. If she was silent, he accused her of being at fault for laying there like a corpse, and the abuse would begin. If she defended herself, his rage erupted that much sooner. But he never left her with bruises that could be seen or stop her from doing chores.

"Mama, biscuit, please. I found fishies!"

"Oh, did you? Well, there should be a few left." As she found the biscuits in the basket, Leah warned, "Don't try and catch them again, lambkin. Last time you fell in."

"I know how. I know how," he insisted, snatching the biscuits from her and running back to the stream.

"Then be careful, love," she called out. Despite the hardships, William had thrived here. He lost his chubbiness on their journey, but had grown taller, his features—all but his darkening brown hair and light blue eyes—her own. For the sake of her sons she had tried to put money aside with the hope of one day getting on the stage and going to California. Twice now, Roddy had discovered her hidden cache of money.

He claimed it as his, although some money was given to her from grateful travelers for the meals she offered. She made use of the wild greens, trout, and sage hens the size of turkeys, along with meat from the pronghorn antelope, rather than offer the standard station fare of bacon and beans.

The fort trader, William Carter—Judge, most

called him—had given her another opportunity to
earn money. He was a true Virginia gentleman who
let her trade her dried herbs and salted meats. She
knew Judge, as well as others, was aware of her
troubled marriage, but there was nothing he or
anyone could do.

Leah roused herself to look around, carefully
scanning the wooded area across the stream bed
where William, shoes and stockings off, waded
near the bank to catch an early-stirring trout. They
had been free of raids through the long, bitterly
cold winter, but everyone warned that spring
would bring the Cheyenne and Sioux war parties
out again.

She touched her rifle. She had been forced to
learn to shoot and carried it everywhere with her
when she left the safe walls of the stockade. When
they arrived here to take up the duties of station
keeping, it had been late July. The elder trees had
been in flower and the gooseberries ripe.

By December, word came of the shameful Sand
Creek massacre that led to escalating Indian troubles.
A Colorado volunteer militia regiment slaughtered
Cheyenne women and children, thus provoking the
Cheyenne to join with the Sioux. All the trails
west, the Oregon, California, and Bozeman, as well
as the forts that guarded these routes and every
Overland home station and swing station, were
subjected to raids. The Indians struck like lightning, and their home station was particularly vulnerable, for the Indians prized the strong stage
horses.

Far to the north she could see the Wind River
Range, and realized how long she had been here.
James was stirring, William laughing as he
splashed up the bank, likely because the fish tried

to nibble his toes, and she had to call an end to their free time. It was worth whatever price Roddy demanded to see William with a smile as he came to her call.

After months of delay, Trev finally arrived at Fort Kearney. He had an adjustment to make wearing a blue uniform again, but it wasn't as bad for him as for others, for he had worn one for two years. Once he had given his oath with the understanding that he would be sent to the western frontier to keep peace with the plains Indians, not fight his comrades in the war, Trev and the other galvanized Yankees, as they were called, were kept separated from the other prisoners while Washington dickered over their status and whose responsibility their rations and new uniforms fell to.

But once at the fort, Trev had not wasted his time. He had searched and been rewarded to discover a former West Pointer, now Colonel David Harrington, was on assignment here. Trev had requested a meeting and now waited outside David's office.

Ushered in minutes later, Trev instantly saw the changes the years had brought. David was no longer the lanky, sallow-faced boy. His hair had touches of gray in the dark brown color, and his face bore the deep lines worry forced on a man. David's greeting was less than Trev had expected— cold, actually—until his aide closed the office door behind him and left them alone.

David came up out of his chair and around the desk to give Trev a bear hug. "Damn, but it's good to see you. I've your record here, and admit, Trev, I was surprised to see that you had taken the oath."

"It's a long story," Trev answered, taking the seat in front of the desk as David returned to his behind it. "But I won't bore you. David, I need a favor, and you're the man in position to grant it. I want an assignment to Fort Bridger."

"Just like that? Surely there is more you are going to tell me?"

Trev knew this was no time for reluctance. "There's someone—"

"Ah, Cooper's wife, I'll bet. Half the men at the fort talk about her." He looked up and quickly judged Trev's tense expression. "I hear she is lovely, but they talk about her cooking and kindness. She has made their station one of the best." David paused, and toyed with the papers on his desk. "As a friend, I'm asking if there'll be trouble between you and Cooper if I do assign you out there?"

"Cooper can't make trouble for me. I know too much about him. As for myself—" Trev knew it would be easy to lie, but couldn't. "I'd like to kill him, but I won't. I didn't when I had a chance. But there was once something between his wife and me. I just want to be close by if she needs me. If the war—"

"Jesus, Trev, say no more. My brother lost his wife to another man after he was wounded at Shiloh. Cost him an eye." Heaving a weary sigh, David pushed his chair back and opened his bottom drawer. He withdrew a bottle and two glasses, pouring out drinks for them.

"I'll do this for you, Trev, but I want to warn you that you won't have it easy. The Indians have been brutalizing the stage stations to get the horses. They've burned out settlers and nearly destroyed the telegraph lines. And the Union commanders and soldiers aren't going to accept you. Expect mistrust, Trev. And I'm afraid you'll have to remain a noncommissioned officer."

"I don't care, David. I'll be a private if that's what it takes. Prison taught me to take orders."

"Trev, keep your bitterness hidden. There are men out here who escaped from Andersonville. You'll find no sympathy from them."

"I don't want any."

"All right. Since you've served a tour in the Southwest, I can arrange for you to have a detail of nine men. You'll ride escort to the stage between Cooper's home station and the fort."

"When?" was all Trev asked as he accepted the offered drink.

"Would next week be too soon?"

"David, after surviving hell, I hope it's not too late."

Leah had a week of warning to arm herself against seeing Trev again. Wally Colfax, one of the stage drivers, brought the news of the new officer and patrol that would be stationed there. She expected Roddy's outburst, but it never came. Nor did he turn on her. When liquor loosened his tongue, he brooded that Trev would reveal what he had done.

She fully understood his fear. The men out here—traders, soldiers, even travelers—all seemed to want a fresh start. They were more likely to admire a man's fighting skills against the hostiles, or his drinking ability, than ask him which side he fought on in the war. The reports that reached them of the South's steady retreat and lack of weapons, food, and supplies brought the daily expectation of the South's surrender.

To avoid problems with Roddy, Leah kept to her own daily routine. Despite repeated warnings that the warming weather was sure to bring Indian raids, she escaped down to the stream with her children.

Luis, the young stock tender, had come fishing with her. Leah left the quilt where James sat playing and walked down to the creek to see the fish William caught with the Mexican boy's help. She was halfway between her sons when she noticed the sudden silence. And the sense of danger from that silence came as suddenly.

"Luis, bring William. Leave the fish and come to me," she ordered, spinning around to run back to her baby and her rifle.

Wild yells exploded from the woods across the stream. Leah threw a look over her shoulder and saw four mounted Indians break from the trees. Luis had a struggling William thrown over his thin shoulder and was running toward her. There would be no time to run back to the stockade. She snatched up her loaded rifle, ignoring little James's cry, screaming for Luis to hurry as she began firing. No matter how prepared she thought she was, she was shaking as she tried to aim at the Indians. Eagle feathers decorated their hair and trailed from long skins on their shoulders.

There were six shots in her Colt rifle, but Leah forgot Wally's instructions to count each one. Luis had grabbed James and was running up the hill behind her when she realized her rifle was empty. The first raider was almost upon her. Leah wanted to run, wanted to make sure her children were safe, but she ran out from beneath the tree into the path of an oncoming rider. Swinging her rifle like a club, she battered his leg, but before she could hit him again, another Indian crowded her between the horses and wrenched the rifle from her hands.

A kick to her lower back sent her staggering, her fall stopped by whoever gripped her hair. She couldn't scream—the pain had taken her breath— but she clawed at whatever was within reach, afraid to even look up at her attackers. Another blow brought her to her knees, where she remained, chest heaving, while her fingers dug into the earth. She gathered her strength and came up in a rush, flinging dirt at the Indian leaning out of his saddle to grab hold of her.

A roaring filled her ears. She didn't understand why the Indian suddenly pitched backward, away from her. Shoving her hair from her face, she saw one Indian holding her rifle high, his horse rearing up while he yelled what sounded like a challenge. It was then she heard the steady firing from the top of the hill and the shouted order for her to get down.

With her face buried in her hands, Leah huddled on the ground. Seconds, minutes, she was never sure how long the shooting continued, or when it stopped. Time didn't matter. Her sons were safe.

The gradual realization that the shooting had stopped brought the sound of *his* voice calling her name.

She believed herself strong. She thought she had accepted the loss of Trev in her life. Leah thanked God every day for the gift of having Trev's son. She promised herself at each sunset that she wouldn't destroy herself with the endless longing she had for Trev. But the sound of his voice calling to her proved she wasn't strong at all.

The rich caress of his voice brought back memories. Memories of love and hope. Memories and dreams of Trev. With an anguished moan, Leah tore the grass from its roots. Trev wasn't her hope. He wasn't her love. He would hate her for his imprisonment.

Tears of fright streamed down her cheeks as he turned her over. She felt him pry open her hands, which still clutched earth and grass. The need to be held by him, comforted and cherished, ripped through her. She shook with the force of that need.

But Trev wasn't gathering her into his arms. He wasn't whispering of missing, of longing, of the same need. Trev wasn't even looking at her. His gaze, all his tense concentration, was on her hands as he slowly brushed them clean.

"My children?" she finally whispered through parched lips.

"Frightened, but safe. And you? Are you hurt, Mrs. Cooper?"

The hiss of her indrawn breath cut into the quiet. Leah attempted to swallow, but there was a knot constricting her throat. Every fear that he would hate her came rushing back.

"Mrs. Cooper, the other soldiers are concerned. Are you all right?"

It took Leah moments to understand that he was not only reminding her who she was, but warning her they were not alone. But his curt manner cut into her. Were they to pretend to be strangers? She couldn't. No one could demand the strength such a role would take.

She tried to jerk her hand away. Trev gently shackled her wrist with one hand. "You've cut yourself," he murmured, unable to look at her as he opened the knot of the bright yellow bandanna around his neck. Her hands were all he dared to touch, though he wanted to hold her. Hold Leah and rock her against him until the terrified look in her eyes disappeared. He knew the strength he would need to demand of himself when he saw her again, but not this much. Not when he felt as if his insides were being torn apart.

The shuffle of feet and murmurs of the soldiers behind him reminded him they were watching. He didn't dare linger over a woman who wasn't his. Could never be his. And the rush of renewed anger the knowledge brought forced him to make short work of wrapping her hand while he knelt at her side.

A quick look showed him that the blaze of life in her eyes had faded. He longed to whisper words of hope to bring them back to life. He needed to know the tears that spilled down her cheeks weren't those of despair, but of joy. Every nerve in his body screamed with the need to feel her sweet body pressed to his, to feel alive once more. But the others were crowding closer, wondering what was taking him so long.

Leah barely heard the other soldiers state the reassurances that her children were safe. She could feel Trev's withdrawal, longed to speak freely to him, but bit back the words. She stole a look at his harshly drawn features. There were small scars. Dark shadows beneath his eyes. He was thinner, but still had a taut, dangerous aura about him. She didn't have the courage to pull away when he helped her to stand. Leah had been starved for too long and the need to be near him ruled her now.

"Will you be able to stand by yourself, Mrs. Cooper?" Trev asked as if fighting to keep his emotions from being revealed.

Once again she had to hear his curt, polite, distanced voice. With it, she absorbed the shock of Trev in a Union uniform. But this time a swift, sharp pain sliced through her. She shuddered violently. An icy cloak surrounded her. And he looked at her with the eyes of a stranger, forcing the pain to spread beneath the numbness. Leah could barely answer him.

"Yes. Yes, I'm f-fine." Leah rubbed her arms, wincing from deep hurt he brought to her, hardly feeling the pain as she put pressure on her cut palm.

"Someone will need to see to that cut," Trev warned.

"I will. I've had to learn to tend so many wounds. So I'll do it. They took my rifle. It was empty. But they took it," she mumbled, filling the silence, keeping him close. "I did what Wally told me. Fired right at them. They didn't turn and run. Wally said they would. They didn't. I forgot to . . . to count the shots. I really did forget—" Leah broke off and looked up at Trev, finding compassion and a blaze of fury. She quickly glanced at each of the other soldiers. Pity and sympathy were in most of their gazes except for three of them. Leah didn't want to think about what was in their eyes. But she couldn't help feeling as if something dirty had crawled over her.

Trev's fury threatened to explode. Leah, his lovely Leah, alone and defenseless, apologizing to them, when her bravery outshone those of some men he had fought with in the war.

"Ain't a need for you to explain, ma'am. You did

jus' fine. But you ain't got to worry. We won't let this happen again."

Trev sent a resentful look at Rye Munroe, but kept silent. Leah was shaken and he couldn't do a damn thing to help her. If it had been any other woman, Trev knew he would have held her. Any other woman would have had the comfort she needed.

She swayed where she stood and he gripped her upper arm, still unable to meet her gaze, which seemed to cry out to him. Trev didn't trust himself not to fall apart and carry her off, stealing what had been denied him. Leah and her love. He had schooled himself to see her again. But never like this. Not bruised and fighting for her children and her life. Not with the knowing eyes of other men watching them.

She was still as lovely as the memory he carried with him, but the girl's innocence and softness were gone. He regretted their loss. In their place, her face revealed the honed strength of a woman who had survived her hardships. It was a look that Trev knew well. His face, like those of the soldiers around them, bore the same stamp. But they were men.

Leah was no longer his little dreamer. From a bitter well inside rose the knowledge that his best friend's betrayal had stolen that from her.

He wasn't sure where he found the strength to release her, but he did, and fired orders to his men.

"Private Randall, you and Private Briggs escort Mrs. Cooper back to the stockade." *Mrs. Cooper.* He swallowed the bile for having to call her that. Trev stood aside as the two young men, both ex-Confederates out of Morton Prison, took up their places on either side of Leah and offered their arms. In that next brief moment their gazes met. Leah's filled with a plea, with a longing and renewed hope. Trev knew his eyes revealed his regret and pain. He had to force out the order for them to leave.

"We gonna track 'em, Cap?"

"Those are our orders. And it's sergeant, Private Butler," Trev reminded him, but without heat, without really caring. Danny Butler was as green as new apples, good-natured about being made the butt of jokes by the others, but one of the most anxious-to-please men that Trev ever had under his command. The boy had been captured by Union forces two days after he had enlisted on his seventeenth birthday. After four months at Rock Island, working the burial detail with Trev, Danny had taken the oath the first time it was offered to him. There were times when Trev wished he had a little of the boy's resilience.

Trev's gaze had never left Leah's retreating figure. He was distracted by the childish voice calling her "Mama." She was still flanked by the two privates, but knelt with arms open to hug the little boy flinging himself at her. *William*. Trev had to close his eyes briefly. The sight was too painful, the need to know if the boy was his son too sharp an edge that tore at him.

"We'd best be moseyin', Sergeant. Them hostiles ain't gonna wait 'round for us."

The reminder tore Trev from the past. He hid his gratitude, but focused on his corporal. Dooley Matthews was Danny's opposite. Trev had instinctively trusted the older man. He topped Trev by a good six inches, his lanky frame as easy moving as his slow drawl. Dooley never talked about the war, where he was from, or if he had a family. But the man had a savvy about surviving, which was apparent when he chose to speak. From the sharp look in his eyes it was a savvy Danny needed to learn. Trev ordered them to team up with three other ex-Confederates from Point Lookout Prison in Maryland. Pender Applewood, Ed Wilson, and Alex Hayden were men Trev had been warned to watch as potential deserters. He sent the five of them back to get their horses.

"Rye, you and Riley come with me. We'll see how far we can track them on foot."

Until the very moment he had to turn away, Trev swore he would not look at Leah and her son again. But he had learned how well-paved the road to hell was with all his good intentions.

"Go on ahead," he ordered, "I want to make sure that Dooley doesn't have trouble with those three." A feeble excuse at best, Trev knew, but he didn't care. He needed the sight of Leah. real, not a vision that haunted his nights. She still knelt at the top of the hill. She had one arm around William, and in the other she held another son. The five soldiers passed her, but he saw that Leah didn't look at them. Her gaze was as steady on him, as his was on her. Only an inner warning that he was lingering too long made him remember his place. Trev turned away and followed his men.

But he couldn't help shooting one last glance back as he crossed the stream, wondering where in the hell Cooper was. He had not seen Cooper when his detail had arrived at the logged walls of the stockade half an hour ago. With the help of One-eyed Pete, the stock tender, they had stripped their horses of gear and turned them out in the corral. There was still no sign of Cooper when

Leah's screams and the shot sent Trev and his men running to find her.

Not once, not even now that she and her sons were safe, did Cooper show up. But he would eventually. And Trev knew he would have to dig deep inside himself not to kill the bastard. Not for what Roddy had done to him and the other Confederates by sending them into hellholes, but for his abusing Leah.

Trev was aware, as he began to block his thoughts and let survival instincts take over, that killing had become anathema to him. Except to protect life. Leah. Her children. This was the one vow he had to keep. It was a chance to regain a measure of self-respect.

He had lost it all: home, dreams, honor, his love, and perhaps a son. Somewhere beneath this vast land's sky there had to be a place for him to start over.

Either that or find his grave.

Chapter Twenty

MURMURING soothing sounds to her sons, Leah watched Trev until the woods hid the last bit of his uniform. She was still shaken by the Indian attack, but an inner turmoil claimed her thoughts that had nothing to do with the attack and everything with seeing Trev again.

She knew he was just under six feet tall, but his body now had a rawhide leanness which made him appear taller. Prison had put its stamp on him; it was there in the hardness of his features, his eyes, even his voice. Where had he gotten those small scars on his face? And what scars were hidden from her, from everyone? That last day when they had been together so briefly and he had told her about his father, she knew he had withheld so much from her. In the same way she always had sensed the darkness in him, Leah had a strong feeling that the darkness, along with the scars prison had left on Trev, had taken root so deeply they would never leave him. Had it been only a year since she had seen him? It seemed a lifetime to her.

Inside her, there burned a need to talk to Trev, a yearning to know again the laughter and pleasure they shared just being with each other. Leah knew her scars were as well hidden as his, but there were times, like now, when the hunger for comfort all but overwhelmed her.

William calling to her brought Leah back with a start. Her sons needed her. They had to come first. There was no one else but her to take care of them. Yet her heart ached for Trev, and her prayers went with him.

Leah wasn't sure which of the privates urged them to get back to the stockade, then offered to take James from her. His smile, as warm as his snapping black eyes, eased not only her fear, but the little boy's as well. The moment the soldier held out his arms to James, the baby went to him.

"Don't worry 'bout me droppin' him, ma'am. I've got six little brothers left at home. Ma always said I did real fine acarin' for them."

"I'm sure you did," Leah answered, seeing the comfortable way he held James. Not at all the awkwardness that Roddy displayed on the rare occasions he held his son. "I'm sorry," she added in a distracted voice. "I don't know your name."

"Private Joe Randall, ma'am. This 'ere's Tate Briggs. Tate, you take that other little fella from Mrs. Cooper so we can get back. Ain't no place to be standin' 'bout jawin'."

"I was gonna do it. Don't need you to give me orders, Joe. You ain't a corporal no more. Private same as me," Tate reminded him.

Leah saw the smiles they exchanged, understanding they were only teasing. Her smile was a mere hint that curved her lips for the way James had nestled his head on Joe's shoulder. Both of her children hungered for a father's love and attention. As long as she remained with Roddy, they would remain hungry. Just as she would.

" 'Sides, Joe, Shelby didn't say—"

"That's Sergeant Shelby to you, Briggs," Joe cut in as he settled James in his arms and started to walk away.

"Yeah, well, anyway—ah, the heck with it!" Tate steadied Leah as she rose to stand up beside him. "Let me take this fine-looking little fella, Mrs. Cooper."

William buried his head against Leah's neck, his small arms clinging to her. "He's shy with strangers," she explained, hating herself for the lie that came so easily now. Her little boy was becoming more withdrawn with every passing day and she knew the blame was Roddy's. It was one more thing for her to add to the simmering pot of hate that was threatening to erupt into a boil. Only the thought of her sons being hurt kept Leah from an open confrontation with Roddy. He wouldn't hesitate to hurt them to get back at her.

But as she walked back to the station with Tate teasing William, she roused herself to hope that Trev and his soldiers would bring laughter back into their lives. Just as they reached the stockade gate, Tate managed to get a shy little smile from William when he gave the boy his cap.

Tate looked back, then said, "You and the boy don't need to worry this'll happen again. Dooley Matthews is one fine tracker an' he'll find them. But your husband must be worried something fierce over where you and the boy are, ma'am."

Leah didn't answer him. William gave up the cap without a struggle when Leah asked for it and returned the hat to the private. Roddy worried? If he was, he certainly had a strange way of showing it. Her face heated with shame, for it wouldn't be long before they would all know about Roddy's concern for her and the boys.

Leah had to wait until she had supper ready before Roddy came into the kitchen. One look told her he had been drinking. He wasn't staggering drunk, not like some nights, but he had that gleam in his eyes that boded no good for her. Perhaps it was her worry over Trev and his men still out there searching for the Indians, or just the thought of Trev being near, that gave her the courage to attack instead of merely being quiet.

"Where were you, Roddy? Couldn't you come to see if we had been hurt? You're always reminding me that I mustn't give anyone reason to talk, but what about you? What kind of a man does it make you, who wouldn't even come to see if his wife and children needed him?"

"Need? You dare talk about need to me?" he demanded, banging his fist on the table. "You got what you deserved, woman. Told you time and again not to leave the stockade. Didn't I? Whatever happened was your fault. But I guess you ain't all that much. Even the damn Indians didn't want you."

"I—I run-runned w-with Lu-Luis."

Leah froze. The spoon she had been using to stir the stew pot dripped on the floor. William's stammering could trigger Roddy's abuse. Roddy just didn't understand or care that he was the only one William stammered to.

"If you had a decent woman for a mother, boy, you wouldn't have had to run anywhere." Roddy ignored the boy standing nearby and pulled out the bench. He glanced at the table, rubbed his eyes, then shot a glaring look at Leah. "There's only one plate."

"I ate with the boys," she murmured, gesturing for William to come to her. When he refused and stood by Roddy's side, his little face turned up looking for attention, Leah felt her heart squeeze with agony; William begged, and Roddy ignored him.

"You saying I'm late again?"

She turned to ladle the stew into a bowl for him. James was already asleep and now she had to get William to bed before Roddy started on him. Without answering, she set the bowl in front of him.

"Serve me. Show me what a good little wife I've got."

"It's not a wife but a slave you want, Roddy." But she said it without heat, having repeated it too many times to matter anymore. These were the small humiliations he heaped upon her; there were others, the ones that kept her walking the floors at night. "William, come with mama. It's time for bed."

"No. Leave him right where he is." Roddy reached out to shackle William's small wrist and pulled the boy closer. "You set right down there, next to me," he ordered Leah. "I want to see if having Indian hands on you changed you any."

"Roddy, don't do this. Please." She closed her eyes for a moment, then sat to one side of him. Leah took William's other hand within hers, feeling how chilled his skin was. "Let me put him to bed, Roddy. He's had a shock today and James was cranky by the time we—"

"You saw him, didn't you?" he interrupted, shoveling in a mouthful of stew. He chewed noisily, motioning with his fork for Leah to push the plate of bread closer. William tugged against the grip on his wrist, but once more Roddy ignored him. "Answer me, *wife*. You did see him."

"Let William go, Roddy. You can do whatever it

is you need to me, but let him go." His blank stare forced her up and around the table. William started to whimper when Leah tried to pry Roddy's thick fingers off her son's thin arm. Roddy didn't say a word, just kept on eating while she silently struggled to get him to release his grip.

"If you don't stop, Leah, I'm gonna give that boy something to remember. Something you won't be forgetting, either."

The soft-voiced threat made her look up at him. Hate poured from his eyes as they went from her to William, then back to hold her gaze. "Go sit down, Leah." With a rough shake to William's arm, he added, "Stop that whimpering, boy. You remember what I did to you the last time. You'll get more of the same."

Leah didn't sit. She grabbed the poker from the fire. "Not this time. Not ever again, Roddy. You let my son go or I'll use this on you."

He threw back his head and started laughing. "You threaten me? Figuring that bastard's gonna take you and these brats in?" He moved suddenly, shoving William aside, not even glancing when the boy fell and Leah cried out. Roddy blocked her way when she tried to go around him to get to her son.

Leah ducked his fist, but he caught her around the neck with one big hand, bringing her up short. "Go to bed, William. Please listen to mama. Go. Now." Roddy's fingers tightened, cutting off her breath.

"I'll fix it so he won't want you. No man'll want you."

The furious pounding on the door stopped him with his fist in midair. He shot a murderous look at Leah, but she was gasping, her fingers clawing at his hand. Roddy let her go.

"Get inside with your son." He didn't wait to see if she obeyed him, but went to the door. "What the devil do you want?" he demanded of the soldier standing there.

"Shelby and Hayden tangled with the Indians. We need your wife, Mr. Cooper," Danny Butler told him.

"She ain't touching them. You go find someone else to tend them."

"There ain't no one else."

Roddy knew the truth of that, but he started to close the door anyway.

"I'll be right there, Private," Leah said from behind him. "But I'll need someone to stay with my children since my husband still has work to finish." She refused to look at Roddy as he turned to face her. "Unless they are able to be moved here? I have everything I need and—" Leah cut herself off as she realized that Trev was one of the men hurt. "How badly are they wounded?"

"Sergeant Shelby's got a gash in his side and Hayden got a bullet crease on his head. If you don't mind, Mr. Cooper, it would be better for them to come here. Our quarters ain't what you'd call clean. That last detail sure left—"

"Please," Leah interrupted, "go get them. I'll get my things together."

Roddy closed the door, then rounded on Leah. "You bitch! You couldn't wait to get him into my house. You can't wait to get your hands on him. I wish to hell they had killed him."

"I'd do the same no matter who was hurt, Roddy, and you know it. I've never lied to you about my feelings for Trev. You married me knowing that I loved another man. I'm only sorry you found out who it was." Leah knew she should stop, but while she would not berate Roddy for his claim that this was his house, she had no intention of letting him believe she would betray him.

"Roddy, it's not Trev being here for me that's eating at you. You're afraid he'll tell what you did to him and those soldiers that day. It's that and your own failures that make you turn on me and the boys. Stay here. Watch me, if you're so worried that I'll disgrace you."

She walked away and heard the door slam in answer. Leah gripped the doorframe to their small bedroom until she stopped shaking. Roddy was wrong. Wrong about this being his house, wrong about her. The station belonged to the stage company, just as the meager furnishings did. And Leah knew that no matter who was hurt, she would tend them as best as she could.

Gathering up her herb basket and clean rags, she set water to boil. If this was the result of the first day Trev was here, what would the following days be like? Once again the knock at the door stopped her musings.

William came into the kitchen just as Trev and Hayden entered with the help of Tate and Joe. Leah couldn't force herself to look at Trev, but then he thanked her and she had to turn. How she managed to swallow her cry, she never knew. His shirt was blood-soaked on his left side. Leah crushed the linen rags in her hands.

"Mrs. Cooper," Trev said, demanding her attention, "we appreciate your offer. Especially after what you've been through today. But please take care of Hayden first. That bullet crease knocked him off his horse and his bruises are worse than mine." He didn't wait to meet her gaze, for he couldn't. His rage grew when he saw the reddened marks on her neck. And then there was the boy.

Trev moved the bench nearer to the table, saw the unfinished plate, and once more wondered where Roddy was. But little William stood there watching him, and Trev felt an ache that turned to a razor-sharp pain when he saw fear in the boy's eyes. Hayden was seated across from him, and Leah was already washing his head wound, with her back toward Trev. Tate hovered at her side, ready to give whatever help she needed. And Trev had to fight from going to the boy, from making a move or saying a word that would give him or Leah away.

"I'll go tend to the horses," Joe said. "Unless you'll need me here, too, ma'am?"

"No, I can manage with just Tate," Leah answered. She heard the scrape of the bench being pulled nearer to the table and wanted to look behind her to see where William was. But to turn around meant she would have to see Trev again, and she wasn't ready for it. Hayden moaned when she spread his cut to clean out the dirt that had been ground into the wound. Leah, without realizing it, made the same soothing sounds she murmured earlier to her sons. And when she tied off the bandage, there was no more time to avoid seeing Trev.

"Tate, you'll have to help Alex back to the room." Trev ordered. "The others should have it cleaned by now."

"I wanted to do it," Leah began, then stopped herself. She couldn't tell him Roddy had forbidden her. William whispered to her and Leah rushed to her son. Picking him up, she smiled when he rubbed his eyes. "Sergeant Shelby," she called softly, "let me tuck my son into bed. I'll be right back."

Trev nodded, unbuttoning his bib-front shirt, conscious that Leah was watching him. He wouldn't turn around until the men were gone. When he did he found Leah was gone too. He gazed around the kitchen, the big iron pots testimony to the cooking she did for the stage passengers. Dried bundles of herbs hung from the wood rafters, filling the room with pleasant scents. He shot a look back at the doorway where Leah had disappeared, assuming the two rooms jutting out from the back of the building were their bedrooms. Across from where he stood, another table with two benches piled on top blocked off yet another doorway.

It had to lead to the sutler's store that Roddy managed, and the bar. He had never seen Leah's home once she had married Roddy, but even to his eyes, there was little here to suggest a woman's personal possessions.

Leah rushed back into the room, quickly tossing out the pan of water, rinsing it, then filling it with fresh hot water. She set it on the table, avoided looking at Trev, then realized how foolish she was behaving.

He was about to yank off the blood-soaked neckerchief he had pressed against the gash on his side. "No, Let me wet it first," she said. But the intriguing shadows playing over his body from both the lamp and firelight held her still. Trev looked up at her, and Leah read too much in his eyes, suddenly aware that they were alone. And just as aware that Roddy could come in at any moment.

"Please, Trev," she whispered huskily, stepping forward. "It'll bleed again if you just pull it off."

His eyes narrowed at the change in Leah's voice. The very softness of hers made his own harsh and clipped. "If you touch me, Mrs. Cooper," he stated flatly as a reminder to both of them, "I won't be—"

"You need my help. I told you I had to tend wounds and injuries. There's no one else." She didn't wait for his consent, but took up a clean cloth and, after wetting it, barely squeezed it before she brought it to his skin. At the first scrape of the cloth to his bruised flesh, Trev's breath hissed between his teeth. Leah told herself the tremor in her hands was just the events of the day catching up to her. When she managed to peel away his makeshift bandage, she told herself it was the pain that caused his body to tense. It had nothing to do with her touching him. Nothing at all to do with the enforced intimacy of closeness as she leaned over to wash his bare flesh. And he meant nothing by splaying his hand over her hip to steady her. But even as Leah repeated this over and over to herself, she knew she lied. A low sound of distress escaped her lips, and she worked faster.

"How did you let yourself get so close to them?" she asked, trying desperately to distract herself from the hundred other questions she wanted answered. She could only be thankful that the wound was shallow and wouldn't need stitches.

"They had split up and we did, too. Only we didn't know they banded together a ways up the trail." Trev stopped himself for a few moments. He couldn't tell Leah he had been thinking about her, forgetting the most basic rule of survival. Nothing, but nothing should distract a man when he was tracking an enemy. "Anyway," he went on, "they were waiting for us. Once Alex went down, the four of them jumped us. I guess I got lucky." He closed his eyes, letting every nerve ending absorb the gentle, slow way her hands moved over his skin. The pain of the wound receded, and in its place the deeper ache he had been carrying with him for so long began to spread. Hunger that he had denied, buried, and thought he controlled now surfaced.

"Trev?" Leah cupped his cheek with one hand. "How can you say you were lucky? You were hurt." When he didn't answer her, she began to spread a salve over the gash, then tore strips from the big squares of linen.

He wondered how he let himself make that slip. Did he really tell her he was lucky? That was from the past, when he had gone looking for a knife blade with his name on it. How many times had he said as much to Robert? Robert. He was buried in the past, too. When Leah leaned over him again, Trev brushed his chin against her hair, remembering the feel of its silky weight free and sliding over his skin. He tried to control his elemental response to her, but if anything, Leah's touch became more gentle, almost caressing.

"Leah? Do you know what you're doing to me?"

His voice was husky and so, so soft, shimmering through her, but she glanced up, saw desire in his eyes, and retreated. "I'm sorry if I hurt you. I want to make sure there are no bits of thread stuck to the wound."

"Well, finish it. I can't take much more." Curt and harsh, the words snapped out, but Trev couldn't help it. He felt the enticing whisper of her breath across his bare flesh, her fingers unconsciously rubbing the hair on his chest. All the while her eyes darkened. He knew Leah, knew she had to be aware of what was happening. But she moved her head just then and the lamplight revealed the bruises on her neck. Trev had not forgotten about them.

He slid forward before she could move, capturing her between his spread thighs. Bracing both hands on her hips, he held her still. "I know you didn't have those marks on your neck from the attack. I want to know why Roddy put his hands on you again. And what's more, Leah," he demanded softly, "I want to know if—"

"No." When she met his gaze, his eyes weren't soft at all. She denied him with a quick shake of her head.

Trev lost his patience. He yanked her against him, his head thrown back to look up at her. "Why, Leah? How many times? Because of me? I want to know."

Leah clutched his shoulders, closing her eyes, fighting not to tell him. She thought of her endless struggle to escape Roddy, and knew if she said one word to Trev, she would never fight alone again. The temptation was there, not for herself but for William and James. From her deepest memories came the reminder of Trev's dream, and all who had denied it to him. He had longed to heal, not to hurt. If she told him about Roddy, she knew Trev would go after him. Roddy hated Trev enough to kill him. She couldn't risk that. Her silence was Trev's protection.

"The baby grabbed me. That's all it is." With a hard shove that caught him unaware, she managed to pull away, but the table edge blocked her from freedom. "Don't interfere."

"If you won't tell me, I swear I'll go after Roddy. A child's fingers didn't make those marks, Leah.

It's more than past time for me to confront that bastard. I haven't forgotten what he did to you."

"Stay away from him, Trev." Leah wrapped her arms around her waist to keep from holding on to him. She wanted to be in his arms, resting her head on his shoulder, turning back time, freezing it forever in a place where they had loved.

"Leah?"

The caress he made of her name almost undid every sworn promise she had made to herself. She wanted Trev free of the taint of death, needed him to have his dream. She would sacrifice everything but her children to see him find the love they had been denied.

"Trev, please let me finish binding up your wound. I—I can't . . . someone, might come . . . just please let this be done." Tears burned her eyes, but she fought to keep him from seeing them.

He rose and placed both hands on the table's edge, caging her. Trev leaned into Leah so that she was forced backward and had to look up at him. Her hands came up to rest on his shoulders of their own volition. She never knew where she found the strength not to pull him closer and once again taste heaven from his lips.

His knuckles whitened as he kept himself from taking her into his arms and holding her as he had yearned to from the moment he saw her lying in the dirt. "Leah, how much more will you have us denied? I can't have you, but I won't stand by and see him hurt you again. I will not," he stated in an even softer, more deadly voice, "ever let him put his hands on you again. He should have been with you today, or forbidden you to leave the stockade. Doesn't he care?"

"Listen to me," she demanded, digging her fingers into his shoulders. "You have no right. I knew the danger. I took the risk—"

"Why? Why would you risk your children, yourself?"

"I—I needed to—leave it be, Trev." She couldn't look into his eyes any longer. They were intense with a meld of desire and rage. "I told you, you have no right to ask. No rights at all. Roddy is my husband. What he does—"

"He put the fear in William's eyes, didn't he?" No longer able to stop himself, Trev caught her up against him, holding her tight. For a moment he allowed himself to bask in the fulfilled need of having Leah in his arms, of feeling her body pressed against the length of his. He smoothed her hair with one hand and with the other tilted her face up. "Whose right is that, Leah? Roddy's? Or mine?"

"Mine," she whispered without hesitation, knowing she could say nothing else. "The right is mine, just as William is mine."

"Two things kept me alive in prison. Finding you and keeping you safe and wondering if William is my son. You deny me both."

With a wrenching despair Leah stared at him. "Yes, Trev, I deny you."

Someone whistled outside and Trev shot a look over his shoulder. He had to let her go, but even as he told himself this, he was brushing his lips against hers. "If once," he murmured against the trembling fullness of her mouth, "you told me you loved him, I would walk away from you, Leah. But the love in your eyes is for me, and nothing will make me leave you until it is gone."

"You don't know what you're saying. Let me go before someone comes in. Please, Trev, understand that you can't stay here. You must get another assignment. There'll be trouble with Roddy. More than before. I can't see you hurt again. I can't live with knowing that—" She closed her eyes and turned her head. "You are making a heaven and hell for me, Trev," she said after a few moments.

"It's better than what I've lived with," he snapped, letting her go. But his gaze promised he wasn't done.

Leah gathered up the linen, her fingers clumsy, her body shaking. She barely managed to tie off the ends of the bandage when a soft knock at the door caught her attention.

"Who's there?" she called out, stepping away from Trev.

"Private Randall, ma'am."

"The door's open," Leah said, but was already walking across to open it herself. "Come in," she offered.

"No need, ma'am. I brought over a clean shirt for the sergeant. Thought he could use it and some help to walk back."

"I'll be right with you," Trev answered, making no move to take the shirt that Joe handed over to Leah.

She closed the door to keep the night chill out, then slowly walked back to give Trev the shirt. Leah watched him struggle to pull it over his head, wanting to help, not daring to touch him again. She picked up his discarded shirt and held it when he tried to take it from her.

"I can wash and mend it. You'll need this, Trev."

The burning throb of pain from his wound forced Trev to hold his side when he moved toward her. Leaning close, he whispered, "To hell with my needs. My only concern is what you need."

Leah didn't answer him. She twisted the cloth of his shirt, waiting for the door to close behind him. She heard Trev's ragged breathing and had to look up.

"Thank you again for all your help, Mrs. Cooper."

He said her name like a curse and Leah shivered. "Rest a day or so to let that gash heal," she managed to say, because of Joe standing there, looking from Trev to her. And she needed a last word, a last look. "If you should start bleeding again, or need—"

Shimmering rage exploded in Trev's eyes. "I haven't stopped bleeding."

Leah saw him close the door. She glanced around the empty room, then down at the blood-stain on her faded gown. "How much more, dear God?" she whispered, unable to touch the stain. She raised Trev's shirt to her lips and stared at the widening dark spot her tears made on the blue cloth. "Lord, help me. I love him so. I love him and I'm so afraid of what will happen if he stays."

James whimpered in his sleep. Leah knew the bars on her cage would never open. Like a trapped animal she wanted to crawl away and hide. But when James cried out, she was reminded of her place. Mother. Roddy's wife. And never, ever more than Trev's memory.

Chapter Twenty-One

TWO days later, under a sky that promised rain by day's end, Trev had his patrol mounted to escort the stage to the fort. He had stayed away from Leah, and Roddy kept from his sight. Hayden, still complaining of dizziness, was being left behind, but Trev felt uneasy about it. The soldier had demanded Leah's attention, playing on her sympathy. Trev had been spared warning him away from her, afraid of what Roddy might do to her. Both Rye and Joe managed to get to Hayden before him.

Wally, driving today, called out to Trev from atop the stage, anxious to get started. Luis, standing by the stockade gates, opened them at Trev's signal. Dooley led four men out, with the stage following. Trev was about to join them when a bellow of rage came from the sutler's store. Huber, the relief driver, was over near the corral, closer than Trev but not quicker.

"Take them out, Rye," Trev ordered, telling himself he was not going to interfere, just as Leah begged him not to.

But when a child's high-pitched, fearful cry ripped through the air, followed by another yell, nothing was going to stop Trev. He was off his horse and running before Huber was halfway across the yard.

The door was open, but the overcast sky and dim interior offered little light. The crowded stacks of flour and barrels hid Roddy from him. Brine and oiled leather melded with the musty smell of the store.

"Cooper?" A scuffling noise sent him running down the only clear aisle.

"Little bastard! Come outta there."

Trev saw the bulk of Roddy's body bend over. He came even with the counter just as Roddy dragged a whimpering William out from beneath a table stacked with blankets. The child's cry was enough reason to go after Roddy, but it was the sight of the belt looped in his hand that sent rage into Trev.

"Put it down, Cooper. Fight me, not the boy." Glass crunched under Trev's boots as he leaped at Roddy. He dodged the belt swung at him and landed a solid blow that sent Roddy staggering.

"Get out, boy. Go to your mother." It was all Trev managed. Roddy's fist slammed into his jaw, rocking his head back. The second blow forced Trev against the stack of barrels and only the fact that everything was so tightly packed into the store saved him from falling.

Roddy came at him again, swinging the belt at Trev's face. Ducking his head, Trev threw up his arm and caught the sting of leather. The gash on his side opened and he felt a burning tear. Behind him he heard Huber with William, but he couldn't spare a look to make sure Huber was taking the boy outside.

"I'll teach you to come between me and mine. They should've killed you in that damn prison. But

you won't get away from me. I swear you won't!"
Enraged that Trev managed to land his fist again,
Roddy dropped one end of the belt. He snapped
the leather like a whip, and even in the dim light
Roddy saw the glitter of the thick metal buckle
land on his enemy's back. Again and again, he
wielded the belt, beating Trev back down the aisle,
never letting him get close enough to use his fists.

Trev took every blow, luring Cooper outside,
where he would have room. "C'mon Cooper. Hit
me again," Trev goaded, staying out of his reach
now. "Can't fight like a man, can you? Women and
children don't fight back, do they?" Only the
cleaner smell of air told Trev he was close to the
door. Just as he was about to step through the doorway, Leah came rushing in behind him. The moment Trev turned his back to protect her from
being hit, Roddy lunged at him.

With a shove, Trev sent Leah out the door. He
took the full brunt of Roddy's weight and went
down beneath him. Splinters from the raw wood
frame tore through his shirt.

But the pain was nothing to the searing force of
Roddy's big fist slamming into his wounded side.
Trev couldn't breathe. He felt as if a knife had cut
him open again. Black lights danced in front of
his eyes. From a distance he heard Leah.

"Get off him! Roddy, please, you'll kill him. Stop
it! Somebody stop him!"

"Christ, Leah, get the hell away from him," Trev
muttered, gathering himself to try to dump Roddy
off. He felt the hem of her gown against the back
of his head. Roddy had his hand spread over the
back of his head and Trev sucked in air the moment his head was lifted. "Get away, he shouted,

bucking, unable to get Roddy off, and eating dirt when his face was banged against the ground.

Trev went still. His only hope was to have Roddy think he had knocked him out. Leah was shouting and still close. Then he saw her fall backward, unsure if Roddy shoved her or if she stumbled.

With an enraged cry Trev jammed his elbow back, the grunt of pain a pure satisfaction as he twisted and heaved himself free. He kicked Roddy's shoulder, swiping at his eyes, going for him with fists that seemed apart from the rest of his aching body. He spit blood and felt his eyes closing, but nothing stopped him.

"I swore you'd never hurt her again. I swore it," he cried, not even making an attempt to see where his blows were landing, just striking out over and over.

Roddy butted his head into Trev's stomach, sending him staggering backward. Trev knew he couldn't take much more of the beating. He wasn't anywhere near recovered from the deprivations of prison.

"Use your gun, soldier!" Huber shouted.

Shaking his head, Trev glanced down at his sidearm. The distraction nearly cost him his life. Roddy grabbed a pick from the jumble near the store's door and flung it at Trev. Only Leah's scream made him move aside at the last possible moment. Roddy's rage at missing Trev poured out in a steady stream of swearing and filth. He held his fists high and once again came at him.

"The gun! Use your damn gun before he kills you!"

But Trev made no move to do so. He swayed where he stood, trying to brace himself for the next blow. Roddy swerved at the last second and went for Leah.

"No! God, no!" Trev heard himself cry from far off. He heard a shot that kicked up the dirt at Roddy's feet, stopping Roddy cold. Through a haze of sweat and blood he saw that two men were standing on either side of Roddy, holding rifles on him. Then he looked down and saw the gun in his hand. It wasn't his Colt, but the smooth grip fit his hand as if made for him. He stared at the long barrel, stared at it and saw Leah's face reddened with the imprint of Roddy's big hand. He saw the marks on her neck, the fear in her eyes. He saw William. Fear. Heard the whimpers. And then Trev looked up to where the men held Roddy Cooper.

He brought the gun barrel up until he knew he would have a clean shot at Cooper's heart. He didn't need the use of both eyes; one was enough to sight in on his waiting target. His finger was swollen but he gently began to squeeze the trigger. One shot. That's all it would take. Roddy would be dead and Leah free. One . . . single . . . bullet . . .

"Trev, you'll never forgive yourself if you kill him," Leah whispered at his side.

He didn't turn to look at her. He couldn't.

"Trev, please. No more deaths. No more blood."

"He'd have hurt you again. He was going to beat William with his belt."

The soft, chilling deadness of his voice cost Leah whatever hope she had of reaching him. Her whisper carried no farther than Trev. "I love you. Don't do this."

His hand shook; even bracing his wrist with his other hand couldn't stop the trembling that beset him.

"You stopped him from hurting William. That's

all that really matters, Trev. He won't do it again. Roddy's a coward. You know that," she rushed to say, so afraid he would stop listening, so afraid that he would pull that trigger. "You're hurt. Come away from here. Let Huber and Pete see to him. Come with me, Trev," she repeated, very gently touching his extended arm. The same trembling that racked his body held sway over hers.

"Don't let hate consume you, Trev. It's what your father wanted."

"No!"

"Yes, Trev," she insisted, then pleaded. "He never wanted you to know love. Love is what makes you strong. Your father didn't want a son who could be gentle or tender. He despised those soft emotions. You know he did," Leah begged, gripping his arm. "He tried to mold you into the same destructive man that he was. But you wouldn't let him do it. You're so strong, Trev. You were never afraid to show me how gentle you could be. You do know how to love? Remember?" She barely murmured the last, parched as she was, but Leah refused to give up the hope of stopping him.

"Remember us, Trev. Remember our love."

"Leah, stop—"

"I can't. I've bargained with the devil and he's finally had his fill of me. God answered my prayers and let me see you again. And I—"

"God had nothing to do with it," he ruthlessly cut in. "I would've torn this country apart to find you again. But I knew where you were. Where that bastard had taken you. Nothing, not the damn Union force could've stopped me from coming here."

"Then don't destroy what we had. If you kill Roddy, you will kill all hope of realizing your dream to heal. Trev, look at me!" But she went on when he refused. "Will you let Roddy win? Roddy and your father?" Leah ducked beneath his arm and stood in front of him. Trev didn't take his gaze from where Huber and Pete held Roddy. And she was stricken by the feral gleam in his eyes.

"Get out of the way, Leah."

The snarl of his voice only reinforced her need to stop him. Her fingers clenched around the cloth of her gown. His face was battered and bleeding, but she was afraid that if she touched him, Trev would explode.

"Shoot him and you'll crucify yourself. And me."

He could no longer ignore Leah's words or the urgency in her voice. And the love she held out to him. Trev closed his eyes. A shudder ripped through him and pain threatened to overwhelm his battered body. Trev barely managed to fight it off and stay on his feet. He had listened to everything Leah had said, but he still wouldn't lower the gun.

"Why, Leah? Why now?" he asked in a hoarse, ragged voice.

She knew what he was asking her. Why had she stripped away any hope of their past remaining secret from all but Roddy. Leah knew the answer, but she deliberately let him think she had misunderstood what he had asked her.

"William wanted a peppermint stick. Roddy wouldn't let him have one. He yelled and William tried to get the jar down from the counter by himself. It fell and broke. The rest—"

"Damn you! Is it my son that he beats?"

His furious whisper lashed her. Leah lowered her head, shaking because she had gambled and lost. She couldn't even summon a prayer for help.

"Answer me, Leah!"

"Does it matter so much? He's a little boy. My son, Trev. And he pays for my sins, my guilt, my past," she said in an odd, flat voice. "And he needs me," she added, defeated enough to walk away.

She couldn't stay and watch Trev destroy himself. She would not see Roddy die. The guilt was all hers. She had brought the three of them to this moment.

"Leah!"

Trev's voice almost stopped her, but Luis was near the corner of the store with her sons. She had to remember her place and it wasn't by Trev's side. She had lied to him when she said the devil was done with her. He was laughing over every step she took away from her love and back into hell.

Remember us. Remember love. Your father wanted to mold you. Hate consumes. Destroy your dream. I love you. Love you. Leah's words pounded in his mind, and the bloodlust surged hotter with each repetition Trev made of them.

He stared at the wavering figures of Pete, Huber, and Roddy. He thought of Leah proclaiming the sins and the guilt were hers. If he pulled the trigger, they would be his as well. And he wanted to do it, consequences be damned. But so would he damn his love.

Trev slowly lowered his arm to his side. The weight of the gun pulled at him. "Leah?" he whispered as the ground rushed up to meet him.

The nightmare waited beyond pain. Trev welcomed the pain and fought off the mist that veiled his mind. Leah calling him. Leah needing him. He twisted and turned, aches and bruises setting his body on fire with every move, but he couldn't escape.

"Where are you?" he cried out. "I can't see you, Leah. Oh, Christ! Stop her. I don't want to listen. I can't . . ."

"Hush, love. Hush."

"Leah? Where are you? I need you. I want to see you. I've got to find you." In Trev's mind, the mist dipped and swirled, rising to a thick dark gray so that he couldn't even hear her faint whisper. Again and again he cried out. Struggling to wake. Needing to put an end to the torment.

And then there was a warmth enfolding him. Soft, sweet murmurs eased his torment. Tension slowly seeped from his body and he sought the comfort this new dream offered.

"Leah," he whispered, the feel of her long hair brushing against his bare flesh, so real that he stopped fighting and let every exquisite touch sink deep into his soul, where he hungered.

How many nights had he dreamed of gathering her into his arms, his hands smoothing her hair? His every breath was filled with the scent of her. Leah. His love. His life.

Time had stopped for him. Peaceful contentment cradled him until pain receded and desire kindled with the need to taste her lips. An aching groan came from deep inside him when he felt cool drops against his mouth. Trev licked his lips and slowly roused himself with the understanding his lips were wet with tears.

"Don't cry, my love," he whispered, opening one eye, for the other was swollen shut. The darkness of the small room off the men's barracks was near absolute, but he didn't need to see. Leah was in his arms. Real. Not the devil's trick. Not a dream.

Trev tried to speak. Her lips closed softly, gently over his. Her fingertips lightly held his face still, but nothing could have made him move. Love seeped its balm into him from her kiss, from the tears she shed, and the sweet, breathless way she said his name.

The trembling warmth of her mouth sent heat licking through him. Leah curled her body closer to his like a small bird seeking the safety of its nest. Trev welcomed her, welcomed the release from the loneliness that had plagued him. He held love in his arms, tasted its healing power from the deepening heat of her kiss and knew again the deep feeling of being whole.

His hand caught the length of her hair, drawing it up slowly against his chest. He held it while he cradled her head and rocked his mouth against hers, taking every bitter moment of the past, every agonizing hour they had been lost to each other, and he gave back his love, his hope, his intense need for her.

And Leah gave as well, just as she had from the beginning, all of herself, all of her heart, with nothing held back from him. There was a clawing hunger to know again the tenderness and gentleness which only Trev had given to her. For her, time stopped. They were alone in the world. Her well-hidden wounds were salved by his deepening kisses. This man that she loved was healing her spirit. She longed to heal his as well.

"Trev?" she whispered, lifting her head, unable to stem the flow of her tears. She brought his hand to her mouth, kissing the skinned flesh, wishing she could take all of his pain away with so simple a gesture. Because of her he had suffered. Leah felt she offered him so little.

His hand turned within hers and caressed her cheek. "Why did you come? I would have spared you anyone knowing about us."

"I had to. Luis stayed with me and the children. I couldn't sleep worrying about you. Huber said he and Pete had cleaned you up and gave you whiskey to sleep, but I had to know—had to see you for myself."

He drew her head down to his shoulder. "Where's Cooper?" The question had burned his tongue from the moment he realized that Leah was not the devil's haunting.

"When you passed out, Roddy tried to go after you again. Pete and Huber stopped him. They locked him in the store. I didn't even go to see him, Trev," she confessed, tension gripping hold of her. "I didn't even want to see how badly he was hurt. When he—"

"Hush. Don't say more. We've been through so much, Leah. Stay here beside me." He shifted to his side, ignoring the pain from the beating, and gathered her close. "You my love, are all that I need." And as he brought his lips to hers, Trev knew he must not allow anything to come between them now. Whatever time Leah had stolen for them, he had no choice but to take. His broken spirit was beginning to feel the healing power of her love and he fed off the strength that love gave to him.

Once there had been the raw lightning of passion between them, but now Leah felt a deeper, stronger bond that made passion shimmer to life. She was afraid of hurting him and broke their kiss, but she couldn't stop touching him.

From the blackest pit of his nightmare Trev couldn't stop thinking about Leah being forced to take Roddy to her bed. A hard lump twisted into a knot in his stomach, the pain more intense than any bruise. Leah was so giving, and he, her first lover, knew how sensual she was. Jealousy reared its ugly head and he battled to block it.

"What's wrong?" Leah sensed the sudden change in him and tried to back away, but he held her tight. "Trev, the time is long past for lies or for us to hold back anything from each other. If you want me to go—"

"No!" He took her mouth with a desperate urgency fed by the need to wipe the guilt clean that because of him she had had to marry that bastard who abused her.

With one hand caught between their bodies and the other gripping his shoulder, Leah offered him no resistance. Trev had his demons to fight, just as she did. His kiss was fierce with a possessive demand that took and took. She gave, but took as much, for passion burst to life within her, a passion that went beyond physical desire to be strengthened by her love for this one man.

There was no risks. No conscience. Leah needed him and would not deny herself one moment of the completeness he brought to her. She knew his body as well as her own. Knew its heat and its power. And with Trev—Trev alone—she knew her power as a woman. It had been so long—too long—that she had been denied her rights as a woman. Rights that Trev had taught her, even as he fulfilled them.

Leah twisted beneath him as he settled himself over her. Her body was taut with need, but softened to the hard fit of his. Memories flashed of every time they had made love. Memories that were all she had lived on. Her hands were frantic moving over him, so afraid he would be snatched away from her. The stinging nip of his teeth, instantly soothed by the lave of his tongue, made her cry out.

Trev drank that cry and the softer, pleasure moan which followed. "I swear to you," he promised between stringing kisses down her bared, arched throat, "he'll never touch you again."

"Trev, don't—"

His lips silenced her.

And when the kiss ended, Leah held his face between her hands. "Don't hate me, but Trev I can't make love with you now. I never meant for you to think that I would. Listen," she insisted when he tried to jerk his head back. "William wakes with nightmares. I need to be there for him."

There was the temptation to coax her to stay, to give them both what they needed. He wasn't wrong about Leah's wanting him; she was trembling with passion. But he slowly eased himself to her side and, with only the promise of a future, found the strength to deny what his body craved.

Leah sensed what the denial cost him. She was already paying for it. She listened to their ragged breathing, unable to help herself from reaching out and placing her hand over Trev's heart.

"You're angry with me."

"No. I can't be. I hoped for a little time before I said this. But after what happened today, there is no time. The detail will be back with our supplies sometime tomorrow. I want you packed and ready to leave with the boys."

"Trev, you'll—"

"Just listen," he said, looming over her in the dark before she could rise. "We can't stay here.

You and your children can't. Once before I offered to take you away from him. Now there is no choice, Leah. I didn't kill him," he grated from between clenched teeth, fighting the desire and emotions that churned inside him. "Not today. But there'll be tomorrow or next week. You can't live with him. You can't tell me you still want to honor any damn vows you made to him when he's broken those of God and man!"

"No! No, I won't tell you that. But it's you, Trev. Will you break your oath to the army? I—"

"Break this one? Do you believe anything matters to me but you?" His hand was shaking when he smoothed her hair back from her face. "I didn't want to run."

"They'll hunt for you."

"I don't matter. It's you and the boys. It won't be easy, Leah. I can't lie and say it will. The hardship—"

"Trev, oh, Trev," she cried. "I thought I understood what love was. But you're willing to sacrifice everything—"

"Love, listen to yourself," he whispered, drawing her up so he could hold her. "Do you think I could ever make up for what you've suffered because of me? Oaths and honor are small weights, Leah, when measured against the love I have for you." He treasured the way she held him, the feel of supple strength in her body, and prayed the tears were those of happiness. He had to release her or he simply wouldn't. "Leah, I'll let you go now, but understand, it's for the last time."

"The last time," she repeated, pressing a quick hard kiss to his lips, then leaving him before the temptation to stay could overwhelm her. She closed the door to his room carefully behind her and shivered in the night chill. Her heart was so full of love that she cast her gaze skyward and whispered, "Thank you, dear Lord, for bringing my love back to me."

She didn't want to think about escape; she only wanted to breathe life into the hope that she and Trev would be together, making a new life for themselves and keeping her children safe.

But as she ran across the compound back to her sons, an insidious whisper cautioned her to beware. What Trev had proposed seemed all too easy. Leah argued with herself as she opened the door to the kitchen and saw that the fire had nearly died. Why shouldn't it be easy for them? They had been through enough.

Yet the warning persisted. Would the Lord allow her to cast aside the vows she had made before Him? Would Trev be able to break the oath made on his honor without a fearful retribution being demanded of them?

Leah didn't know the answers. Without bothering to light a lamp, she went into the small room where Luis slept with the children. William was curled up on the single bunk with Luis. She smoothed the quilt over them, reassured by their deep, even breathing that their sleep was peaceful. James no longer slept in his cradle—he was too active—so Leah was careful not to make any noise when she pulled one of the chairs away which kept him from rolling off the bunk.

She pulled the edge of the quilt down, for James had a tendency to crawl beneath it. But even in the dark, she realized something was wrong. His breathing ... "James," she whispered, having to force herself to reach out and touch her son.

Leah didn't understand. She tore the quilt off

the bed. Lifted the rolled blanket. "James!" Panic choked her breath. She stood, frozen, crushing the wool in her hands, unable to believe that her baby wasn't there.

Chapter Twenty-Two

L EAH'S screams tore through the night. Trev jackknifed off his bunk, grabbed his gun from the holster hanging on the post, and ran outside. The rain that had been promised all day burst with a sudden downpour and he couldn't see for a moment. Bootless, shirtless, he ran across the compound yard, his only thought that Roddy had gotten out and was hurting her.

He burst through the kitchen door, cursing the darkness inside. "Leah! Where are you?" When the screams stopped, his heart missed a beat. Softer then, he called her, making his way into the room.

An animal whimper came from behind him. Trev cocked his gun, swirling around, and dropped to one knee, ready to fire. He never knew what stilled his finger on the trigger. From the doorway came Leah.

"Trev?"

"Sweet Christ! I almost shot you. What the hell happened?" He was up and started to walk toward her when Pete and Huber came in.

"Missus? What's all the ruckus?" Huber, first through the door, asked. "It's wetter than a cow's tit, an' you'll pardon me for sayin' so," he grumbled, slapping water off the floppy brim of his hat.

"I was trying to find out," Trev said, his voice

sharp with warning. He found the lamp on the table and lit it.

"Stop your jawing and get inside, you skinny old coot," Pete muttered behind Huber. Like Trev, they were barefoot, carrying their rifles, and Pete tried to hold the top of his union suit together as Huber made room for him to come inside.

Trev turned to Leah. Her face was bleached of color and her eyes were huge and dark. "What happened?"

She shook her head, gesturing behind her into the dark room. Pete adjusted his eye patch and started forward, but Trev motioned him back. He touched her arm but she jerked away from him.

"Bring me the lamp, Pete. I can't see." Trev wasn't sure Pete had heard, but the spry old man was quick to do as he had asked. "My God!" Trev didn't hear Pete echo that and more. He went to the bunk and looked down at Luis and William. Both were bound and, he guessed, gagged with the rags on the floor. When he tried to rouse Luis, he saw the lump on the back of the boy's head. Rage choked him. He had to force himself to touch the smaller boy, the child who could be his son. Bile rose and he gagged. William's body was almost lifeless. "He hit them? That bastard hit them." He heard the disbelief in his voice. His mind shied away from what he was seeing. It was without thought that he reached down and withdrew the knife from his boot. He no longer had handmade sheaths, but merely a piece of rawhide a harness maker had sown in place. Trev cut through the rope binding the boys and he lifted William into his arms.

The boy's head lolled to one side and Trev saw the lump and crusted blood that had come from the blow. He turned to Leah. "Why? What kind of an animal—"

But Leah wasn't looking at him. Her fist was pressed to her lips and he could see her shake. Trev followed her gaze to the other bunk. The empty bunk.

And he saw his love's eyes were lifeless. A blinding coldness spread inside him. "He took James? He took the child, Leah? Tell me," he demanded in a soft voice, afraid to let the rage escape him.

"I couldn't find him, Trev. When I came back I couldn't find my baby."

He knew she was in shock; he had seen enough in the war. But never had the sight of those same vacant eyes along with her puzzled voice ever pierced him like a knife thrust to the gut.

"Will you help me find James? Will you?"

Leah's voice rose shrilly, shattering the silence that had held all of them. Trev thrust William into Pete's arms. His walk was slow, so unlike the fury churning, demanding action from him. "Leah, we need you to make some coffee. The fire's nearly dead and it's cold in here. Huber will help you. Won't you?" he asked the man hovering in the doorway.

"Sure thing, missus. You come along with me."

But when he reached out to take her arm, Leah snarled at him and backed into the corner between the wall and the chest.

Trev's stomach lurched. She was like an animal at bay. Her eyes were wild, darting from one to the other, but never settling on William or Luis. He was torn about what to do. She needed him, but he needed to find Roddy. Roddy and James. He held out his hand to her, unashamed that it was trembling.

"Come here, Leah. You know I won't hurt you. No, one here will hurt you. I need you, love. I'll find James for you. But I want you to come to me."

"He took my baby."

"I know, love. I'm going to get him back. James'll be safe. I promise you that." Trev held his gaze to hers, but she wasn't seeing him. Her hands were splayed against the logged wall, clawing at the wood, but he knew she wasn't even aware of what she was doing. He heard Pete moving around behind him, but not even that distracted Leah. He hurt for her, the pain nearly dropping him to his knees and he prayed. He bargained with God, and he begged Leah to come to him.

The sound of water splashing into a basin behind him made Trev thankful that Huber and Pete were here to take care of Luis and William. He didn't even realize he still held his knife until he saw Leah staring at it. With care, he brought his hand up and let her see him toss the knife on James's empty bed. What he never expected was Leah's lunge for the weapon.

"I'll kill him!"

Trev grabbed her before she got hold of the knife. Her hands clawed at him. Searing pain shot from his swollen eye. Trev had one wrist in his grasp and he used it to twist her around so that he pressed her back against his chest, with his own arms locked over hers.

"Easy, love. Easy," he murmured, feeling the icy chill of her body. He hoped to warm her with the heat of his, and rocked her gently, until the fight went out of her. The rippling shudder that went through her body as her first sob came was both a curse and benediction for him to feel and hear.

He turned her and cradled her head, thinking of the time that Roddy had been gone, listening to the rain pound on the roof. Leah didn't cling to him, nor did he feel tears. And he ached to shed them for her.

"It's God's punishment," she murmured after a few minutes in a flat voice. "I was so happy and he took my son away to punish me."

"No! No one is punishing you. Roddy took James. Roddy is the bastard who'll pay."

"The little one's coming around and Luis is awake," Pete informed them.

"Go to William, Leah," Trev whispered, tilting her face up to his. "He needs you now. You've got to be strong for him and for me. I can't leave you like this, but I can't let Roddy have more of a head start."

"He ain't the only one gone," Huber said from where he stood at the doorway. "Figured it best I check on Hayden. Recovered right quick, since his horse and gear are missin'. But you'll have hell's own time tryin' to track 'em in this rain."

"He's right," Pete added, setting down the basin he had used to wash the boy's wounds. "Be best if you let Huber or me come with you. We know the country and you don't."

"You'll find them, Trev?" Leah asked in a trembling voice.

"I'll find them," he promised, looking toward the bed when William cried out.

He didn't see the way Huber and Pete stared at him, but Leah did. She heard death in his voice and saw, as she roused herself, that the promise of death was in Trev's eyes. Was there never to be peace for them? This is what she had been warned about; this was the retribution demanded. James for Trev. Her mind whispered that over and over as she dragged herself to the bed and cradled William to her breast. She couldn't summon tears. She rocked back and forth, wondering how she would ever pay the price.

Huber motioned for Trev to come into the kitchen with him. With a last look at Leah, Trev followed him. The stock tender handed him a cup of coffee and at his first sip, Trev mumbled his thanks for the whiskey Huber had added.

"Didn't want to say more in front of the missus, but Roddy took more'n the boy. He cleaned out every box of cartridges an' near as I remember, 'bout eight repeatin' rifles. Took most of the whiskey, too."

"How the hell did he get out, Huber? You told me—"

"Said he was locked up tight an' that's jus' what he was. Don't think any of us figured that door over there locks from inside the store."

Trev followed his gesture to where the extra table and benches were piled against the door leading to the store. It wouldn't have taken a man of Cooper's strength much effort to shove them out of his way. Roddy had to have made his escape while Leah was in his room with him. Trev glanced toward the doorway. Leah must have realized it by now. She would be blaming herself that James was gone, but he kept thinking of what Roddy would have done to her if he had found her here. He slugged down the coffee, needing its heat, needing to wipe out the bitter taste coating his mouth.

"Since you found Hayden missing, Huber, do you know if he went with Cooper?"

"Three horses is gone an' a mule. Can't rightly figure where they'd think of headin'. Injuns stirrin'.

Ain't safe for two white men alone. Me an' Pete an' Wally been keepin' an eye on Cooper. Wouldn't surprise me none at all to find out he's tradin' with them Cheyenne. Here, fill your cup. You ain't in no shape to ride out after them."

"There's no one else." Trev told him. "I can't leave the station with only one man here. My detail won't be back with supplies until late afternoon at the earliest."

Huber noisily drank his coffee, smacking his lips when he was done. "Know you ain't wantin' to hear this now, but iffen you'd listened to me, the missus would be wearin' widow's weeds an' been better off."

"You're right. I don't want to hear it. What I want from you is a likely direction they could have taken. And if you've warmed up your belly—"

"An' my cold feet."

"And your cold feet, Huber. I'll need help saddling my horse. And a spare. I can ride in relays and make better time." Trev sipped at his second cup, knowing nothing would take the inner cold away, but racking his mind for some idea of where to begin searching. Thunder rumbled off in the distance and the rain was still a steady downpour.

"Hear that? You think you can find peas in that soup out there? That's what it'll be like. Lookin' for peas in thick soup." Huber didn't bother with coffee this time. He filled his cup from the jug of whiskey he had taken from the store. He offered some to Trev, who refused.

"I think you should give some to Leah, Huber."

"Well, here. Take it."

"No. You do it. I don't think she wants to see me."

"Horse dumplin's! Feelin' sorry for yourself?

Ain't a one of us could've figured him to pull off gettin' out. As for that Hayden, I've seen his likes before. End up with his boots planted. See if I ain't right. Ain't either of 'em fit to be called a man, an' that's a fact."

Trev listened to Leah's crooning voice coming from the bedroom just as Pete joined them. "How are they?"

"Hurting, all three of them," Pete answered, helping himself to both the coffee and the whiskey. "I heard you say you're going after them alone and I'll add to what Huber told you. You're a fool to try. Wait till light. The damp never hit my bones, which means the rain will stop before long. Once it starts drying up, you'll have prints like a map to follow."

There was an urge to reject what made perfect sense for Trev. He needed to do something, not stand around and wait for the rain to stop. He kept thinking about little James. He was Roddy's son and therein lay the boy's protection. But then, his mind countered, what kind of a father would take a young child from his mother?

He listened to Huber fill Pete in on what he had found missing and Trev paced, his glance constantly going to the bedroom doorway. Finally he couldn't take any more. He stood undecided for a few moments, then abruptly went to the bedroom. Leaning against the frame, he watched Leah. William had his head nestled in the curve of her shoulder, where her hair cushioned him. Luis was curled up at her side and her hand absently stroked his head. All of them had their eyes closed and Trev drank in the picture they made for him.

Leah's hair held no sheen from the lamp. It was

as dull and lifeless as the eyes she opened and directed at him. "Have you found James?"

"Not yet. I'm—" Trev stopped himself. She had closed her eyes and shut him out. There were so many things he wanted to say and not one of them what Leah needed to hear. Defeated by the moment, his shoulders slumped and Trev lowered his head.

"Don't come back to me without my baby," Leah stated in an odd, soft voice.

Trev felt the knife twist inside him. He spun around and ran for the door. He'd never utter another useless promise to her, only to himself.

The rain had slackened just as Pete had said it would. Trev stopped thinking and headed for his room. His gun wanted cleaning. He had no time. Once dressed, he went to the barn and once more found himself facing Pete and Huber. But he had sealed himself against their arguments. "The only thing either of you can do is pick out the best horse for a spare."

Trev smoothed the blanket over the big bay's back without thinking. When he hefted his saddle, he staggered before he caught his balance and swung it up onto the horse's back. He knew Pete and Huber were watching him, knew they thought him a fool. And maybe he agreed with them. He was in no shape to ride. But James belonged to the woman he loved. He had no choice.

Huber got on the other side of the bay and swung the cinch belt under the horse's belly so Trev could grab it. "You got enough muscle to knee this critter?"

A grunt was Trev's answer as he kneed the horse's belly and yanked the cinch tight. He was careful to wrap the excess leather so it wouldn't rub the bay's hide, for he had no idea how long he would be riding.

Pete handed over the canteen he filled and a packet of food. "You didn't eat, so take it. And when that detail gets back, I'll send Dooley and Rye after you." He held the bridle as Trev mounted, sharing a look with Huber for the exhaustion that marked Trev's every move.

"Don't send Rye. He's got sense. More than me. Tell him to keep watch over Wilson and Pender Applewood. They were close to Hayden. If he deserted, they might make a run for it, too. Send Tate with Dooley. He's a good shot."

"Here, now, you 'bout forgot this," Huber said, handing Trev his hat. "You take care. That missus is gonna need someone."

"Yeah. Her son." Trev pulled his hat low, then urged the bay out at a walk. He crossed the muddy compound yard, thankful the rain was now a drizzle.

Just as he reached the gate, a chill prickled its way down his spine and he had to turn around. Leah stood by the back door with William in her arms, watching him.

He remembered her last words. *"Don't come back to me without my baby."*

Trev knew what death felt like. It had to be the same black coldness that encompassed him at this moment. He set his heels to the horse and rode out. And the pain in her eyes followed him.

Only Huber and Pete saw the glisten of her tears. They witnessed her faltering steps and heard her call him back.

Chapter Twenty-Three

THE trail Trev followed was heading north. Why would Cooper and Hayden risk riding into Indian territory? Unless Huber had been right and Cooper was illegally trading with them.

A wind whipped his damp clothes and he huddled beneath his poncho to conserve his body heat. Trev longed to spur his mount, but the footing was slippery for both horses and he dared not risk injury to either one. He skirted the Sweetwater station, manned with the same amount of men as he had, sure that Cooper and Hayden had done the same. Hayden especially wouldn't want to be seen by soldiers, deserter that he was.

Through grasslands just showing signs of greening, he rode, keeping a wary eye on the river ahead. It turned abruptly and passed through a ridge. Devil's Gate was the name of the chasm. Trev struggled to recall the map he had been given at the fort.

It wasn't the map he remembered but the crusty old scout who warned him of the gate being a favorite place for the Indians to ambush immigrant trains.

The walls rose, gray granite streaked with black from bottom to top. Trev judged the height at well over three hundred feet while he rode through an area no more than thirty feet wide.

The gelding Huber had chosen for his spare tugged at the lead rein. Trev didn't bother to look back. He knew he should let the animal's instincts be a guide, since his were less than sharp, but he had no choice. He had to go on through the chasm.

This is the way the trail led. Out of Devil's Gate and on to sage flats and barren hills.

Trev checked his back trail, pushing himself to continue, but wishing he wasn't alone. If he was ambushed by a raiding party, Cooper and Hayden would get away. There would be no one to follow them. A feeble sun rose and his stomach growled in warning. He searched for a spot to safely stop, for his strength was ebbing with every minute. The ridges were crested with pines and the slopes showed clusters of aspens. Far beyond them, to the northwest, loomed the mountains, their peaks still white with winter's snow.

Beneath the sheltering overhang of rock, Trev dismounted for a breather. Huber had packed jerky and Trev helped himself to that and water. He couldn't understand why he hadn't caught sight of Cooper and Hayden. A few hours' lead was all they could have had.

He deliberately avoided any thought about Leah. He needed a clear head. Any emotions could cloud his judgment. Still chewing the last of the jerky, he switched the lead rein to his horse and mounted the gelding. The ground was already drying and he set off at a fast walk, driven by the urgency of how much time had passed.

At the mouth of a gully the gelding shied, nickering before Trev could stop him. And the answering nicker that came from somewhere up ahead chilled his blood. He withdrew his rifle from its boot and flowed down out of the saddle, crouching to present as small a target as possible.

The wind came blowing hard from the mountains and he cursed it, trying as he was to hear any sound that would warn him of what he could expect to encounter. He cursed Huber as well for choosing that damn horse. A glance showed the gelding was trained to obey the ground rein, for he and the bay were at ease, chomping at the early spring grass. But Trev didn't trust this sign that there was no danger.

He moved forward around an outcrop, keeping the rifle close to his body to prevent a glint of metal from giving any warning. As suddenly as it had come, the wind died away. And he heard a faint sound, almost like a mewling.

No matter how he strained to hear more, that was the only sound that came to him. That and the sudden thunder of hoofbeats coming in behind him.

Trev swiveled around to fire, jerking the rifle high when he saw army blue and the flash of sunlight on brass. He eased his finger off the trigger as soon as he recognized Dooley and Tate.

They drew rein near his horses and he stepped out from his cover, motioning them for silence.

Dooley reached him first. Leaning close to Trev's ear, he whispered, "Cut your track and Indian sign about a mile back. Careless of you."

There was nothing Trev could say to defend himself, but he gestured toward the gully. Once again the faint mewling came to them. He watched Dooley for a reaction, glad the man was as puzzled as he was. At least he hadn't lost all sense. Tate remained with the horses and Trev gave over the lead to Dooley as they started into the gully.

"Jesus!" whispered Dooley, coming up from a crouch. The smell of death waited for them around the rocks. Ever cautious, he took the time to search the rocks above them before he went forward.

Trev saw the horse. Stiff-legged, on its side with two arrows through its throat, several in its saddle. The other horse was down, too, but from where Trev stood with Dooley, he couldn't see if it was wounded. And that faint mewling sound came again.

The ground was churned mud, showing signs of a struggle. Dread filled Trev as he started forward. The dead horse had an army brand and he knew it had to be the one Hayden had stolen.

"I figure there were eight, maybe twelve riders. Two men wouldn't have had a chance, Sergeant."

"But where are the bodies?" Trev had to know what happened to Cooper, but more, he feared for James. "Would they have taken the boy? You know the Sioux, Dooley."

"Those arrows aren't Sioux. They're Cheyenne."

"And the mule is gone." Trev made his way past the dead horse and knelt by the other. The animal raised its head and struggled to rise, but Trev held it down, soothing the horse with his touch and murmurs. He glanced up at Dooley on the other side, uneasy that they were in a crease which left them blind.

There was a sharp exclamation from Dooley. "Well, I'll be damned." He had untied the blanket knotted at its four corners and slipped over the saddle horn. "Mrs. Cooper is going to be one happy mother."

"James? You found James." Trev scrambled to his feet and came around to Dooley's side. "That was the mewling sound I heard," he said as Dooley lifted the little boy up. The baby's eyes were squeezed shut and his small hands were curled into fists pressed to his mouth. But at the sound of the men's voices, James opened his mouth to cry.

"Here," Dooley said, "you take him. I'm not big on holding babies."

Trev did so gladly. "Easy, little one." He tried to see if the boy was injured, but there was no blood. Offering a prayer, his elation was slow in coming that the boy was safe and he could bring James home to Leah. He rushed back to where Tate waited with the horses, firing off orders for his canteen and blanket roll. The boy was soaked, still making those faint mewling noises.

"Bet he cried himself out, Sergeant. That's why he ain't howling now. Any idea how long he was alone there?"

"None. Maybe Dooley can figure it out. Go help him, Tate. There's an injured horse and one that wants burying." Trev tore off his neckerchief and set James down on the blanket Tate had spread. He wet the cloth and washed the boy's face, then soaked the end in the water and gently opened his mouth.

A hint of a smile creased his lips to see the eager way James sucked the cloth. "Thirsty, huh? Well, we'll have you back to your mama soon." The boy's hair was as pale a blond as Leah's, his eyes gray with a hint of blue. Trev caught himself looking for a resemblance to Roddy, realizing it didn't matter. This was Leah's son. Just as she claimed William was. They were hers, and it was all the reason he needed to protect them with his life.

Trev used his knife to cut off a corner of the blanket, carefully opening the soaked cloth surrounding James so that he could replace it. The wrapper was wet and Trev discarded it, once more cutting off a length of the blanket. He slit a hole in the roughly cut rectangle, sliding it over James's head like a poncho.

Very gently then, Trev lifted the baby into his arms and cradled him. Smoothing his forehead with one finger, Trev rocked him in his arms. He had been given the gift of this child's life. Leah's child. And now, by right of the love filling him, his. Trev swore it as he lowered his head and gently kissed the baby.

"Shelby!" Tate whispered, coming at him on the run. "Get down. Dooley spotted smoke coming from that far ridge."

"Maybe the Cheyenne couldn't wait."

Tate's gulp was loud enough to make Trev look at him. A cold sweat broke out on the private's forehead and he wiped it impatiently, before resettling his cap on his head. "Guess it's me and Dooley going after them?"

Trev gazed at the baby. He wanted to bring him back to Leah. Needed to. But it wasn't Tate's responsibility to go after Cooper or Hayden. He cupped the baby's head with his hand and lifted him to his lips. Pressing a quick, light kiss on his head, Trev handed him to Tate.

"You take him back."

"But I can't ride—"

"We can't take the baby with us, Private. If Dooley and I are between you and those Cheyenne, you'll have a better chance of making it."

James lifted his head from Tate's shoulder and solemnly stared at Trev. His small arm reached out for him. "Get going, Private," was all Trev could manage. He shook his head, thinking he was reading more into the baby's gesture than was really there.

Trev handed over his neckerchief. "Make sure you give him more to drink." He held the boy briefly while Tate mounted, then handed him up to the private. "Get going. And don't stop for anything." He took up the reins of his bay, the gelding, and Dooley's hammerhead roan. The horse was the ugliest he had ever seen and when he tried to bite Trev, he knew he had a disposition to match.

Dooley was waiting for him a little ways from the dead horses. "Had to slit this one's throat. Leg was broke. I didn't want to risk a shot. Look up there, Sergeant."

"Forget the sergeant," Trev shaded his eyes and saw the faint rising smoke. "Campfire?"

"Might be. Seems right strange to stop in midafternoon and make a fire. If it was a hunting party and they were hungry, I might not worry. But if Hayden and Cooper were just riding along, there was no reason to attack them."

"Unless Cooper had something they wanted."

"True enough. Huber said he cleaned out the cartridges and all the rifles. Pete said he might of been trading with them right along. Maybe he promised them more than he could deliver."

"Like our supplies that you brought back," Trev answered. "Listen, Dooley, you can go back if you want. I've got to go on. I can't leave—"

"Ain't going. I'm with you all the way."

"Then mount up. I won't rest until I know what happened."

Dooley studied the ground as they kept the horses to a walk out of the gully. Twice he dismounted and walked a ways before he came back to where Trev waited.

"Smoke's still rising and you can near smell it."

"Can you tell how many came this way?"

Dooley set his cap back on his head. "Two riding double for sure. A packed mule and my best guess is ten Indian ponies. You real sure about going on?"

"I'm sure. There's no choice for me."

"Well, see that shoulder? We can leave the horses there and make our way up on foot."

Trev gazed to where Dooley was pointing. They would have the cover of the trees a good way up the slope to shield them. He rode along behind Dooley, not wanting to think about Cooper or Hayden. Trev didn't want to speculate on what they might find. Whatever Cooper got, it would never be enough for what he had done to Leah and the children.

Dooley cautiously led the way across a grassy ledge, then into a sparse grove of aspens. He kept checking the trail ahead, and Trev kept watch there as well as on their back trail. The last thing they needed was to get caught.

The stink was subtle at first, but as they rode on, Trev began to gag. His horse was tense, ears pricked forward, shying at the shadows. Dooley was having the same trouble. Trev called a halt and saw the knowledge in Dooley's gaze. "We've both breathed the same stench before," Trev said.

"Yeah. Burned flesh. Whatever we're going to find up there won't be pretty."

"Move out, Dooley," was all Trev answered. One way or the other, he had to know. He couldn't go back to Leah with any doubt about Roddy. He breathed through his mouth to avoid the stench. Trev had had enough of it during the war. Just as he had had enough of death.

They were climbing now, the breeze growing stronger and the cover of the trees thinning. Far to the southwest, Trev caught a glimpse of an eagle soaring and envied the bird of prey his freedom.

"This is as far as we ride." Dooley was out of his saddle with his rifle in hand almost as soon as he spoke.

Trev followed suit, tying the reins to a low limb just as Dooley was. There was no sense in having the horses get spooked and run off. This was not country that a man wanted to be on foot. And the stench was overwhelming.

There was a trail of sorts up through the scattered trees and boulders. Both men were careful to step lightly and look first so they wouldn't dislodge a rock. Trev shared a look with Dooley when they began hearing moans.

Trev stepped closer to Dooley. "Listen to me," he whispered against Dooley's ear. "I don't want you to risk your life. Not for the likes of those two."

"You going?"

Trev nodded and started forward, but Dooley's hand on his arm stopped him. He gestured with his rifle to a split in the rocks. "There's a crease down there. And the smell. And I'm still with you."

Once again Trev nodded, for the words went no further than his ear. Dooley was right about the crease. And the smell. Trev flattened himself against the rock, his stomach churning.

There were two stakes in the ground. Hayden, recognizable by his dark hair, was tied to one,

Roddy the other. Neither man had a stitch of clothing left on. Blood ran from cuts. Trev saw a severed hand on the ground, saw Indians holding knives, but it was the two arrows being heated by the fire that made his bile rise. He signaled Dooley and backed down and away, thankful the Indians were making enough noise snapping their whips at their victims that they didn't hear them.

When they went far enough, Trev stopped.

"You can't just leave them, Shelby. Doesn't matter what they've done. No man deserves to die like that. They're killing them by inches."

"I saw." Trev turned away. He swore he wouldn't kill again. They had no hope of rescuing the two men, not outnumbered as they were. And to do what Dooley suggested meant going back up there and shooting them.

Trev stared down at his hands. So much blood had touched them. But he had never killed for revenge. No matter how tempted. He was never able to kill his father, whose cruelty ruined so many lives. He couldn't kill Robert, not even when he had begged, not even when he confessed his betrayal. Now there was Hayden and Cooper.

An animallike wail of pain sent shivers up his back and cut into his thoughts. There was no more time to think about it. Dooley was already turning, running back, and Trev had to follow. He cocked his rifle as he ran. And it wasn't until he once again flattened himself against the rock that he realized Dooley had taken the place he had had before. Dooley was now aiming at Hayden, and that left . . .

Christ! He couldn't do it. He couldn't shoot Roddy. Bitter bile, thick and choking, rose in his throat. He wanted to call out to Dooley, tell him, but the other man was already sighting down his barrel. Once more, time ran out. Trev had to bring his rifle up. Had to look down its barrel at Roddy Cooper. Had to do it now, because if he and Dooley were to get out alive, the shots had to come together.

The trailing length of what appeared to be a scarf of eagle feathers came into his vision. A calmness pervaded Trev's mind and his body. Another cry split the air. Then a long, drawn-out moan. Trev could feel Dooley staring at him. Could almost hear the silent question of why was he waiting.

At that moment Trev couldn't have answered him. He had brought his rifle sight up to Roddy's forehead. Trev blinked. It wasn't possible that Roddy could see him, with the blood that was running down from his head. But Trev swore his eyes were on him.

No! No, you bastard! It's no more than you deserve!

The click of Dooley's hammer being cocked sounded like a shot to Trev. He cast him a fast look, and gave him a curt nod.

They fired simultaneously. And as one, the two men were up and running.

Trev leaped from rock to rock, but Dooley turned as wild howls came from behind them. Trev cursed him. Dooley fired his rifle until it was empty.

"Go!" Trev shouted, dropping down to one knee and squeezing off two shots. One Cheyenne went down; another took a graze to his upper arm that didn't slow him down at all. The rest of the Indians, cheated of their captives, were swarming up and over the rocks, coming after them. Trev fired again. He missed and swore. Then he was running down the slope, dodging trees, rock, and brush.

Dooley was holed up behind a tree that barely concealed him. He was trying to reload as Trev ran by. "Run, damn you!" Trev yelled, turning and squeezing off his last two shots.

Rock chips flew as the Indians returned fire. Trev broke out in a sweat, expecting to feel the slam of a bullet in his back at any second. Dooley came up alongside him. Both ran for all they were worth.

Trev slid on loose scree. Dooley grabbed his arm to steady him.

"I'm loaded. Get the horses."

Trev couldn't argue. There were at least four Indians shooting at him and Dooley. Danger fed a rush of blood that kept him going. Panting, knowing he had only minutes or he wouldn't make it, Trev slid his knife from his boot and cut the tied ends of the reins. He grabbed hold of them quickly, for the horses smelled blood and tried to rear, and the gelding broke free.

His bay pivoted. Holding the reins of Dooley's horse made it difficult to mount. Trev got his boot in the stirrup and looked up as he climbed into his saddle. Dooley was swinging his rifle at the Indian closing in on him. Two more were nearly on him. Trev threw his knife. His aim was off because of the restive moves of the horse, but he bought Dooley enough time to fire his pistol and warn the other two back.

Under the steady barrage of fire from Trev's pistol, Dooley got his horse. The animal was already at a run when he swung himself into the saddle.

"I'm empty, so we ride!"

"Keep down. I don't want to lose you!" Trev yelled back.

Without exchanging another word, they rode hard for the gully. Trev knew they would have a little time to reload and make a stand. The only thing that had saved them was that the Cheyenne had to go back for their ponies.

Trev saw the land in a blur. Exhaustion was overtaking him. He could barely stay in his saddle and a quick look showed Dooley in little better shape. Twice he caught himself slipping. He had to thread his fingers into the bay's thick mane, then lean forward until his head rested against the horse's neck.

His eyes closed. Pain throbbed behind the swollen one. An agonizing groan tore from his lips. Even with his eyes shut for a few moments, he couldn't wipe out the sight of Roddy's last look. Deep in the rational part of his mind, Trev knew there was nothing else he could have done. But he was beyond allowing rationale to rule.

He didn't realize the bay was slowing to keep pace with Dooley's hammerhead roan. He couldn't rouse himself to care. Leah had her son. One promise he kept from so many empty ones made.

"Shelby! Shelby! Can you make it to the gate?" Dooley drew rein and kept his roan to a fast walk, bringing him up alongside Trev's horse. He reached out and shook him. Repeated the question again. Trev's mumble made no sense to him. Dooley took matters into his own hands. There was no more sign of pursuit, but he knew that didn't mean a thing. The Cheyenne could be circling around them. The war party was big enough to split up. Another look at the way Trev was slumped over his horse made Dooley believe he was on his own.

He set his heels to the roan, knowing the bay would keep pace, and decided to make a run all the way to the station.

"You hang on, Shelby. Just hang on."

"Have to," Trev muttered. "Got to . . . go back."

Doolcy pulled up once they entered Devil's Gate. He helped Trev dismount and tucked him into a crevice while he went back to scout their back trail.

Trev forced himself to eat more of the jerky. He was a danger to Dooley and himself without the strength to lift his gun. He emptied his canteen trying to rid his mouth of the taste of bile and when Dooley came back to report, he was able to stand on his own.

"Not a sign of them. Can't understand it, but I'm not one to question a bit of luck."

"Yours, Dooley. Mine ran out a long time ago. Just pray it holds." Trev couldn't look at him. He squinted through his good eye and grabbed hold of his saddle horn to pull himself up on his horse. "You intend to stand there and test your luck?"

"Not me. But you're a hell of a man to ride with, Shelby. There's not many I'd say that about."

"If you knew—"

"About what happened at the station with Cooper? Huber told me and Tate. Not too much," he added, once again setting a fast pace. "Still think you're a hell of a man." Dooley saw no point in telling Trev he had reported the Indian raid to the commander at Fort Bridger. Or the rumors he had heard about Cooper and the way he treated his wife. The way Dooley saw it, and knew he wasn't alone, Shelby did them all a favor.

He was reminded of that when they finally saw the stockade of the home station. He saw Trev rousing himself to sit up as they rode through the gate.

Riley Tucker spotted them and let out a yell. Men came out of the barracks at a run. Trev saw Joe, Tate, and Rye Munroe, but shook his head when he realized that he was either seeing double or there were too many men here.

There was only one face he wanted to see and his gaze went to the doorway, where he hoped to find Leah. The door opened as he dismounted, ignoring the slaps on his back, the questions shot at him from too many. But it wasn't Leah who came out of the door into the yard. The uniform was blue. The man was a stranger, but the rank was captain.

"Sergeant Shelby! I'll see you in my quarters immediately."

"That's Captain Hanibal Dorsey, Trev," Rye whispered. "Fresh from school with about as much sense as a daisy."

Trev didn't answer Rye or the command. He slipped his rifle out of its boot and started walking away.

"Sergeant! You come back here!"

Dorsey's voice grated on Trev's ears. The babble increased and still he walked away.

"Trev?"

He stopped dead. Soft as it was, Leah's voice cut through the noise, the whoops as Dooley recounted what had happened. Trev turned slowly. She was halfway across the yard, poised for flight. *To me, Leah. Run to me.* He had eyes for no one else. He closed off his hearing to all but her whisper of his name. Trev didn't see, hear, or feel the wrath of the captain at his side, shouting orders, demanding obedience, grabbing hold of his arm.

Leah was running to him.

Trev shoved the rifle at the captain's chest and walked forward.

"I'll have you confined to quarters, Shelby! I'll bring you up on charges!"

"Do it," Trev returned, opening his gunbelt and letting it fall.

"I'm ordering you to come back here, Sergeant. I'll strip you of your stripes! I'm not done with you."

"Go to hell, Dorsey," Trev said loud enough so that every man heard him. "I'm the one who's finished."

"Court-marshaled, Shelby! You hear that? Thrown out of the army. Disgraced!"

"I'll push a broom and muck out stables, Dorsey. But I'm done with killing." Trev meant every word for the captain, but he said them to Leah. His gaze held hers. He searched her dark brown eyes for what he most needed. Forgiveness.

"Stop him! I want that man escorted under guard to the barracks."

Not one man moved. They couldn't. Pete and Huber had picked up Trev's weapons and stood guard. They weren't alone. Trev's detail joined them.

"This 'ere's the Overland Stage's home station, Captain Dorsey," Huber stated. "An' it's home station business that wants fixin'."

Trev couldn't acknowledge Huber's support, or that of the other men. Leah was so close, her breath mingled with his. He closed his eyes when she reached up with her hand to touch his bearded cheek.

"Forgive me, Trev," she whispered. Her lips were dry. She couldn't summon enough moisture to say more.

"I killed him, Leah. I'm the one who asks for forgiveness. It doesn't matter why I did it. But I killed Roddy."

It wasn't the stark words of his confession that made her cradle his face within her trembling hands, it was the pain she saw in his eyes. "You brought James back. You came back. That's all that matters, Trev. You're safe." Leah was aware that others listened. But she had no shame. Someday she would tell Trev of her own guilt for wishing Roddy dead. Someday when they had time, and a long enough chance to rebuild a life with love.

Love in her eyes was all Trev saw as he took her into his arms. His head dropped to her shoulder and he nestled his face against her neck.

Leah held him tight. "Come with me, Trev," she murmured, the weariness of his body and spirit bringing a well of love and compassion. She slid her arm around his waist, stepping to his side. The sun was beginning to set and cast their shadows before them.

"Wait, Leah. We need to talk."

"We will, Trev. We will. There's time now, my love." She couldn't say more, but she could show him. From the deep pocket of her apron, Leah withdrew the gold double heart ring. She closed her hand around it, then uncurled her fingers and brought the ring to her lips to press a kiss on it. Then she offered it to Trev.

With a bewildered look he took it. "Where—"

"I've had it since that day the Union soldiers captured you."

"All this time I thought I lost it." He took a few

faltering steps. It was only Leah's strength that lent itself to him so he could walk beside her. "How did you know it was mine?"

"It was warm. Warmed by love, and the gold gleamed as though someone had constantly touched it. From the moment I picked it up, I just knew the ring belonged to you."

At the doorway, Leah slipped free of him and turned. "Huber, I want you and Pete to keep everyone away. Including you, Captain Dorsey." And when she turned back, it was to see Trev framed in the doorway. Her love. Strength tempered by gentleness. She had never loved him more than at this moment when the sun seemed to be pouring its last rays on him. His spirit, his immense courage, and his quiet pride whispered to her.

It wasn't a time to smile. It wasn't a time for tears. But it was long past time for her to love. And it was with love that she went into his waiting arms, her heart filled with joy. For there had been no shadows, no darkness around him.

Trev closed the door. But he wasn't caged. For the first time, he was free.

Epilogue

She kissed the scars on her lover's body, blessed in the aftermath of their passion by the bonding of mind, heart, and spirit. Love graced and enriched the passion Leah had shared with her husband over the years. Love that they cherished and nurtured for the precious gift that it was. And when she pressed a last lingering kiss to Trev's lips, Leah rested her chin on her folded hands crossed over Trev's chest and gazed at him.

"I love you, Trev."

"Do you know," he asked, gathering up the pale sheen of her hair, his gaze riveted to her face, "that I never want you to stop saying those words?" Five years only made the elegant lines of her face seem more beautiful. His breath caught. In the muted light of the lamp in their bedroom, her eyes glowed with her joy. He never tired of seeing it. Never tired of loving her, or of being loved in return.

He lifted her hand to his lips, kissing the palm, then the ring she proudly wore. His ring. His wife. "Are you sorry that we moved from Boston?"

"No. Although I wonder why you keep asking me. I loved being with your sister and her family, Trev, but it wasn't what you wanted. We agreed to give this a try." Leah glanced at the dresser top, where Trev's new medical set of specula rested in a velvet-lined wooden case. Each of the ivory handles were inscribed DR. TREVOR SHELBY. It was her birthday gift to him.

"Trev, we're both needed here on the reservation. It's our chance to make dreams come true. I've already had three new students at school. And you can't deny," she teased, tapping the cleft in his chin, "that you take as much pleasure in what you learned about Indian medicine as what you have taught.

"We've been happy, and the children—"

"Ah, yes, thankfully the little darlings are all asleep," he said, gently rolling her to her side and raising himself above her. There were dreams alive in her eyes now and he prayed he would always be able to make them real for her. "I love you," he murmured, bringing his lips to hers. "Love you. Love . . ." And with each word, he scattered kisses across her face, then lowered his head to nuzzle the sweeter flesh of her breast.

They had struggled so long and so hard to be together that Trev knew Leah felt as he did; every moment was a precious gift to treasure.

Her shivering sigh was all a lover could want to hear. But Trev heard another noise, a softer one that brought his head up with a jerk.

"That came from the loft!" he whispered, rolling quickly to the other side of the bed. "Where did you throw my pants?"

"My nightgown, Trev. I can't find it."

"If you weren't such a wanton . . . throwing clothes . . . here," he said grumpily, throwing the nightgown toward her. He hopped about, trying to get his pants on.

"Hurry," Leah's muffled voice warned as she slid

the gown over her head and grabbed the quilt at the edge of the bed.

"Papa?"

"I'm coming, Will." Trev heard Leah laughing while he swore beneath his breath as he tried to close at least two of the buttons on his pants.

"James had a bad dream," William announced at the doorway. He came in, for there was always welcome in his parents' bed, and dragged James along in his wake.

"Your sons, Trev—"

"My sons? Yours, Mrs. Shelby, don't know how to sleep at night. Do they?" he asked with mock intensity as he turned up the lamp and looked from eight-year-old William's face to James, who was nearly six.

Trev dropped to a crouch and held out his arms. "Come tell Papa what's been chasing you this time."

James tugged free of William's hand and ran to Trev. But even as he cradled the boy with one arm, Trev eyed the strange way William just stood there.

"Will?"

The boy didn't answer, but the small face peering around his nightshirt told Trev what was wrong. "You, too, Bell? Up on the bed, the lot of you." He saw with pride how Will lifted two-year-old Isabella up to his mother and then ran around to ensure a place beside Trev.

Amid giggles and laughter the children squirmed and finally settled down. Leah on her side, with Bell curled up next to her, thumb in mouth, her dark brown eyes as wide as her mother's. Trev leaned against the headboard, James on one side, his little rump pressed to Trev's hip, and William, with Trev's encouragement, sat up beside him.

Trev rumpled Will's hair and tucked his head against his shoulder just as Leah remarked with a thankful sigh, "At least Matthew is asleep."

"Tell us again how Dooley saved your life, Papa," James murmured, closing his eyes.

"That's why Matthew got his name," Will added, looking up at his father with adoration.

And Trev hugged his first son, the son of his heart, his gaze meeting Leah's. They needed no words. Their shared look said someday they would tell them. But someday was far off in the future, where tomorrows waited.

"We live for today, Trev," Leah reminded him, and herself as well. "The good memories of the past are ours to cherish, but we will always have the dreams of tomorrow. Always," she repeated. "Our vow. One we will keep as long as we have love in our hearts."